For my wonderful husband Richard Dunn, for making our own Mallorca adventures possible.

I also dedicate this book to the many people on the island who work tirelessly and with passion to improve the welfare of Mallorca's numerous stray and unwanted cats and kittens.

CHAPTER ONE

'You're replacing me with a soap star?' I hardly recognised the tense, high-pitched voice as my own. 'Seriously?'

My boss, Barry Jones, leaned back on the faux-leather executive chair behind his desk. He squinted at me with unnerving blue eyes, and I could tell I was not the only one surprised by my uncharacteristic outburst. He was doubtless wondering what had happened to the easy-going Laura Lundon. Had he possessed an atom of empathy he'd have realised my recent bereavement had something to do with the change.

Barry cleared his throat, sat up straight, and brushed what look liked cigarette ash from the sleeve of his shirt. All his clothes were black – a strange colour choice for a heavy smoker who also had a flaky-scalp problem.

He picked up his Bard FM-branded biro and twirled it between the fingers of his left hand. This habit of his reminded me of a majorette with a baton and, for a moment, I pictured Barry in a short skirt and a blonde wig going through a routine. I had a powerful urge to bat the pen away but tucked my hands under my thighs instead.

'Laura, you are not being replaced.' He brought my attention back to the troubling conversation. 'It's a promotion … if you'll just hear me out.'

I'd been presenting the weekday afternoon show for ten years. Not once had I considered moving to another show or radio station. Some people thought I was unambitious, but the truth was that change and I were as compatible as a TV box set and a full night's sleep.

Barry had been station manager for only two months, so perhaps he didn't know me well yet. *Time to put him straight.*

'But I love what I do and the listeners like it too. You told me last month my audience figures were the second-best on the station.'

'That's why I need you on breakfast.' His tone was grudging. 'Between you and me, that show needs a shake-up. I'm making it double-headed and you're the female I want on it.'

A shake-up? My mouth hung open and I must have looked like a cod on Sainsbury's fish counter. Billy Ryan was not only one of my oldest and dearest friends, but also a popular and award-winning radio presenter.

Of course, a small part of me felt flattered that Barry had chosen me for the station's flagship show, where I'd be working alongside someone for whom I had a ton of respect and affection. But be bright and bouncy on-air at six thirty in the morning? Not even if my mattress were on fire. It would take more than the prospect of presenting with Billy to change my night-owl lifestyle.

My thoughts returned to the afternoon show. 'But … Odette Williams?'

The twenty-something actor had been in the

popular TV soap *Westhaven*. But after only three months, Odette's character met a grisly, ratings-boosting death. The next day the tabloid papers published a grainy screenshot of the murder scene, with ex-boyfriend Gavin holding a bloodied hammer as he stood over her lifeless body. The full-colour image quite put me off the strawberry smoothie I'd been slurping.

'She did a good job covering for you when you were off,' Barry said. 'A record number of listeners phoned in.'

It was uncharacteristic of me, but I whipped out my hand from under my leg and slammed it down on the glass desktop. The sharp sound startled my boss; his pen flew from his fingers up into the air and down onto the floor with a clatter. He continued to look at me as though nothing had happened.

'Her screen boyfriend had just murdered her character in one of TV's most gruesome soap deaths.' The pitch of my voice had risen again. 'No wonder people wanted to talk to her. Speak to Dan; he'll tell you what she was like to work with.' I gulped, hoping my producer would forgive my blurted indiscretion.

My boss peered at his laptop screen as he tap-danced his nicotine-stained fingers over the keyboard.

'I'll do that. He needn't worry, I'll soon lick Odette into shape.'

That was something I didn't want to picture. Barry's 'hands-on' reputation made me grateful to be five years older than him and lacking the long blonde hair and pneumatic breasts he favoured in his female conquests.

'It's a done deal, Laura.' He folded his arms, leaned back again, and looked me in the eye. 'We signed the contract yesterday over lunch. Odette starts in two weeks' time and you start breakfast the same day.' He glanced at his screen. 'Monday the twentieth.'

'Without talking to me first?' A lump rose in my throat.

Any decent manager would have waited a few days after my return from compassionate leave before breaking this life-changing news. I swallowed hard and took a deep breath. A whiff of smoke lingered in the air, suggesting he'd had an illicit cigarette by the window before this awkward meeting.

'How does Billy feel about this?'

Barry appeared to be studying some dandruff that had settled on his desk. I guessed he wasn't contemplating a change of shampoo.

'He's coming off breakfast.' He avoided eye contact with me. 'I'm giving him a new Sunday morning show.' He pushed the flakes together with an index finger. 'He's getting on a bit now for the early starts.'

Getting on a bit? Billy had recently turned sixty but could easily pass as being in his early fifties. He'd been on the breakfast show ever since I first joined Bard FM as a news reporter. If he worked only one day a week, how would he manage financially? And I knew he always spent Sundays with his elderly widowed mother, who lived in Oxford. He would be heartbroken to lose his show, and if this change damaged our friendship, I'd be devastated.

'By the way, Laura, Billy doesn't know this yet. He's not back from holiday till Monday, so this conversation stays within these four walls.' He spread his arms to indicate what was holding up the ceiling.

No need to mansplain, Barry. Those walls now felt as though they were closing in on me. At last, Barry looked me in the eye. 'Understood?'

'Understood perfectly.' I coughed and shifted in the chair. 'Who will I be presenting with, if it's not Billy?'

'It'll be you and Quentin. Male and female. It's the dog's whatnots on breakfast shows.'

My stomach flipped over. I knew only one person called Quentin.

AFTER ESCAPING from Barry's office, I went straight to what served as the radio station's kitchen-slash-staffroom. The small windowless space had a table and chairs, a cupboard full of mismatched crockery, a fridge, and a worktop. You could make a hot drink, a slice of toast, or microwave a Marks & Spencer lasagne into bubbling life. But it was also a refuge in times of stress and a place to find a few minutes' peace and thinking time.

I slumped on a chair, trying to ignore the lingering aroma of cremated toast from someone's breakfast. My first day back, doing the job I loved, was ruined. It took only that short meeting with Barry to extinguish the joy of my return to my daily routine.

I looked into the open cake tin on the table. I'd brought it in that morning, filled with home-made brownies for my workmates. Just for once, I wished my radio friends weren't so enthusiastic about my baking; only a few measly crumbs remained in the bottom of the tin. I licked the tip of my finger and stabbed at them, transferring them one by one to my tongue, as tears slid down my cheeks.

Those few chocolatey morsels reminded me I still had to cancel the booking I'd made for the weekend in Vienna for Zeller's birthday later in the month. Even though I didn't like going abroad, being away anywhere with her was always fun.

Zeller had been a travel writer who'd visited dozens of capital cities. It was ironic that she'd never been to Austria's capital and eaten its famously sinful chocolate cake. It was also ironic that twelve months after beating breast cancer, a massive stroke had extinguished her life like a sudden draught snuffing a candle flame. My beloved aunt was only seventy-one when she died.

CHAPTER TWO

I usually spent the hour after my show with Dan, my producer, going through the running order and details for the next day. But just before my show had ended, I received a message from Barry asking me to see him in his office as soon as I was off-air.

Oblivious to what awaited me, I told Dan I'd see him back in the production office, but when I returned later from the staff room, I found a yellow Post-it Note stuck to my computer screen: *Barry's called me in. Back soon.*

I knew what that meeting was about and would have given my signed copy of *Mary Berry's Baking Bible* to be a fly on the wall.

While I waited for Dan, I checked through the running order for the next day. He still hadn't returned, so I flicked through the diary to see what he'd arranged for the rest of the week.

Although my stomach was still churning from Barry's news, I couldn't help but beam when I saw the name Gil McGill scheduled for Friday's show. My resourceful producer had booked an interview with the famous rock star, who was the new owner of a Tudor manor house in Warwickshire said to be the haunt of a resident ghost. It would be the highlight of the week.

'Pub – now!'

I looked up to see Dan, his pale complexion flushed. He didn't sit down but threw his notepad and biro onto the desk. The slap of the notebook landing made a few colleagues turn their heads.

'He's told you, then,' I said in a quiet voice as we both shut down our computers and gathered our things to leave for the day.

'Fire exit stairs.' Dan tipped his head towards the door to the external metal staircase. 'If I see Barry again today, I'll deck him.'

'WELL, that turned into a crappy first day back,' I said, sipping Perrier in The Oak Inn. 'It won't be a good one for Billy, either, on Monday.' He and his friend Greg were in Barcelona.

'He'll be gutted, poor sod.' Dan took a slurp of his Guinness, licked the creamy foam from his top lip, and put down his glass. 'But Quentin Lowe? Barry must have heard about your history with him.'

'Oh, he knew all right. He believes we'll be "a dream team" because listeners will love hearing two people bickering at breakfast time.'

'Sounds like home,' Dan said. 'My parents' arguing is what gets me out of the house early and at the gym before work.' He grinned. 'Nothing to do with Daisy, of course.' My producer had a huge crush on his nubile personal trainer.

'Haven't you asked her out for a drink yet?'

'I was *this* close.' He held up a finger and thumb that were almost touching. 'We got chatting last week, waiting for a free treadmill, and she told me I reminded her of Louis Theroux. Talk about a turn-off.'

We laughed out loud – although I secretly shared Daisy's opinion – and the three elderly regulars at the bar turned to dispense disapproving looks. Then my thoughts returned to what I still referred to as the Dark Days, when I worked on the drive-time show with Quentin. Resentful about my appointment as his co-presenter, he did everything possible to belittle me and make my life miserable.

'Remember when he used to introduce me as his "travel tart"?' Quentin had moved from a larger station, and Bard FM's owner (who visited the station only once a year, before Christmas) considered him such a catch that he told the station manager to give him free rein to format the show. He formatted me as the travel and weather reporter (aka "travel tart") and himself as the star turn.

'Nobody gets away with stuff like that now' – Dan shook his head and made quote marks in the air with his fingers – 'not in these "Me Too" times.'

I appreciated my friend's attempt to reassure me but knew the chauvinistic Barry wouldn't side with me if any problems arose.

When Barry's predecessor realised my relationship with Quentin was on the verge of going nuclear, he gave me the opportunity to become the new afternoon show presenter. It was a position I'd cherished for a decade.

Quentin's time at Bard FM ended soon afterwards. One night, after everybody had left the building and an automated programme was on-air, he sneaked back into the station with a listener. He'd invited her for a private after-hours tour … of each other. Well, it would have been private if Quentin had read the memo about the new security camera in the production studio.

According to my male colleagues (who gleefully watched the steamy footage before our former boss deleted it), the young woman had all the attributes of a professional contortionist. They weren't so envious the next day when the station manager sacked Quentin. And now Barry had employed him again for the station's most important show. Inexplicable.

Dan swallowed the last of his Guinness and stood up. 'Something stronger this time?'

'Why not? G&T please.' I didn't have to drive anywhere that evening. 'I was going over to Mum and Dad's for some advice, but they've just started dance classes on Monday evenings.'

'Can't picture your dad doing an Anton du Beke,' he said.

'Neither can I … he's got two left feet. But *Strictly Come Dancing* is Mum's favourite TV show, and he likes to keep her happy.'

I watched him walk with care from the bar back to the table, his brimming pint glass in one hand and my gin in the other, the bottle of tonic protruding from his jeans pocket. His mouth was fixed in a silly grin, and between his teeth he gripped two bags of salt and vinegar crisps.

He reminded me of Gofer, the Labrador puppy and sibling-substitute my parents bought me on my seventh birthday. Whenever anyone came to the front door, our crazy pooch would rush to greet them, his tail wagging and a scatter cushion from the sofa held fast in his jaw; he'd then drop it at the visitor's feet. *Happy days.*

'Oh Dan, what would I do without you to make me laugh?'

He put down the drinks and unclenched his teeth, releasing the bags of crisps onto the table.

'Don't say I never buy you dinner.' He gave me an exaggerated wink. 'Now, I need you to cheer me up.' He pushed his black-framed Theroux-style glasses back up the bridge of his nose. 'How am I going to turn that soap "star" into a radio presenter?'

CHAPTER THREE

Twenty-seater cinema. Heated indoor pool and Jacuzzi. Snooker room. Temperature-controlled cigar cave. My eyes widened as I looked at the captioned interior images of Butterwick Hall on the upmarket estate agent's website. Each photo had the word 'Sold' emblazoned across it, but I found no mention of the property's selling price. If you had to ask, I figured, you couldn't afford it. Gil wouldn't have needed to ask.

The image of the impressive wine cellar made me groan, and I clicked straight to the next one. *Ugh.* I couldn't think about wine that Friday morning; feeling no more positive about the prospect of working with Quentin again, I'd finished a bottle of Sauvignon Blanc before going to bed – my second indulgence in alcohol that week on a school night. *Just call me Lush Lundon.*

According to the website, Henry VIII once stayed a few nights at the Tudor hall with a mistress. It was a good chat-up story for Gil, but I imagined anyone with lady-of-the-manor aspirations would find the twenty-first century comforts and conveniences more appealing.

I guessed the Fender Stratocaster guitar ace bought the place for reasons other than its historical interest and wondered if he even knew the stories about Butterwick Hall's rumoured ghost—

'You're early today.' I looked up to see Dan, who'd just arrived. He shrugged out of his leather bomber jacket and hung it over the back of his chair.

'Reading about this place Gil bought.' I grinned at my producer. 'Quite the pad for wild rock star parties. Maybe he'll invite us to one.'

He laughed.

'Let's not hold our breath on that one. Coffee?' He didn't wait for an answer but, as he did every day, went to make our hot drinks. Who'd make my coffee in future? It was unlikely to be Quentin.

I'd come in an hour earlier than usual that morning to retrieve and save sound files of recent interviews. If the breakfast show didn't work out (I wasn't optimistic), some audio material to send with job applications to other radio stations would be essential. Using my editing suite on my home laptop, I would compile a showreel of my best clips.

Once I'd saved what I wanted, I started doing research about my guest. As I'd lain awake in bed during the night, the ceiling swirling above me, I told myself the interview with Gil was going to be the best I'd ever done. Thanks to Google, I now knew everything from his shoe size (a whopping fifteen) to his favourite coffee brand (Illy), to his first job (undertaker's assistant). Perhaps he had already encountered ghosts?

When Dan returned and placed a steaming mug of coffee on my desk, he lowered his voice.

'Did you get to speak to your folks last night?'

I'd contacted them each day that week, intending to go over one evening for some of their wise counsel.

'No. Most unlike them, but they've been out all week. I hope I'll have better luck this weekend.'

THE WEEK PASSED QUICKLY and with no further mention of the imminent changes to the breakfast show, which would remain a secret until Billy was off-air on Monday morning at ten o'clock. I felt sick every time I thought about the effect the news would have on him and the whole team.

Apart from Barry and Quentin, Dan and I were the only people aware of what was going to happen, so there was no conversation about it in the office. It was almost as though I had imagined the scenario with the boss. Until late Friday afternoon.

The interview with Gil had been a great success, even though his overbearing PR manager insisted on being in the studio with us. His presence didn't stop Gil sharing some hilarious stories about life on tour. Afterwards Dan took a selfie of the three of us – without Mr Overbearing – in the studio.

As he left, Gil said he'd invite Dan and me to the housewarming party he was planning for July. Although he would doubtless forget about the invitation before then, we were already debating the possible dress code and etiquette with regard to taking a bottle of wine to a super-wealthy person's party.

As I sat down at my desk, an email notification flashed onto the screen: it was from Barry and headed 'Quentin'. Perhaps my old adversary had decided against moving back to Bard FM after all? Now that would have been the perfect end to what had been a brilliant Friday. I opened the message, hoping.

Quentin's coming for a meeting on Monday morning at eleven o'clock about the new show. You may wish to come in earlier to join us.

May? I was supposed to be the co-presenter. Of course I should be there. I stormed out of the production office. If the door hadn't had an anti-slam mechanism, it would have rattled the windows in their frames.

BARRY DIDN'T SUBSCRIBE to the staff benefits of an open-door policy. I knocked, then walked straight in before he could reply – almost a crime, in his view. He looked up, face flushed, and snapped shut his laptop.

'I'd appreciate it if—'

'A quick word, please, Barry?'

'Okay.' He glanced at his fake Rolex. 'Make it speedy, though. Due at a drinks do at the town hall in ten.'

'This won't take long.' I dropped into the chair opposite my boss and paused. *Just go for it.*

'I've been thinking about what you told me on Monday.' I almost sounded calm. 'But I can't work with Quentin again, so I'm giving you a month's notice of my resignation. You'll have it in writing before I leave for home.'

Barry leaned his elbows on the desk and steepled his hands, an ugly sneer on his face.

'Got another job, have you?'

'No. But, as you know, Quentin and I worked together in the past, and it's not an experience I care to repeat. I'd rather be unemployed.'

'You disappoint me, Laura. I thought you'd be up to

the challenge, but you're behaving like a petulant child.' He picked up his pen and twirled it between his fingers in that annoying way of his. 'Resignation accepted. No need to work your notice – just let me have it in writing, then you can go.'

'What do you mean?'

'Clear your desk. Leave the office. You'll get your full month's pay, of course.'

'But … my show—'

'I can't risk you saying anything negative on-air. This is standard industry practice, as you must be aware. I imagine Odette will be delighted to start earlier.'

I stood up with such force that the chair tipped and crashed to the floor behind me. Pick it up yourself, I thought, with a last glare at Barry. I stormed out, leaving the door wide open.

OUTSIDE THE PRODUCTION OFFICE, I took a few deep breaths. I could do this. Aware of a few of my colleagues glancing up from their work, I made no eye contact with anyone and said nothing as I stomped to my desk. I opened a new Word document on the computer and thumped out my brief letter of resignation.

Without speaking to anyone, I strode over to the printer, removed the sheet of paper, and signed it with a flourish, before folding it into an envelope on which I'd written Barry's name in angry capital letters.

No way would I deliver it in person, so I walked to the row of pigeonholes near the door and slid it into the one labelled *Station Manager*. Alongside the photocopier, I found a carton containing reams of copy paper, which I removed and dumped onto the floor. I took the empty

box back to my desk and transferred my personal possessions from each drawer into it. I couldn't look at Dan in
case I burst into tears.

'What's going on?' he hissed across our desks.

'I'm out of here,' I muttered.

Everyone else was trying to appear focused on their
work, but an expectant silence hung over the room.

'Whaaat?' Dan's face was a blur through my tear-
filled eyes. 'Tell me—'

His phone rang, and he answered it, stony-faced. No
prizes for guessing who was calling him. Dan banged
down the receiver and, without looking at me, scribbled
on a Post-it, which he handed me across the desk: *Told not
to talk to you. Will call you later.*

He strode out of the room, cursing under his breath.
With tears trickling down my cheeks, I gathered my
possessions and headed for the fire exit door for the final
time.

'ARE you still able to take Fergus out this evening?' Miss
Barker's booming voice made me jump. I'd been so deep
in thought, trudging up the stairs in my apartment block,
I almost dropped the box I was carrying.

'Sorry to startle you, dear,' my downstairs neighbour
called up the staircase from her doorway. 'I saw your car
arrive and wanted to catch you on the way up, just to
make sure.'

With all the events of the day, I had forgotten my
promise to walk Miss Barker's Westie that evening. The
retired head teacher was going to Birmingham for a
reunion dinner – one of her rare social engagements. To
be at the restaurant for the pre-prandial sherry and

canapés, Warwickshire's slowest driver needed to depart before it was time for Fergus to go walkies.

'Of course, Miss Barker,' I called back. 'I'll just put my stuff upstairs and change. Be down in ten minutes.' I hoped a cold, wet flannel held against my eyes for a minute or five would reduce the impact of my crying. My downstairs neighbour had a blunt manner, and if she spotted evidence of tears, she wouldn't hesitate to ask the reason for them.

Fergus and I went for a brisk half-hour walk along the canal towpath, which was rich in interesting scents for his twitching black nose. His short tail was in non-stop wagging mode as he snuffled at the grassy verges; he, at least, was happy. I took deep breaths of the cool spring air, as if to fill the hollowness I felt inside.

Bard FM had been a daytime home and workplace for so long, I'd never imagined myself leaving to work anywhere else. My closest friends worked there, and it would be hard not to see them every day.

Over the years, I'd helped train new colleagues, been to farewell parties for others, and even attended the funeral of one who had died far too young. In all my time there, Quentin was the only person to leave the station suddenly, clutching a black bin bag of his possessions.

At least I walked out of Bard FM with my things in a box. And I'd never had sex in the production studio – far too dangerous with all that electrical equipment around.

MY NEIGHBOUR HAD GIVEN me a spare key for her apartment so I could let Fergus in for his dinner after our walk. He headed straight for his food bowl in the kitchen and, after I'd stroked his head and told him to be a good boy, I left the key and the leash on the hall console table and went upstairs to my home.

Leaving my mobile phone on the coffee table while I was out was a deliberate policy, and it was no surprise on my return to find several texts, missed calls, and WhatsApp messages from workmates. My resignation and sudden departure had shocked everyone, but I couldn't explain yet why I'd left the job I loved.

I read everything but wasn't in the mood to reply. Just as I was about to switch the phone off, Dan rang me.

'Got you at last. How are you, Laura?'

'Feeling numb,' I said. 'Can't quite believe I'm finished at the station, although I guess it'll sink in soon.'

He offered to come round. And bring wine and a takeaway pizza.

'Thanks, Dan, but I'm having a bath and an early night. I haven't slept well at all this week.'

'Okay. As long as you're sure.' He paused. 'How about breakfast tomorrow at Huffkins? Ten o'clock?'

Irresistible. Dan was persuasive, and if I saw him in the morning, it would give me the rest of the day free. I still needed to catch up with my parents, although the news I'd wanted to share on Monday had since changed.

AN ELECTRONIC TUNE interrupted a bizarre nightmare in which I was interviewing Boris Johnson on *Desert Island Discs*. It was a relief to wake up and not see the prime minister facing me, running a hand through the messy mop on his head.

Despite a dull headache and tightness in my shoulders, I answered the phone before I spotted it was Billy calling. At least he'd waited until a decent hour; even at the weekends my friend was up just after five in the morning.

'Hello, Billy. Are you home again?'

'Yes, I am, sugar plum – and full of the joys. But how are you, now you're back at work?'

His cheerful tone suggested he didn't know I'd left the station. In a voice still thick with sleep, I told him things were fine.

'I *have* heard you sound better.' Billy's concerned tone was evident. 'Listen, Laura, my contact at The Swan's offered me a couple of prime tickets for tonight's performance of *The Provoked Wife*. Hilarious, they tell me – and a Restoration romp may be just the tonic you need. Fancy a luvvie night? Drinks at The Mucky Duck first?'

Under normal circumstances I would have snapped up the invitation because our theatre nights out were always fun. Billy had good contacts in the Royal Shakespeare Company and the theatrical set's favourite watering hole; they usually treated us to the best seats and a complimentary drink in the eighteenth-century pub.

I also appreciated Billy's old-fashioned manners. He was the only man I knew who opened doors for me, and when we were walking anywhere together, insisted on being on the kerbside of the pavement.

As much as a night out would be a welcome tonic, it would be impossible to be my normal self with him, knowing the news that awaited him on Monday.

'Oh, thank you, Billy, that would've been a real treat,

but I'm busy all this weekend. I'm sorry. Catch up soon, yeah?'

He sounded so upbeat after his holiday, and it pained me to know his world would be turned upside down once he returned to work. I wondered if his jolly mood was anything to do with Greg, the man he went to Barcelona with; they often went away together. It was funny: I'd been a friend of Billy's for years, but I knew little about his romantic life.

IF DAN COULD TELL on Saturday morning that I'd cried a bath's worth of tears the previous evening, he was too discreet to mention it. As we sat having a mid-morning breakfast together in the busy Stratford café, I told him Billy was back and in good spirits.

'Shame that's going to change on Monday,' Dan said. 'Anyway, we're here to talk about you. What did your folks say about your news?'

'They still don't know. I left them an answerphone message again last night to call me, but they haven't so far.' I gave a wry laugh. 'Wish I had such a busy social life.'

I expected Dan to make one of his usual comments about Andy being away so much but, for once, he said nothing about my often-absent boyfriend.

'What are you going to do about a new job?'

'First, I'm going to make a showreel, then look online for suitable presenter vacancies.' I sipped my coffee. 'If you hear of anything, you know what to do. Zeller left me a little money and her house, so I should be okay for a month or two.'

'Well, if you need a reference, give them my details.'
He grinned. 'I'll write one that'll do the business for you.'

'Aw, thanks, Dan. I'm going to miss you so much,
wherever I go.' I swallowed hard and looked into the
bottom of my empty cup. 'Fancy another coffee?'

Before he could answer, my phone vibrated and
shimmied across the table. I'd left it on silent mode but
could see it was Mum calling. At last, she was returning
my calls. With one hand over my right ear to block out
the café chatter and clatter, I answered the phone.

'Hey, Mum … I've been trying to—' I listened,
grimaced, and glanced at Dan, who raised an eyebrow.

'Okay, Mum. Please don't cry. I'll just get the car and
drive straight—'

The line went dead. I dropped my phone into my
handbag and pulled out a ten-pound note, which I
dropped onto the table.

'Here, this was on me.' I stood up. 'Sorry, Dan, gotta
go. I've never heard Mum in such a state.'

He stood too and placed his hand on my shoulder.

'Try not to worry. Probably still grief over Zeller.
Takes a long while to get over the loss of a sibling.' He
paused, and I guessed he was remembering his younger
sister, Penny, who died at the age of fourteen after a
horse-riding accident. 'Want me to drive you?'

'Thanks, Dan, but I'll be fine.' I stood on tiptoes and
kissed my friend on the cheek. 'See you soon.'

As I strode down the road towards home to collect
my car, I repeated a silent prayer: *Please God, don't let it be
cancer. Please God, don't let it be cancer.*

CHAPTER FOUR

'Mum, I'm here!' I called out as I opened the front door of my former home, using my old key. Sobbing came from the lounge, and I rushed through to find Mum hunched on the sofa next to Dad. He had one arm around her shoulders; she was crying into his Fair Isle sweater. He looked up and gave me a weak smile.

'Hello, love, thanks for coming. I was in the greenhouse when your mum rang you. We'd agreed not to tell you yet, but it's been playing on her mind since the funeral, so I think the time has come.'

It occurred to me they could have been avoiding my calls during the week, instead of being out living their best social life. I'd never seen Mum in such a state, not even on that awful morning when she found our elderly dog Gofer had died in his sleep, curled up in his basket.

'Tell me what?' I looked from Dad to Mum and back to Dad, whose expression revealed no discernible emotion. 'You're not getting divorced, are you?'

Dad's bushy salt and pepper eyebrows shot up

towards his widow's peak. 'Of course not, love. Whatever gave you that crazy idea?'

It *was* crazy. Mum and Dad were the happiest couple
I knew. Perhaps they were selling the house, planning to
tour Europe by campervan, and feared breaking the
news to me? No. I'd inherited my unadventurous spirit
from them; they were unlikely to be giving up their home
comforts for a life involving a one-foot-square shower
cubicle and a chemical loo.

I couldn't bring myself to mention the C-word;
which of them was most likely to be ill? They had always
been healthy, although both looked peaky at that
moment.

'Well, whatever, it must be something serious,' I said,
looking at Mum's tear-streaked face. I knelt on the floor
in front of her and took her hands in mine, giving them
a reassuring squeeze. Hospitals made Dad queasy, but
now I was without a job I could accompany Mum if she
needed regular treatments.

'How about I make us all some tea?' Dad knew the
perfect remedy for difficult moments. As he headed
towards the kitchen, I clambered up from the floor, sat
down next to my mum, and put my arm around her
shoulders.

'Whatever it is, Mum, we'll get through it together,' I
said, sounding more positive than I felt. 'As a family.'

My well-meant words brought on a fresh wave of
sobbing and tears. At last, Dad returned and poured us
each a mug of the steaming brew from the old Brown
Betty teapot. I moved to the nearest armchair so he
could resume his position on the sofa. How could I have
even considered that an impending divorce might be the
reason for Mum's state on the phone earlier?

Dad took a sip of his tea, then put his mug down on a coaster. Mum still hadn't touched her drink.

I looked at the steam curling up from my mug for a few moments before speaking.

'Have you or Mum got … a serious disease?' I couldn't say 'cancer'. Not after Zeller's illness.

'Thank God, no. It's nothing like that, love. Apart from the odd creaky joint, I think we're both in pretty decent health for our age.'

I exhaled. But this good news didn't explain Mum's distress.

'You know we love you,' he blurted out. 'We've raised an incredible, loving daughter and couldn't be prouder of the woman you've become.'

Mum's shoulders were shaking, and if I'd stood up then, my legs would have been too. Where was this conversation going?

'Thank you,' I said in a quiet voice. 'You did a super job as parents, so most of the credit's yours.'

'There is no simple way to tell you this – which is why your mum's so upset …' My father chewed his lower lip as he did when grappling with a complex clue in *The Times*'s cryptic crossword. 'The thing is … although we raised you as our own daughter … almost from birth … we're not your biological parents.'

That news wiped the matter of losing my beloved job right out of my mind.

BACK AT MY first-floor flat on the other side of town, I kicked off my shoes and dropped my bag in the hallway. A quick look in the mirror revealed a tear-stained face and puffy eyes. I hadn't cried like that since my ill-fated marriage ended after only six months.

I went straight to the coffee table in the living room where I put down the book Dad had given me and collapsed onto the sofa.

A headache was looming, so I closed my eyes and rubbed circles on my temples, hoping to keep the pain at bay. I thought that losing both my aunt and my job were the worst things to happen to me since my late twenties – when my husband left me for Kevin, our postman – but this latest news eclipsed even that.

What my parents told me was like a storyline in a TV soap – the type in which Odette Williams might have a part. However, this was not the result of a scriptwriter's creativity, but authentic life. My life. One with a landscape rocked as if by an earthquake. All because of one shocking and incredible conversation.

How could the three people I trusted most have kept such an enormous secret from me all my life? I replayed the shattering scene in my head.

'It was Zeller's wish to keep it from you,' Dad said in a firm voice, in response to my outburst after he'd told me. He stood up, red-faced, and walked over to the roll-top desk by the window. My heart was pounding as he picked up a hardback book and brought it back over. With a shaking hand, I took it from him but couldn't find the words to respond.

Dad became emotional then, but I was too shocked to do anything but scoop up my car keys and handbag and storm out of my old family home. A ground-floor window rattled after I slammed the front door. It was wrong to leave like that, but it stopped me from saying something I would later regret.

'I am *still* Laura Lundon,' I repeated aloud to myself

during the short and speed-limit-breaking drive back to my apartment. 'I am still *me.*'

In the quiet of my home, curled into my sofa, I somehow dozed off. When I woke up – my neck stiff and mouth as dry as Weetabix in want of milk – I had no idea how long I'd been asleep or, for a moment, even where I was. Then I spotted Zeller's pristine publication in front of me on the coffee table. Had I read *Deià Dreams* before? The title was unfamiliar, but Dad told me it was Zeller's debut travel book.

Even before I was old enough to read them, my aunt would put aside a signed first edition of each of her published books. She gave me the initial instalment of the collection on my thirteenth birthday. Those and her subsequent books lived on the top shelf of my bookcase.

I stood up and padded across the Turkish rug – a gift from Zeller after a trip to Istanbul – to check the titles. Each book contained a personal dedication to me in her exuberant handwriting. Why was there no copy of *Deià Dreams*?

Zeller's passion had been travelling the world and writing about her experiences. In contrast, I was a geography dunce at school and didn't enjoy foreign travel. There'd been a teenage holiday in a Normandy gîte with Mum and Dad, a wet weekend in Paris with my long-term boyfriend, Andy, and a friend's raucous hen party in Amsterdam. My passport spent most of the time tucked away in my underwear drawer.

What did I know about Mallorca? I skimmed the newspapers every day at work and heard the office chatter about the reality TV show *Love Island,* filmed at a luxury villa there. To me, the largest of the Balearic Islands was a mixed bag of everything from drunken Brits jumping from Magaluf hotel balconies to a messy end on the concrete below, to celebrities – of varying degrees of fame and undress – flaunting their money and perma-tans on gleaming motor yachts or beside glittering swimming pools.

The mountain village of Deià had been the haunt of famous people for several decades, but Zeller was unlikely to have been there because of its celebrity appeal.

As a travel writer, she focused on the cultural aspects of places she visited. She excelled at finding interesting locals and telling engaging anecdotes. As I scanned the titles on the spines of her books, I recalled her story about the chicken-intestine crackers in a restaurant in Bali. Of Zeller's many travel tales, it was a favourite.

But whatever had she found to write about in a mountain village in Mallorca? Curiosity overwhelmed me. I returned to the sofa and picked up the hardback copy of *Deià Dreams* with both hands, as though it were as precious as the Gutenberg Bible.

The pristine book's cover illustration was a watercolour painting of a young Zeller standing in profile on a huge rock, one hand shading her eyes as she gazed at the azure Mediterranean.

I flipped to the inside flap of the book jacket, where I found an old black and white photograph of her. Even though it was an old photo, I could see her likeness to her sister. How ironic that people had told me how much I looked like Mum.

I swivelled around on the sofa, put my feet up, and flicked through the pages of the thick book, seeing the numbers grow: one hundred and ten … one hundred and ninety-two ... two hundred. Zeller hadn't been short of inspiration.

As the crisp, cream-coloured pages fanned past, I was sure I caught a faint hint of Reminiscence Patchouli – Zeller's favourite fragrance. Her frequent travels through duty-free enabled her to spray herself with apparent abandon at all times. I could always tell when Zeller had been in a room.

I stopped fanning through the book for a moment, remembering when I was maybe fourteen or fifteen. On Zeller's return from a trip to Madrid, she presented me with a tissue-wrapped parcel tied with a cream velvet ribbon. After I ripped off the wrappings (hoping for a box of exotic Spanish chocolates), I found a bottle of Chanel Cristalle. Zeller had bought me my first proper perfume, and my confectionery cravings melted like chocolate left too close to a log fire.

Chanel Cristalle was still my fragrance of choice on special occasions but, as an infrequent overseas traveller, I didn't have the luxury of regular duty-free purchases. For everyday use, I bought whatever fragrance I most liked from the two-for-one offers at Boots.

The velvet ribbon from that gift of perfume was among my treasured mementoes, which I kept in a carved wooden casket Zeller brought me back from the Philippines. Sitting on my sofa with my thoughts, I realised for the first time how much she must have thought about me while she was travelling.

I started flicking through the book again. Somewhere towards the end, I found something tucked inside. With care, I removed two sheets of folded notepaper.

It was the onion-skin writing paper Zeller always used, whether penning a newsy letter during a longer assignment or scribbling a hasty pre-trip note to cancel her newspaper deliveries. When I was around five years old, I asked Zeller why she wrote on 'funny paper'.

'Because it weighs almost nothing,' she replied. 'When you're flying, it's important to travel light so you can fit plenty of clean knickers in your suitcase.' The word 'knickers' sent little-girl-me into fits of giggles, which caused a minor accident in my own.

I doubted that I'd found a shopping list Zeller had absent-mindedly slipped into the book and mislaid. But my hands trembled too much to unfold the pages.

'Wine,' I said aloud to the room, needing something to slow down the thoughts cascading through my mind. In the kitchen I poured a generous glass of Sauvignon Blanc from the fridge and retrieved a box of tissues.

I didn't often drink alcohol when I was alone, even less when it was still daylight outside. Reading a letter from a woman I'd always believed to be my aunt but who was, in fact, my biological mother? That called for help. After a long sip of the chilled white wine and a deep breath, I sat back, unfolded the pages, and began to read.

CHAPTER FIVE

M ay 28th, 2008
         Darling Daughter,
    As you'll see, I am penning this on my sixtieth birthday.
Perhaps I am facing my mortality?

    At times, I am sorry that you will learn the truth when it is too
late for us to have a normal mother-and-daughter relationship.
Instead, I wanted you to have that with my sister, who's been a
wonderful mum to you. But I hope you agree the affection between
us was more than that of an aunt and her niece.

    I fell in love during my stay in Mallorca, but I realised it
wasn't going to last. Life is too short to commit to someone you don't
care for with all your heart. My passion was fuelled by the beau-
tiful environment, the sun, the sea, and plentiful wine. Those influ-
ences remained, but the infatuation faded. Unlike your mum, I
didn't ever find 'the one', but I've never regretted staying single.

    Your biological father gave me the most precious gift: you. Even
if I had loved him enough, I didn't want to stay longer on the
island, although I'll admit Mallorca's natural beauty and tradi-
tional culture enchanted me.

    When I returned home pregnant with you and learnt that your mum and dad were unable to have their own children, I saw it as a sign from God and knew what I had to do. My sister was desperate to start a family, but it was impossible for her to conceive.

I'll never forget their reaction when I made my offer. The indescribable joy on your mum's face is a memory I've revisited many times since. She has always said you were the most treasured gift she could ever have received.

We spent endless hours discussing everything, but I had the final say in choosing your name. We agreed I'd be a big part of your life, and that's why, when they moved from Lichfield to Stratford as new parents just after you were born, I relocated too. I bought the house behind theirs so I was able to see you every day I wasn't away on my travels.

Our only disagreement was about when to tell you all this. Your mum and dad were adamant they wanted you to know as soon as you were old enough to understand. I insisted that you should grow up believing they were your parents and I was your aunt. I'm still convinced it was the best decision in the circumstances.

You may find all this difficult to come to terms with, but I hope one day you'll accept that this was my wish … and mine alone. I would hate you to blame your parents for not telling you before.

This has been a Herculean secret for me to keep. Remember when I asked you to stop calling me Aunty? I told you it made me feel old. The truth is the word stabbed at my heart, even though I'd done what was best for us all.

I must have written millions of words in my lifetime, but this letter has been my most challenging piece of writing. And you may never get to read it because if, God forbid, my sister dies first, I shall explain all of this to you in person and ask for your forgiveness.

Darling Laura, the unveiling of this family secret will have shocked and upset you, but I hope you will forgive us all and continue to treat your mum and dad as your parents. The three of us have always loved you as a daughter.

Although you're not an enthusiastic traveller, my greatest wish is that you'll visit Mallorca one day. You were conceived in a beautiful mountain village, which makes Deià a part of you, just as you're a part of me.

Your loving mother,

Zeller

'All the things we might have done together,' I wailed. The combination of tears and ink would render the writing illegible, so I put down the fragile pages and reached for a tissue.

We had become closer since my divorce and move back to Stratford. Accompanying her to some of her morning chemotherapy sessions had further strengthened our relationship. I couldn't believe I'd never see her again.

I remembered shopping trips, occasional spa days, and evenings chatting over supper and wine at each other's homes. How had Zeller kept a gargantuan secret like this from me during those intimate occasions? Even on that evening when we drank two bottles of Pol Roger between us to celebrate a book award. So much for *in vino veritas*. The headache from Hades the next morning put me off champagne for months. Well, a few weeks.

We had a lot of fun together over the years but, as memories came back to me, I knew I had sometimes hurt Zeller's feelings more than I could have realised at the time. As a teenager, it seemed uncool to be hanging out with an aunt and, like many teens, I preferred spending my free time with friends rather than family. I flushed with shame at the memory of one occasion.

'I'm going to Paris on Saturday to check out a new hotel,' Zeller said. 'How about coming with me? We'll have dinner on a boat on the Seine, a night in five-star splendour, and do Disneyland.'

Despite France being 'foreign', I would have snapped

up the opportunity to spend a Parisian-pastry-packed weekend with Zeller now. The sixteen-year-old me grimaced.

'Thank you, but Disneyland's for kids. Anyway, I'm going ice skating with Meryl this Saturday.'

My rude and selfish attitude must have hurt Zeller, and if mine was typical teenage behaviour, I was glad I hadn't had children.

I reread the first few paragraphs of her letter and stopped at the mention of 'the one'. Was Andy Webb 'the one' for me? We had fun and were fond of each other but – for both of us – it was a convenient relationship that coasted along with few problems. We both loved our jobs and understood each other's work ethic. Although we sometimes spent a night together at either Andy's or my apartment, we didn't share a home. My failed marriage had made me wary of any arrangement threatening my independence.

Andy's freelance wildlife cameraman assignments often took him away for extended periods. Some women wouldn't want a partner with his lifestyle, but I respected the importance of his career to him.

My boyfriend's latest assignment was a long one in Japan, filming for a TV documentary series. He'd been there for a month, and I didn't expect to see him in person again for at least another month or two.

We kept in touch by email because of the eight-hour time difference, although he had made a WhatsApp phone call to explain how sorry he was that his work schedule wouldn't allow him to fly back to the UK for Zeller's funeral.

Andy and I hadn't exchanged emails for a couple of weeks. His last one had been a follow-up to his phone call, restating his regret that he couldn't be with me when we said a final goodbye to my aunt. I still needed to reply to that. I considered phoning him instead. But although it was early evening in Stratford-upon-Avon, it was the middle of the night in Tokyo; my hardworking boyfriend would be fast asleep.

I needed friendly company, and thankfully I wouldn't have to wait long.

THE DOORBELL RANG. I wasn't expecting visitors, but even a couple of Jehovah's Witnesses on the doorstep would have been a welcome distraction. When I opened the door, I couldn't help but smile. Dan stood there with a grease-stained paper carrier bag in one hand and a bottle of wine tucked under his arm.

'I decided not to ask first this time,' he explained as I ushered him in. 'Just checking in with you after that phone call from your mum this morning. Brought supplies.'

'Ooh, thank you,' I said. 'Smells delicious.'

'From that new Indian place near the theatre. Thought we should try it.'

He handed me the carrier bag, which emitted spicy aromas. I rarely ate Indian cuisine, but the tantalising aroma reminded me I'd missed lunch.

Dan followed me into the kitchen, where I warmed some plates under the hot tap while he pulled a couple of cans of lager from my fridge. We agreed to eat first, talk later, and were soon sitting at my breakfast bar tucking into enough chicken jalfrezi, onion bhajis, and basmati rice to feed the whole of my apartment block.

After putting the dirty dishes to soak in the sink, Dan opened the wine and we moved through to the sofa.

'How was your mum?' He poured two glasses of the Sauvignon Blanc. 'All okay?'

No way was I sharing what I'd learnt earlier in the day; I needed time to process it all first.

'Yeah,' I said in the breeziest tone possible, 'it was grief, as you suggested.'

'At least your dad's supportive. Mine was useless with Mum when my sister died. Spent most of his time in the pub getting sozzled.'

I thought of all the support Dad had given me when I moved back to Stratford after my marriage ended. 'I'm lucky. My dad is a real gem.' He was always there for Mum and me, with a hug, kind words, or practical help. But he wasn't my biological father, and neither of my parents had any idea who had contributed his genes to me.

At that moment I realised there was only one way forward. If I wanted to know his identity, it would be down to me to find out. Despite how I felt about going abroad, I knew I'd soon have to travel to Mallorca.

CHAPTER SIX

S unday was a lost day. Let's just say I remembered why I'd sworn off Indian food last time. What a pity; it had been tasty, if a little fiery. I crawled out of bed mid-morning, switched on my phone, and found a WhatsApp message from Dan.

OMG, what was in that jalfrezi? In the loo all night. Hope you're OK.

I replied that I shared his pain and wished him a speedy recovery. Then I turned off the phone – noting there was no communication from Mum and Dad – and returned to bed. The frequency of my bathroom visits slowed down, and I even managed to sleep, albeit in a fitful way between weird dreams. I woke with a start after one dream, wondering what Zeller would have done if her sister hadn't wanted children. Would I have been put up for adoption? Or worse? Somehow, I fell back to sleep.

When I woke again, the sun was setting behind the trees on the other side of the canal.

Wrapped in my dressing gown and nursing a cup of

tea, I sat at my laptop and listened to the first of the radio interviews I'd saved onto my thumb drive. Creating a new showreel was going to be more work than I'd thought.

DAN CALLED me from Bard FM after eleven o'clock the next day.

'Morning. You better?' He sounded his usual self.

'Fine now, thanks. Slept most of yesterday, but that was preferable to moping around the place, mourning for my job.' I remembered it was Monday. 'How's Billy? Has Barry told him yet?'

'Yeah, he has. And Billy didn't take it well, as we expected. He left the station straight after the meeting, without speaking to anyone.'

Bad news. I sighed, blowing out my cheeks.

'I'll call him later.' My day was clear, apart from working on my new showreel. Billy was one of my dearest friends, and I would be there for him if he needed to talk.

DESPITE MY CALLING Billy's phone several times that Monday, he didn't answer. Who could blame him? I'd done the same on Friday evening after I left the radio station. By mid-afternoon, I was worried about the lack of response. Billy was gregarious and, as he lived on his own, relished any opportunity for conversation.

It was impossible to concentrate on anything. At five o'clock, I grabbed my bag and coat and strode across town to Billy's place. His apartment was on the ground floor of a converted Victorian detached house, and when he didn't answer the doorbell, I tiptoed over the immaculate lawn at the front of the building and peered through the window into my friend's sitting room.

He wasn't there. I'd just turned to walk to the parking area at the rear of the property when I heard a woman's voice from above.

'If you're looking for Billy, I think he's gone away somewhere.'

I looked up to see his upstairs neighbour leaning out of the window. Billy had told me he had a new neighbour, and this was the first time I'd seen her.

'Oh. Thank you. I don't suppose he said where he was going?'

'We didn't speak. I saw him dash to his car, carrying a small suitcase. Drove off at quite a speed and messed up the gravel.' She pulled the window shut with a bang.

My shoulders slumped and I sighed. Perhaps he'd gone to stay with Greg for a few days? I'd try his mobile again later and if he didn't answer, send him an email.

I took a different route home through the town centre, passing a travel agency I'd never taken much notice of before. It had dedicated its window display to holidays in Mallorca, with a poster of Deià as the centrepiece. I paused for a moment to look at it and then spent the rest of my walk home knowing I was going to honour Zeller's wish and visit the island.

THE NEXT DAY I was up early for a brisk walk along the canal towpath, hoping the exercise and fine spring weather would brighten my mood. I still hadn't been able to speak to Billy; instead, I'd sent a short email of commiseration to tell him I was available if he needed to talk anytime.

Back at home, I put on my apron for some baking therapy. I love making delicious treats and, although I say it myself, friends rave about them. Whatever I'm creating – muffins, cookies, or bread – it gives me valuable thinking time. That morning my mental meanderings resulted in three-dozen chocolate and walnut muffins, twenty large cookies, and a Victoria sponge. And I don't even like Victoria sponge.

A delicious aroma wafted through the apartment, and I had to smile despite the pile of used bowls and baking tins by the kitchen sink. If I kept all those tempting goods at home, I'd comfort-eat my way through the lot in a few days.

I put the cookies into the Delft cookie jar Zeller had bought me from the Netherlands and stretched to place it out of easy reach on the kitchen's highest shelf. The Victoria sponge and two-dozen muffins went into a large cake tin, and the remaining muffins in a smaller one.

Alice, who ran the local soup kitchen for the homeless, would be grateful for the larger tin. During a recent radio interview, the warm-hearted woman had revealed the shocking number of people who relied on the cheerless place for their meals. I hoped the home-baked goodies would brighten their day.

In my odds-and-sods drawer, I found a length of red velvet ribbon which I tied into a bow around the smaller tin. My peace offering was ready.

THE SUN SHONE from a blue sky studded with cotton-wool clouds, and birds were singing in the treetops. I strode to Roseberry Avenue, planning my apology on the way. As I passed Dad's Volvo parked on the drive, I waved to my parents' neighbour, who was mowing his front lawn. My heart was racing as I stood at the familiar door.

After storming out of Mum and Dad's house on Saturday, it wasn't appropriate just to breeze in as though nothing had happened. I'd since read and reread Zeller's letter several times and realised I should have been less hasty to condemn them for keeping the Big Secret from me. It was time for an apology.

I pressed the doorbell and waited, chewing my bottom lip. Only a few moments later, Mum opened the door. Her eyebrows raised when she saw me, but what I noticed most was that she looked her usual cheerful self, with no trace of the distress I'd witnessed on Saturday. I realised then what a huge relief it must have been for my parents to unburden themselves of the family secret.

'Darling! This is a lovely surprise.' She gestured me in as though Saturday had never happened, but I sensed she understood why I hadn't let myself in.

Inside, I handed over the ribbon-wrapped tin.

'Peace offering, Mum. I'm so sorry for my reaction on Saturday.'

She put the box on the hall table and hugged me where we stood near the foot of the stairs. Like me, she hated tension.

'I shouldn't have taken it out on you and Dad,' I said, as she released me and smiled.

'I wish we'd found a better way or time to break the news to you. I'm afraid the matter had been playing on my mind ever since Zeller died, and I was dreading having to tell you. It must have been an enormous shock.'

'To be honest, I haven't been able to stop thinking about it. But Zeller's letter made it clear it was her decision, and hers alone, to keep the truth from me. I can't imagine how hard it was to keep that secret.'

Mum picked up the cake tin and turned towards the kitchen.

'I'll put the kettle on and tell your dad you're here.' He was in his greenhouse, sweet-talking his tomato plant seedlings. I followed Mum, hoping Dad would be as forgiving.

～

'THESE ARE DELICIOUS, LOVE,' Dad said, peeling the paper case from his second muffin. He chewed for a few moments with a satisfied smile on his face. 'Well, if all else fails, how about opening a bakery or café?'

I'd told my parents their daughter was now an unemployed person in need of a new challenge.

'Can't quite see that happening, Dad. Not in Stratford, anyway. Rents are too high.' I beamed at him. 'I'll take the compliment, though.'

Mum poured a second cup of tea for us all, and intuition told me she had advice to go with it.

'Is there a rush to get another job? You've worked hard for years. You could use some of Zeller's money to have a proper holiday first, instead of those short breaks you usually take.'

'Funny you should mention that.' I put down my teacup and smiled at my parents. 'I've been thinking about going away before I start looking for a new job.' Zeller had left me ten thousand pounds and 14 Ophelia Drive – her house backing onto my parents' property. 'A couple of weeks in Mallorca shouldn't eat into my inheritance too much.'

The two pairs of eyebrows opposite shot up towards the kitchen ceiling. Dad slipped his hand over Mum's on the table.

I held up my hands as though facing a gunman.

'I admit going abroad isn't really my thing, but I've started reading Zeller's book about Deià and already I'd like to see the place for myself.' It would have hurt their feelings if I'd told them I was also curious to find out the identity of my biological father.

'Isn't it a bit too soon for that?' Mum frowned as though she deduced my wish to visit had another purpose. 'Wouldn't you prefer somewhere with no links to Zeller? Until you've come to terms with things? You once said you'd like to return to Cornwall, and it is lovely in May.'

Ah, yes. Cornwall. Andy and I had stayed in Fowey for a long weekend the previous October. It was a memorable trip: 2018's Storm Callum treated us to lashing rain and fierce winds, and we were confined to the B&B's flock-wallpapered lounge with our Kindles for most of our stay. On our drive home – we left earlier than planned – Andy had to change his car's punctured tyre in a deluge on the side of the motorway. We wouldn't forget Cornwall.

But the main reason the Cornish weekend stuck in my mind was that over dinner on the first night, Andy asked for my views on marriage. I remember my stomach lurching, fearing he was about to propose. My brief experience of being married had put me off another trip up the aisle, so I was more than relieved he didn't drop to one knee and produce a small velvet-covered box containing a diamond ring.

Instead, we had a frank conversation and discovered neither of us wanted to get married, or even live together, despite having been a couple for nine years. We were both content with our somewhat unconventional relationship. To celebrate our mutual agreement on this matter, we made overenthusiastic love that night. And broke the cheap double bed in our room.

'Cornwall would be beautiful now, before the summer holidaymakers arrive,' Mum said, jolting me back from the thunderous crack in that Cornish B&B bedroom to the present.

With no job or other commitments, and extra money at my disposal, the circumstances were perfect for taking a holiday, wherever it was. I leaned across the kitchen table and squeezed Mum's free hand.

'Well, nothing's decided yet, but I'll tell you if I book something. Now, who'd like that last muffin?'

Arrived safe and sound in Palma de Mallorca. Smart hotel. Room has a sea view and balcony. Cloudless sky and it's warm! Tell you all about it when I'm back. Lots of love, L xx

After pressing send on the WhatsApp message to Mum, I switched off my phone. It was an update to my earlier message saying I was on my way to Mallorca. I hoped Mum wasn't upset that I didn't take her advice and choose Cornwall instead.

The day after I made peace with my parents, I'd sat hunched over my laptop at home, searching for vacancies in the radio world. Other than a late-show presenter's job on a station in Dundee, I found nothing.

Spring had taken a sabbatical, and driving rain pelted against the living room window that morning. I could see the canopies of the ash trees on the far side of the canal swaying in the wind. Shivering, I got up to switch the central heating on. As the radiators gurgled back into life, I did an internet search for Mallorca. A webcam revealed blue skies and the gentlest of breezes stirring palm fronds on the seafront of the island's capital.

Within the hour, I'd booked my flights and hotels. I would spend the first nine nights in Palma and then a week in Deià. With less than twenty-four hours between the booking and the flight departure, I had little time to stress about flying and my first solo trip abroad.

Before I packed my suitcase, I wrote a long email to Andy, telling him about leaving my job, Zeller being my biological mother, and my imminent trip Mallorca. He replied less than an hour later, expressing his sympathy for recent events, and telling me to have fun on my holiday. Then I sent Dan a message to tell him I was going away and let him know Billy's neighbour had seen him dash off from home with a suitcase.

By Thursday afternoon I was in another world, sitting on a director's chair on the balcony of my hotel room on Palma's seafront. So far, I'd survived the flight, not lost my luggage, and nobody had mugged me or seized me for a life in the slave trade. It was a promising start to my first foreign holiday on my own.

I took in the impressive panoramic view, stretching around the Bay of Palma. In the distance, the sun shone its spotlight on the city's famous Gothic cathedral, La Seu. The guidebook I'd bought at Birmingham Airport, to distract me during the dreaded flight, recommended a visit.

Dazzling white motorboats moored in the harbour's sparkling Mediterranean waters reflected the intense light. A few floors beneath my room, I could see the hotel's outdoor swimming pool. How warm would the water be in May? I wondered.

My sunglasses were in the depths of my handbag, so I closed my eyes and took deep breaths, feeling the release of tension in my neck and shoulders. I intended to relax while I was in Palma and there was no reason not to start straight away. I'd not had lunch but craved something Spanish: a siesta. My need for sleep was greater than my need to eat. And that king-sized bed was calling out to me.

THUNDER? An earthquake? No. It was my stomach rumbling. I picked up my phone from the bedside table to check the time: seven o'clock. Almost four hours of slumber. I hauled myself off the comfortable mattress and padded across the cool tiled floor to the bathroom for a shower, before dressing and putting on some make-up. I checked myself in the full-length mirror; at least I no longer looked exhausted.

Away from the temptations of my baked goods, I hoped I would lose a little weight during my stay in Mallorca. Since Zeller's death, I had been comfort eating, drinking more wine than usual, and not sleeping well. My appetite soared whenever I was short of sleep, and the results were reflected in the mirror.

That evening, though, a glass of cava and a decent dinner would start my holiday in style. I spritzed myself in my duty-free purchase of Chanel Cristalle, picked up my handbag, room key, and Mallorca guidebook, then went down to the lounge bar.

THE HOTEL WAS HOSTING A CONFERENCE, and after a long day cooped up in a meeting room, every delegate was slaking his or her thirst. I sat in the corner of the large lounge on a squashy-cushioned sofa, away from the chattering mass standing in clusters by the bar.

After the barman brought my glass of cava and a small dish of roasted local almonds, I picked up my book and began reading.

'Hello, hello, hello,' a male voice said, startling me; it was so close to my ear I could feel the man's warm breath. He was British, and I guessed he was one of the conference delegates as he and his two companions were wearing suits and loosened ties. I didn't reply but gave them what Andy called my 'stern face'. The three guys, who looked in their late twenties, were oblivious to my expression.

Fortified by the beers they were carrying, two of them sank onto the sofa facing mine. The third sat next to me and flashed a cheeky grin in my direction.

'What's a pretty girl like you doing on her own?'

'Trying to read my book in peace.' I flashed my not-so-pretty stern face again. 'If you don't mind?'

'Bit boring though,' he said. His two friends grinned and nudged each other. The red-haired one, who bore a passing resemblance to Prince Harry, spoke.

'Need to work on your technique, Kev.'

I sighed and glared at the man sitting next to me.

'They're right, Kev. Perhaps you could practise on someone else?'

'Whoa, lady! That's not friendly, is it?' His voice had become louder, and from the smell of beer on his breath, his thirst level must have been stratospheric after a day in a conference room.

'How 'bout coming clubbing with us?' It was Ginger, sitting right opposite me, his chest puffed out like a pigeon as he delivered his own chat-up line. 'We'd show you a good time.'

All three burst into raucous laughter. I gave an exaggerated sigh and slammed my book shut. I stood up and took my bag, book, and drink to another sofa and cursed beneath my breath when I saw the persistent trio had followed me, carrying their drinks. Kev swayed a little as he walked.

Determined not to walk out of the bar before I finished my cava, I ignored them. They plonked themselves down around me, egging each other on to try their luck again. I lowered my head and was trying to concentrate on reading about some Arab baths in Palma when something extraordinary happened.

CHAPTER EIGHT

'D arling, sorry I'm late.' I frowned, wondering if this person had mistaken me for someone else. An attractive olive-skinned, dark-haired man, around my age, leaned down to kiss my cheek. My heartbeat quickened, and my face became hot. I noted a subtle but delicious aroma of unfamiliar aftershave. The stranger placed the metal case he was carrying onto the floor beside me.

My mouth opened, but nothing came out. If this scene had been in a movie, anyone watching would have deduced I'd never seen this man before. Not my three unwanted companions; they downed the rest of their beers in one and as they scurried off, I heard the word 'boyfriend'.

The stranger watched them walk away, then sat down on the opposite sofa and gave me a disarming smile. Perfect teeth. *A toothpaste commercial model?*

'Sorry,' he said, not looking the least bit apologetic, 'but I was having a swift beer at the bar and could see those guys were annoying you. Thought I should come to your rescue.'

It took a few moments for me to string a coherent sentence together.

'Yes, they were. So, thank you – very quick-thinking of you.' I stretched out my hand and laughed. 'As we're already on kissing terms, I should introduce myself: I'm Laura. Laura Lundon.'

His handshake was firm and sent an unexpected warm tingle down my spine.

'Carlos McCloud.' His first name sounded Spanish, but his surname and accent suggested he was British.

'Pleased to meet you, Carlos. I think I owe you a drink. What can I get you?'

'A G&T would slip down well, thank you.'

A member of the bar staff was heading in our direction, so I stuck my hand in the air like a schoolgirl asking the teacher for permission to go to the loo. Carlos spoke in Spanish to the uniformed man and I heard 'gin tonics' in the rapid exchange of words.

'I don't imagine you came here looking to rescue any damsels in distress,' I said.

He laughed and patted the metal case on the floor beside him.

'No. I'm a freelance photographer. Just finished a shoot in the kitchen here. New chef, new dishes.'

'Sounds like an interesting job.' I thought of Andy for a moment. What a coincidence both men worked with cameras, albeit my boyfriend shot moving images.

'It is. Most of the time.' Carlos gave a nod of acknowledgement to the barman who'd arrived with our drinks. I signed the bill, charging it to my room account, and we clinked glasses.

'*¡Salud!*' he said, making eye contact.

'*¡Salud!*' The appendix in my guidebook included a

list of useful words and phrases, and I'd already learnt the expression for 'good health' or 'cheers'.

'That's about the limit of my Spanish. It's my first visit to Spain.'

'And you chose Mallorca. You'll love it. Like this hotel?'

'What's not to like with the views here?' I replied. 'I found it online and thought it'd be perfect for a first visit to the island.'

'How about having a taste of its gastronomy this evening?'

I hesitated for a moment. Was it sensible to go off with someone I'd met less than an hour ago in a hotel bar? I had only his word that the metal case contained photographic equipment, rather than weapons for restraining and torturing gullible female tourists.

'You'd be hopeless at poker.' Carlos gave me a wide grin. 'If it makes you feel safer, I meant eating here in the hotel. The manager invited me and a companion to have dinner tonight … some company would be nice.'

The rumbling sound from my stomach wasn't the only reason I accepted his invitation.

A GUITARIST PERCHED on a stool in the corner of the restaurant terrace played lilting Spanish classics on an acoustic instrument. With his face tilted upwards, he appeared to be lost in the music, and amazed me by not looking at his hands as his fingers danced over the frets. The ambience made me wish Andy was more romantic in his choice of places to stay when we went away.

Our round table offered a spectacular view of the bay and the city lights winking into life as the sky darkened. The sommelier had already poured cava for us, and Carlos raised his glass towards me.

'To your first holiday in Mallorca.' His eyes were the colour of espresso coffee, and when they met mine, that tingling happened again. *Perhaps I'm allergic to the hotel shower gel?*

'I'll drink to that.'

He glanced down at his copy of the leather-bound menu. 'Decided? Or could I suggest something?'

'Thank you, but I've already seen what I'd like.' I promised myself I would try some traditional local dishes during my stay on the island but, having missed lunch, I was ravenous and wanted to eat something familiar. As the menu was in several languages, including English, my choice was easy.

After a hand signal from Carlos, the waiter came over and took our orders on an electronic device. My dinner companion ordered a bottle of local red wine, having first asked for my colour preference.

Conversation flowed as we waited for our starters to arrive, and I learnt that he was born on the island. He owed his Christian name, glossy black hair, tanned skin, and seductive brown eyes to his Spanish mother; his surname came from his Scottish father.

'I studied photography, which had been a hobby since I was a kid,' he said. 'After college, the bright lights of Barcelona lured me, and I got a job as an in-house photographer for a lifestyle magazine. It taught me a lot, but I missed Mallorca.'

His thirtieth-birthday gift to himself was a ferry ticket back to Palma, where he invested his savings in a well-maintained second-hand Canon camera, a couple of new lenses, and a set of business cards.

'I became a freelance photographer,' Carlos said. 'It

took a while to get established, but a decade or so later, I have a decent reputation and can be a bit more selective about the jobs I take.'

'And you get some nice perks, like this free dinner tonight?'

'Sometimes.' He laughed. 'I've shot photos in villas and on superyachts I'd never have seen otherwise. And met a lot of famous people – some pleasant, others not so. Sounds glamorous, but often it's just a quick news photo for the local press.'

The waiter arrived at the table with our starters. Carlos had ordered a gazpacho, which I knew was cold soup. Not for me. I'd chosen a Caprese salad, scattered with the largest basil leaves ever. My plate looked like a work of art: fat dollops of creamy mozzarella, drizzles of extra virgin olive oil, shiny green basil leaves, and a dusting of cracked black pepper and salt flakes, on a bed of luscious, sliced tomatoes. They tasted even sweeter than the ones Dad nurtured in his greenhouse.

We were both hungry and said little as we devoured our first course dishes, but as soon as we'd finished, the conversation resumed.

'Whereabouts in England are you from?'

'The Midlands.' As he'd never lived in the United Kingdom, I wondered if he'd heard of my hometown. 'A place called Stratford-upon-Avon.'

'William Shakespeare's birthplace? I've seen photos on Instagram, but although I've been to Scotland to see relatives, England's still on my list of places to visit.'

'Yes, Shakespeare's our claim to fame,' I said. 'Like Mallorca, we get our fair share of tourists too.' I took a thoughtful sip of the full-bodied red wine, which would go straight to my head after the drinks I'd already had on an empty stomach. Pausing gave me a few moments to consider how much personal information I should share with him.

'I'm a presenter on a radio station in Stratford.' I didn't expect we'd see each other again and wasn't going to bore him with my recent work and personal problems. This evening was a chance to forget all the crap for a few hours.

Carlos showed a genuine interest in my job and asked questions about the people I'd interviewed and where my love of radio had come from.

We continued to chat as we ate our main course dishes: for Carlos, roast shoulder of lamb (which looked similar to the way Mum cooked it on a Sunday), and for me, a huge grilled sea bass, ordered without garlic, which occupied the whole plate. A bowl of golden French fries and some gloopy home-made mayonnaise accompanied the dish. The weight-loss hopes were fading fast …

'*UNA PAUSA, POR FAVOR*,' Carlos said to the waiter who removed our empty plates. We both needed a brief break before dessert but continued chatting about our backgrounds. He told me he'd never known his Spanish mother, who died only months after he was born; his father had raised him with early help from a live-in German nanny.

It was not a surprise to learn that someone as good-looking as Carlos had had several girlfriends – two had been Spanish fashion models. I was curious to hear he'd been single for six months and, emboldened by alcohol, asked why.

'Women always complain I'm married to my camera.' He treated me to that disarming smile again.

'My working hours can be erratic and, as a freelancer, sometimes I need to cancel dates at short notice for an urgent job. But anyway, I've not yet met anyone I'd want to share my life with long-term.' He picked up his wine glass. 'How about you?'

'I was married in my late twenties,' I said. 'Lasted less than a year and put me off doing it again.' I didn't tell him about Andy, for no other reason than this was a one-off dinner with someone I'd just met.

My dining companion glanced at his wristwatch. 'Sorry, Laura, I've an early start tomorrow. Do you mind if we order dessert now?' He raised his hand to attract the waiter's attention, then winked at me. 'Something *mallorquín* this time, perhaps?'

'Sounds good to me.' I wondered if I should have been more adventurous and chosen local dishes for my first two courses. The roast lamb had, according to my companion, been cooked to perfection.

Carlos ordered us both the traditional almond cake, known on the island as *gató*. It was light, moist, and accompanied by a generous ball of almond ice cream. You had to like those nuts, of course, but I did; I would find a recipe for the cake before I returned home and add it to my baking repertoire.

'That was delicious,' I said, after dabbing my mouth with the linen napkin. 'Thank you, Carlos, for a wonderful first evening in Mallorca. It's been a promising start to a much-needed holiday.'

'You're very welcome. Thanks for your company; it was fun.' He pulled his wallet from his pocket. 'I don't suppose you'd like to do something tomorrow night?'

I hesitated at the unexpected invitation. Not because of any uneasy gut feeling about Carlos, or other plans I had for the next evening. Andy was on my mind. Then I remembered his email, telling me to have fun on my holiday. What harm would it do to spend a few more hours with this friendly local showing me some of his home island?

'I'd really like that, thank you.'

'Excellent.' He removed a note from his wallet for a tip and slipped it under the pepper mill. 'Not sure when my shoot'll be over but give me your number and I'll call you afterwards to arrange a time to pick you up.'

Having tapped my number into his phone, he stood and pulled my chair out for me. Then we thanked and shook hands with the maître d' before leaving. Carlos's impeccable manners reminded me of Billy, and I couldn't help wondering how my friend was.

We said goodbye in the hotel foyer and he gave me a quick kiss on each cheek. Cheek kisses and hugs were common greetings even between men, I'd noticed in the airport arrivals hall earlier that day. Then my dinner companion left, taking his aluminium camera case with him but leaving a hint of his sandalwood aftershave with me.

My enjoyable evening and meal with a good-looking man, in Andy's absence, was no reason to have a guilty conscience ... but those chaste cheek kisses had quickened my heartbeat more than they should have.

CHAPTER NINE

Have you ever noticed how the morning following a large, satisfying dinner, you can be ravenous? In the hotel's breakfast room, a smiling woman wearing a 'Hostess' badge greeted me. Having ticked a list on her clipboard, she invited me to sit anywhere I liked.

I liked the look of the buffet, so I chose a table close to the spread of tempting items. This meant I ate about four times more than I should have. But at least I was open about my greediness and not stuffing bananas and bread rolls wrapped in paper napkins into a handbag in a furtive manner, like one woman I spotted.

Between visits to the buffet, I checked for phone messages and emails. Mum had replied, wishing me a wonderful holiday and telling me to be careful. And there was a brief SMS message from Billy:

Shocked and hurt about breakfast – and devastated you've left. xx

I tapped out a quick reply, letting him know I'd contact him within the hour. He had been there for me when Zeller died, comforting me after the shock of her fatal stroke, and had stood in for Andy, who'd been unable to come back from Japan for the funeral. The least I could do was be there for him at his own low point.

BILLY ANSWERED after the first ring.

'Hello, Laura, I didn't expect you to ring while you were on holiday. I heard you'd gone to Mallorca.' His usual melodic voice sounded flat in tone, and there was no hint of any surprise that I'd chosen to travel abroad. That was ominous.

'I've been thinking about you.' I paused. 'I'm furious with Barry for what he's done. Are you off-air now until your new Sunday show starts?'

He gave a feeble laugh. 'No. Quentin couldn't start until next week, so Barry had no choice but to leave me on breakfast. But he's threatened to terminate my contract if I say anything negative on-air.'

'But … I came to see you on Monday evening and the woman upstairs told me you'd left in a hurry, with a suitcase.' I hesitated. 'I assumed you'd gone to stay with … a friend.'

'No, nothing like that. My washing machine broke down and I needed to get to the launderette before it closed. I'd run out of bin bags to put the dirty stuff in, so used a case instead.'

Mystery solved.

'Anyway, when Barry gets complaints from listeners, he'll realise he's made a terrible mistake,' I said.

'Like he did by forcing you to leave. But I want you to know that if you'd accepted Barry's proposal, it wouldn't have affected our friendship in the slightest.'

I noticed music in the background and realised he was still in the studio, doing what would be his last Friday breakfast show.

'Have to go now, song's ending.' He blew me a kiss down the line. 'Let's have a drink when you're back.'

I wished him luck for Sunday and promised to call him when I was home again.

IT WAS ALMOST eleven o'clock when I left the hotel and was met by bright sunshine and a pleasantly warm day. Unlike the overcast skies and rain of home that morning. The walk along the promenade towards the cathedral took longer than expected, and when I arrived at last, the cool air inside felt like an injection of energy.

I sank onto a pew, marvelling at the surroundings and colours of the stained-glass windows. For almost half an hour, I sat watching tourists move with due reverence around the monumental Gothic building. Believers were seated around me, heads bowed temporarily in private prayer, before they returned to the routine of daily life in the vibrant city.

Did Zeller ever visit the cathedral? Had she even come to Palma? So far, I'd read nothing in her book to suggest she left the mountains, let alone ventured into the island's waterfront capital.

In the cathedral's serenity, my mind wandered. I thought about Zeller, Mum and Dad, Andy, and Carlos. By the time I stood to leave, I was swathed in a sense of calm that had been missing for many weeks. Perhaps it was down to the cathedral's architectural beauty and humbling size? Perhaps I was becoming more spiritual? One thing was certain: I needed a caffeine fix and a bite to eat for lunch. I had no idea what time I'd be sitting down to dinner that evening.

The exit was through the inevitable gift shop. The souvenirs on display ranged from religious icons to pure hot-off-the-boat tat from China. My modest purchases were a postcard to send to Mum and Dad, and one for my neighbour Miss Barker, having remembered I hadn't told her I was going to be away.

When I emerged, blinking in the brightness, the full heat of a Mallorcan mid-May day hit me. It felt like a fine summer's day back in Stratford-upon-Avon. Sitting under a parasol on the terrace of a nearby café, I shuddered at every sip of my bitter Americano as I studied both map and guidebook to get my bearings. If this was a watered-down coffee in Mallorca, whatever would an espresso be like?

AFTERWARDS, I wandered through the old town's narrow lanes, lined with shade-providing buildings on either side. Many of the handsome sandstone properties would once have been grand homes. A cluster of doorbells on the wall outside suggested some of these were now divided into apartments.

Through wrought-iron gates I saw shady courtyards with handsome arches, external staircases, and stone-walled wells. How many zillions of selfies and tourist snaps featured these photogenic places?

One of these buildings – described in my guidebook as *palacios* – was now a cute-looking boutique hotel with a well-shaded courtyard bistro. A tinkling fountain in the centre made the place irresistible.

THE RESTAURANT EXPERIENCE in Palma differed from eating out in Stratford-upon-Avon. Nobody pressured me to vacate the table after the server cleared it at the end of my meal. According to my guidebook, the time spent chatting with companions after a meal was the *sobremesa* – meaning 'over the table'. Eating alone made that impossible, but the staff didn't hurry me to leave after I'd finished my lunch.

My eyes widened when I noticed what time it was. For almost two hours I'd lingered there, despite having had only a salad and a slice of irresistible almond cake for dessert. Between courses, I'd searched online on my phone for a recipe; I was going to make the cake as dessert for a supper-and-gossip evening with Dan and Billy once I was back in Stratford. Before I left Palma, I would buy Mallorcan almonds to take home for authenticity.

It was only my second day in Mallorca, but I'd already noticed that the Mediterranean lifestyle was more laid-back than the English one. As much as the slower pace appealed to me, I still drummed my finger-tips on the table while waiting for my bill; it was my first taste of the *mañana* culture.

As I STROLLED along the seafront road to my hotel, I felt my phone vibrate in my hand. I grinned when I looked at the screen and saw a WhatsApp message from Carlos:

Hi Laura. Having a good day? 18.00 tonight OK to pick you up?

I'd just passed a bench, so I walked back to it and sat

down to tap out my reply. To my surprise and slight
consternation, I was impatient to see him again – in only
two hours' time. In my head I skipped the rest of the way
to the hotel; my feet hurt far too much from all the
walking to do it for real.

CHAPTER TEN

'Wow! This lot must be worth millions,' I said as I climbed out of Carlos's Toyota RAV4 that evening. I was wide-eyed, surveying the rows of huge white motor yachts moored in the marina.

Carlos laughed. 'Maybe even billions, Laura. It's a paparazzi paradise, with lots of international celebs and the occasional member of European royalty here in the summer.' He guided me by my elbow as we crossed the road towards the waterside, behind a passing yellow Ferrari.

As we strolled, he pointed out some of the boat names. I took photos of a few of the impressive vessels to send to Dad. His fantasy lottery-win purchase was a motor cruiser on the River Avon, though the wash from any of the luxurious boats in Puerto Portals would knock the riverbank anglers from their fold-up fishing stools.

'Let's stop for a drink,' Carlos said after a while. 'Wellies is a favourite here.' As we sipped alcohol-free cocktails and watched the constant stream of people strolling along the waterfront, we played 'Spot the

Facelift'. Were they trophy wives, or just afraid of the possible competition from the younger women who paraded around with high hemlines and hope in their eyes?

The marina was also home to designer boutiques where the window displays of mannequins wearing glitzy clothes showed no prices. Even if I could afford to buy them, I doubted these boutiques stocked anything in a size sixteen. I was more interested in the number of bars and restaurants in the marina. I'd never seen such a display of wealth and could tell it was a magnet for the rich. And the famous, I thought, doing a double take on spotting a familiar face.

'See that guy in the red shorts?' I said, tipping my head towards the man who'd walked past with his gaze fixed ahead of him.

Carlos turned to look.

'Gil McGill. Spends a bit of time on his boat here in the summer. Every time, a different girlfriend.'

'You *know* him?'

'Not as a friend, but I've photographed him a few times. He's a lot friendlier than most celebrities.'

'It's a small world, isn't it? I interviewed him on my radio show only last Friday, believe it or not.' It was incredible that we should be in the same location at the same time. Nautical Gil had shed his rock star image and blended in with other wealthy boat owners, wearing tailored shorts, a crisp linen shirt, and navy-blue deck shoes (I smiled to note he was sockless, unlike some of the British socks-and-sandals holidaymakers I'd noticed in Palma that morning). Only Gil's ponytail gave him away.

A week had passed since our interview, but I doubted he'd recognise me out of context, and I had no intention of interrupting his private time on the island. But I was intrigued to know which floating gin palace was Gil's.

'I promise I'm not a groupie,' I told Carlos. 'Just a journalistic sense of curiosity because he mentioned his boat.'

He laughed. 'Come on, I'll show you.' He left a note from his wallet on the table to cover our drinks, then we left the terrace, walking arm in arm. I couldn't help my smug smile, being in this glamorous marina in warm evening sunshine with my handsome new friend – no nips, tucks, scary injections, or bank-account-draining clothes required.

We stopped a short distance from the boat so Gil wouldn't see us. Carlos raised his hand and discreetly pointed out a large Sunseeker motor yacht.

'That's it. She's called *Sueños* – Spanish for "dreams",' he said in a low voice.

I took a discreet photo on my phone to send to Dan later, knowing he'd be surprised too by the coincidence. We hadn't walked far back towards the main promenade when someone overtook us on the path. It was Gil, now wearing cream linen trousers, a denim shirt, and Birkenstocks (size fifteen, I knew). Dressed for dinner, I assumed, and in a hurry.

He glanced over his shoulder, then stopped and turned, throwing open his arms.

'Carlos, amigo! What brings you here?'

'Just an evening stroll.' Carlos released my arm, and the two met in a man hug, patting each other's backs. As they stepped apart, Gil looked at me and smiled.

'Laura Lundon … if the gin hasn't addled my brain. What're you doing in Mallorca?'

'Hello, Gil.' I smiled and shook his extended hand. 'Even radio presenters have holidays sometimes.'

He laughed and turned to Carlos. 'I was on Laura's show just last week. Best interview I'd done in ages. She rocks!'

The unexpected compliment flushed my cheeks.

'Sorry, gotta go,' he said, glancing at his chunky wristwatch. 'Meeting Isabella for dinner. But if you're back in the marina this week, come to the boat and we'll have a few bevvies.'

We thanked him and he strode off to meet his date for the night.

'Isabella?' Carlos raised one eyebrow. 'The last time I photographed him, a Russian blonde called Saskia was wrapped around him like a second skin.'

We both laughed at the way Gil McGill fitted the typical stereotype of a rock star a little past his prime. Drinks on *Sueños* probably wouldn't happen, but I couldn't wait to see Dan's face when I told him about the invitation.

'I thought we'd have a bite to eat here,' Carlos said, stopping at the entrance to a smart eatery with floor-to-ceiling windows facing a dazzling motor yacht moored only yards away.

The restaurant manager recognised him and led us to a table for two by the open window. The sun was just above the horizon and had turned the sky and the surface of the Mediterranean golden. Everything appeared to glow, and I couldn't stop smiling.

'You like it, then?'

'It's beautiful here.'

'You're beautiful,' Carlos said in a quiet voice. Okay, I might have imagined that.

A petite server, carrying menus almost the size of her torso, arrived at our table.

'*Buenas noches,* Carlos.' The young woman flashed him

a coquettish smile as she handed over a menu. My dinner companion appeared to be one of the restaurant's regular diners.

IT WAS ONLY my second evening with Carlos, but it felt as though we'd known each other longer. Conversation with him was easy; he was a good listener and an interesting talker. I could have told him about Zeller and my job situation, but I didn't want to spoil our enjoyment or share too many details of my personal life. I probably wouldn't see him again.

'I've got a free Saturday tomorrow,' Carlos said suddenly. 'If you're not doing anything, we could visit my favourite part of the island.'

'Well … I've not made any plans yet,' I said. Just then, his phone rang. He looked at the screen.

'Sorry, Laura, I need to take this. Back in a few minutes.' While he was outside, I thought about his offer but reminded myself I'd come to Mallorca to find out who had shared his genes with me. Carlos was becoming a distraction – albeit a pleasant one. But he didn't yet know I was spending a second week on the island, so when I was in Deià, I would be able to focus on my mission.

'Sorry about that. Work thing,' he said as he sat down again. 'Well, are you up for an outing tomorrow?'

I smiled. 'Sounds good to me. Where are we going?'

'I think I'll keep it a surprise.' Carlos grinned at me. 'But I'm a hundred per cent sure you'll love it.'

CHAPTER ELEVEN

'Nice,' Carlos said, giving me a smiling appraisal as he opened his car door for me outside the hotel. 'That colour suits you.'

When did Andy last compliment me on anything I was wearing? I hoped my flushed cheeks didn't clash with my coral linen dress. To our mutual amusement, it was almost the same shade as the shirt Carlos wore.

'You don't look too bad yourself,' I said, admiring the smart cream shorts and navy deck shoes he'd paired with the shirt. As he slid into the driver's seat, I grinned. We were off on a magical mystery tour.

We left the city along a road lined with trees laden with purple-blue blooms, which Carlos told me were jacarandas. After a few minutes travelling in comfortable silence, I looked sideways at him, admiring his strong jawline.

'Are you going to tell me where we're going?'

'Out for lunch. It's a surprise, so I couldn't possibly tell you.'

'Okay, if I must, I'll be patient.'

He glanced at me for a moment, causing another quickening of my heartbeat. And not because he'd taken his eyes off the road ahead. Perhaps I needed to see a cardiologist when I returned home?

'What one thing about you would surprise me?' This was a question I'd used to garner interesting answers from past radio guests.

'I play the ukulele,' Carlos said without hesitating.

'Really?' I turned to look on the back seat of the car. 'Shame you didn't bring it with you so you could prove it.'

'You're here till next Saturday, aren't you? I'll drive you to the airport and serenade you at the departures gate. Something to remember me by.'

I laughed, despite knowing I wasn't leaving when he thought I was. *Should I tell him?* Several minutes' silence passed before he spoke again.

'Right. Your turn to surprise me.'

I didn't have to think long. 'Last summer I won first prize in a baking competition at the Stratford Festival. I make a mean chocolate brownie.'

Carlos smacked the steering wheel with one hand.

'My kind of woman!'

Soon, the fields either side of the road gave way to the impressive mountain peaks that had looked so distant not long before. The change in scenery was sudden and dramatic.

A roadside sign showed we were on the way to Valldemossa. I'd read that Chopin stayed there one nineteenth-century winter with the French writer pen-named George Sand. Although Chopin's lover wrote a largely uncomplimentary account of their stay, my guidebook suggested a copy of *A Winter in Majorca* was an essential souvenir. I planned to buy the book for Dad, who, as a retired English teacher, was an avid reader.

My first glimpse of Valldemossa made me gasp. It was a cluster of stone houses with terracotta-tiled roofs, beneath what Carlos explained was the Carthusian monastery where Chopin had spent that miserable winter. I couldn't wait to arrive and explore but heard the car indicator clicking before the main road reached the heart of the village. Where were we going?

It soon became clear. We passed a sign for the Valldemossa Hotel and Restaurant and pulled into its car park. The attractive stone-built property sat on a hilltop overlooking its beautiful surroundings.

Carlos parked, switched off the engine, and smiled at me.

'What d'you think?'

'Is this where we're having lunch?'

'Looks like it.' He winked at me.

After we'd climbed what must have been a hundred steps up to the hotel entrance, we paused to take in the glorious views all around us from the large terrace. The honey-coloured stone building had forest-green external window shutters, and the sight of the interior arches, tiled floors, and wooden ceiling beams took my breath away.

The hotel would be perfect for a romantic break, and I was sure the beds would be sturdier than the one Andy and I had broken in the Cornish B&B. When he returned from Japan, maybe I could persuade him we should come for a long weekend? An injection of romance would benefit our relationship after our longest-ever time apart.

'Shall we go through?'

I blushed, caught thinking of a future visit with my boyfriend while I was with someone else kind enough to bring me here for lunch.

'Yes, let's.'

We walked into the restaurant, where a waiter led us out to the cobbled terrace and our table.

'Stunning views,' I said, gazing at the sea-blue tiled tower of the monastery building on the adjacent hilltop. Only two other couples were lunching there, and it almost felt as though we had the place to ourselves.

'I'm pleased it meets with your approval, ma'am.' Carlos picked up his glass and raised it towards me. 'A toast to Valldemossa and the Tramuntana mountains.'

'To Valldemossa and the mountains.' We clinked glasses and took the first taste of well-chilled cava. As Carlos had to drive, we were having only one small fizz before we ate.

'I can't believe how soon we arrived in a different landscape,' I said. 'Seems like another world, but we got here so quickly from Palma.'

'It's only around twenty-three kilometres, which makes it a popular weekend escape for us urbanites.'

If my home was in one of the many blocks of apartments we'd passed on the outskirts of the island's capital, I'd want to flee the city for this beautiful village whenever I could.

'Have you always lived in Palma?' I was curious to know more about my lunch companion.

Carlos poured olive oil onto his side plate and dipped a piece of warm bread roll into the green-gold pool.

'No. We used to live here in the mountains until I went to an international senior school near Palma. The school run twice a day would have been too much time on the road, so we moved to an apartment in Palma, where my dad still lives.' He took a bite of his bread and, after swallowing, continued: 'He was a boat captain in Port de Sóller, and when we moved home, he became captain on a Spanish politician's yacht in Palma. El Capitán – that's what everyone calls Dad – retired a few years ago.'

'Did you live here in Valldemossa?' My heartbeat quickened. I'd studied my map of the island over breakfast and knew that Deià wasn't too far from where we were. Could I ask him to take me there?

'No, but I know this village well and I'll show you around after lunch. Every visitor to Mallorca should see Valldemossa.'

The waiter arrived, carrying a large flat pan with some ceremony. Carlos had ordered paella in advance as a surprise for me and, although I wouldn't have chosen it from a menu, the aroma of seafood and saffron was tantalising. Our server spooned steaming heaps of the rice dish onto our plates, then we set about the important business of eating. As tasty as the food was, I couldn't wait to explore the village.

'I THINK we can say you've seen Valldemossa.' Carlos smiled at me, setting butterflies dancing in my stomach. *This shouldn't be happening.*

We sat on the terrace of a smart café, drinking orange juice squeezed fresh to order and watching tourists wander the streets, mobile phones held aloft as they tried to follow their online maps.

We'd visited the former home of Catalina Tomàs, the island's only saint, and been to a short piano recital of

Chopin compositions. As we sat listening to the music, Carlos put his hand over mine and gave it a quick squeeze.

He mouthed 'Okay?' at me without making a sound. I smiled and nodded; I was way more than okay.

His touch made my heart race, despite the small but irritating voice in my head prodding at my conscience: *Andy. What about Andy?* It's totally innocent, I replied silently. A holiday fling that won't go any further. I glanced sideways at Carlos and saw he was watching me. As our eyes met, my heart was beating so hard it sounded like an unwanted percussion accompaniment to the pianist's rendition of Chopin's 'Raindrop' Prelude.

'Another drink?' He interrupted my thoughts, which brought me back to our terrace table at the café.

'No, thanks, all good to go,' I replied. 'I'm keen to see where we're going next.' He'd told me that lunch and the visit to Valldemossa were just the start of our excursion in the mountains. I'd never have guessed how that day would end.

CHAPTER TWELVE

'I'm taking you to the village where I was born,' Carlos said, raising his hand to request the bill. 'Deià's one of the most famous places in Mallorca – and, in my opinion, the most beautiful.'

If I'd been standing, my legs would have given way.

'Deià?' My voice was almost a whisper.

'You okay?' He frowned. A handsome frown it was too. 'You sound a bit … strange.'

I concentrated on sounding normal. It was too late now to tell him the full story, so I offered a shorter, alternative version.

'I'm fine, thanks. It's just a coincidence because I'd wanted to visit Deià. An older friend of mine was there for a few months writing a book about it.' I coughed to clear the lump in my throat and blinked hard. 'She … died in April, and I thought I'd like to see the place that inspired her and maybe meet anyone she might have known there.'

After Carlos had paid the bill, we left the café to return to the car.

'I am sorry about your friend.' He took my hand in his and gave it a gentle squeeze. 'Do you know when she was there?'

He came to an immediate halt when I told him.

'We were living there then!' He sounded as excited as I felt. 'I was only a toddler, but Dad might have met her. If you like, I'll arrange for you to have a chat with him.'

Unable to speak, I nodded. He pulled his mobile phone from his pocket, his fingers poised over the screen.

'Monday morning any good?'

'That'd be great,' I squeaked. Perhaps this was why fate had brought us together. Moments later, Carlos was speaking to his father. 'Eleven thirty's great, Dad. See you then.'

He disconnected the call and returned the phone to his pocket.

'All fixed. I'll pick you up and take you to Dad's. You'll love him, by the way.'

Excited about the prospect of talking to someone who might have known Zeller, I acted out of character. As we stood in the middle of the quiet lane leading back to the hotel car park, I threw my arms around Carlos and kissed him on the lips. Just a brief meeting of our lips, you understand. A kiss of gratitude.

'Thank you so much. This means a lot to me.'

'Then it means a lot to me too,' he said, a broad smile on his face. 'Now, come on. Places to see, things to do!'

WE ROUNDED a corner on the picturesque coast road high above the Mediterranean and were almost there. I could see the village nestled beneath the mountains and felt a wave of unexpected emotion wash over me. Before Carlos could notice, I quickly brushed away a tear from my right cheek.

This was the village where Zeller had fallen in love with the man who fathered me. Somewhere over there he could be sipping a cold beer on a terrace, doing the newspaper crossword, or tending the plants in his garden. Maybe he'd since married and had other children, who'd be half-siblings, and grandchildren too.

If I found out who he was, I had no intention of turning his life upside down by knocking on his door and announcing myself as his daughter. One father was sufficient for me, and Dad was the best. I only needed to know who the man was and get a sense of why Zeller fell in love with him. In my excitement, it didn't occur to me he might no longer live in Deià.

As we approached the village, I wondered which of the rustic stone cottages huddled below the hilltop church had been the one where they'd conceived me. I hoped they'd made love in a cosy home and not in the back of a steamy-windowed Seat car in a secluded lane. Zeller was such a practical person I couldn't bring myself to think about her in the throes of passion anywhere.

'Oh, it's … stunning,' I said, pushing lurid thoughts aside. I glanced at Carlos, who was concentrating on the road ahead of him. Although he must have seen the view a zillion times, he wore the now-familiar grin that made me feel warm inside.

We drove into the heart of the village, where he manoeuvred the car into a parking space more suitable for a Fiat 500 than his four-by-four.

'I hope you have room for a spot of late-afternoon tea,' he said, taking my hand again as we crossed the road. I supposed it was because vehicles drove on the other side of the road in Spain and he feared I'd look the wrong way before stepping off the kerb and be hit by a car.

We were in front of the entrance to Belmond La Residencia – the same hotel I'd booked for the second week of my holiday. It looked even more fabulous than it had on my laptop screen in rainy Stratford-upon-Avon. I had to suppress a giggle of elation, knowing I'd be staying there soon. For an entire week.

Carlos led me along a path, past ancient olive trees and perfumed, bloom-filled rose bushes, towards the terraces. I was almost lost for words at the unexpected beauty of the place and its setting.

'Here okay?' He pointed out a two-seater outdoor sofa with a spectacular view.

'More than, thank you.' I was almost sorry I hadn't told him about my staying a second week on the island. But I reminded myself, I had things to do in Deià, without any distractions. Carlos hadn't stopped beaming since we'd come through the gates, and I couldn't ruin his surprise by telling him I'd already discovered the place on the internet.

He'd booked an English-style afternoon tea for us, which arrived on an exquisite bone china tea service. Our server, whose badge bore the name Francisco, told us the design was unique to the hotel and was in homage to the late Catalan artist Joan Miró, who had a studio in Palma. I'd read in my guidebook it was now a museum.

'We have a number of Miró's original artworks inside the hotel,' Francisco said as he poured tea into the elegant cups. 'Do have a look before you leave.'

I gave mental thanks that we wouldn't be washing up. I remembered Dad's suggestion that I could open a café as an alternative to another radio job. If I ever did, my chosen tableware would have to be bounceable rather than posh.

'Good thing we walked off lunch.' Carlos piled cream onto his raspberry-jam-topped scone. He appeared to be one of those fortunate people who can eat whatever they like without gaining weight.

I doubted that our amble around Valldemossa had been enough to work off the calories in our delicious paella and I was glad we'd skipped dessert. All my recent eating and drinking would soon show on my waistline.

After our sumptuous tea, we went to look at the Miró paintings and then strolled into the village. We wandered the narrow lanes and the stone steps up to the church and the small Deià municipal cemetery. My personal tour guide showed me the stone slab marking Robert Graves's burial place. The simple inscription gave the writer's name, birth and death dates, and the word *Poeta*.

Carlos and I took photos of each other against picturesque backdrops of cypress trees, ivy-clad houses, towering mountains, and the Mediterranean. I asked him why he used his iPhone, when he owned high-quality photographic gear.

'The pro stuff's too conspicuous when I'm not working, and these have brilliant cameras.'

We also took some selfies, although I wasn't going to post them on my little-used Instagram account, in case Andy spotted them and misunderstood the apparent cosiness of the images.

I'd already looked at Carlos's Instagram photos the day after I met him – just to be sure there weren't any pictures of him with an obvious partner or any similar-looking, dark-eyed children. When I checked his feed early the morning after our visit to Deià, I saw a photo of the two of us. And smiled.

WAS THERE a lane or alley in Deià we didn't walk along
that afternoon? My favourite had been the one where
Carlos lived as a child. The old stone house had the
customary terracotta roof tiles, small windows with
typical Spanish wrought-iron bars, and a narrow sliver of
garden at the front, where the current residents had
placed hand-painted flowerpots bursting with scarlet
geraniums.

'I had an idyllic childhood here.' He had a wistful
look on his face. 'We were both sad to move away, but
you've seen the road between here and Palma. Dad
couldn't do that journey twice every day and work too.'

'Whoever lives here now has looked after the place at
least.'

'That's true.' He gave a last glance up at what had
been his bedroom window. 'Ready to leave yet? I have
one more stop on this magical mystery tour.'

Whatever next? I thought, as we drove back in the
direction of Valldemossa. I'd had a good look around
Deià, and although Carlos had no idea where Zeller
might have stayed, he gave me a useful introduction to
the place. I would explore further and talk to a few
people after I returned in a week's time.

Not long after leaving the village, we turned right off
the winding coast road into a lane, passing an impressive
manor house signposted as Son Marroig. We left the
Toyota in the busy car park and walked to a small
outdoor bar; it wasn't much more than a hut with a large
terrace of tables and low stools. It didn't have the sophistication of the bars in Puerto Portals, but the panoramic
view was the reason so many people were there.

'They come for the sunset,' Carlos explained. 'In

another ten minutes the sun will disappear below the horizon, turning the sky and the sea golden.'

I picked up my phone and went to the edge of the terrace to take photos. I'd never seen such a spectacular slice of scenery or a more romantic setting.

'I brought my first proper girlfriend here,' Carlos said when I returned to our table. 'Marga, her name was. I had a scooter then and she sat on the back, her arms tight around my waist. I thought it meant she fancied me, but it turned out that riding pillion terrified her. A week later she dumped me for a guy with a car. I still bear the emotional scars,' he joked, patting his heart with one fist.

We laughed and finished our cold drinks. Carlos stood and took my hand.

'Come and see this.' We watched in silence as the sun slipped down out of sight. Some nearby Japanese tourists clapped their hands; nature's spectacle was over for the day.

Carlos turned to me, lifted my chin with a delicate touch, and kissed me on the lips. It was a long, delicious kiss that had nothing to do with gratitude. As our mouths parted again, the Japanese group burst into another round of applause.

THE JOURNEY back to Palma was over too soon, and my heart sank at the now-familiar sight of the seafront road known as the Paseo Marítimo and the illuminated sign of my hotel in the distance.

'Is there somewhere near here you could park overnight?' Forward of me, I know, but I didn't want my day with Carlos to end. I'd been missing the intimacy of being physically close to someone and wanted the comfort of falling asleep in this man's arms. We were already so in tune with each other I knew he'd understand my subtle suggestion.

'I'm sure I can find a place.' He turned to look at me. 'But I must warn you I haven't brought my toothbrush.'

'Lucky I always carry a spare. New and still in its packaging. If you don't mind it being pink.'

As we walked from the car to the hotel, my heart was racing. Years had passed since I'd been with anyone other than Andy, and we hadn't made love for what seemed ages.

The porter tipped his cap as we emerged from the revolving door. We said good evening and strode towards the lifts. Once inside, Carlos kissed me again, harder this time. A kiss filled with mutual longing. I felt as though my legs were melting beneath me. Breathless, we came out of the lift and scuttled along the marble-tiled corridor to my room. Before shutting the door on the world outside, Carlos hastily hooked the 'Do Not Disturb' sign over the handle.

CHAPTER THIRTEEN

'Aye, it's a fine view,' the man nicknamed El Capitán said, making a sweep of the Bay of Palma with his muscular right arm. 'When you've worked on boats all your life, it's impossible to live anywhere without the sea in sight. Carlos jokes that I have seawater running through my veins.'

We were on his apartment balcony, which had a table and four chairs and, in one corner, a lounger. He stood looking out, stroking his beard which still had traces of its original auburn. I wondered for a moment what my first impression of his son would have been if he'd looked like a younger version of Captain Birdseye and inherited his father's red hair and ruddy complexion, rather than his mother's Andalusian colouring.

'Drink, lass? I'm having a glass of *tinto*.'

It was a little early in the day for me to be drinking wine, but maybe it was what they did in Mallorca. I didn't want to be unsociable.

'That sounds good, thank you.'

'Sit yourself down, Laura. I'll be just a moment.' He

went inside, and I heard cupboard doors opening and closing.

I wondered who owned the gleaming yachts and motorboats down in the marina. Were they all famous people like Gil McGill, enjoying some privacy and rare anonymity afloat on the Mediterranean?

'As you do,' I muttered at the exact moment that El Capitán came back onto the terrace carrying a wooden tray.

'Beg your pardon, lass?'

'Oh, only musing,' I said. 'I interviewed a rock star recently on the radio and he told me he owned a boat in the Med. I had no idea where, but Carlos and I bumped into him in Puerto Portals on Friday. It's a small world.'

Carlos's father used a fancy corkscrew to pull the cork from the bottle.

'Saw plenty of their type when I had my charter yacht in Port de Sóller. The tales I could tell you …' He poured two generous measures and passed me one glass.

'¡Salud!' he said, as we clinked glasses then sipped. 'It's Mallorcan. From Ribas, the island's oldest winery. Been in the same family since 1711, believe it or not. It's organic and worth looking out for in restaurants here.' He held his glass up towards the bright sky, appraising the wine's rich garnet hue.

Carlos had brought me to the apartment and introduced me to his father, before leaving for a photoshoot with a famous rugby player who was holidaying on the island. El Capitán soon put me at ease, and a few minutes after arriving, I took a deep breath and felt my shoulders loosen.

In the lift going up to the sixth floor, Carlos had taken my face in his hands and given me a gentle kiss on the lips.

'Being with you is great,' he said. 'I want to spend as much time with you as I can before you go home, but I hope you understand I couldn't turn down a job for *Hello!* magazine.'

'Of course!' *Even though I'm enjoying every moment we're together.*

We arrived at the sixth floor. Outside the apartment door, Carlos paused to explain that I should address his father as Capitán, as the full El Capitán only applied when talking about him, rather than to him. Thank goodness I didn't need to learn Spanish, I thought, as Carlos pulled out a key and opened the apartment door.

'Hey, Dad? We're here!'

～

'HELP YOURSELF,' El Capitán said, pushing the dish of glossy black olives and tiny gherkins across the low table towards me. I'd never eaten an olive in my life – the black ones reminded me of the summer holiday when I'd volunteered to look after Roger, the school rabbit. Which meant cleaning out his cage every day. I did like pickles, so I stabbed one with a cocktail stick and nibbled it in a dainty fashion, not wanting to be caught with a mouthful of food when I needed to speak.

'Carlos said you're looking for information about a writer who was in Deià in the seventies.'

'Yes, that's right.' I put down my glass and composed my thoughts. 'A friend of mine. Her name was Zeller Floyd.'

My host frowned. 'Was? She got married?'

I couldn't believe my luck; it sounded as though Carlos's father had known her. The downside was having to break the news to him.

'No, she never married,' I said. 'But I'm sorry to tell you—' I coughed away the lump that had risen in my throat and excused myself. 'Zeller died last month … a massive stroke.'

The man's broad shoulders slumped, and he bowed his head for a moment.

'Och no, that's tragic. She was a wonderful woman, and it's been my life's biggest regret that we lost touch.' His voice caught in his throat, and he took a mouthful of wine then went inside the apartment. A trumpeting sound from within told me he was blowing his nose. I felt awful delivering such upsetting news.

A few minutes later, he returned to the terrace, holding a silver-framed photo.

'My late wife. Carlos's mother.' He handed me the framed black and white photograph. 'Her name was Laura too. The pronunciation's different, because she was Spanish, but the spelling's the same.'

'She was beautiful.' I saw the genetic connection between this dark-eyed young woman and her good-looking son. 'How awful to lose her so soon after Carlos was born. I am so sorry.' With care, I stood the framed picture on the table so we could both see it.

'Aye, heartbreaking. If it hadn't been for Carlos, I'm not sure I could have continued living.' He picked up his drink again, swirling the remaining wine around the bottom of the glass. 'I was sure I'd never find another woman I could love.'

He told me he'd employed a live-in au-pair-cum-nanny called Ilka to help with his son after Laura's death.

'She was kind and efficient, but she kept talking to Carlos in German and I didn't want her to confuse the poor bairn. To be honest, it was a relief when she told me she had to go back to Frankfurt to look after her sick father.' Ilka's departure put El Capitán's ability to run full-day charter trips at risk as he couldn't take his toddler son on those.

'I used to take him to the port and on short trips, but some customers weren't keen on a boisterous toddler being on board. Meeting Zeller was my salvation. She walked into the bar where I was having a beer one evening.' He paused and smiled. 'Carlos was playing on the floor with a toy car and he pushed it right in her path, so she had to jump out of the way to avoid it.' He laughed. 'Anyway, we got chatting and hit it off straight away – and Carlos seemed to like her too.'

El Capitán stood and poured us more wine. At this rate, his son would have to pour me into his car when he returned.

'We spent more than an hour together over a cold beer or two, and before she left she offered to look after Carlos at my home whenever I had full-day charter trips booked.' He laughed. 'She used to lug her portable type-writer with her, but he was such a handful, I don't think she got much writing done.'

He told me that Zeller sometimes stayed for a drink or a bite to eat – which she would make – after he arrived home from work.

'I shouldn't say this, but your friend wasn't a good cook then.' He almost whispered, as though she were in the next room and might hear him. 'But she made up for it by being a convivial supper companion and becoming a very dear friend.'

'You've surprised me. I never saw her have much to do with children.' The irony.

He raised one bushy eyebrow and stroked his beard.

'Did you know your friend was pregnant when she left the island?'

How to reply? I paused.

'Yes, her sister told me recently.' That part was true. 'But it was long before my time, of course, and Zeller never spoke about it.'

'Then I suppose she put the bairn up for adoption.' He shook his head, a sad expression on his face. 'To be honest with you – and I've never stopped regretting this – I should have told Zeller I'd fallen in love with her. But she was such a free-spirited lass, and I didn't want to frighten her off with such talk.'

I could see tears pooling in his eyes and I looked out to sea, feeling dreadful to have resurrected painful memories.

'When she told me she was pregnant, I asked her to marry me. In my heart I knew she was too independent to settle down, so I shouldn't have been shocked when she left Mallorca a day or two later without even saying goodbye. It was the last I ever saw or heard of her. My foolish pride stopped me from trying to find her.'

He pulled a large, crumpled handkerchief from his pocket and blew his nose again. The noise was so loud it almost drowned out the hooter of the enormous cruise ship manoeuvring out of the port.

'I can't apologise enough for bringing all this back to you,' I said, my voice catching in my throat. Should I put my arm around his shoulders and comfort him? I wished Carlos would return.

And then I didn't. Trembling, I placed my glass on the table. I had a tight feeling in my chest and gasped for breath. Could I be having a panic attack? Or worse, a heart attack? Sentences echoed in my head: *We became close friends … I fell in love with Zeller … When I heard she was pregnant, I asked her to marry me …*

Drinks and supper together at his house? Perhaps

they'd had dessert upstairs in El Capitán's double bed. Was it a coincidence the name Zeller had chosen for me was the same as his late wife? Did I need any further clues?

Everything pointed to the fact he'd fathered the child of the woman he believed was my old friend. I couldn't now bring myself to tell him the terrible truth: that I was his daughter. Or that I'd had sex with his son at the weekend (not that I would have told him that anyway) — or, as circumstances suggested, sex with my half-brother (and three times to boot). The wine and the gherkins were threatening to revisit the terrace.

The unsteadiness in my legs as I stood up had nothing to do with the wine I'd drunk.

'I'm so sorry about everything, Capitán, but I have to go,' I blurted out. 'Feeling sick. Maybe something I ate last night.'

'The bathroom's through—'

I didn't give him the chance to finish. Snatching my bag from the floor, I almost ran out of the apartment to the lift, one hand over my mouth. Out on the street, I threw up in a potted palm flanking the marbled entrance to the building.

Hunched over the terracotta, sweating and holding my stomach, I heard a passing well-dressed local woman say something to her companion. I didn't need to be a linguist to guess it was 'another disgraceful drunken British tourist'.

My hotel was about fifteen minutes' walk away, but I couldn't risk bumping into Carlos on his way back from his assignment. How could I explain that the woman I'd said was an old friend was, in fact, my mother? And that he was almost certainly my half-brother? If only I'd told him the full story from the start.

I straightened up, took a deep breath, patted my hair into place to make myself look more presentable, and walked to the edge of the pavement, where I stuck out my arm to flag down an approaching taxi. If the driver noticed the unpleasant vomit splatter on my dress as he slewed his car to a halt at the kerb, his face revealed nothing. He did, however, open his window.

I climbed into the back seat, gave him the name of my hotel, and told him in slowly enunciated English I'd give him a good tip because the journey was so short. As the taxi pulled away from the kerb, I closed my eyes and replayed the morning's conversation in my head.

CHAPTER FOURTEEN

Back in my hotel room, my mobile phone rang within the hour. Carlos, of course. I paced back and forth, leaving the phone to ring until he gave up waiting for a reply. Then I undressed, put my vomit-stained dress to soak in the washbasin, and sank into a hot bath, a cool damp flannel draped across my forehead.

When I emerged, pink-faced and swathed in a vast fluffy towel, I noticed Carlos had left a message on my mobile. Yearning to hear his voice again, I listened to what he'd said.

'Are you okay, Laura? Dad said you felt ill and rushed off. Call and let me know if you need anything. An English-speaking doctor, perhaps?'

Maybe a one-way ticket to the other side of the world and a dose of amnesia? My eyes welled with tears. What had begun as a bit of holiday fun had quickly become more meaningful. Carlos's concern suggested the feeling might be mutual.

I took a can of Perrier from the minibar, resisting the

siren call of the half-bottle of Sauvignon Blanc. To distract myself, I sat on the bed and checked my email inbox.

The subject of one new message caught my eye. It was from a radio station I'd written to about vacancies. The heading read: 'We're interested'.

I gasped and clicked to read the full message, scanning first and then rereading it with care. The online advertisement had been vague but intriguing, and I now learnt it was a new station in Bristol, expected to launch late summer. They were already talking to potential presenters and wanted to meet me for 'an informal chat'.

I put aside my family issues for a few moments as I reminded myself that I had no job to go back to after my holiday. My quick reply explained I was away in Spain and, after playing email ping-pong for a few minutes, we arranged a meeting in Bristol for the day after I returned to the UK.

The city was too far from home to commute, but a move to another part of the country could be beneficial. I'd lived in the same town as my parents since my divorce and their proximity meant it was easy to rely on Dad's help with any DIY or car problems. Moving away would force me to solve my own difficulties; now I was forty-one, it was time I became self-sufficient.

I googled 'properties to rent in Bristol' and was scanning the screen when the room phone rang. In an absent-minded fashion, I forgot to ignore any calls and answered.

'Hello?'

'Laura, it's me.' My heart sank. Carlos. 'I've been calling you on your mobile but kept getting voicemail. I was really worried – are you all right?'

Hanging up would have been cruel, but I couldn't tell him what I had learnt at his father's apartment.

'Yes, I was sick earlier, but I'm fine now, thanks. Sorry to worry you.'

'No need to apologise. The important thing is you're okay.' He hesitated. 'Do you fancy a light supper tonight? There's a restaurant in an old windmill I'd love us to try.'

If only. 'I'm sorry. I have to fly back to the UK this evening. Unexpected work problem.' I had a mental picture of the two of us at a candlelit table in a windmill. *Don't torture yourself.*

'Thank you so much for everything, Carlos. I've had an amazing time with you and I'll never forget this trip. Or you.'

'Is that it, then?' I heard the disappointment in his voice. 'I wish you didn't have to cut your holiday short. We've had such fun together.' He sighed. 'I'm free the rest of today. Could I come for a farewell drink, then drive you to the airport? Then we can say a proper goodbye?'

Tears trickled down my cheeks as I pictured him at the other end of the phone. I couldn't speak, but he filled the silence.

'I'll bring my ukulele and serenade you, as promised.'

'Sorry, Carlos, I don't have time for a drink – I still have to pack.' That was true: my empty case lay open on the bed and my clothes hung in the wardrobe. I swallowed the lump in my throat. 'And I've already booked a taxi.'

'Cancel it, Laura. Please. When do you need to leave?'

I gave in to his insistent tone and told him six o'clock.

'I'll be waiting outside at five to six. See you then.'

Although it would hurt him, I knew what I had to do.

Seeing him again would be too hard. I folded my clothes and packed them into my case before adding the rest of my things. The stained dress in the basin was too wet to pack, even after I'd vented my frustration by wringing it out several times. I left it on a hanger, dripping over the bath. Maybe it would fit whoever serviced the room after I'd left.

At just before five o'clock that afternoon, I checked out at reception, having explained I had to cut short my stay. Minutes after I'd settled my bill, I climbed into the back of one of the taxis on the rank outside and fastened my seatbelt.

The driver hefted my suitcase into the car boot as I looked out at the hotel, bidding a silent goodbye to what could have been. The friendly porter stood outside, raised his uniform cap, and gave a small bow. I waved goodbye, biting my lip to stop myself crying.

IT WAS fortunate I could check into La Residencia earlier than planned. The taxi driver wasn't big on talking (or perhaps didn't speak English), which suited me fine. A Spanish talk show blared from the radio; the contributors babbled all over each other, and I wondered how anyone could make sense of the chaotic conversation.

The trip to Deià took us past landmarks familiar from the weekend – although it seemed a lifetime ago. Was it only Saturday night Carlos and I made love and fell asleep in each other's arms?

THAT SUNDAY MORNING, my heart had sunk when I woke to find his side of the bed was cold. He must have been careful not to wake me, and for a few minutes I wondered if sex had always been his ultimate goal. Then I remembered I'd been the one to suggest spending the night together.

I found his handwritten note on the console table. He'd left to fetch his photographic equipment from home for a sunrise shoot with a famous Spanish TV presenter. He had other plans later in the day but promised to pick me up on Monday morning to take me to his father's apartment at the agreed time. I blushed and smiled when I read Carlos's last sentence, then folded and tucked the note into my handbag. I could never have imagined what a fateful Monday it would be.

NOT LONG AFTER LEAVING VALLDEMOSSA, the physical and emotional exhaustion of the day overwhelmed me. I slept the rest of the journey until the driver braked to go through the gates of the Deià hotel. With haste, I wiped a slick of drool from the side of my mouth only moments before the hotel porter opened the taxi door for me.

CHAPTER FIFTEEN

'You must go up and visit the Mirador,' Javier, the waiter, said to me when he brought a pot of coffee to my poolside table for my second day's breakfast at the hotel. 'The views are spectacular.'

After spending the previous day lazing by one of the hotel's swimming pools, alternating between dream-drenched sleep and bouts of reading Zeller's book, I needed some physical activity. A walk would shake off my sluggishness.

The words 'up' and *mirador* (the Spanish for 'view-point') ought to have warned me what to expect. By the time I arrived at the hotel's 'Poets' Walk', on the approach to the Mirador, I was puffing like the Shake-speare Express heritage steam train. Thank heavens someone had installed a row of benches, positioned to take advantage of the jaw-dropping view.

The reason for the 'Poets' Walk' name became clear: the backrest of each bench bore a line from a different poem. One of these resonated with me and, after looking around to make sure nobody could hear, I read the words aloud in voiceover fashion.

'You can cut all the flowers, but you cannot keep spring from coming.' On return to my sumptuous room, I would google the poet, someone named Neruda.

After taking a photograph of the bench, I sank onto it, grateful to kick off my sandals for a few minutes. My heart was still pounding from the steady climb, and my calf muscles were as taut as guitar strings. But the view made the unexpected exertion more than worth it; high above the hotel buildings and the village of terracotta-tiled cottages, a warm breeze wafted heady scents of rosemary, lavender, and wild fennel. Birdsong and fluttering leaves provided the soundtrack.

I removed my straw sun hat and ran my fingers through flattened hair damp from the heat. Now I was over forty, I should start an exercise regime; goodness knows I needed one. After my holiday, though. I sat and smiled to myself, taking in the gorgeous scenery and allowing random thoughts to drift through my mind.

I wondered which of the stone houses clustered below had been Zeller's temporary home. It was such a beautiful place; no wonder she stayed longer than planned.

Less than a week had passed since that blissful afternoon in the village with Carlos. Within forty-eight hours of our visit, I'd uncovered the identity of my biological father – which had been my main reason for coming to Mallorca.

I was going to use the rest of my holiday to get to know Deià better, by exploring and reading more of Zeller's book. Top of my list was relaxation, because I needed downtime to deal with the recent traumas in my life. La Residencia had become my luxurious refuge from the outside world. The perfect hideaway home from home.

Home. A year from now, where would I be living? I wanted to keep my canal-side apartment in Stratford and not live in the mortgage-free house Zeller had left me. It was too near my parents' home and much larger than I needed.

If I had the job in Bristol, I could rent out my flat, sell the house, and buy a small townhouse with a garden. I'd read that Clifton was a desirable neighbourhood with a vibrant foodie scene. It would be a fresh start.

I delved into the straw basket on loan from the hotel and found my refillable water bottle. After glugging the entire contents, I pulled out Zeller's book. One more chapter before I strolled down to the heated swimming pool for an energising dip, then a snooze in the shade.

The night before, cosseted by cool Egyptian cotton sheets, I'd read about Zeller's morning swims in the cove. With a rolled towel tucked under her arm, she used to walk down to the rocky beach of Cala Deià to dive into the clear waters of the Mediterranean. The swim and the half-hour walk each way were her daily exercise.

Before the first tourists arrived for a day on the popular little beach, she was back in the village, bashing out her daily word count on her Hermes Rocket typewriter. I'd never swum in the sea – strictly a heated swimming pool girl, me – but I intended to retrace Zeller's steps, if only for a paddle.

The loud bray of a donkey startled me. Javier had told me about these weed-devouring creatures, whose job was to keep the mountainside vegetation in check. One of the four-legged workers stood at the gate leading to the lookout point and the path further up the mountain.

I pulled my phone out from the basket again to take

a quick photo. Mum loved donkeys and she'd appreciate the picture.

WHEN I EMERGED DRIPPING from the pool and wrapped myself in the hotel's towelling robe, I noticed Javier setting the terrace tables for lunch. I strolled over to thank him for the Mirador recommendation.

'You're welcome,' he said with a slight bow of his head. 'Anything you need to know about the hotel, or Deià, please ask me.'

Looking at the village from my lofty vantage point, I'd wondered how many residents from Zeller's era were still in the village. Could I find anyone to talk to about her? Of course, 1978 was a long time ago, but …

'You may be able to help me with something. I had an author friend who stayed here for several months in 1978 and I'd love to find someone from that time who's still living here. Do you think there is anybody?'

Javier gave an enthusiastic nod. 'Yes. My grand-mother. She's lived here all her life.' He glanced at his watch. 'My shift ends at three. I could take you to meet her if you like. She doesn't speak any English, but I can translate.'

'If it's not too much trouble, that'd be fantastic. But will your grandmother mind?'

'Not at all. She loves company.' He glanced over at the main hotel building. 'Shall we meet in reception just after three?'

AFTER SHOWERING AND DRESSING, I strode down to the village shop and bought a bunch of flowers as a thank-you gift for Javier's grandmother. When I returned, the off-duty waiter was in reception, ready to leave.

As we walked to his grandmother's house, I told Javier a few details about Zeller, to help him start the conversation. Within ten minutes we arrived at a small stone cottage. Unlike some properties we passed on the way, the shutters were open. A white-haired lady sat in a high-backed chair next to the window and waved when she saw us.

'My *abuela* likes to know what's going on in her village.' Javier gave me a meaningful look. 'She doesn't go out often these days – too much traffic, she says – but still manages to keep up with the local gossip.'

After the introductions, we sat chatting. I gave Javier my questions, and he translated for the elderly lady, then translated her replies into English for me. It was a novel experience, but the conversation soon found a rhythm.

'I'm afraid she doesn't remember names very well,' Javier said, 'but she says quite a few Englishwomen were staying in the village back then.'

'Please tell her that Zeller used to go to the beach early every morning for a swim. She might have seen her.'

Despite the Mallorcan language being a total mystery to me, I could see this snippet of information had triggered a memory. Javier's grandmother beamed, and a torrent of the local language fell from her mouth, accompanied by much arm-waving.

Javier looked at me with a puzzled frown on his face.

'She thinks she remembers her.' He sounded uncertain. 'A woman who kept a donkey in her garden and used to ride it down to the beach each morning. She had long red hair, worn in a ponytail.'

My shoulders slumped. Zeller on a donkey? Not likely. And she'd always kept her chestnut-brown hair in a manageable, chin-length bob for convenience when travelling.

'Not Zeller, I'm afraid.' I kept a smile on my face when I said this to Javier, not wanting to disappoint his grandmother. Perhaps the lady's memory wasn't as reliable as her grandson thought? Then I remembered the book in my shoulder bag. I pulled it out and pointed to the black and white photo of Zeller as she was then, on the inside flap of the jacket.

'Ah!' The woman clapped her hands together. A rapid exchange between grandmother and grandson made me lean forward in my seat.

'Yes, Laura, that worked.' Javier beamed and rubbed his hands together. 'Your friend rented an old place right at the bottom of the village.' He paused for a moment, and his brow knitted. 'My *abuela* could be mistaken but remembers your writer friend spending a lot of time with a Scottish widower everyone knew as El Capitán. She was often at his house … sometimes late at night.'

His grandmother's eyes brightened, as though recalling this had been a delicious topic of village gossip back in the day. I imagined she now had few contemporaries in Deià with whom to share her decades-old memories.

'Thank you, Javier,' I said. 'And please thank your grandmother. She's been really helpful.'

The elderly lady stifled a yawn, making her rheumy eyes water. I guessed it was time for her nap, so we said our goodbyes with the customary hugs and kisses and left. Javier went one way, towards his home, and I returned to the hotel, wondering if Zeller had known her visits to El Capitán's home were the talk of Deià's locals.

When I collected my room key from the hotel reception, I noticed a small sign for a rental car company. Perhaps I should step – or to be more accurate, drive – outside my comfort zone? It would be a pity not to see a little more of the island while I was there.

'Is it possible to hire a car for just a day tomorrow?' I asked the girl behind the desk, who wore a badge bearing her name. 'Nothing too fast … and as small as possible?'

'Leave it with me.' Clara smiled and handed me my key. 'I'll call your room and let you know.'

If only I'd checked the weather forecast before I later signed the contract to hire a Fiat 500.

CHAPTER SIXTEEN

A nother drop of sweat trickled down the back of my neck. I wiped it away with one hand and gripped the rented Fiat's small steering wheel with the other. I fixed my eyes on the narrow country lane ahead, dreading an encounter with a tractor or bus. *Oh, this awful humidity.*

When Javier brought coffee to my breakfast table that morning, he warned me a storm was coming later. I'd glanced up at the cerulean-blue sky and wondered whether he'd read the forecast for another island.

By the time I finished breakfast, cleaned my teeth, and checked my latest emails, grey clouds had swept across the blue and swallowed the sun. The speed with which the weather changed surprised me. If I was lucky, I'd be inside the car if it rained.

I threw what I needed into the straw basket and went to reception to collect the keys to my rental vehicle.

'It's the white one parked just outside,' Clara said. 'Have you decided where you're going today?'

'Not sure yet. Maybe you could suggest a small town

with a few shops and somewhere to have a decent coffee and lunch? Away from the mountains?' I wouldn't admit to feeling cautious about driving abroad for the first time.

'Santa Maria's worth a visit.' The receptionist reached down into a drawer and produced a map which she spread on the reception desk. 'You could do a winery tour there too if you're interested.' She drew a circle in red ink around the town on the map, then wrote the name of two wineries on a separate piece of paper, before handing both to me.

'Thank you, Clara, that sounds perfect.' Who needed sunshine? I was going on an excursion and my pale skin would appreciate a break from the sun's rays.

CLINK, clink. The sound of bottles knocking together in a carrier bag accompanied me as I left Macià Batle, one of the Santa Maria wineries Clara had mentioned. I'd bought a bottle of Mallorcan Manto Negro for Mum and Dad and one for Billy, who was a connoisseur of all things wine related.

I remembered the Spanish word for red wine was *tinto*, which seemed appropriate; if the bottles broke during the flight home, I'd have a suitcase full of tinted clothes.

A few fat drops of rain spattered onto the windscreen as I fastened my seatbelt and glanced down at the map on the passenger seat. At least it was an easy route back to the mountains. I set off through the small town, past the smart interiors shop where I'd had a delicious cup of coffee and lunch in a long garden so magical it could have had fairies living at the end of it.

Once more on the country lanes, I noticed the wind was strengthening. I had to grip the steering wheel with both hands to prevent any sudden powerful gusts wresting the Fiat 500 from my control. Feeling vulnerable in such a small car, I wished I'd stayed in Deià. Or hired a Sherman tank.

The roadside trees bent back and forth; their trunks looked ready to snap, in what I was sure was a gale-force wind. They didn't look as robust as the mighty oaks or horse chestnuts of England.

A green snowstorm of leaves was falling ahead of me, and I eased off the accelerator, torn between driving at a sensible speed for the worsening conditions and putting my foot down to reach the hotel as soon as possible.

'Please, please don't let a tree fall on me,' I muttered. At least I wasn't yet in the mountains, where I'd spotted roadside signs warning of potential rockfalls. Some of those rocks were enormous boulders seemingly perched on top of others on the side of the coast road. Could strong winds dislodge them? I hoped not, as I still had to drive past.

The urgent trill of my mobile phone in my straw basket in the passenger footwell startled me. I was sure it would be Carlos calling, as he'd done several times since I'd moved to Deià. After having listened to his first message, I knew I couldn't torture myself by hearing his warm voice again.

I tried not to think about him arriving to take me to the airport only to find I'd already departed. Ignoring the electronic tune, I focused on keeping the car under control as the wind buffeted the small vehicle.

The sky had become darker, and in the distance I saw an obstruction in the road. A fallen tree perhaps? As

I slowed and approached it, I saw a person bending over awkwardly and struggling to pick up an object from the tarmac.

I checked the rear mirror and, with no other traffic in sight, switched on the hazard warning lights and brought the little white Fiat to a halt, partly on the verge.

The noise of the wind blowing through the trees and a sudden clap of thunder startled me as I climbed out of the car. I considered jumping back in and driving off at speed before the storm could worsen. But the person struggling with what looked like a fallen signpost was a woman. How could I not at least try to help her?

'Hang on!' I yelled into the wind. 'I'll give you a hand.' As I ran towards her, the bruised clouds above shed their load.

BY THE TIME we'd dragged the sign and its broken post through the open gates of the woman's property, the heavy downpour had drenched us both.

'Won't you come in and shelter till this darned storm has passed?' An American accent.

'Thank you, but I'd better fetch the car first.' I'd parked it on the grassy verge, but the two wheels on the driver's side were still on the carriageway and visibility was so bad it could cause an accident. I could only just see the blinking hazard lights through the deluge.

When I returned and parked in front of the old stone house, the woman stood at the open door holding a large, clean towel for me.

'The kettle's on for a hot drink,' she said. 'I've put the electric fire on, so go sit by it. You don't want to catch a chill.'

I kicked off my sodden sandals just inside and entered, dripping. 'Some storm, eh?'

As we pulled rush-seated wooden chairs closer to the small electric fire, we exchanged names. Marylou Benton didn't volunteer her age, but I guessed her to be in her fifties. Shorter than me, she was lean and looked fit, with well-toned arms and calves, and skin that revealed a life-long love affair with the sunshine. Her puffy eyes suggested she'd been crying not long before I arrived on the scene. Wrestling alone with a broken sign must have been stressful, I supposed.

'Just gonna change these clothes,' Marylou said, standing up. She padded towards one of the three doors at the far end of the room, leaving a trail of drips in her wake. 'Can I lend you anything to change into?'

'Thank you, Marylou, but I'll be fine in front of this fire.' I doubted the slender woman would own anything large enough to fit me.

When she disappeared into what was presumably her bedroom, I looked around at the L-shaped space encom-passing sitting, dining, and kitchen areas. One interior wall was built from exposed stone and had a small window. Like many of the properties I'd seen in Deià, the latter had iron bars as well as the glass. The grate in the large fireplace still held ashes and part-burnt logs – although I doubted a fire had been necessary for a long while. An adjacent wicker basket contained a tangle of kindling sticks.

The old cooker in the corner could have come out of the ark; Noah might even have been the last person to clean it. Evidence suggested that Marylou was no domestic goddess. I watched the fierce blue flames licking the bottom of the aluminium kettle, which soon emitted a shrill whistle. Before I could get up to switch off the gas, the woman returned.

'Sorry to keep you, hon,' she said. 'I can't thank you enough for stopping. Twisted my back somehow yesterday, and it hurts like hell. I'd never have managed without your help.'

Even as we'd grappled with the breakaway sign in the torrential rain and fierce wind, I'd noticed the name on it. I wondered what this American woman's story was and how she came to be living in the Mallorcan countryside. A tremendous crack of thunder rattled the glass in the window frames, and flashes of lightning lit up the room through the closed slatted wooden shutters.

'Anyone would have done the same,' I replied, although I doubted my own words. I rubbed my wet hair with the towel. 'Do you often have storms like this in Mallorca?'

'No, but when we do, we sure know about 'em!' Marylou pointed to a zinc bucket on the floor of the lounge area. 'That's catching the rain coming through the darned leaky roof.'

It was only then I noticed the rhythmic sound of water dripping onto metal. The house had a third-world vibe that didn't chime with La Residencia's luxury or Palma's sophistication.

'You're a tourist, right?' Without waiting for a reply, the woman turned to one of the wall-mounted kitchen cupboards. 'Tea? Coffee?'

'I'd love a tea, please.' I shivered and thought longingly of Mum and her Brown Betty teapot. 'And, yes, I'm a tourist. My first visit to Mallorca.'

Marylou opened a cupboard and pulled out a yellow box of Lipton tea bags and a couple of mismatched mugs.

'Here. One English tea, made the American way.' She placed the steaming mugs on the time-scarred pine table and sat down opposite me.

She wouldn't have won any prizes for making tea, but the weak brew ticked the boxes for hot, wet, and comforting.

'You're running a cat refuge here?' I'd seen the illustration of a feline on the fallen sign, and tilted my head in the direction of a shabby armchair, where a fluffy ginger cat appeared oblivious to the increasing number of meteorological explosions.

'That's Calvin. After Calvin Coolidge, one of our red-haired presidents,' Marylou said. 'He's my darlin' boy. The others are all outside, poor unwanted kitties, in their—' Her voice caught in her throat and a single tear slid down each of Marylou's cheeks. The storm had upset her. Having a leaky roof and an emergency bucket for drips would have upset me too.

'You okay?' I reached across the table and laid my hand on the American's tanned forearm. She pulled a tissue from a pocket in the paisley-patterned kaftan she'd changed into.

'I'm sorry.' She sniffed, then blew her nose. 'I've had some bad news and I don't know what to do.'

'Would it help to talk about it?' People told me I was a good listener – a useful quality in radio interviews – so it seemed natural to offer a sympathetic ear.

She sniffed again and wiped a tear from her cheek.

'It's my mom. She has only about a month to live. Cancer. She's in Florida. I'm here.'

I blew out my cheeks in a loud sigh.

'That's awful. I'm so sorry.' I squeezed Marylou's arm and looked down at the table to hide the tears welling in my own eyes.

Zeller's sudden death had been a terrible shock; we'd had no chance to say goodbye or tell her we loved her. At least a terminal illness gives notice and time to say and do all the important things. This American woman had a chance to be with her mother before it was too late.

I swallowed the lump in my throat. 'Well, you should go to her. You really should.'

'I know … and I want to,' she sobbed. 'But I have this place. I can't leave the kitties and nobody round here's gonna look after them for me.'

Which is when I did something insane.

CHAPTER SEVENTEEN

The wind had eased, and the rain stopped by the time I climbed out of the car back at the hotel and returned the keys to reception. The sun even made a belated appearance to prepare for its nightly sunset show. Optimistic waiters carried stacks of seat cushions from inside the bar back out to the terrace, casting defiant glances towards the sky. Maybe a G&T before I did anything else? After all, it had been an eventful day.

Minutes after I sank into one of the comfortable chairs and ordered, a waiter delivered my drink and a bowl of salted almonds. Relieved to have survived the day without damaging the cute little Fiat, I gazed out at the Mediterranean and took some calming deep breaths.

I couldn't believe how the weather had changed while I was out. Or that I had volunteered to help Marylou. Was I capable of running a cat refuge for up to a month? When I was growing up, there had always been a dog in the family, but I didn't remember having anything to do with cats. Soon I'd be looking after Refugio Marylou's felines, including Calvin – whose look of disdain suggested he thought I wasn't capable of the job. *Perceptive puss, that Calvin.*

My offer to take care of the refuge during Marylou's visit to Florida had seemed the ideal solution to her problem – she could be with her mother until the end came. I had no job to go back to anyway, so could cope with a few more weeks on the island. It would give me some quiet time to think about everything that had happened recently and make some plans.

Marylou assured me that looking after the cats wasn't difficult, although I realised the work would be more physical than being a radio presenter. The upside of that could be a downturn on the bathroom scales.

We arranged that on the Saturday lunchtime when I checked out of La Residencia, I'd take a taxi to Refugio Marylou and she'd show me what I had to do in her absence. She would then drive me to the airport so I could fly back to England to sort a few things out before returning for the duration of her stay in Florida.

There was one obvious benefit to staying at Marylou's place: I thought I'd have an opportunity to see more of the island and maybe find out more about Zeller's time in Deià. And I'd only have to buy food for myself and fuel for Marylou's car.

In the meantime, I was going to make the most of my remaining time at the renowned Deià hotel.

'We'll have a beautiful sunset this evening,' the waiter said, pausing by my table to look out at the Mediterranean. 'Would you like another drink?'

For the price of one G&T at La Residencia, Dan and I could both have drinks *and* crisps at The Oak Inn back at home. Although I missed Dan's company, I knew where I'd rather be sitting. That would be yes to a second drink, then.

At that moment my phone rang, and by coincidence, Dan's name and Louis Theroux-like photo appeared on the screen. I answered in a low voice to avoid disturbing other guests nearby.

'Dan! This is a lovely surprise. Everything okay?'

'Sorry to disturb you on your hols, Laura, but there's something I thought you should know.'

'Sounds ominous,' I said, my heartbeat quickening. If anything had happened to my parents, their neighbours would have contacted me, I was sure.

'It's probably nothing important, but I thought you should know somebody's been at the station asking for you.'

'A listener, I imagine, wondering where I was.' My departure had, after all, been sudden and without explanation.

'No. It was a guy who sounded as English as you and me but said his name was Carlos. He had Sandra on reception all of a flutter, with his Latin good looks.'

Thank God I was sitting down. It had to be the same Carlos.

'What did he say?' My voice sounded as shaky as my legs felt.

'He asked to see you. Said you'd left Mallorca without saying goodbye.' Dan sounded puzzled. 'I thought you'd gone for more than two weeks?'

Just as Zeller left the island without saying goodbye to El Capitán, I'd done the same to his son.

'It's complicated, Dan,' I said. 'He's someone I met on my first night here and we spent a bit of time together last week. Then I discovered something about him that meant I couldn't see him again. I told him I had to go home but changed hotel instead.' If only I hadn't told

Carlos where I worked. Correction: used to work. 'What did you tell him?'

'I had no idea who he was or whether he was someone you'd want to hear from, so I said you weren't working at the station anymore and I had no idea where you'd gone.'

I puffed out my cheeks and gave an audible sigh. 'Oh thanks, Dan. Did he sound angry?'

'Wouldn't have said angry. Disappointed, more like.'

'Thank you. It's a complicated saga, but I'll tell you everything when I'm back. I warn you now, it'll be a two-bottles-of-wine conversation, so we'd better make it a Friday evening.'

Dan laughed. 'You're on. Gotta go. Barry's heading my way.'

'Miss you, Dan – don't miss Barry though. Bye … and thanks for letting me know.'

My hands were shaking as I put down the phone. It was incredible that Carlos had flown to England to find me. It appeared he might like me as much as I liked him. What a tragic mess.

My dinner was booked for eight thirty, which gave me time to have a spa treatment. I drained my second G&T and waved goodbye to the busy waiter as I left the terrace. A relaxing massage had never been more neces-sary than it was at that moment. Besides, indulging myself with pampering treatments would be impossible once I was in residence at Refugio Marylou.

My LAST DAY and a half at La Residencia passed too quickly. Despite my original intentions, I didn't follow in Zeller's footsteps by walking down to Cala Deià's stony beach. Nor did I visit the open-air restaurant perched on the rocks on one side of the cove. Still, I reminded myself, I'd be on the island for a few more weeks yet.

Instead, faced with a month of physical work at Refugio Marylou, I made the most of every moment at the hotel, enjoying the delicious cuisine, swimming in the largest outdoor pool, a couple more wellness treatments, and even a painting lesson from the resident artist. At least I'd proved I could rule out art as a future way to make a living.

I was almost tearful on my last morning as I said goodbye to Javier and thanked him again for taking me to see his grandmother. All the staff had been so friendly. It felt as though I was leaving my second home (a lot more luxurious than my own home, I must add) when I clambered into the taxi Clara had ordered for me. Would I ever return to this piece of paradise?

HAVING COLLECTED me from one of Mallorca's most iconic five-star hotels, the taxi driver wasn't prepared for the contrast when we arrived at the rusty gates of Refugio Marylou.

He swivelled in the driving seat and frowned at me.

'*Es correcto?*'

It didn't take a working knowledge of Spanish to understand him.

'*Sí, correcto,*' I said, my spirits sinking. Muttering to himself in Spanish, he climbed out of the driver's seat to retrieve my case from the car boot. Even though the sun was shining, the place looked even shabbier than when I'd seen it during the storm. What had I let myself in for?

CHAPTER EIGHTEEN

'Welcome back,' Marylou said, her arms outstretched to give me a hug. Had she thought I might change my mind and not return?

'Coffee? Tea? Something cold?'

I remembered the tea she made on the day we met, and opted for coffee.

'Go sit yourself in the garden.' She waved her hand in the direction of the door. I went outside and wandered to the back of the house, passing the cats' enclosures at the side of the property on the way. They all seemed to be asleep, curled into furry balls within the units and cat pods inside the enclosures.

'Garden' was a generous description of the land at the rear of the house; the patch was terraced with old terracotta patio tiles, many of them cracked or broken, but I spotted a few herbs drooping in a cluster of clay pots.

An enormous old fig tree dominated the rest of the space, a sparse lawn of broad-bladed grass. The tree's leafy canopy provided the perfect shade for the small bistro table and two metal chairs underneath. I sat down, breathed in the delicious scent of the tree's leaves, and gazed at the pastoral scene beyond the property.

'Beautiful, isn't it?' Marylou arrived, carrying two mugs of coffee. 'Sometimes all you can hear are the lambs bleating. It won't be peaceful like this when I'm back in Florida.'

'Is that where you're from?'

'Gee, no. It's the state where folks go to retire and play golf.' She laughed. 'We're Nashville folks, but Mom fell in love with Miami after a golfing holiday there. Can't stand the place, myself.'

AFTER WE'D FINISHED our drinks, Marylou showed me around the small house and the cat enclosures and explained everything I needed to know. The list of chores seemed overwhelming, and I was already doubting my ability to look after the place. Then she added that the little house – or *casita* as she called it – was off the grid.

'Er, what does that mean?' My stomach felt as though it were sinking to my knees.

'No worries, honey,' she said. 'The solar-powered electricity system pretty much looks after itself. Just don't put too many electrical appliances on at once or you'll blow a fuse.' If there wasn't enough sunshine, she told me, the generator would start and stop automatically as required. 'If you hear a deep rumbling sound, that'll be the genny.'

There was more. The hot-water boiler was fuelled by butane gas, which came in orange metal containers. Marylou showed me how to change the gas container and relight the water heater. She might have been lean, and around a decade older than me, but she was strong and had no apparent difficulty lifting the heavy gas bottle. When I tried it, I'm sure my arms lengthened by an inch.

I prayed the gas would last until her return, or I'd be taking cold showers. An unfortunate incident with a Bunsen burner during my schooldays loomed large in my memory; the sound of fire engine sirens still made me blush.

My duties would also include driving household rubbish and recycling to Santa Maria, where I'd find bins allocated for different materials. *What, no collection?*

'But you won't need to worry about the septic tank,' Marylou said. 'I just had it sucked out.' As a lifelong townie, I had no idea what that was, but it didn't sound pleasant. How did this woman manage everything on her own?

'I don't know if I'll remember all this,' I said, shaking my head from side to side. The more I heard, the more I regretted my impulsive offer to look after the place in her absence. If only I'd made the most of my foray into the luxury lifestyle at La Residencia and not gone out exploring. Instead, I was facing a massive challenge, armed with a generous dose of imposter syndrome.

Marylou patted my arm. 'Don't worry. I've written you a bible of everything you need to know, right down to the places where you'll get a decent cup of coffee and bite to eat. And if you have any problem with the property itself, you can always ask Oddo.'

Oddo? I frowned, thinking what a cruel nickname that was.

'He's my landlord … lives next door. He's German

but speaks English. I'll take you to meet him before we leave.'

Ah, Otto. The American pronunciation of her land-lord's name had thrown me.

Sure enough, when we went back into the kitchen, a blue ring binder with the word 'Bible' written in large scrawling letters across the front was on the table. From the thickness of the contents, it seemed an appropriate name. I flicked open the cover and found Marylou's email address on the front page.

'Do you have a phone number too, so I can WhatsApp you if there's a problem?'

She shook her head. 'I'm not a WhatsApp kinda gal, honey!' She laughed, a throaty sound suggesting she'd once been a heavy smoker. 'What with the time differ-ence and cost of international phone calls, I think we'd best stick to emails, if that's good for you.'

After she'd covered everything to do with the cats and the house, Marylou and I walked to Otto's house, which was the nearest property. Flushed in the face, he answered the door after several minutes, wearing a bathrobe; he didn't invite us in. Although brief, the intro-duction was enough for me to notice the way he looked me up and down as though my clothes were transparent. As we walked back to the refuge, I noticed two cars on Otto's drive and guessed he had female company.

And finally, there was Marylou's ancient Renault Express. The insurance policy covered any driver, and the old vehicle would be my transport while she was away.

'Use it whenever you like,' she said. 'Might as well explore the island while you're here.'

It looked too old and battered to drive all over

Mallorca, but I hoped to find time to visit Deià again and have that paddle in the cove.

'She can be a bit testy though,' Marylou warned as we climbed in after loading my suitcase into the back. 'It may take two or three goes to kick her into life, but she usually starts eventually.'

Usually? Eventually? My heart sank again; matters of a mechanical nature were not my forte. Dad always dealt with any problems with my beloved old Mini and I couldn't imagine him being willing to hop on a plane to tinker with this piece of French engineering.

Marylou was taking me to the airport for my flight back to the UK. I had things to do, including attending my interview for the radio job in Bristol. I also had to pack suitable clothes for my temporary new role as cat refuge manager.

My return flight to Palma was booked for the same day Marylou would leave Mallorca. She was going to meet my inbound flight and take me back to the *casita* to settle me in; then I'd drive her to the airport for the first leg of her journey to the States, before returning to the sanctuary. Exhaustion set in just thinking about all the driving involved, before I even started looking after the cats.

CHAPTER NINETEEN

My flight took me to Bristol, where I was meeting the owner of the city's future new radio station on the Sunday morning. The plane landed early evening and I checked into the budget hotel I'd booked.

Because I didn't know Bristol, I'd thought about looking around the city centre, but there'd be another occasion to do that. An occasion when I didn't fancy a long, hot bath, a decent cup of tea, and an early night. Besides, I had to find something to wear for my meeting the next day. I hefted my suitcase onto the bed, sprang the locks, and threw back the lid.

I riffled through the contents of the case and pulled out a clean but crumpled long-sleeved dress. Zeller had taught me the trick of hanging creased garments in the steamy ambience over a bath. As the bath filled, I poured the entire contents of the small plastic bottle of hotel bath gel into the water. The toiletries weren't luxurious like those at La Resi, but as I sank down into the scented water, I closed my eyes and imagined I was back in Deià.

THE NEXT MORNING, it was a relief to find my dress showed no signs of its international travels. I showered, dressed, and breakfasted in time for my taxi's arrival at nine o'clock.

Kevin, the station owner, had given me the address of a former tyre sales depot in the process of being converted into a radio station. He was waiting outside, wearing a yellow construction worker's helmet with Kev written in marker pen on the front.

I looked at the building, trying to imagine myself working on an industrial estate on the periphery of Bristol. So much for my daydream of working in the heart of the vibrant city centre, a choice of tempting artisan bakeries and cafés within easy-walking distance.

'Let me show you around,' Kevin said after we'd introduced ourselves. He handed me a spare helmet to wear inside the building. 'Sorry, it'll mess up your hair, but Health and Safety means it's essential – even though nobody's working on a Sunday.'

After explaining his encouraging vision for the premises, we went for a coffee and informal chat in a nearby spartan, canteen-like café. Few customers were there that morning but the aroma of fried food hung in the air, and the coffee tasted like mere hot water compared to what I'd been drinking in Mallorca.

The less than salubrious location wasn't the only reason our conversation was not what I'd expected. Although Kevin's well-thought-out plans for the radio station impressed me, he had some bad news: his principal investor had pulled out of the project.

'I'm in talks with someone else and feel pretty positive about the outcome.' He had a sad smile on his face. 'I must be honest and tell you we're unlikely to launch now until the back end of this year. But if you're still interested, I think you'd be an asset to the station.'

My shoulders slumped and I gazed down into my coffee cup. Could I survive that long without work or a salary?

'Well, thank you for the kind words – and for being open with me. I may have to look for something else in the meantime, but I like what you've told me about your plans, so please still keep me in mind.'

We shook hands and wished each other good luck, then I left the café. The cooking aroma clinging to my clothes wasn't the only reason I felt deflated. It was clear I needed to look for other opportunities, which I'd have to do once I'd settled in at Refugio Marylou.

BEFORE I LEFT MALLORCA, I'd emailed Mum and Dad to tell them I was coming home for a few days and would explain my plans to return to Mallorca for a while longer.

I'd love to have seen their expressions when they read that their travel-phobic daughter was going to spend several more weeks abroad. And I was looking forward to their reactions when I told them I'd be looking after cats.

Mum replied to tell me Dad would pick me up in Bristol after my appointment with Kevin.

'How did the interview go, love?' Dad asked as we left the city.

'So-so. The guy was keen to have me on board and I liked him, but he's lost his main financial backer, which is delaying the launch. I think I'll be looking for other opportunities.'

'I'm sure something will come along.' We travelled in silence for a few minutes before he gave me a brief sideways glance. 'You must have liked Mallorca, to be going back.'

'To my surprise, I did, but it's not really because of that.' I told him about the storm and how it had led me to Marylou and her problem. 'It was because none of us was able to say goodbye to Zeller. It broke my heart this woman couldn't be with her dying mother only because she had nobody to look after the cats.'

'Making it possible for her to go was a kind and selfless act.'

And a crazy one.

We fell into a comfortable silence and it wasn't long before Dad's steady driving pace lulled me into a deep sleep. I didn't wake until the car stopped outside my parents' house.

'Your Mum's doing a Sunday roast. Leg of lamb. She thought you'd be hungry after all the foreign food.' Dad winked at me as he switched off the engine. Mum was one of life's feeders and couldn't have imagined how much delicious food I'd eaten in Mallorca.

I also knew my parents were expecting to hear all about my holiday. They would, however, be hearing an edited account of my eventful two weeks.

'Wow, THIS IS DELISH,' Dan said, lifting another forkful of almond cake to his mouth. 'I thought Mallorca was all fish and chips.'

'That's Magaluf, Dan. Not that I went there. The

island's covered with almond trees, and this is one way they use the nuts.'

He gave me an update on Bard FM and told me Odette was, as he'd expected, 'challenging' to produce.

'And how's Billy now? I tried to reach him last night to invite him too, but no luck.'

'Haven't seen him since he did his last breakfast show. His mum's not well and he's staying at her place during the week, so there's been no chance to catch up. Rang him a few times, but he didn't answer.' Dan lifted his plate towards me and grinned as I cut another slice of the almond cake I'd made. 'His new show sounds good though.'

Poor Billy. His mum lived in Oxford and it would be an early start for him to take the M40 up to Stratford on a Sunday morning. At least the roads would be quieter at the weekends.

Dan took another mouthful of cake and chewed for a few minutes. A small, thoughtful frown slowly appeared on his face, then he asked the question that almost made me choke on my almond cake.

CHAPTER TWENTY

'Well? What was it with this Carlos guy?'

I put my cake plate down on the coffee table.

'We're going to need another bottle of wine.' I hauled myself off the sofa and went to the kitchen. I didn't intend to give him the full story about Carlos, but I was ready to tell him what I'd found out about Zeller.

I returned with a bottle of Mallorcan red wine, a Ribas I'd bought in the grocery store in Deià before I left. Swaddled in unworn clothes for its flight, it had survived Ryanair's baggage handling.

Dan sat, his head cocked to one side, as I told him about the day Mum had phoned me in tears when we were in Huffkins café. He gasped when I told him Zeller was my birth mother, and my eyes prickled with tears. Dan shuffled along the sofa towards me and put his arm around my shoulders.

'That must have been a helluva shock.'

'It was. I was horrible to Mum and Dad and stormed

out of the house. It wasn't their fault Zeller wanted to keep it secret while she and Mum were both alive.'

I told him about Zeller's letter and how she'd hoped I would visit Mallorca one day.

'You know I'd rather have my holidays in this country, but I felt compelled to see the village where she'd stayed and try to find out who my birth father was.'

'And did you?' Dan asked in a soft voice.

'That's where Carlos comes in. He's a freelance photographer, born on the island to a Scottish father and Spanish mother. She died when he was a baby.'

I stood and paced the room, my hands thrust into the front pockets of my jeans. After composing my thoughts, I sat back down on the sofa.

'Carlos came to my rescue on the first night of my holiday. I was having a drink in the hotel bar and being hassled by some half-pissed English guys. He was at the bar, could see what was happening, and pretended to be my boyfriend to get rid of them. We had dinner together in the hotel afterwards.'

I took another slurp of my wine and couldn't help but smile. That had been such an enjoyable evening.

'I wasn't expecting to see him again so didn't tell him much about my life, except that I was a radio presenter in Stratford-upon-Avon. But we saw each other again the next evening and then the day after that, when he drove me into the mountains and we went to Deià. Guess what? He was born and spent his childhood there. It's so beautiful, Dan.' I reached for my phone on the coffee table to show him the photo I'd taken from La Residencia's Mirador.

'Wow! I didn't know you'd taken up mountaineering.' He handed my phone back.

'Ha ha. Almost killed me, walking up there. Anyway,

I'd told Carlos that Zeller was an old friend who'd been staying in the village, and it turned out Carlos and his father were living there at the same time – although Carlos was just a tot then.'

'You didn't tell him she was your birth mother?' Dan was wide-eyed.

'No. Well, it's taken me this long to tell you – and you're one of my closest friends. We'd only just met, so it didn't seem relevant. Besides, I needed to come to terms with it all myself first.'

'And have you?'

'I'm working on it.'

I told Dan that Carlos arranged for me to meet his father at the Palma apartment where he now lived.

'Carlos had a photo shoot that morning, so it was just me and his dad, who was charming.' I outlined our conversation and how everything pointed to the Scot being my biological father.

'His late wife – Carlos's mum – was also named Laura. Too much of a coincidence, don't you think? But I couldn't leap up, throw my arms around him and tell him I was his daughter. He might have had a heart attack.' I picked up my glass and drained the last drops of red wine.

'Understandable. And this would make Carlos your … half-brother?'

I burst into tears.

'Oh no!' Dan said, pulling me into a hug. 'You didn't …?'

'We did,' I sobbed into his chest. 'Just the once. Well, three times. On the one night. I was so lonely …'

Dan stroked my hair and spoke in a soft voice.

'I'm not surprised, Laura. Andy's been away ages,

and he was up in Scotland for a couple of weeks before he went to Japan.'

'I haven't only been unfaithful to Andy, I'm also pretty sure we committed incest on some level.' I shuddered, pulled away from Dan and made eye contact with him. 'And what makes it worse is Carlos and I – it sounds cheesy, I know – had something I hadn't experienced before. He was so lovely ...'

Dan smiled and wiped a tear from my cheek with his hand.

'Oh, I wouldn't worry too much about being unfaithful on one occasion to Andy. He's not likely to find out, and you're not engaged or anything. Besides, you may not be the only one feeling lonely – if you get my drift.'

Dan was right, of course, although I couldn't imagine Andy being unfaithful. He was too much of a workaholic, but that possibility made me feel less guilty about my behaviour.

'Anyway, I told Carlos's father I had to leave because I was feeling ill, which was true. I actually threw up in a potted plant outside his apartment building, like a drunken holidaymaker. I arranged to check out of my hotel in Palma that afternoon and into the one I'd booked in Deià, a few days earlier than planned.

'When Carlos phoned me later, I told him I had to fly home for work reasons. He insisted on seeing me again and taking me to the airport, but I left Palma before he arrived. I just couldn't face telling him. And I suppose that's why he came looking for me. Closure.'

'He must like you an awful lot to have done that.' Dan held out his plate. 'Do you think we need more cake?'

He was another of those fortunate people who can

eat anything and not gain an ounce. *Why are they always men?* I took the plate from him, grateful for the change of subject.

'And maybe some more wine?' I offered as I stood to go to the kitchen.

'That too, thanks. Any chance I could kip on your sofa tonight? Don't think I should drive home.'

'Of course you can, Dan. And there's even enough almond cake for breakfast.'

DAN LEFT after breakfast the next morning, having promised not to tell anyone about our previous evening's conversation. He was a Scorpio and loved keeping secrets, so I knew my story wouldn't become the talk of Bard FM later.

Once he'd departed, I sorted clothes for my trip back to Mallorca. What was the dress code for running a cat refuge? I chose old pairs of shorts, well-worn T-shirts, two summer dresses, linen trousers, a loose tunic top, towelling bathrobe, ballerina shoes, trainers, and three pairs of flip-flops. And in case I had the urge (and time) for lunch at La Residencia, I packed my smart coral linen dress and one pair of strappy sandals. I hadn't been a Girl Guide for nothing.

Despite phoning Billy several times since I'd been back, he hadn't answered. Perhaps he still didn't feel like talking to anyone, with the added pressure of his mum being ill. I didn't leave a message, and he didn't use WhatsApp, so I sent him an email before I packed my laptop into my cabin bag.

Hello Billy. I hope you're okay. No reply from you on the phone, hence this email.

I'm still furious Barry took you off breakfast and hope you're enjoying your new Sunday show. I've just returned from my holiday in Mallorca – but I'm going back again almost straight away! Long story ...

Dan was here last night. He said your mum's sick and you're staying in Oxford. I hope she recovers soon.

When we're both back in Stratford let's catch up. Lots to talk about!

Take care, Billy. Miss you.
Lots of love, L xx

~

MUM AND DAD drove me to Birmingham Airport for my Wednesday early morning flight, having insisted I cancel the taxi I'd booked. They were looking after the keys to my apartment and promised to visit once a week to empty my mailbox and water my plants.

'Have a safe trip, darling,' Mum said, hugging me before I went through the security gates. 'Keep in touch too, we'll be worrying about you.'

I was worrying about myself, although I wouldn't have admitted it to my parents.

'And watch out for those Latin lotharios, love.' Dad took his turn to wrap me in his arms. He had little to worry about there; I doubted there were many male predators in Marylou's rural part of Mallorca.

'I'll be spending all my time looking after the cats. Their teeth and claws will be far more dangerous than anything on two legs.'

I turned and waved as I passed through the security barrier. No going back now.

CHAPTER TWENTY-ONE

Cats fed – check; cats watered – check; litter trays cleaned – eeuugh – check; enclosures locked – check.

It was my second day at Refugio Marylou, and I was working through the list I'd made to get me through the first few days until routine set in.

When I'd hugged Marylou goodbye at Palma airport, I reiterated my hope that I could do the job she'd entrusted to me. A serious dose of doubt bugged me.

'Honey, anyone who can fog a mirror can look after those cats,' she said.

On my first evening I realised the American had meant only the refuge's assorted felines and not her own grumpy, pampered puss.

Entering the kittens' enclosure, small furry bundles charged towards me, desperate for food and oblivious to the potential danger of two size-five human feet. A tiny grey kitten ran halfway up my bare leg and its needle-like claws piercing my skin made me screech. The noise scattered the kittens to their safe places.

The older cats would rush towards me and swarm around my legs, their fur and whiskers tickling my skin as they mewled insistently for food. At least they didn't try scaling my legs as though they were trees.

When I put the full bowls on the ground, the cats dived into their food as though in a race. While they scoffed, their tails stood erect, like a row of flagpoles. With their focus locked on eating, I could stroke even Harry, the most nervous of them all. The pale ginger cat appeared not to notice I was doing it. I'd read about him in Marylou's bible: somebody had tied him inside a sack and dumped him next to a roadside rubbish container.

Like a seasoned biographer, Marylou had documented each cat's sad backstory, accompanied by a photograph. On my first night at the refuge, while reading these stories, tears had streamed down my cheeks. How could people be so cruel to animals?

Her own long-haired ginger tom had also made my eyes water. I hoped the thorough washing I'd given the angry scratch on my left forearm would prevent an infection. I added iodine and protective gloves for Calvin's future grooming sessions to my shopping list.

From his armchair throne in the kitchen, the imperious feline watched me as I forked wet food from a tin into his china bowl. His breakfast looked like the salmon pâté from the French deli next door to the Bard FM studios, but its aroma was more gross than gourmet. This was his usual food, but the haughty cat seemed indifferent to his meal. I wondered if he was missing Marylou.

I'll get to that in my own time, the pampered puss appeared to be thinking, when I put the bowl in its usual place on the kitchen floor.

'You're not getting away without your grooming,' I

said in a mock-stern voice, brandishing the cat's brush. Calvin stood on his chair, arched his back as he stretched, turned around, and sat down again, treating me to a view of his back.

I sighed and dropped the brush onto the kitchen table.

I summoned my inner Arnie Schwarzenegger. 'I'll be back.' *Not until I have gloves, though.* The famous line from Arnie's movie *The Terminator* passed Calvin by and not a hair on his head stirred.

'And don't let that delicious food go crusty in this heat.'

I hurried out of the stuffy room to escape the strong fishy aroma. *Oh my God, I'm talking to cats now.* I needed to make some human friends while I was on the island, for some proper conversation.

It was still only spring, but the old house was stuffy and uncomfortable; how did Marylou survive without air conditioning?

THANK God I didn't have to sleep in the small spare room, with its single bed and the world's smallest window. Marylou had insisted I use her own bedroom during my stay. She made up the double bed with fresh bedding and showed me where to find more clean linen when I needed it. I had to use the spare room cupboard to store my clothes, but at least I didn't have to spend my nights in the smaller cell-like bedroom.

Although I wasn't an early riser back at home, I woke at first light in Mallorca. Perhaps it was the promise of a day when anything could happen after I'd finished my cat duties.

By mid-morning I was usually ready to make a cafetière of coffee and take it outside to drink. Underneath the fig tree's leafy canopy was the coolest place, and I'd become addicted to the fig leaves' heady scent.

This was my time for thinking, planning, and dipping into Zeller's book. As I read, I noted points of interest. I intended to find a few hours one day soon to visit Deià again, but if that didn't happen, I would spend two or three more nights at La Residencia once Marylou was back. By then, I would be desperate for some pampering and relaxation before I returned home to start the next chapter of my life.

After skimming through my notes from the previous day, I removed my bookmark and started reading.

A WEEK HAS PASSED since I arrived in this tiny mountain village. Already I've met six local women named Maria, four called Cati (after the saint born in nearby Valldemossa), and seven men with the name Josep. Nobody stood at the altar of the hilltop Sant Joan Baptista church to witness their child christened Jason, Jennifer, or any other popular English name.

It's common for islanders to have the same Christian name as their parent or grandparent. It may seem unimaginative, but it's the tradition here and throughout the island.

'Doesn't it cause confusion?' I asked Cati, the friendly woman behind the pharmacy counter, when I went to buy something to ease an annoying cough. She laughed and told me everyone has their own nickname, distinguishing them from others with the same Christian name. From now on, I shall think of her as Cough Drop Cati.

I met a Clive last night; he didn't tell me whether he had a nickname, but I imagine he's the only Clive in the village. He's five years older than I am and has lived in Deià for years.

After the sun went down and the day-trippers left, I strolled out for some cool air and to find a bar where I wouldn't be the only female customer. I took my pen and notebook with me, so the astute locals will guess I'm a writer.

Clive was sitting at a table in Paco's, sipping a beer, and we were soon in conversation. Almost two hours later, I stood up to leave and he offered to walk me home.

'Thanks for the offer, Clive, but I'll be fine,' I said. I wanted to be alone so I could plan the five hundred words I was going to write before bedtime. I did, however, accept his kind invitation to join him for lunch on Saturday.

I WROTE 'CLIVE' in my notebook, underscoring it twice. If only I'd found out what El Capitán's proper name was. Could it be Clive? El Capitán Clive was pleasingly alliterative. Zeller didn't mention little Carlos playing on the bar floor, though. Was this how it all began? I'd have a lot of explaining to do if I were to contact Carlos's father again. But that was not going to happen.

Something interrupted the whirlwind of thoughts going through my mind. *What was that?* It was late morning and the cats would be snoozing in the shaded nooks and crannies of their enclosures, as usual. The cicadas' incessant buzzing was often the only sound at that time of the day – yet I was sure I'd just heard a vehicle nearby.

I stood up, slipped my feet into my flip-flops, and flip-flopped to the front of the house, just in time to see a dusty black van leaving through the open gates at the end of the long drive.

Then I noticed it: a large cardboard box on the

ground in front of the old wooden door. Whatever could
it be?

CHAPTER TWENTY-TWO

'Ah, you're the kind person Marylou told me about,' Silvia said, smiling. I'd just introduced myself to the vet who looked after the refuge cats when they needed treatment or vaccinations.

The smiling woman opened the box and lifted out the two wriggling black kittens.

'What cute little *gatitos*!' She placed the tiny creatures side by side on her consulting room's stainless-steel counter. They mewled and huddled together, trembling and unable to make an escape bid. Their ears were huge and out of proportion with their scrappy little bodies.

'Poor things, they're terrified,' I said. 'How could anyone be so cruel?'

'They're lucky. At least someone brought them to the refuge.' The vet picked one up and placed it on the counter-top weighing machine. 'It's not uncommon for people to drown unwanted kittens – or just dump them in the countryside to fend for themselves.'

'That's appalling.' Tears pricked the back of my eyes. 'I suppose these little guys are fortunate then.'

The machine's digital read-out showed the kitten's weight as four hundred grams.

Silvia picked up the furry bundle in one hand and used the other to examine the small animal with care, peeking into orifices and lifting the base of its tail, while it made indignant kitten noises, flaying at the air with its tiny paws like a cornered boxer.

She put down the squealing creature and repeated the process with the other, identical kitten.

'Some people will, I'm sorry to say, dispose of kittens rather than pay to have their cats neutered. It is a matter of education … and cost, of course.'

Marylou had told me Silvia did some veterinary training in Bristol, which explained her excellent, if sometimes formal, English. It also raised her awareness of the difference in attitudes towards animals between the British and her fellow Spaniards.

'You have two healthy little boys here, about four weeks old.' The vet placed the second kitten back beside his brother on the counter. 'But they should still be with their mama, so they're a bit underweight. I will give you some special formula to feed them for a week. Bring them back in seven days and we'll see how they're doing.'

'Okaaay,' I said, letting this news sink in. I bent to pick up the box from the floor.

'No. Leave that. It's too big for them and they'll feel more secure in something smaller. Wait a minute.' She left the room, and I stood waiting, one hand placed on each kitten's back to stop them escaping.

'What am I going to do with you, little guys?' I spoke in a soft voice, feeling their trembling backs under my hands. 'I don't think Marylou expected any additions to her family of feline waifs and strays.'

Silvia came back into the surgery clutching a wicker cat carrier. 'This should do.' She placed the basket, a folded towel inside, on the counter. 'It's old, but it'll be fine for transporting these two.'

'Any special feeding instructions?'

'Oh yes, definitely. You must give them a bottle every four hours. Don't worry, I'll give you everything you need.'

'Every four hours? Including nights?'

'I am afraid so, Laura.' After placing the kittens inside the carrier, she secured the clasps then smiled at me. 'It is tough but rewarding, and at this age at least they won't need you to stimulate them to poo or wee.'

Don't ask, I told myself, relieved not to have that duty as well.

'Please keep them isolated and warm for the time being. And don't let that bully Calvin anywhere near them.' The vet turned and started opening cupboards and drawers, assembling the items I'd need for the next week. She had long black hair, tied back in a scrunchie, and had a kind face and manner.

'I am writing some instructions' – she laughed – 'but please excuse my written English.'

Afterwards, she handed the piece of paper to me, on which she'd also written her mobile phone number.

'If you have any problems – whatever the time – WhatsApp me.'

I hesitated, skimming through the notes and taking in the unexpected new responsibility.

'You'll be fine.' Silvia patted my arm. 'The hardest thing will be telling them apart – they look identical.'

I slipped the handles of the carrier bag containing the feeding stuff over my wrist and picked up the cat carrier.

'Thank you so much, Silvia. See you next week.'

'You are welcome.' She laughed. 'And good luck choosing names for those little *niños*.'

As I walked through the waiting room, where an elderly man sat with his grey-whiskered Jack Russell, Silvia's hearty laugh echoed in my ears. It was fortunate Marylou had such a generous and sympathetic vet on hand. I liked her from the moment we met and hoped we could become friends.

THE KITTENS HAD TRAVELLED to the vet's surgery in petrified silence. On the return journey they were still petrified ... but no longer silent.

'Hush, guys,' I said, having checked in the rear-view mirror to make sure the carrying case hadn't slipped from under the seat belt. Two little side-by-side faces looked back. I couldn't help but smile at their indignant expressions, even though I knew I had a mammoth task ahead of me.

Marylou liked all her sanctuary residents to have a name and their photograph in her records, and this was something else I needed to do before I immersed myself in feeding duties.

Perhaps some music would calm them? I turned on the car radio and pressed the search button to find a station. Within moments, I was singing along in a soft voice to 'Celebrate the World'. I hadn't heard that Womack & Womack track for ages.

'Got it!' I smacked the steering wheel with one hand. The perfect names for two kittens I'd have trouble telling apart: Womack and Womack. 'I'm a genius!' My mewling passengers in their basket on the back seat showed no signs of being impressed. One problem solved. Feeding every four hours around the clock wouldn't be as easy.

SOMETIME AFTER THREE in the morning, I was sitting on the bed in my bathrobe, cradling a kitten. Womack, for sure. I'd never felt as tired in my entire life. It occurred to me this would have been the inhumane hour my alarm would chirrup me awake if I'd moved to the breakfast show. I shuddered at the thought; at least my current interrupted nights were a temporary inconvenience.

Although I preferred to sleep during the hours of darkness, there was undeniable joy in sitting up in bed, eyelids at half-mast, with a warm kitten snuggled into the crook of my left arm. The first Womack sucked with all his strength on the teat, enjoying the kitten-milk formula and purring with contentment.

'Hey, slow down, little man.' His brother, head resting on my foot, watched the proceedings with a surprising degree of patience. The next bottle was keeping warm wrapped in a towel. Being a cat 'mum' was already proving to be quite exhausting. Only another six days (and nights) to go, I told myself, yawning so widely I heard my jaw click.

A ROUTINE SET IN. At around seven in the morning, I padded through to the kitchen to make two bottles of formula for the kittens, then went back to bed to feed them. They seemed to enjoy being on my lap, sucking with increasing strength at their bottles.

Once fed, they fell fast asleep curled up together in their basket in the bedroom, and I got up to deal with Calvin and the refuge cats.

On the day I visited Marylou to learn about my duties, I'd found the place too quiet, but now I was aware rural life had its own sounds. When I had my breakfast, sitting at the table under the fig tree, I could hear birds, the dongling of sheep bells in the field behind the property, a nearby cockerel with a dreadful sense of timing, and the occasional rumble of a tractor. Nature's music was becoming a balm for my soul and the perfect soundtrack for deep thinking.

I often thought of Carlos and wondered whether our relationship would have developed further if I hadn't made the awful discovery. To be frank, it was unlikely to lead to anything serious; we lived almost a thousand miles apart. And there was the matter of my existing boyfriend, who would eventually return to England from Japan.

That morning, I was still sitting on the bed, feeding the second Womack. He wriggled in my lap, and I could feel he had the hiccups. I tried not to laugh at the surprised expression on his sweet face when his little body went into spasm.

'Come on, little boy.' I put the bottle on the bedside table and stood. 'Time for your snooze.'

The kittens slept in Marylou's room with me, although I put them into their carrying case at night. During the day, I let them have free run of the bedroom. Whenever I went to fetch them for their feed, they had somehow got onto the bed and were asleep – one with his head resting on the other's body. They looked adorable and I took a few photographs to send to Mum.

I was making breakfast for myself when my mobile

phone alerted me to a new email. It was from Billy, but there was no subject heading. He hadn't replied to the one I sent before I returned to Mallorca. Perhaps he was now getting over his disappointment about losing his weekday show and felt like communicating again.

But it wasn't the bright and breezy message I'd hoped to receive. *Oh no.* Tears filled my eyes as I read the few sentences for a second time.

My dear Laura,

I'm afraid I have the most dreadful news. Mum died at the weekend. It was sudden and unexpected as her consultant believed she was on the mend. I'm devastated.

I wanted to let you know as you'd met Mum a few times. The funeral will be on Friday 14 June at Oxford Crematorium. Your presence would mean everything to me. I'm sorry not to phone, but it's too soon to be able to talk about this.

Much love,

Billy

My poor friend was having an awful time. Of course I should be there to support him. When Andy couldn't return from Japan for Zeller's funeral, it was Billy who held my hand and handed me his clean handkerchief for my tears.

But was it feasible to travel to the UK and back in one day? An internet search for flights revealed it was impossible to make the trip without an overnight stay there. Even if I put out extra food for the cats, I had to consider the risks. What if another Icelandic volcano eruption delayed or cancelled the return flight? Or worse still, the plane crashed – although that was, I hoped, unlikely. I was committed to my responsibilities at Refugio Marylou.

Breakfast had lost its appeal, so I spent some time writing and editing a suitable reply to Billy, who had no idea why I was in Mallorca. I explained I was in sole charge of a cat refuge and unable to leave my feline charges. I paused before pressing send, wishing I could speak to him on the phone. But he'd said it was too soon to talk, so the electronic message would have to do.

CHAPTER TWENTY-THREE

'I bring you these from my garden,' Otto announced in German-accented English. Marylou's landlord stood on the doorstep, wearing surfer shorts, Birkenstocks, and a smile. No shirt. His chest glistened with sweat.

His right arm was around a large plastic bowl full of plump red tomatoes. Who would have guessed he was the type to grow his own produce? Or own any Tupperware?

He was, though, the type to leer at women. I'd noticed that before, when Marylou introduced us. He was doing it again, and this time I was alone.

I knew the small *finca* – a house with land – Marylou rented had once been Otto's home. His wealthy father had lived in the neighbouring property, a much larger and less rustic house.

When his father became too ill to live on his own, Otto moved in to care for him. In due course, the elderly man died and his former home became his son's permanent residence.

Marylou saw his vacated finca advertised to rent. It

was an affordable option for the American, who wanted a place where she could live and fulfil her dream of opening somewhere to care for some of Mallorca's many unwanted cats. Her plans to build enclosures in the garden didn't faze her new landlord.

'I don't need to tell you why the rental price was low,' Marylou had said, looking around the room. 'It ain't Buckingham Palace, for sure. But it's my home.'

My mind snapped back to the present. Where were my manners?

'Thank you very much, Otto, how kind of you. They look tasty.' The aroma of the tomato stems reminded me of Dad's greenhouse on a warm summer's day. *Caprese salad for lunch.*

As he handed me the bowl, I forced a smile, which I knew didn't reach my eyes. The man made the hairs stand up on the back of my neck. Although I looked forward to eating the freshly picked tomatoes, I wanted him to leave. Despite the warmth of the day, a shiver ran down my back.

'It is very warm today,' Otto said in his accented English. 'You will invite me for a cold drink before I go?'

Licking Calvin's food bowl clean had more appeal than spending time in this man's company, but he was Marylou's landlord. Did Spanish law allow him to come in whenever he wanted? I shuddered, then reminded myself he'd been neighbourly and brought me a generous quantity of his home-grown tomatoes.

'Yes, of course,' I said, opening the door wider. I pushed it shut behind him to keep out the heat, and he followed me. I'd spread my paperwork all over the pine table, so I placed the bowl on the worktop.

'What would you like?' I called out, peering into the fridge. 'I can offer you water, juice, Sprite, or beer.'

'Any white wine?' He startled me; I hadn't heard him come right up behind me. *Damn. He must have seen the Sauvignon Blanc.*

I removed the open bottle and, irritated by his invasion of my personal space, banged it onto the table. I crossed to the shelves to fetch a wine glass for Otto and a tumbler for my water. A chilled white wine would have been enjoyable, but not in this man's company. As I stretched to reach the glasses, I felt fiery breath on the back of my neck and detected a strong whiff of alcohol mixed with sweat and suntan oil.

'Let me help you.'

'It's okay, I'm fine.' My voice sounded an octave higher than usual. I stepped to one side, away from him, but Otto grabbed me from behind and wrapped muscular arms around my waist.

'Stop right now!' I yelled. His right hand pawed at my left breast and I felt him nip the back of my neck with his teeth.

'What the bloody hell do you think you're doing?' My heart pounded as I stamped on one of his feet, wishing I'd been wearing shoes. With pointed heels. The surprise move enabled me to pull myself away from Otto's grasp. He yelped and bent to check his foot for damage.

'Get out! Now!' I pointed to the door. Otto spat out something in German. Whatever it meant had a threatening tone. I was sure he was able to hear my heart thumping.

'Marylou is always grateful,' he said. His thin lips had curled into a cruel smile. 'You single women with only cats for company need a man sometimes. I could give you a memorable time.'

Otto grabbed my left wrist and squeezed hard. I

wrenched myself free and lurched forward, snatching my mobile phone from the table.

'Out! Or I'll call the police.'

'Okay, I go,' he snarled. 'But you will regret this. My rental agreement with Marylou is informal, and you may soon wish you had accepted my offer.'

'Fat chance!' I spat back at him, not caring whether he understood the colloquial English.

'Funny you say those words,' Otto replied. 'I do find you quite fat. I don't think I would like your body pressed against mine after all. *Auf Wiedersehen.*'

He spun around and strode to the door, which he flung open then slammed behind him, startling Calvin from his snooze on the chair. Growling, I took two strides to the kitchen worktop, picked the ripest-looking tomato from the bowl, and hurled it after him. On impact with the door, it split and dribbled seeds down the wood.

With a shaking hand, I poured a large glass of the white wine and sank onto the sofa. The wine disappeared in three desperate gulps.

My heart pounded as I wondered whether Otto would return later. As the owner of the property, he doubtless had a door key. Would he let himself in one night? If I screamed, there was nobody around to hear me. I found a wooden rolling pin in a kitchen drawer to put by the bed … just in case.

If only I could turn to a friend in Mallorca. As helpful as Silvia was, I didn't know her well enough yet to tell her about the incident. Would she think I'd encouraged Otto in some way? Had I, without intending to?

For the umpteenth time, I regretted not telling Carlos about the true nature of our relationship. Having an older half-brother to defend my honour would be useful, but it was too late to explain everything now. After the way I'd treated him, he probably wished he'd never met me.

One person did need to know what had happened. Once I stopped shaking, I went to sit at the table, swept all my papers aside, and opened my laptop to compose an email.

Hi Marylou,

How are things there? You and your mum are always in my thoughts.

The cats are all okay – including Calvin, who sleeps most of the day on his chair.

I paused, wondering whether to mention the additions to the refuge. Next time, maybe.

I thought I should let you know I've just had a difficult 'situation' with Otto. He brought me a bowl of tomatoes from his garden this morning. He made a serious pass at me and I had to fight him off. Things got unpleasant, and he stormed out of the house, saying I'd regret turning him down.

I think he'd been drinking before he arrived, so perhaps this was out of character and it'll all blow over.

Anyway, I needed to tell you my side of the story in case you hear a different version from Otto.

Send me an update when you can.

Best wishes,

Laura

DAYS PASSED, with no reply from Marylou. After checking my emails yet again, I snapped my laptop shut and sat at the kitchen table, elbows on the pine tabletop and my head in my hands. If only I'd insisted on having a phone number for her; the lack of communication was driving me nuts.

As I hadn't seen or heard from Otto since, I hoped he'd forgotten the incident – or chosen to pretend it didn't happen. With any luck, Marylou's landlord would be too embarrassed to face me again.

I swallowed the last of my coffee and put the empty mug into the sink with my breakfast bowl and spoon. The washing-up would have to wait until later; it was market day in Santa Maria and I liked to arrive early before finding a parking space became a nightmare.

A visit to this weekly event was a Sunday morning treat. I enjoyed trawling the stalls for plump fresh fruit and veg to load into Marylou's old straw basket, like a local. I'd buy a loaf from the sourdough bakery there to enjoy with a local goat's cheese I'd discovered. Another reason I looked forward to a few hours in Santa Maria was the chance to mingle with other people. Much more time with little human contact and I'd be walking on all fours like the cats.

I showered and dressed, then checked my reflection in the mirror. '*Muy bien,*' I said aloud, practising a few words of the Spanish I'd acquired. Almost impressive.

My healthy glow no longer came courtesy of blusher and, despite Otto's cruel remark about me being fat, I had shed several pounds in weight. *How many calories do I burn each morning cleaning out those cats' enclosures?*

Enough to have an *ensaïmada* later, I decided. This sweet, local speciality pastry, although made with lard, would go well with my mid-morning coffee while I was out.

Before I left, I locked all the windows. The property – like Otto's – was in an isolated location, and Marylou had warned me the old practice of leaving rural homes unlocked when going out was no longer advisable.

A padlock and chain for the property's gates seemed a good idea, and I added the items to my market shopping list. What happened with Otto had made me realise how vulnerable I was on my own.

Then I slid my precious laptop out of sight under the sofa at one end of the room and grabbed my shoulder bag and the battered straw basket for my purchases. Time for my morning out. But when I opened the front door, my plans changed.

CHAPTER TWENTY-FOUR

A plain white envelope was on the doorstep, held in place by a large stone. Even on a weekday, there was no postal delivery service to this property; Marylou rented a post office box in the local Correos and collected any mail once a week. Someone had delivered this in person; I had to buy that padlock and chain. My breakfast rose in my gullet as I bent to pick up the missive, suspecting its contents were about to ruin my Sunday.

I STORMED through the open gates and up the gravel path towards the neighbouring stone house. Otto's Doberman, Bruno, strained at the end of a heavy leash, baring his teeth and snarling. His thick leather collar, studded with metal spikes, only enhanced the impression this was a dog you wouldn't want loose about the place.

'Oh, for God's sake, shut up!' I yelled, hoping the beast couldn't smell the fear in me. Stomping past, I gave

him a wide berth. At the front door, I made a fist with
my hand and pounded on the oak like a woman
possessed.

'Open up, Otto,' I shouted. 'Your car's here so I
know you're in.' I waited a moment, then hammered
again, using both hands this time. Not a sound came
from the house.

'What a delightful surprise to see you here.' Sarcasm
dripped from his words.

I gasped and turned around, startled to find Marylou's landlord behind me. He wore the briefest of lime-
green Speedos and a pair of matching flip-flops. Kermit
the Frog came to mind as I pictured Otto sunning
himself on a giant lily pad on a pond in his back garden.
If I wasn't so furious, I'd have laughed out loud.

'What the hell is this, Otto?' I waved the typed letter
in his face. Written in poor English, it would have been
amusing if the contents weren't so serious. It was from a
lawyer's office in Palma. Otto's lawyer's office.

'It is clear, is it not? I want you and those wretched
cats out of my property by July the twenty-ninth. I am
selling the finca.'

I'd already worked out what that meant. 'But that's
only six weeks away. What about the rental lease with
Marylou?' How would I break this devastating news to
the American, who already had enough worries about
her mother? Whatever would she say?

He laughed. 'Lease? Did she not tell you?' Otto stood
with his legs apart and hands on his hips, flaunting his
manhood in front of me. 'There was no official rental
agreement. We sealed the deal in our own way.'

I shuddered at the memory of what he'd hinted at on
That Awful Day. The thought of Otto and Marylou
thrashing about on the double bed where I slept at night

filled me with both nausea and anger. How could she be so reckless?

'You're doing this to spite me, Otto, because I wouldn't have sex with you. Well, you know what? I'd rather never have sex again than have it with you. You're a complete and utter bastard!'

If only I could have hit him, I'd have felt better. But my clenched fists remained by my sides. I couldn't add an assault charge to my existing troubles; if I were festering in a foreign jail, what would happen to the refuge?

My shouts set Bruno barking again and Otto strode over to the dog, shouting something in German. Would he let the beast loose? Even chained up, the Doberman terrified me.

'I'll find a place for Marylou to live – and better than your damp hovel. But the cats? What about them?'

'*Fick dich!*'

He spat out the words, which I guessed weren't an apology. Crouching down beside his snarling dog, muttering in German into its ear, he unclipped the chain but kept his hand inside Bruno's studded collar.

'Now get off my land before I set my dog on you. Unless, of course, you want to change your mind about sleeping with me?'

As I turned to stride away, I had an overwhelming urge to pick up a rock from the path border and smash it into Otto's skull. This was real life, however, and not an episode of *Midsomer Murders*. Instead, I kicked the gate on my way out.

∾

How WOULD I find a home for the refuge and Marylou in such a short time? I spent almost all night tossing and turning, my hair and skin damp with sweat, trying to think of solutions.

Once or twice, a bright idea came to me, only for nagging realism to bat it aside. Just as I was at last drifting off to sleep, I heard a cockerel somewhere not too far away crowing in the dark. I sat up and looked at Marylou's alarm clock on the bedside table. Four in the morning. Great timing, Mr Cockerel. I hit the pillow again with a thump, closed my eyes, and breathed deeply in and out in pursuit of sleep, praying for the perfect solution to come to me in a dream.

LATER, as sunlight sliced through the shutters, painting bright stripes across the bedroom wall, I threw back the sheet and hauled my weary body off the mattress to face the new day. When I looked in the mirror at my wayward hair, I saw Helena Bonham Carter as *Harry Potter*'s Bellatrix Lestrange. After a cool shower, I changed into what had become my cat-duty uniform: baggy shorts, an old T-shirt, bathrobe, and flip-flops. I'd managed to tame the witchy hairdo.

If only I'd visited my hairdresser in Stratford before returning to Mallorca. My hair was long enough to pull into a scrunchie, and a few grey roots showed. Finding someone to cut and colour my light-brown hair was another task to add to what was becoming an unwieldy mental list. I needed time. I needed a hairdresser. But most of all, I needed coffee.

As I waited for the kettle to boil, I fired up my laptop and checked my email inbox. Still nothing from Marylou. Perhaps when she read my latest news, she would find the time to get in touch.

Was it my imagination or were the cats and kittens feeling my anxiety? As I began my routine of feeding, watering, and cleaning, their meowing sounded more urgent than usual, and the way they clustered around my feet made it difficult for me to move.

'Hey guys, I have work to do here,' I said, bending down to stroke Harry's ginger head. He was no longer nervous of me and liked to greet me by rubbing the side of his face against my leg. He was stealing my heart. I would ask Silvia what the procedure would be for taking him back to England.

Perhaps the cats were intuitive enough to detect my mood from the tone of despair in my voice. 'I've got more chance of winning the Nobel Physics Prize than rehoming you guys – and *I* almost blew up the school science lab!'

∾

IT WAS Wednesday before I sat down to focus on the dilemma I faced. I'd spent the past couple of days in a state of denial, hoping that I would wake up in the morning and find it had all been a terrible dream. But reality hit me that morning, after I'd fed the cats.

Brainstorming beckoned. I made a pot of coffee and sat indoors at the pine table. Armed with a pen and notepad, I jotted down ideas – however absurd – as I thought of them. The most achievable one was finding new homes for as many of the moggies as possible. But I would also search for someone willing, or mad enough, to rent me a property as an alternative home for the refuge. And, of course, for poor Marylou.

My initial enthusiasm waned when I realised my inability to speak Spanish was going to be a hindrance, limiting me to communicating with the island's British community.

First, I emailed Silvia to ask whether she knew anyone looking for a cat or kitten. I gave her a brief explanation of the dilemma the refuge was facing, telling her about the eviction notice but not what Otto had done to me.

She phoned me less than ten minutes after I'd hit the send button.

'*Hola*, Laura, I got your email and I'm shocked,' she said. 'What did Marylou say when she heard?'

'That's the problem, Silvia. I've sent her two emails, and she hasn't replied.' My voice broke and I swallowed hard.

'Oh Laura, how awful for you. Listen, I was going to phone anyway to invite you for lunch this Sunday. Tomeu's making a paella, and between the three of us, I'm sure we'll be able to come up with some ideas.'

My shoulders fell to where nature intended them to be.

'You're so kind, Silvia. I'd love to come for a paella, thank you. What time should I arrive?'

'I'll come and get you,' she said. 'We're eating at our place in the country and it's difficult to find. Is two o'clock good for you?'

Place in the country? 'Ooh. Sounds intriguing … and perfect. Thank you, Silvia.' I was becoming used to the locals eating lunch later than we did in England. Back in my radio days, I'd have finished my lunch not long after twelve o'clock.

I'd had no idea Silvia owned a place in the countryside. Would it be large enough to accommodate the cats' enclosures temporarily, if necessary?

Carlos had told me many Palma residents had a rural bolthole for weekend escapes. But Silvia lived in Santa Dolores; with fewer than twenty households and a dusty bar, the hamlet was far from a manic metropolis.

Silvia's husband had died when her only child, Tomeu, was five years old, and though I'd not yet met him, I knew mother and son were close. Teenage Tomeu was the man of the house and hoped to study graphic design at college when he finished school in a year's time. Perhaps he could put the word out at school about adopting a cat or kitten?

That phone call improved my day. It was time for a celebratory biscuit with my second cup of coffee. As I nibbled the shop-bought cookie, I realised how much I was missing my therapeutic baking sessions. I decided to risk using the oven – or the Dragon, as I'd named this flame-throwing piece of kitchen apparatus – and make a batch of shortbread as a contribution to Sunday's lunch with Silvia and Tomeu. Even Calvin's nose twitched when the delicious buttery aroma of baking filled the room later that morning.

'WHAT A BEAUTIFUL PLACE!' I said to Silvia when we arrived early on Sunday afternoon. Her countryside bolthole wasn't far from the refuge but would have been impossible for me to find. Access was along a bumpy earth track off a rural lane, and I imagined bits of Marylou's old Renault would have fallen off as it crossed the rough terrain.

We arrived at an old stone property, which was tiny

and in the middle of a patch of land that I could see was too small to accommodate the cats' enclosures.

Silvia explained that the building had once been where her grandfather stored his tractor. Her father inherited it from his father, sold off most of the surrounding land, and converted the building into somewhere to spend time at weekends in the countryside with his family.

'When Papa died, my sister and I inherited it. We share the place, but Aina lives in Barcelona now so rarely uses it. Because my surgery is in my home, coming here feels like a proper break from work.'

Silvia pointed to the terrace, where Tomeu was heating olive oil in a paella pan over a firepit. She had brought him over before coming to collect me, and he appeared to have everything under control.

'Tomeu loves it here,' she said. 'He's in a band with a few friends, and this is a great place for them to practise. They can't disturb anyone with their enthusiastic playing. Come and see inside.'

She led the way. I noted the fall in temperature as we entered the simply furnished open-plan room, where I saw an old sofa, log burner, table and chairs, an ancient cooker, and a humming fridge. A threadbare rug covered some of what looked like a cement floor. Silvia pointed to a door in the corner. 'The loo's there if you need it.'

I glanced again at the cooker in the corner. It was the same model as the one Marylou had, and appeared to be almost as old. Silvia must have noticed, because she laughed. 'If we cook, it's often outside. Food always tastes better outdoors, no?'

'I have to agree.' We stepped out into the hot sunshine again. 'Smells pretty amazing too.'

Half an hour later we were sitting at the rustic

outdoor table and benches, under a large parasol, spooning generous helpings of the aromatic rice dish onto our plates from the paella pan in the middle of the table.

'Tomeu, that was sensational,' I said afterwards, wiping my mouth with a paper serviette. 'That was the most delicious paella I've ever had.' I didn't mention I'd never tried it until I came to Mallorca, or that this was only the second paella I'd ever eaten. The teenager blushed at the compliment.

After we'd stacked the crockery and piled it into the outdoor-kitchen sink, I retrieved the foil package of home-made shortbread from Marylou's straw basket. Tomeu had made a pot of coffee and was pouring the dark brown liquid into earthenware cups.

'A little contribution from me, to say thank you.' I opened the package and placed it in the centre of the table.

'Proper shortbread! I love it.' Silvia leaned across to take a piece and glanced at her son. 'Tomeu and I have talked about your problem, Laura. He's a talented artist and has offered to design a poster for my waiting room, appealing for people to adopt a cat or kitten. Would that help, do you think?'

I beamed at Tomeu. 'That'd be brilliant – but only if you have time. I don't want to disrupt your studies.'

'It will be my pleasure,' he replied. He must have been the politest teenager I'd ever met. I could have hugged him for being such a supportive son to my new friend. 'I can also make some duplicates to put up at school – if the principal agrees.'

'Calvin is booked in for his annual vaccination this Wednesday,' Silvia said. 'By then, Tomeu's poster will be on the wall.' I blinked away tears; these people were so generous and thoughtful.

'Thank you both,' I said, swallowing the lump in my throat and reaching for a second piece of shortbread. 'It'll be a brilliant start.'

'I'll email you a copy of the poster too,' Tomeu said. 'You could use it on social media.'

Oh dear. Social media. I rarely used it, but the teenager's suggestion was a sensible one. It was time to refresh my lapsed skills.

Just as I was leaving, I remembered to ask Silvia if she had a mobile phone number for Marylou and, sure enough, she did. She wrote the number on the back of one of her practice's business cards and I slipped it into my basket, relieved to have a more reliable form of contact. Tomorrow, at an appropriate hour, I'd phone her … however much it was going to cost.

CHAPTER TWENTY-FIVE

On Monday morning, after tackling the routine daily chores, I put my mug of steaming coffee on the kitchen table, plonked myself down on one of the rickety dining chairs, and switched on my laptop.

Facebook first. I groaned when I logged onto my account; my last post had been a few photographs from Bard FM's Christmas 2018 party. It was a bittersweet memory. I'd loved most of my time working there, and seeing the photos reminded me I was missing my friends as well as the buzz of working in radio.

Not one of my Facebook friends was on the island, and it was unlikely someone from the UK would come all this way to adopt even the most appealing cat in the sanctuary. Harry had that title and I had designs on taking him back home if I could.

A picture paints a thousand words. Why did that phrase pop into my mind then? I closed Facebook and did a Google search. A few keystrokes later, photos of dogs of all breeds, shapes, and sizes filled my screen. The

Instagram account was in the name of @findingthemhomes and based in Ontario.

'Genius!' I punched the humid air with my fist. It had to be worth a try. By that evening, I'd created the Moggies in Mallorca Instagram page and posted my first photograph: Womack and Womack sitting on the bed. One of them had his head tipped to the side; the other was licking his brother's neck. Although they would be better off if someone adopted them, part of me wanted them to remain at the refuge. Bottle-feeding them for a week had bonded us.

I wrote a suitable caption, explaining they were looking for a home together if possible. With an email account also set up for the page, people could contact me if they were interested in adopting any of the cats featured each day. I sat and looked at the screen for about ten minutes, waiting for any response. *Nada*. Of course, it would take time to build an audience. Despite this depressing thought, I had at least taken positive steps towards rehoming some of my charges.

Over the next few days, I was going to photograph as many of the cats and kittens as possible and post one picture each day on the Moggies in Mallorca Instagram page. In the meantime, I did some research into hashtags and wrote a list of suitable ones for the posts I was going to create.

At the end of what was a long period in front of a screen, my eyes felt ready to pop out of their sockets. I needed to get out of the house. But first, I had something important to do.

IT TOOK a few moments before I heard Marylou's phone ring. I waited, planning how to explain the predicament we were in. And waited. There was no reply. I frowned and disconnected the call.

After I'd fed the cats, I had a shower, changed into clean clothes, and drove to a cosy Italian eatery I'd been to before in Santa Maria. Owner Luigi treated me as though I were his best customer, fussing over me and paying me compliments on my choice of dishes. That evening I was also his only customer as it was still too early for locals to be eating dinner.

Just as my pizza – the size of a small circus ring – arrived at the table, I heard an electronic ping from my handbag. I delved in and retrieved my phone, hoping Marylou had seen my attempt to reach her and returned the call ... or that someone was enquiring about adoption. The email wasn't what I'd hoped for but it made me sit upright and grin.

Hi Laura!

Sorry I haven't been in touch for a while. Been manic here in the last weeks of shooting. Just got back after the crew's wrap party. Yay! Filming's over at last, and earlier than expected.

Before I fly back to the UK, could I come and see you in Mallorca? On Thursday this week if that suits you?

Let me know ASAP please, and I'll book the flights.

Love Andy x

PS: I hope the catsitting's going well.

I glanced at my watch. It was the middle of the night in Tokyo; I imagined the party had been a lively and late affair. They seemed to have been away from home such a long time. I'd send him a reply before I went to bed, just as he'd be starting a new day.

Although my pizza was both tasty and satisfying, I

couldn't resist a celebratory tiramisu for dessert. I was sure when Andy knew the predicament I was in, he'd offer to stay and help. Fingers crossed he didn't have another assignment lined up.

Back in the car, parked in the middle of Santa Maria, I phoned Marylou's number again. After ringing a few times, a man answered with a hesitant 'Hello?'.

'May I speak to Marylou, please?' I guessed he was a friend or neighbour. But he said nothing further and the line went dead. *How strange.* I assumed it was a transatlantic connection problem and dialled again. This time, I heard the persistent ring telling me my call was unwelcome.

My heartbeat was racing and I felt queasy. It could have been the combination of pizza and tiramisu, but I feared I'd phoned at a bad time. Had Marylou's mother just died? I dropped my phone into my bag and fired up the noisy old Renault.

THE BIRDS WERE NOT the only ones singing early the next morning. Andy would be here in a couple of days, and I couldn't wait to see him. We'd been apart for the longest time in our history as a couple and had some catching up to do. Perhaps being with my boyfriend again would stop me thinking so often about Carlos.

I threw back the sheet and almost sprang out of bed, having remembered my dream about being back on the radio. There was an English station broadcasting on the island; I'd heard it playing Womack & Womack on the day I took the kittens to the vet. My subconscious must have been sending me a message: *Get yourself an interview, Laura!*

Before I did anything else, I searched online and found the contact email address for the aptly named Britannia FM. Then I composed a note to the station manager, explaining the cat refuge's predicament and asking about the possibility of doing an on-air appeal.

I wondered whether to mention my radio experience but decided against it in case anyone thought I was angling for a job there. I didn't expect to get a reply for a day or two, so the ping alerting me to a new message from them only a few minutes later surprised me.

Hello Laura,

Thank you for your email. Yes, happy to give you some airtime. Don't suppose you're free today? Our afternoon show guest just cancelled, so we have a slot to fill. Would 3.15 work for you? Let me know soonest please.

Map of studio location attached – in case you can make it.

Mike Collins, Station Manager

Yes! I punched the air in triumph, then typed my reply. Three fifteen would be perfect. I'd be back from Palma in time for the evening feed.

I was a little late doing my feeding and cleaning duties that morning but figured the cats would have understood if they'd known what was going on. Most of them were now used to me, and only one or two still cowered in a corner until the food bowls were on the ground. The others liked weaving around my ankles, demanding their breakfast and making it almost impossible to move without treading on a paw or tail.

'I've got important work to do today,' I told them as I started emptying the contents of the litter trays into a large black bag. 'Even more important than this stinky job. Trying to find a new place for you all to live.' It was a good thing nobody was around to hear my one-sided conversation with the cats. I was looking forward to talking to a human being again later and being on the radio again, even if only as a guest.

After a coffee, I had a shower and washed my hair, then dressed for a visit to Palma. It was already thirty degrees outside, so I chose loose-fitting linen trousers and a tunic top for comfort. My plan was to leave early for the city, have a pre-interview wander around the old town, and a bite of lunch – wearing Marylou's wide-brimmed straw hat and my sunglasses, in case of Carlos sightings.

First, I needed to find out how to buy a train ticket at Santa Maria station. No way was I going to drive Mary-lou's car into the centre of Mallorca's capital. Driving on the wrong side of rural roads was quite enough, thank you.

WHEN THE ON-AIR studio light went out, I removed the headphones and placed them on the desk in front of me, opposite Molly, the presenter.

In case Carlos might listen to the station and hear the interview, I asked Molly to introduce me by only my first name. She asked me very few questions and let me talk for longer than I expected.

'Thank you for giving me so much time.' I smiled at her.

'No. Thank you for making it easy for me.' The presenter sighed. 'I've been doing this job only a month, so it was great to have someone with plenty to say, without me having to prompt them.'

Molly told me she'd been a holiday rep in Magaluf, but after an over-refreshed holidaymaker threw up all over her one evening, she resigned. A job in radio sales seemed less messy, and when Britannia FM's afternoon presenter left to become a club DJ in Ibiza, Mike had persuaded her to try presenting. The red rash on her neck suggested she was finding it stressful.

The song 'Hotel California' was ending, so I stood up. We shook hands and I left before she needed to speak to her listeners again. I trotted down the stairs, hopeful that one or two cats might find a new home because of the interview. As I stood at the bottom of the staircase to restore the audible alerts on my phone, a man's voice took me by surprise.

'Laura?' The silver-haired man looked to be in his fifties and had an attractive smile. 'Sorry – didn't mean to make you jump.' He held out his hand. 'I'm Mike, the station manager.'

'Yes, I'm Laura.' We shook hands. 'Pleased to meet you, Mike, and thank you for letting me come in today. It's all a bit of a mess, and I thought this would be the best way to reach the local English-speaking community.'

'It was an interesting listen. And you did more than reach someone,' he replied with a smile. 'I've just taken a call from a man who owns a superyacht here. He'd like to donate five thousand euros towards the cost of relocating the refuge.'

My phone slipped from my grip and clattered on the floor. I seemed to have lost my ability to speak. I put one hand on my chest; my heartbeat had quickened.

'Did you say five thousand euros? Seriously?'

Mike bent to retrieve my phone, glanced at the screen, and handed it to me.

'Your lucky day: it's not broken and, yes, five thousand euros. I've just emailed Rupert's contact details to you. He said to call him tomorrow.'

I hesitated for a moment. Could this be a hoax?

Rupert – if that were his actual name – could be one of those men who lures women into his orbit with spurious offers and promises. I'd have to be cautious but didn't want to appear ungrateful.

Mike let out a hearty laugh and slapped his thighs. 'No need to worry – I can vouch for Rupert. He's a wealthy, salt-of-the-earth type who likes to support causes he cares about. He told me he's a cat lover.'

'Phew,' I said. 'That's a relief. Sometimes people who phone radio stations are a little ... odd.'

Mike laughed again. The laughter lines under his eyes suggested he enjoyed life. 'Come on, I'll walk out with you.'

He opened the building door for me, and we went out into the bright afternoon sunshine.

'My guess would be you've got radio experience,' he said as we stood under the shade of the building's awning. 'I don't suppose you're looking for a job? You have an attractive voice and tell a story well.'

I laughed. 'You've rumbled me. Yes, I've been a presenter for over ten years. I appreciate the offer, but I'm only on the island until Marylou returns, then it's back home for me.' *And no job.*

'Pity. We could use someone like you. If you change your mind, get in touch. And let me know if you need any more publicity. Happy to assist.'

'Thank you, Mike. I really value your help.'

We said our goodbyes and did the Mallorcan cheek-kissing thing before I set off in search of a taxi back to the railway station, humming 'Hotel California' and almost skipping along the pavement.

When I arrived home, I found two emails from people interested in adopting a cat. I had a few phone calls to make the next morning and one to make that day. Before I went to change clothes to deal with the cats, I tried Marylou's number again. No reply. *Should I be worried?*

CHAPTER TWENTY-SIX

The next morning, I attended to my emails as soon as I'd fed the cats and done the usual cleaning.

A brief email from Dan told me he attended Billy's mum's funeral in Oxford. He'd also been out for a drink with Daisy, his personal trainer, and a second date was already in the diary. He hadn't had a steady girlfriend for almost a year, and I hoped things would work out for him this time.

Nothing had arrived from Marylou, and I'd given up hope on that front. She was either hopeless at checking her emails or was concentrating all her efforts on her mother; in her shoes, I knew I'd be doing the latter.

I dealt with the two enquiries about adopting a cat and, after a couple of quick phone calls, sent both enquirers – one English, one with a Scandinavian name – a map to Refugio Marylou. If they didn't change their minds in the meantime, I was expecting them that afternoon.

'RUPERT SPEAKING.' Our generous benefactor answered my call almost straight away.

'Hello Rupert, it's Laura … Mike Collins gave me your number.'

'Ah! Cat woman,' he said. I tried not to laugh at the alarming mental picture of me wearing Halle Berry's skintight *Catwoman* suit from the movie.

'When Mike told me about your offer, I couldn't believe it. Thank you *so* much for your generosity.'

'You're welcome. I love cats but, as I live on my boat, it's not practical to have one of my own … so this is the best way I can help.'

He was sailing to Corsica at the weekend for a couple of weeks, so we arranged to meet in Palma on Friday morning. We were going to set up an account for the refuge with his donation. I'd be the signatory until Marylou returned to take over.

COMMUNICATIONS SORTED, I showered and dressed for my visit to the vet with Marylou's own cat.

'Come on, Calvin. I don't have time for this.' Although he usually spent most of the day – and night – asleep on his armchair, he leapt off his seat the moment he saw me enter the room with his wicker travelling case.

'Tactical error, Laura,' I told myself as I dropped to my knees and peered under the sofa. Calvin had positioned himself out of reach and was hissing his fury through a cloud of dust bunnies. No way was I going to stretch out and try to grab the loose skin on the back of his neck – a little trick Marylou had shown me to pacify cats.

Subterfuge. I stood up and went to the kitchen

cupboard, opening doors and drawers and making the
sort of noises that meant feeding time for Calvin. He was
a substantial cat with an appetite to match, and after I'd
opened the tin of tuna I'd intended to have with salad for
my lunch, I could see him peeking out from under the
sofa. I forked a little of the fish into his food bowl and
mashed it well to release the aroma. Nostrils twitching,
he came and stopped at my feet, looking up at the
worktop.

I placed his dish on the floor and gave him the
chance to enjoy a taste. Meanwhile, I put on the heavy-
duty gloves I now wore during grooming sessions. Thus
armoured, I made a sudden lunge and grabbed Calvin,
then bundled him into his case and secured it before he
could give me the scratching I deserved for my
deception.

A glance at the clock on the wall told me I'd spent
almost half an hour trying to catch Marylou's feisty
feline.

'It's fantastic.' I stood in front of Tomeu's adoption
poster, which was impossible to miss on entering Silvia's
waiting room. 'Your son has a lot of talent for his age.'

'He gets it from his late papa,' Silvia said wearing a
proud smile. 'Paco was a well-known artist on the island.'
A loud meow from the carrier at my feet reminded us
both we had other business.

'Bring him through.' I followed her into the consulta-
tion room.

'He's in a feisty mood. Be careful.' I lifted the basket
onto the metal-topped counter and stepped back a few
paces, figuring I'd be the first in line for an attack.

'Don't worry. He'll behave himself now he's here.'

Well, goodbye fingers, I thought, as she opened the carrier. Calvin hissed and then stepped out as though this were his favourite place (after his raggedy armchair, of course). Silvia stroked his head and spoke to him in a quiet voice, in words I didn't understand. Marylou's cat responded with a low, rumbling purr.

'Contrary creature.' His complete change of character amazed me.

Silvia laughed, then checked his ears, prised open his jaw to look at his teeth, and weighed him.

'Calvin, you've put on a bit of weight since I last saw you.' Silvia looked at me. 'I've just had some diet-food samples delivered, so I'll give you a few to see how he gets on.' I didn't mention I had to resort to bribery with treats at grooming time or, as I'd done earlier, to catch him.

He didn't flinch when Silvia injected him and, after giving him another head rub, she picked him up and placed him back in the cat carrier. Mr Compliant.

To my surprise, he appeared to sleep all the way home, which gave me some quiet time to think about seeing Andy the next day. My heart rate quickened as I imagined us entwined in each other's arms in bed, making up for all the weeks we'd been some six thousand miles apart. I hoped I wouldn't call him Carlos by accident in the throes of passion.

BEFORE THE POTENTIAL ADOPTERS ARRIVED, I read Marylou's bible cover to cover for instructions about adoptions. I didn't remember seeing anything when I'd read the book on my first evening.

The procedure for newcomers was clear: give them a name, take their photograph, and record their date and manner of arrival, along with any known backstory. I'd done all this for Womack and Womack. When the potential adopters arrived, I wanted the refuge to appear professional. *There must be a form for adopters to sign to acknowledge their responsibilities.*

I phoned Silvia, who answered after a couple of rings.

'*Hola*, Laura. Is Calvin okay?'

'Yes, he's fine, thanks. Silvia. May I ask your advice, please? I've got some people coming this afternoon who may be interested in adopting a cat.' I crossed two fingers as I spoke. 'Anyway, I've been through the bible Marylou left me but can't see any procedure for adoptions. Shouldn't there be a form for new owners to sign?'

Silvia laughed. 'As far as I know, Marylou never actively tried to rehome any cats. I think she enjoys having them there for company.'

Oh dear. My American acquaintance was in for a ton of disappointments when she returned to Mallorca. Whenever that might be.

'I have an adoption form that a large animal refuge here uses. I'll find it in my files and email you a scanned copy for guidance. Okay?'

I thanked her again, aware I was doing a lot of that.

The vet emailed me the form within fifteen minutes. After some technical wizardry – or to be more accurate, sheer fluke – I linked my laptop to Marylou's printer and printed off the document, then set about creating something that looked official for Refugio Marylou.

I produced four copies of my masterpiece: two for each adoption – we'd both sign and keep a copy. Mine would go into a new 'Adoptions' section in the bible. I hoped their own copy would remind the adopters of their responsibilities.

Each cat had its own passport containing details of vaccinations, which Marylou kept in an old biscuit tin on top of her wardrobe. I went to fetch the tin so I wouldn't forget to hand over those important documents.

I WAS DRINKING iced tea under the fig tree when I heard a car horn at the front of the house. Expecting visitors, I'd unfastened the gates and jammed them open with rocks. The gates, like much of the property, needed serious maintenance. Whoever bought the place from Otto would have to be keen on do-it-yourself. Or have the money to pay someone else to do the many jobs necessary to make it a decent home.

When I went to the front of the house, a young couple was climbing out of a VW Golf. They asked if they'd found the right place and I remembered that the fallen sign which had started this whole saga was still lying broken behind a gatepost.

'Yes, this is it,' I said. 'Welcome to Refugio Marylou. Come in.'

Gary and Claire followed me into the house. They were a friendly young couple who told me they lived in a modern house in Portals Nous. I remembered the village because Carlos and I had driven through it on the way back from nearby Puerto Portals marina, where we'd bumped into Gil.

Gary was a yacht chef soon going to sea for three months, and his wife wanted to add a cat to their family home. They'd both grown up in families with cats, and as Claire was a freelance graphic designer working from home, any cat they adopted would have plenty of company. And I could tell, plenty of love too.

'Come and meet the cats.' I led them out of the house and around to the enclosures. Once inside, Claire took an instant like to Jet, a handsome black cat who flirted by rolling over to have his tummy tickled.

'He definitely likes you,' I said. So far, Jet hadn't allowed me to do anything other than stroke his head.

'I think I'm in love,' Claire said to her husband. 'Isn't he gorgeous?'

'Looks like this is the one,' Gary said, scooping the cat up into his arms. Jet purred with pleasure as we walked back to the house.

They'd come prepared with a brand-new cat carrier in the back of the car. After they'd signed my forms and kept a copy for themselves, I gave them Jet's passport and waved them off from the front of the house.

'Goodbye, Jet,' I said in a quiet voice as their car turned out of the gates onto the road and out of sight. I wiped a tear from my cheek, sad to see one cat go but thrilled he was going to a loving home.

As I was filing the signed copy of Jet's adoption form into Marylou's bible, another car arrived. I went outside to meet the next potential adopter: Ingrid, a tall blonde woman of about my age, who climbed out of a sporty silver BMW with Swedish number plates.

She rejected my invitation to come into the house, telling me she was in a hurry to get to a business appointment. If she adopted a cat, did she intend to leave it in the car while she attended her meeting?

'I'd just like to see the cats,' she said without smiling.

Ingrid didn't make a good impression on me. I led her to the enclosures, but she didn't want to go inside and instead stood peering through the wire netting.

'That's the one I'd like,' she said, pointing a manicured finger.

'The tabby? That's Bobby. He's a real character.'

'No, no,' she snapped. 'The pale ginger one. Over there.'

She was pointing at Harry. No way.

'I'm sorry, Ingrid, but he's reserved for someone else.'

'Oh.' Her mouth stayed in a tight 'O' shape for a second or two, emphasising the smoker's lines above and below her lips. It reminded me of a cat's bottom, and I had to look away in case I sniggered.

'There's another ginger cat over there ... the gorgeous fluffy one.' I pointed to Clinton. 'He's affectionate and loves to play.'

'No – I don't want one that's going to shed hair all over my villa. I'm only interested in the pale ginger one.'

I turned away from the enclosures and walked back towards the front of the house, speaking to her over my shoulder.

'As I said, he's reserved for someone else. Thank you for coming, and I'm sorry you couldn't be more flexible.'

Ingrid strode back to her car but stopped before opening the door.

'If the other person changes their mind about that cat, please let me know.'

I still hadn't asked Silvia about the rules for taking cats abroad, but I knew I didn't want Ingrid to have Harry.

Without a thank you for my time or a goodbye, she got into her car, slammed the door, and drove off at speed.

'And good riddance to you.' I wouldn't want her to adopt *any* of the cats.

Gary had given me permission to post the photo I took of him holding Jet, on the Moggies in Mallorca page.

'Jet has a new forever home! Get in touch if you'd also love to adopt a gorgeous healthy cat or kitten.'

Within minutes of posting the photo, the 'likes' started. The number of followers for Moggies in Mallorca was growing, and I hoped some of them were on the island and serious about adopting a cat.

When I turned out the bedside light later that night, I settled back onto my pillow with a smile on my face. Tomorrow I'd be back with Andy. I'd invited him to stay with me at Marylou's, but he replied by telling me something I'd never known about him in all the years we'd been together: he was allergic to cats. Maybe I wouldn't be adopting Harry after all.

CHAPTER TWENTY-SEVEN

My boyfriend – for almost a decade – was at the hotel bar, perched on a tall stool. He was clutching a beer and chatting to a young Asian woman sitting on the neighbouring stool; he always was sociable.

His hair was shorter than usual, and he wore smart chinos, rather than his normal uniform of denim jeans.

Andy's email, with news of his imminent visit, had been a wonderful surprise at the end of a day which had frazzled my nerves and left my body rigid like a robot.

I fizzed with excitement at the thought of seeing him again after so long. He was staying for only one night – he had things to sort out in Stratford – but I was sure when he heard about the refuge, he'd offer to come back and help me until Marylou returned home.

We arranged to meet in the bar of the five-star Melia Gran Victoria hotel on the waterfront Paseo Marítimo. Andy's tastes in accommodation had changed since our stay in Cornwall. At least the bed in his room was unlikely to collapse.

I assumed I'd stay the night with Andy, so I fed the

cats early and gave them extra rations late that afternoon. I'd have a decent cooked breakfast before my meeting with Rupert the next day and then return to the refuge. My feline charges wouldn't suffer from having their food later than usual.

With everything going on in recent weeks, I had neglected my appearance. On a day-to-day basis, Calvin's fur had more attention than hair anywhere on my body. After a long, fragrant shower and time deforesting my legs, I slathered myself in Chanel Cristalle lotion and perfume, then put on the only set of matching bra and knickers I had with me in Mallorca. I zipped up the linen shift dress, brought in case an occasion called for smarter attire. I added a pair of strappy sandals, earrings, a slick of lipstick, and a few sweeps of mascara. In Marylou's wardrobe mirror, I saw a slimmer version of my old self. *Bring on the Big Reunion.*

To give me more flexibility in terms of time, I drove to Palma instead of using the train. Listening to Britannia FM, I heard a guest talking about his attempt to paddleboard his way around Mallorca for charity. *Rather him than me.* I wondered if he'd read the previous day's *Majorca Daily Bulletin* report about the increasing number of jellyfish in the Mediterranean because of climate change.

After Mr Paddleboard had finished, the station played George Benson's 'Give Me the Night' and I sang along. Yes, I thought, gimme, gimme, gimme! I felt more like a teenage girl on her way to a second date with a boy she had a massive crush on than a forty-one-year-old off to reunite with her long-absent boyfriend.

Apart from my brief fling with Carlos – which was almost impossible to put out of my mind – it had been ages since I'd had sex. I kept imagining being tangled in luxurious Egyptian cotton sheets with Andy on a king-size bed.

But as soon as I saw him, I realised something had changed. Where were my lustful thoughts or the desire for us to race up to his room? I felt only the warm glow of seeing a very dear old friend after a long absence. Must be the stress, I thought. Once we were alone in his room, I'd focus on him and forget all my problems. Then the fireworks would happen.

Andy must have heard my heels clicking on the marble floor, because he turned his head, smiled, and gave me a wave. He said something to the girl on the next stool, then slid off his own and strode towards me, arms outstretched. Our hug felt good … but not like one of lovers. He released me, took a step back to look me up and down, then grabbed my hand and led me out onto the bar terrace.

We sat at a table under the shade of a parasol, and the barman who'd followed us out took our order. He returned with two large glasses of chilled Sauvignon Blanc and a small dish of crisps.

'Cheers,' we said in unison, chinking our glasses together.

After his first sip, Andy put his glass down on the table.

'You're looking well, Laura. Life good here?'

'Thanks, Andy. All the physical work, instead of sitting on my bum all day, must be having some effect.' I paused. 'Things are a bit more complicated than I expected – I'll tell you later – but the change of scene is helping me come to terms with everything about Zeller and the radio show. Mallorca's a beautiful island and I like it more than I thought I would.' I drank some more of my wine. 'You're looking good yourself. How was the filming?'

Andy glanced into the bar, then looked back at me. 'It was great. And that's why I'm here.' He took a longer slurp of his drink, then looked into my eyes. His smile had morphed into a serious expression. 'I'm returning to Stratford – but not for long.'

I allowed the words to sink in for a moment or two, wondering why.

'Another assignment?'

'In a way.' He averted his gaze to take a keen interest in his wine glass. He ran an index finger around its rim, and I could tell he was composing his thoughts.

'I've accepted a job in Tokyo with NHK, the national TV company. It's an amazing opportunity and I've fallen in love with the country. I've got things to sort out in Stratford, then I'm going back.'

How did I not fall off my chair? Was he going to ask me to go with him? My heart was pounding. Whatever would I reply? *I mean, Japan is a lot more foreign than Mallorca. I don't think I'm up for karaoke bars and raw fish.*

'Wow! I'm shocked. I didn't see that coming.' After a pause, I leaned across the table and rested my hand on his arm. 'Sorry … I should say congratulations, Andy. Not an opportunity to pass up, I guess.'

He didn't ask me if I wanted to join him in Tokyo or tell me I was almost certain to get a job on an English-language radio station. Without putting it into words, he'd conveyed that this move heralded the end of our relationship. How could we be a couple when he lived and worked in another time zone on the other side of the world?

Don't be sick, I told myself, wishing I hadn't drunk wine on an empty stomach. I took a few discreet deep breaths. Andy glanced through the window into the bar, and I had a moment of realisation.

'That girl you were chatting to?' I tipped my head towards the bar entrance. 'I guess she's not someone you just met?'

'Laura, I don't know how to tell you how sorry I am. You're the last person in the world I'd want to hurt, and I didn't mean it to happen.' Andy reached across the table and took my hand, looking into my eyes.

'Her name's Ichika. When I met her, she reminded me of you. I missed you, and I was so lonely. It kinda went from there.'

Reminded him of me? From what little I'd noticed, Andy's dainty new love appeared to be a clothes size six, whereas I was a sixteen (or maybe down to a fourteen after all my hard work and anxiety).

He told me they were both in the same karaoke bar one evening and, emboldened by Japanese rice wine, sang Sonny & Cher's 'I Got You Babe' together on the small stage. *Andy in a karaoke bar? Another change.* Afterwards, they spent the rest of the evening chatting. Their choice of duet now seemed prophetic, but at least Andy did tell her he had a long-term girlfriend in England.

'Because of you, we decided just to be friends,' he said, 'but we both lived in the same apartment block and saw each other most days. I found out she worked in TV and we had a lot in common. We grew closer and realised we wanted to be a couple.' He said he couldn't break the news to me over the internet. 'I owed it to you – and everything we've had together – to tell you in person. And Ichika wanted to meet you.'

It was hard to take in all this news.

'I must admit it's the last thing I expected, but I am happy for you. On both job and relationship fronts. I mean it.' I pulled away my hand, picked up my glass, and poured what remained of my wine down my throat. 'Well, aren't you going to introduce me?'

Andy gave me a weak smile, apologised again, and stood. I sighed and watched as he walked back into the bar. I needed to compose myself to meet the woman who'd replaced me in his affections.

'THAT'S WHERE I AM NOW.' I blew my cheeks out with a loud sigh. 'The refuge has to vacate the property by the twenty-ninth of July, and right now, I don't have a clue where we'll go.'

We'd chatted for more than an hour and ordered more drinks, to celebrate Andy's new future. As the waiter uncorked the bottle of cava, my now ex-boyfriend asked about life in Mallorca. Only on recounting the entire saga, from when I'd helped Marylou during the storm, did I realise how stressful the past few weeks had been.

'Either of you have any bright ideas?' I'd noticed Andy's shoulders slump during my telling of the trouble I was in. He shook his head but said nothing, and I wondered if he felt guilty about enjoying himself in Japan while I was struggling.

Ichika, however, beamed and raised one finger in the air. I liked her from the moment we met and, in the circumstances, had to respect her for coming with Andy to meet me.

With her glossy black bobbed hair, skin like porcelain, and beautiful cat-like eyes, I could understand why Andy had fallen in love with her … although I still couldn't fathom out why she reminded him of me.

'Are there any cat cafés here on the island? Maybe you could rehome some cats in one of those. Tokyo has lots of them for *hogo neko*.'

'*Hogo neko?*'

'Rescue cats. These cafés are places where you can have something to eat or drink and get to know the cats. Many of them are up for adoption. Some of the cafés charge an entry fee; in others you pay only for what you consume. The income funds the care of the resident cats.'

Andy jolted upright in his seat, wide-eyed. 'Oh yeah! I filmed in one in Kichijoji.' He laughed. 'I thought it was a cool concept – even though it's where I found out I was allergic to cats.'

'Oh, I remember the rash,' Ichika said, laying a dainty hand on his arm and giving him a loving look. I didn't want to know where it had affected him.

I picked up my phone and tapped 'cat cafés Mallorca' into Google. '*Nada*.' So much for the possibility of rehoming some of the refuge cats that way on the island. 'Valencia or Barcelona seem to be the nearest.'

I had a mental picture of travelling with the cats in cages on a ferry to the Spanish mainland, with me throwing up over the side of the vessel. Even if the cats didn't get seasick, I would heave for Britain.

'Then why don't you open one here?' Ichika said. 'You have that generous donation to get you started.' Andy's new love made the idea sound almost easy.

Why not? I thought. *Just the slight matter of finding out how to do it.* We celebrated Ichika's genius by ordering another bottle of cava.

～

MY NIGHT TURNED out to be a lot different from the one I'd expected. It was fortunate the hotel wasn't full and I could book myself into a room at the end of the evening.

Spread like a starfish across the king-size bed, enjoying the luxury of air conditioning, I reflected on the evening. Ichika was adorable, and I could see she and Andy were in love. So much so, he told me, they planned to get married and start a family as soon as possible. I didn't even know Andy wanted to be a dad. A lot had changed since our conversation during that short break in Cornwall, and what that said about the closeness of our long relationship made me tearful.

But losing Andy wasn't as upsetting as it might have been. We'd often spent periods of time apart when he was away filming. And I *had* succumbed to Carlos's charms, which wouldn't have happened if we'd been more committed as a couple.

I felt a little envious he had found love and was facing the future with hope; I had lost him, Zeller, and my job. And, in the – almost – sober light of a new day, was no nearer to solving the relocation of Refugio Marylou.

Not only was I alone now, I also felt lonely. Part of me wished I'd been more open with Carlos; even if we couldn't have a romantic relationship, having him as a half-brother would be better than nothing.

A few tears dampened my five-star pillow that night. But I wasn't sure whether they were due to losing Andy or not having Carlos in my life. It could just have been all the stress over the refuge. Or even the copious cava consumed.

A DOOR SLAMMED SOMEWHERE in the corridor outside my room and woke me at dawn. A guest leaving for an early flight, I guessed. As much as I enjoyed being swaddled in high-thread-count sheets, I also felt sweaty and had a woozy head and churning stomach. Too much alcohol, I told myself.

In slow motion, I climbed out of bed and padded to the bathroom for a long shower. It helped me feel better, but I realised the longed-for cooked full English breakfast would not be a good idea. I glugged the contents of a small bottle of Perrier from the minibar, unable even to face a cup of black coffee from the capsule machine.

A long, early walk along the seafront, followed by coffee, juice, and a croissant in a café somewhere, would ease the hangover. By the time I met Rupert at ten o'clock, I might even appear responsible enough to manage a bank account of several thousand euros.

Before I left my room, I found a sheet of hotel notepaper and an envelope in a drawer, and wrote a few words to Andy and Ichika. I wished them every happiness for the future and said I hoped we'd stay in touch as friends. The reality was we were unlikely ever to see each other again. I couldn't think why I'd want to visit Japan – it certainly wouldn't be to attend their wedding.

Andy had already put his flat in Stratford on the market and appointed a solicitor to deal with the sale in his absence. Like me, Andy was an only child, and his parents had retired to the Algarve. Why would he ever need to visit Stratford again?

I couldn't face seeing the happy – and no doubt also hungover – couple that morning, so I packed my few things into my shoulder bag and checked out early, leaving my note for them at the reception desk. I deposited my bag in the Renault parked nearby, then walked at a brisk pace to the city centre.

As reflective and woolly-headed as I was that morning, I did at least have a possible idea for rehoming the refuge. I needed to speak to Marylou as a matter of urgency. What had Andy said? No good deed goes unpunished. How right he was.

CHAPTER TWENTY-EIGHT

My meeting with Rupert went well. We met, as agreed, at a café opposite Palma's town hall, and by the time I'd walked there I was feeling more like my normal self, albeit somewhat warm. He, however, looked jaded and admitted he'd been at a party until the early hours.

We chatted over a couple of strong coffees, and I learnt he was a hedge fund manager until he made enough money to fund a lifestyle based on the sea and his love of sailing. The large inheritance from his late father had also boosted his wealth and enabled him to exercise a charitable nature.

After coffee we walked to his bank and, in what sounded like fluent Spanish, he opened the Refugio Marylou account with a deposit of five thousand euros and me as the main signatory.

We shook hands as we left the building, and I promised to let him have a detailed report of expenditure.

'I trust you, Laura,' he said, smiling. 'Good luck with

everything, and if you need any more money, get in touch.'

Knowing there was now a fund I could use to relocate the refuge put a spring in my step, and I was soon back at the Renault.

THE CATS GREETED me with insistent meows, which wasn't surprising as their breakfast was several hours later than usual. I unlocked the house, changed into my working clothes, and attended to my feline charges without further delay.

Back in the house, Calvin woke up and jumped off his chair to come and rub himself against my legs. Unusual behaviour for him, and I wondered if he was at last getting used to me. I'd left him a bumper supper, and a few morsels remained in his bowl, so any guilty feelings about leaving him overnight melted away.

'There you go,' I said, filling a clean dish with fresh food. As I placed it in his usual feeding place, I caught sight of his manky old armchair and realised wherever his future home was, that chair would have to be there too.

Cats satisfied, I took my laptop, mobile phone, notepad, and pen outside to the table under the fig tree, then went back and made a flask of black coffee. I had serious work to do before it became too hot to sit outdoors. Already the sound of the cicadas filled the air, reminding me of the buzz of wires between electricity pylons.

Four hours flew by, as I read all I could find online about cat cafés. The more I thought about Ichika's suggestion, the more practical the idea sounded. Not only would the felines have a new refuge, it would also generate some income to fund their care. This would reduce Marylou's costs and even make it possible for her to pay Silvia a nominal amount for any treatments she did.

But would Marylou want a business? She seemed content to live in the countryside looking after the cats, using some of her own money and the small but regular donations Silvia told me she received.

I sighed, blowing out my cheeks, then ran my fingers through my unruly hair before pacing around the garden. The alternative to a cat café would be relocating to another rural property, preferably within a reasonable driving distance of Silvia's practice.

If I found somewhere suitable, I believed the kind vet and her son could drum up a group of volunteers to help with the move. All I needed was a small house – ideally with a leakproof roof – on a plot of land available for long-term rent, with a landlord unfazed about cat enclosures on the land. If only I knew where to look.

Silvia did so much for the refuge, and I was reluctant to ask for her assistance to find new premises. She was one of the most generous people I'd met, both in professional and personal terms. Not only did she treat Marylou's cats without charging her, but also donated bags of food the practice received as samples from suppliers.

Where to look for a rental property? Why, an estate agent, of course. I ceased my pacing and returned to the rickety chair for some more online research. I found several photos of fincas for rent or sale but couldn't understand the accompanying texts. Apart from my frustration, the strength of the sun filtering through the fragrant fig leaves was giving me a headache. Although it could have been the previous evening's cava coming back to bite me.

I gathered everything up and retreated indoors, where I tried ringing Marylou again. Still no reply. If her mother hadn't already died, I guessed that the situation was reaching a critical stage. *Doesn't she ever check for missed calls?*

My greatest fear was that I'd have to vacate Otto's property before I could contact her. A wave of nausea overcame me every time I thought of this.

THE NEXT MORNING, after my cat duties, I went shopping. My food stocks were getting low and I needed more bottled water for drinking. A tanker delivered the house tap water, and although Marylou told me it was drinkable, I had my doubts. The concrete tank into which the delivery man stuck the hose from his vehicle looked neither clean nor rodent proof. A few days before, I'd seen a rat run up the outside wall of the tank. Silvia might have heard my scream in her hamlet.

I decided to shop in Santa Maria rather than face the rigours of a Palma hypermarket for the first time. I would also treat myself to a coffee in the garden of the interiors store, where I could fantasize about an outdoor space of my own one day.

Zeller's house in Ophelia Drive had a large garden, and although she'd done little with it, except pay a local man to mow the lawn and keep the borders tidy, it had potential. Would it be sensible to move into the property I'd inherited, after all? I could sell my apartment and wait for the new radio station in Bristol to launch, or continue looking for the best job possible.

Until Marylou returned and I went back to Stratford, I could do little about resolving my home or work situations. Besides, I had a huge problem in Mallorca to solve first.

Before going into the small supermarket, I had a coffee and then wandered along both sides of the main street, looking for estate agencies. I found three, all with property photos on display in the windows. Most of the rural properties appeared to be luxurious restorations … with prices to match. But as I was there, I was going to visit each one just in case.

The first business was a small, modern office containing two Ikea-style desks, a couple of white filing cabinets, and original contemporary art on the white walls. Only one person appeared to be working and she looked up as the doorbell tinkled to announce my arrival.

I told the woman I was looking for a small finca for a modest rent. She gave me a tight-lipped smile that didn't reach her eyes.

'Those are in great demand, I'm afraid, but I believe we have two on our books. Take a seat and I'll fetch the details.'

I sat down and she went to one of the filing cabinets. Moments later, she returned with two buff folders.

'This one is quite small, but it has land and is only five minutes' drive from here. And it's available for two years, if that suits you.'

I smiled at this news and leaned forward in my chair. She opened the folder and passed me the prospectus. The attractive house was modest in size and had a climbing rose beside the front door. I scanned the details, feeling increasingly positive. Until I reached the part about the rent.

'Is this figure per *month*?'

'Yes, of course. And that's a reasonable sum for this most desirable area.'

'What about the other property?' I glanced at the second folder in front of her.

'This one's new on our books,' she said, extracting the papers. 'Just a week or two ago. But it's not of our usual standard, and the rent reflects that.' She used the tip of one finger to push the prospectus across the desk, as if the paper were tainted. 'To be honest with you, we have it only because the owner is a close friend of Fraulein Meyer, the proprietor of this business.'

Seeing the grainy photograph made my stomach lurch. I looked at the bottom of the single page and the monthly rental figure. *Scandalous*.

'Thank you for your time.' I pushed the prospectus back across the desk with equal disdain and stood up. 'I don't think you have anything suitable for my needs.'

The conniving Otto was only trying to find a new tenant for Marylou's home, rather than selling it. Not a happy start to my search for a finca.

THE NEXT ESTATE agent's office had a neat bay tree in a white-painted wooden planter on either side of the front door. I peered through the large window at a cream leather Chesterfield facing a wall-mounted screen showing a video of sumptuous Mallorcan landscapes.

Two well-groomed men in branded polo shirts sat at their desks, focusing on the Apple laptops in front of them. It was fortunate neither saw me; when I looked at the window display, every property was for sale, rather than rent, and not one had a price under two million euros. *Time to move on.*

I smiled when I peered into the third premises. The place looked functional rather than fancy, and the photos in the window had faded in the sunlight. A man at a desk inside beamed at me through the glass, so I went in. In contrast to the office's drab interior, he wore a smart linen suit and a watch that could have been a Rolex.

'Hello, you are English, yes?'

'Yes, that's right.' I wondered how people could identify my nationality even before I spoke. 'Do you have any rental properties available, please? I'm looking for a smallish finca not too far from here. One or two bedrooms.'

'We do,' he said, sounding English himself, although he had the blonde hair and unblemished skin of an outdoorsy Scandinavian.

'My name is Klaus Nilsson.' He removed a business card from his shirt's breast pocket and handed it to me with more ceremony than the business warranted. 'Please tell me your budget.'

That was a tricky one; I didn't know what Marylou could afford – or how much rent she paid Otto.

'Er, I can be a bit flexible,' I said, 'but something at the lower end of the market. And it doesn't matter if it's a bit old-fashioned. Or even scruffy.'

'We have a few potential properties, and I'd be delighted to take you to view them.' Klaus smiled. 'These fincas have character and charm best appreciated on a personal visit, rather than looking at a prospectus.'

I should have realised this was estate agent jargon but, uplifted by the positive news, I was deaf to it.

We arranged to meet on Monday morning at ten thirty, when he would take me to see the properties in question. I celebrated this unexpected achievement by going to Luigi's for an early lunch.

How MUCH RENT did Marylou pay Otto? I had no intention of asking him – or even going anywhere near him – but I needed to find out what she could afford.

As she still hadn't contacted me, I had no choice but to rummage through her drawers and cupboards in the vain hope of finding a rent book or anything giving me the information I needed. It appeared Marylou kept little in the way of paperwork, and I didn't find anything that enlightened me.

I knew she kept her valuables and some personal paperwork in the small safe in her bedroom, because she'd told me. Perhaps the rent book was inside? Where was a safe-cracker when I needed one?

I sighed as I sat down on the bed, phone in hand. It was time to phone Florida again. As before, I heard the phone ring and ring, but nobody answered. My gut told me I might be in even more trouble than I thought.

CHAPTER TWENTY-NINE

What if Marylou's mother wasn't sick at all? What if she'd been looking for a way to leave the island without deserting the cats? I couldn't put these unpleasant suspicions out of my mind, as much as I'd liked Marylou on the three occasions when we'd spent time together.

Stretched out on my back on the bed, I was trying to fend off a stress-induced headache that felt like a metal band tightening around my skull.

I had only Marylou's word her mother was dying. And what could have been a well-acted performance of grief. Perhaps she just wanted to escape her responsibilities? Or get away from Otto? *Now* that *would be understandable*. Maybe she'd seen my arrival as an opportunity to leave a difficult situation.

On Monday evening, I'd try to reach her again. By then I might have news about an alternative location for the refuge. At least I could find out what she could afford to pay in rent.

In the meantime, I attended to the cats earlier than

usual, leaving later time free for myself. My plan was to drink a glass or two of chilled white wine under the fig tree in the garden, enjoying the cooler evening temperature. It had been too long since I'd buried myself in Zeller's book; my biological father's identity was no longer a mystery, but I still wanted to learn more about my birth mother's time in Deià.

'WE'LL GO IN MY CAR,' Klaus said when we met at his office in Santa Maria the following Monday morning.

As we approached the first finca, I realised why he'd suggested I travel with him in his rugged Nissan four-wheel drive.

'It's a pretty rough approach,' I said, hoping I didn't have any loose fillings. Klaus gripped the steering wheel with white knuckles as we bounced along the rutted dirt track. I could see a small building ahead of us. *Please don't let that be it.*

It was. He parked just outside the wire-netting fence surrounding the property. One point was in its favour; the plot of land appeared large enough to accommodate the cats' enclosures.

We sat for a moment, looking through the windscreen. Klaus coughed and spoke.

'The owners were renovating it as a holiday home but split up before they did much work. We believe the house is about ninety years old. The fence is almost new.' He turned to me. 'Would you like to see inside?'

Not really. But having bumped our way along the track, it would be rude not to have a look.

As we climbed out of the car, my nostrils twitched. A strange smell hung in the air. I looked around. A few black pigs were snuffling in a neighbouring field, but the breeze was blowing in the wrong direction for the unpleasant waft to be piggy related.

Klaus unlocked and pushed open the front door with some effort, then ushered me in. The house was as small inside as it appeared from the outside. Had I expected something like *Dr Who*'s Tardis?

The smell of fresh paint suggested the owners had recently decorated, and the white walls did create the illusion of a larger house. Like Marylou's place, the kitchen, dining, and living areas occupied one open-plan room. The only bedroom had an adjoining bathroom with a glass-walled shower cubicle and contemporary wall tiles, which appeared to be a recent update.

The place was unfurnished, except for a modern cooker in the kitchen area. Marylou's furniture – assuming it was hers and not Otto's – would fit and, although the space was small, the property was clean; it could be suitable, I thought.

'May I see outside, please?' Klaus led me back out and waited while I walked around to the rear of the house.

I scuttled right back.

'Whatever's that?' I said, one hand clasped over my nose and mouth, the other pointing to where I'd been. 'Looks like a stagnant pond – and it stinks.'

'I'm afraid you've found this property's weak point.' The estate agent avoided eye contact with me. 'The owners started creating a septic tank but didn't finish it. They said they'd get it sorted but, to be honest, that was a while ago.' He shook his head, pulled a pen from his pocket, and scribbled a note on the folder he was carrying.

The stench was awful, and the cats would breathe

that air around the clock. 'I'm sorry, Klaus,' I said. 'The house itself is quite sweet and better inside than it looks from outside. But nobody should live with a smell like that. It can't be healthy.'

He nodded. 'I understand. I hoped the problem would have been fixed by now, but I haven't visited recently. Let's go to the next one. It's only a kilometre down the road.'

CA'N PEPITO SEEMED A BETTER PROSPECT. The small two-storey house sat in the middle of a plot of land. Like the last place, the access lane gave the vehicle's suspension another workout. But I liked the neat dry-stone wall enclosing the land.

Klaus admitted that the approach, a rollercoaster of humps and dips, was one reason it was difficult to rent out the property. Taking the cats to the vet along the rutted track would be a challenging experience for all concerned.

Decoration would have improved the old-fashioned interior but the place was clean, and other than a faint mustiness from the house having been closed for some time, nothing noxious assaulted my nostrils. The surrounding terrain was flat and laid to scrubby grass, with a paved area under a holm oak tree that would be perfect for Marylou's table and chairs.

'I like it.' I smiled at Klaus. 'The house is fine and has enough land for the cat enclosures at the—'

'Cat enclosures?' He frowned.

'My friend runs a small cat refuge – fewer than twenty cats and kittens.' Tightly pursed lips had replaced the estate agent's smile. 'They're no trouble at all,' I added.

'Your friend? I thought this rental was for yourself.' His accusatory tone made me frown.

'I don't believe I said that. The refuge owner is in the States, spending time with her dying mother. In her absence, I'm looking after the cats and arranging the relocation for her.'

I explained the lease on her current property was expiring and the owner wanted to sell the place — keeping one hand, with two fingers crossed, behind my back.

Although Klaus said he understood, his expression told a different story. 'However, the owners are most insistent they don't want tenants with animals. I'm afraid you've wasted my time and yours by not telling me about this "refuge" before.'

He strode over to his Nissan, climbed in, and started the engine. Did he intend to drive off and leave me there? How would I return to Santa Maria? Would I even find it again? I ran to his vehicle, wrenched open the passenger door, and hauled myself in, just as he was releasing the handbrake.

The estate agent offered no further viewings, and the return journey passed in silence. When he dropped me off outside his office, I apologised for the misunderstanding and thanked him for his time. He wished me luck, adding, 'You'll need it.'

I was past the stage of needing luck. What I needed was a miracle. Of epic proportions. I drove home and prepared for another afternoon of keyboard-thumping online research.

～

AN EMAIL from Ichika was a pleasant surprise. The brief message from her and Andy thanked me for my note and wished me success with the cat café. I smiled, despite feeling a little sad that Andy hadn't written himself. The cat café idea had seemed a good one at the time, but I knew my inability to speak Spanish was a huge barrier to making it happen.

Could I enlist help from someone I'd met on the island? I made a list. Mike and Molly at the radio station could be useful. Gil McGill? No; he was a visitor, like me, and I doubted that he spoke more than enough Spanish to order drinks, a gastronomic dinner, and chat up a sexy señorita. I wrote El Capitán and Carlos, then sadly crossed out their names. Too complicated.

Luigi at the trattoria in Santa Maria? Maybe not. He was busy with the restaurant, and although he was friendly and ready with open arms for a hug whenever I arrived, I didn't know him well enough to enlist his help. Rupert had already done a lot, with his generous donation. Perhaps when he returned from Corsica?

That left Silvia and Tomeu. What would I do without them? Their help had been invaluable, but I didn't want to become a nuisance.

I had never had a lot of friends, preferring a small circle of intimates. For once, I wished I'd surrounded myself with an abundance of acquaintances. My phone rang and broke my train of thought. I swiped the screen to answer the call.

'*Hola* Laura, how are things?'

Pretty crappy, I wanted to say. Not appropriate English to teach a teenager.

'Fine, thanks, Tomeu. And how are the studies going?'

'*Poc a poc.*' I knew this was the local way of saying

'little by little' or 'slowly'. Like my progress with finding new refuge premises.

'Anyway, I'm ringing because my *profesora* at school saw the poster and wants to adopt two cats. Could she come over this afternoon?' My heart skipped a beat. Fantastic news.

We agreed on a plan. Instead of taking the bus from Palma to Santa Maria (where he left his bike each day), Tomeu would travel home with his teacher and I would pick her up at Silvia's house, bring her back to see the cats, and then take her back to her car afterwards.

I gathered my laptop and papers together and went indoors. In a spirit of optimism, I printed some more adoption forms.

'*ADIOS,*' the three of us called, waving outside Silvia's house as Tomeu's teacher drove off. She had come prepared, bringing two carrying baskets with her, and having put one cat in each, she secured the baskets on the back seat. The woman beamed as she drove off, her hand waving goodbye out of the open window.

'Bye, Bobby, bye, Clinton. Have a happy new home,' I said in a quiet voice. Although pleased to have now rehomed three cats, I wished I wasn't doing it without Marylou's knowledge.

'Do you have time for a quick chat?' I asked Silvia.

'Sure. Let's go through. I've no more appointments today.' We went through the house to the pretty patio, adorned with pots of scarlet geraniums. Silvia pulled the scrunchie from her ponytail and shook out her long hair, then went to fetch us a cold beer each. While she was gone, I sat thinking under the parasol.

'You look worried,' she said on her return, pouring the beers into tall glasses. 'Are the other cats okay?'

I assured her they were but said my failure to contact Marylou was worrying me.

'This may make me sound a suspicious person – which I'm really not – but do you think she doesn't intend to come back?' I explained I'd emailed and telephoned her countless times but had no response. Silvia's eyebrows knitted together.

'I'm sure that's not the case, Laura. She loves the island, and her cat refuge means the world to her. She *is* a little scatty about administration and correspondence; that, I know from personal experience.' The vet looked more serious than I'd ever seen her. 'There'll be a good reason she hasn't replied. Her mother's dying, and they haven't seen each other for five years. The remaining time will be precious to them both.'

Silvia had made a valid point. *If I were in the same situation, would I be keeping on top of correspondence? I doubt it.*

'I'm sure you're right.' I swallowed the last of my cold beer and glanced at the time on my phone. 'Fancy an early supper at Luigi's? My treat, to thank you for all your support.'

'Thank you, Laura, what a lovely offer.' She stood and placed the empty glasses and beer cans on the tray she'd brought out. 'Give me fifteen minutes to change out of my scrubs and freshen up, and I'll be ready.'

I sat back and thought about what Silvia had said. Above me, dozens of martins screeched as they circled over her house. Just another element of rural Mallorca's daily soundtrack.

CHAPTER THIRTY

Over a piping-hot lasagne and a crisp green salad, Silvia and I chatted like old friends. We learnt more about each other's past and she showed a genuine interest in radio.

She also asked if there was a man in my life. I explained that my long-term boyfriend and I had just broken up, as he was moving to Japan to be with his new girlfriend.

'I'm so sorry, Laura, that must be hard for you, on top of everything else going on.'

'It was a shock, but Andy and I were apart a lot because of his work. It was perhaps inevitable he or I would meet someone else while he was away.' *As I did with Carlos.*

'Don't let it put you off. I'm sure there's a man out there who's right for you.'

'Only if he's rich, loves cats, and has a spare rural property he'd be willing to rent to Marylou for a rock-bottom price.' We both laughed. 'To be serious, I have more than enough to think about for now.'

I changed the subject to mention Ichika's suggestion
of opening a cat café in Mallorca. Silvia told me she had
visited one in Valencia while attending a conference in
the city.

'It's an interesting concept, Laura. And a good way
to generate funds to support the cats. Some get adopted,
freeing space to take in more homeless kitties.'

'Tough question to answer, but you know Marylou
better than I do: would she be okay with running a cat
café, do you think?'

She gave a loud sigh and shrugged her shoulders.

'I'm not sure she can cook, but that's a job volunteers
could do, I suppose. But I know she wouldn't want to live
in an urban environment.'

That was what I'd feared. I put my thoughts of a
bustling cat café in the heart of Palma out of my mind,
although property rental in the island's cosmopolitan
capital would doubtless be beyond Marylou's budget
anyway.

Silvia leaned across the trattoria table and patted
my arm.

'Don't write it off; it's a good idea.' She paused to
pop the last piece of rocket into her mouth. 'If you have
time, you could make a day trip to Valencia to talk to the
owner of the cat café I visited. Her husband is from
Cardiff, so she speaks fluent English – but with a Welsh
accent. I'd be happy to set up a meeting for you.'

'Where would I be without you, Silvia? Thank you,
I'll give that some thought.'

Luigi arrived, brandishing the dessert menu. 'Señori-
tas! Fresh home-made tiramisu today.'

And every day. Tiramisu it was, then.

❧

THE NEXT MORNING, after feeding and cleaning the cats, I spent some extra time in the enclosures, making a fuss of my feline charges. They were now used to me, and most of them sought a head rub when I was around.

Marylou had placed an old wooden chair inside the enclosure, and I sometimes sat on it, just watching them. After they'd finished eating, they appeared to lick their lips, as though they'd just finished a gourmet platter rather than a bowl of dried cat food. I also enjoyed watching them groom themselves and interact with each other.

I could now brush Rosa, the fluffy black and white cat, who was shedding clouds of fur now the weather was much hotter. She purred like a Porsche when I groomed her and rolled over onto her back to have her tummy brushed gently too. I pulled my mobile phone out of my shorts pocket and took a photo of her looking adorable.

Afterwards I had my customary mid-morning coffee and switched on my laptop. I posted the photo of Rosa on the Moggies in Mallorca Instagram feed and wrote a suitable caption. How could any cat lover on the island resist such a charmer?

The number of followers increased every day, which made me punch the air in triumph. My excitement waned, though, after checking their profiles; most of them were cats whose owners had set up Instagram accounts in their pet's name. Was it worth the effort involved in taking and posting photos and captions every day? I sighed as I closed Instagram and opened my emails.

Dan had sent me an update and a joke which made me laugh out loud and Calvin jump. My friend Sandra, Bard FM's receptionist, emailed to say she was coming to

Magaluf for her holiday in August and hoped we could meet for a drink and a catch-up in the resort. I replied I'd be home by then and would contact her for a night out in Stratford on my return.

Next it was time to check flights to Valencia. I couldn't help but grin when I worked out the flight from Palma took only around forty minutes. Once I was there, an underground train service linked the airport with the city centre.

The cat café website showed its location, and I saw it would only be a short taxi ride from the nearest station. Flight prices were not only lower than I was expecting, but timings worked too. I could travel to Valencia, visit the cat café, and be back at Refugio Marylou in one day. What did I have to lose? I rang Silvia, and she promised to speak to her contact to find a convenient day for my visit.

THREE DAYS later I was reflecting on the previous day's trip to Valencia and El Racó de Gat Café. The owner, Noemi, answered all my questions with ease, though she warned me there could be different restrictions and legal issues in Mallorca.

On the short flight back to Palma, I'd been over everything Noemi and I discussed and realised my priority was to find a suitable rural or semi-rural property within easy driving distance of Palma.

Back at the refuge, I fed the cats and locked the enclosures for the night. It was almost dark, and I planned to spend a couple of hours doing more internet research into fincas for rent. This time, I'd be looking closer to the Palma area.

THE SWEET AROMA of baking filled the house the next morning. Craving comfort food and chocolate, I'd made a batch of brownies. While I waited for them to cool, I jotted down a list of my achievements to date.

Three cats adopted.

Fincas around Santa Maria viewed and discounted.

Moggies in Mallorca Instagram account set up (lots of work for little return, apart from those cosy 'likes').

Visit to El Racó del Gat in Valencia.

My previous research highlighted my severe disadvantage in language terms. I'd found details of rural properties to rent but didn't understand the texts. Not only could I not speak Spanish, but the islanders had their own language, *mallorquí* – a dialect of Catalan.

I needed assistance but didn't want to impose on Silvia or Tomeu yet again. Silvia was busy with appointments and was due to travel to Madrid on Saturday for a veterinary conference.

One person I knew would be more than capable of helping me on the language front. But how would he feel about hearing from me now?

CHAPTER THIRTY-ONE

My stomach was churning as I dialled the number. I had no idea how he'd react to my call – let alone the big favour I was going to ask of him. My feelings of guilt about letting him down hadn't faded.

The phone rang unanswered for what seemed like several minutes. I was on the point of hanging up when the ringing stopped and I heard his voice.

'Hello?'

'Hello, Billy, it's Laura. Is this a good time?'

'Laura! Oh, sweetie, I cannot tell you how lovely it is to hear you again. To what do I owe this unexpected pleasure?'

My shallow breathing returned to something more normal. Why had I ever doubted that he'd understand my absence from his mother's funeral?

'Quite a lot. But first, how are you?'

'Bearing up. I'm at Mum's house.' Billy sighed. 'She left it to me, of course. I was going to sell it, but I'm making it my home instead. I've put my flat on the market.'

'That'll be a long drive to work.' It'd take him almost an hour.

I detected a wry note in his laugh. 'You're a bit behind with the news, sweetie. Not spoken to anyone at the station in the past couple of days?'

'No. Too busy here, I'm afraid.'

'Quick update then: I've left. I told that buffoon Barry what he could do with his Sunday morning show.'

'Oh, Billy! What are you going to do now?'

'I inherited this place and some money, so I'll be fine financially for a while. And I'm converting a bedroom into a production studio for voiceovers.'

'Wow! Good for you.' My old friend was coping well with his big life change.

'I'm itching to get started, but the kit doesn't arrive for a few weeks, so I'm kicking my heels a tad till then.'

Encouraged by this news, I made my offer.

'Fancy a visit to Mallorca? I'd love to see you and, to be honest, I could do with a bit of help with the local language.'

Few people at Bard FM knew Billy's real name was Guillem – Catalan for William. His mother Carme was from Barcelona and married an English surgeon. Widowed for more than a decade, she stayed in the home they'd made together in the leafy North Oxford suburb of Summertown. I knew mother and son often spoke Catalan when alone together.

'There's a spare bedroom here, and I'd pick you up at the airport, so you'd only need to book flights.'

'Well, it'd be lovely to see you,' he said, after a few minutes' hesitation. 'Once my voiceover work starts, I may not have time for holidays.' He sounded more optimistic about his future than I was about my own.

He promised to send details the next day of his flight

arrival, then thanked me and blew a kiss down the phone. I took a deep breath and exhaled. I was looking forward to seeing Billy again – and not just because he spoke Catalan, which would help in the search for new refuge premises.

DESPITE THE EARLY JULY HEAT, housework beckoned. Billy was arriving in two days' time, and I had work to do to make his room comfortable and appealing. Although I always kept my apartment in Stratford tidy, it was a challenge to keep Marylou's little house clean.

As the temperature built up day by day, Calvin shed gossamer clouds of pale ginger fur. Dust from the parched earth surrounding the house blew indoors every time I opened a door or a window, and by the time I'd finished my cat-care duties, I'd neither the will nor the energy to sweep floors and dust.

I allocated Marylou's room for Billy. It was larger and had more natural light than the dingy spare room into which I was moving. It seemed only fair he had the best bedroom when he would be helping me sort out the mess I was in during his 'holiday'.

Using the best of Marylou's clean bed linen, I made up the double bed. By the time I'd cleaned the room's filthy window – which offered a decent view of the countryside – and dusted and polished every horizontal surface, the room looked inviting. I placed a bottle of water and a glass on the bedside table, along with a small vase containing flowers I'd bought in Santa Maria.

Billy had a weakness for my chocolate and walnut brownies, so more baking was another job on my list that day. I was going to make my dear friend the best brownies ever.

I'D BECOME accustomed to the peace in the countryside and winced at the babel of Palma airport's arrivals hall. Multilingual announcements over the public address system punctuated the chatter of excited holidaymakers.

Every time the sliding doors of the baggage reclaim area opened, another flurry of passengers emerged. I found the correct gate and stood alongside others who were waiting to meet arriving travellers. Most of us were holding up handmade signs or portable devices bearing names of people or hotels. For Billy, I'd made a cardboard sign on which I'd written 'Lord Summertown' in black marker pen. The title would appeal to his sense of humour.

It seemed ages since I'd arrived at the airport for the first time, no doubt looking as bewildered as many of those I saw entering the unfamiliar environment. Some passengers dragged their heavy cases towards uniformed holiday reps who stood with clipboards, ticking off names and despatching tourists to the appropriate coaches waiting outside in the parking area.

I spotted a crowd of shrieking young women, dressed head-to-toe in pink and wearing matching cowboy hats; one of them had the word 'Bridezilla' emblazoned in sequins across the front of her T-shirt. *Watch out, Magaluf.*

The electronic arrivals board showed the Gatwick flight had been on the ground for twenty minutes and several other flights had landed before it. I didn't expect to see my friend for a while so amused myself by looking for the most outrageous travelling outfit. There was no shortage of contenders.

'*Hola*, Laura!'

Startled, I spun around and saw Billy standing beside me with a small pull-along case. He drew me into a close hug, crushing my home-made sign against my chest.

'Where did you come from?' I extracted myself from his embrace. 'I've been watching these doors like a hawk for the past twenty minutes.'

'Dear girl, I travel light. Can't stand hanging around a carousel waiting for cases.'

He pointed to the small, wheeled case at his feet. 'Master the art of packing and you can travel with only a cabin bag. I came through the baggage-free exit down there.' He waved his arm towards the far end of the building.

The wisdom of the frequent traveller. I held up the now-crumpled sign.

'Welcome to Mallorca, Billy.'

He roared with laughter. 'The limo outside, is it?'

'Not *quite* a limo,' I replied, leading the way.

As I drove the Renault down the car park ramp, Billy gave an extravagant yawn.

'Didn't sleep too well last night. Mind if I have a little shut-eye on the way?'

'Be my guest.' I needed to concentrate on the busy roads ahead to make it back to the refuge without frightening my passenger.

As my friend snored softly in the seat next to me, I smiled, realising how much I'd missed his company. We had a lot to talk about, and a decent bottle of Mallorcan red wine awaited us back at the finca.

≈

'THIS IS PROPERLY RUSTIC, isn't it?' Billy turned his head to take in his surroundings. 'Does that cooker actually function?'

I laughed. 'It may surprise you, but that very oven has baked you a decent batch of my brownies – even though it doesn't have a working thermostat.'

While Billy went to his room to unpack and hang his clothes in the part of Marylou's wardrobe that I'd cleared for him, I filled the kettle and put it on the hob to boil. When he returned to the kitchen, he'd freshened himself up, and I detected the subtle waft of delicious Penhaligon's cologne that used to linger in the Bard FM studio long after his breakfast show finished.

I picked up the wooden tray bearing the cafetière, mugs, and plate of brownies. 'Garden okay for you?'

'Lead on, lovely.' He followed me out to the garden, where we sat in the shade of the fig tree.

'Before we talk about anything else, Billy, I just want to tell you I was devastated I couldn't be with you at your mum's funeral.' I poured two mugs of coffee. 'But I couldn't leave the cats and didn't know anyone who could look after them for me.'

He leaned across the table and squeezed my hand.

'Don't worry, I quite understood. Although I must admit it amused me to read you were looking after a cat refuge – and abroad, to boot!'

'Thank you for understanding,' I said, offering him a brownie. 'When you didn't reply to my email telling you I couldn't come, I thought you might be angry with me.'

'Silly sausage! I was disappointed, of course, but I understood. I had so much to sort out after Mum's death, I didn't get around to replying to emails.'

I relaxed back on the chair, relieved our long and close friendship was unscathed.

We chatted about the Oxford house for a while. He was settling in well, and his eyes brightened when he spoke about his future work plans. I knew he had many contacts in London and it wouldn't be long before he was voicing commercials and more.

'Dan told me you resigned because Barry wanted to move you to breakfast.' Billy helped himself to a second brownie. 'Dan said it wasn't only because of Quentin, but also you didn't want to replace me. I appreciate that, Laura, thank you, but we'd still have been friends anyway.'

I shrugged. 'For what it's worth, I think Barry made a serious error of judgement taking you off breakfast, and it broke my heart to hear his plans. That's why I turned down your theatre invitation after you were back from Barcelona. I knew what you wouldn't learn until the following Monday.'

He laughed. 'Well, I'm happier than I've been for a long time. I've realised I was in a rut after so many years doing the same show. This is a chance to do something different, and I intend to make the most of this new chapter in my life.'

We sat in contented silence for a few minutes, munching brownies and sipping coffee.

'Enough of me,' Billy said. 'What I'm dying to know is why you're looking after a cat refuge on a Spanish island. I thought you didn't like foreign travel.'

'It's a long story,' I said. 'Are you sitting comfortably?'

CHAPTER THIRTY-TWO

I told Billy all about the evening Mum and Dad revealed Zeller was my birth mother. He nodded when I explained why I'd visited Mallorca.

'It's only natural to want to find out about the place of your conception,' he said. 'In your shoes, I would have too.'

Although I'd given Dan the full story about Carlos, I edited it for Billy, saying the photographer was somebody who introduced me to his father, who knew Zeller back in the day.

I sighed. 'Listening to what this man told me, I realised he must be my biological father.'

'No! That's amazing, Laura. How did he react to finding out he had a daughter he didn't know about?'

'I didn't tell him,' I said. 'Oh, he was charming, and it was obvious how he felt about Zeller, but I just couldn't deal with the situation. I never intended to have a relationship with him. Just wanted to know who fathered me.'

Billy's eyes were wide. 'That's some story. But how

did you come to be running a cat refuge? I wasn't even aware you liked cats.'

I laughed. 'Neither was I, but they're fascinating creatures. I'm considering adopting one to take back home.'

Billy listened with his head tilted. I recounted the saga, from the day of the storm that brought me to Marylou's door, to my current situation. He sat bolt upright, mouth open and eyes wide, when I told him about rejecting Otto's crude advances and finding the subsequent eviction notice.

'Good grief. You should have gone to the police,' he said, frowning. 'And whatever did this Marylou say when she heard?'

'So far, nothing. She hasn't replied to my emails or phone calls, and time's passing faster than I'd like. With no input from her, I'm having to use my initiative and go with my gut instincts.'

'Have you talked to a lawyer?' Billy frowned, stroking his chin. 'The eviction may not even be strictly legal.'

'I considered it. But with the complications of language and local laws, it was possible we'd have to vacate this place before it was all sorted. I decided to press on with finding a solution.'

'Sounds wise, given the timescale. How've you got on?'

I told him about the Instagram page I'd set up for Moggies in Mallorca, about the limited success with adoptions, my futile attempts to find a local property to rent as a new refuge, and then my flying visit to Valencia to see a cat café in operation.

'That's what I'm working on now,' I said. 'I know Marylou's a country girl and won't want to be in Palma, so the ideal place would be a finca in the countryside but not far from the city. It needs to be somewhere Marylou can live and also have the enclosures for the cats.'

I paused to finish my coffee. 'And if there were space to use as a cat café, she could generate some income and create a business she could sell in the future if she ever needed or wanted to.'

I told Billy about the generous donation from Rupert, sitting in the new bank account for Refugio Marylou.

'At least I have some money to put towards the project,' I said. 'It's just the matter of finding a suitable property to rent and getting whatever permits Marylou would need to run the place as a proper business. And that's where I hoped you could help ... because you speak Catalan.'

Billy smiled. *And did he just puff out his chest in pride?*

'You know me. I love a challenge. And this sounds like an enormous one.'

We both laughed and agreed to sit down the next morning to create an action plan. We were going to spend the rest of the day relaxing and chatting. And open that good bottle of Mallorcan red wine.

'Lunch?' I offered, thinking it would be sensible to have some carbs inside us before any alcohol. 'I'm making you a traditional Mallorcan snack, called *pa amb oli*.'

'Delicious, I love it. I had a super one in Palma on my last visit.'

'You've been to Mallorca before?' That was news to me.

'Yes. Been twice with Greg, but some years ago,' he said. 'In fact, I have a distant cousin who lives in the capital. Now I think of it, he may even be useful to us.'

'You're a marvel, Billy. You can't imagine how happy I am to have you here. Missed you so much.'

'I've missed you too.' He held my gaze for longer than usual.

The intensity of the moment made me uneasy, so I stood up and started piling everything back onto the tray.

'Let me give you a hand.' He followed me indoors where together we assembled our *pa amb oli* lunch and the bottle of wine and two glasses, then went back into the garden. As we ate, we chatted about the radio station and our former work colleagues.

'That Odette is a liability,' Billy said. 'After a couple of days, I was too embarrassed to listen. I can only assume she gets away with being incompetent because Barry is having his wicked way with her.'

'Rather her than me.' I shuddered. 'Must be like snogging an ashtray.'

'Gross!' Billy replied with his familiar hearty laugh. It was so good to have his company again.

After a long, lazy lunch and the unavoidable washing-up, I introduced him to the cats and discovered he was a fan of felines. He said the only reason he didn't have one was because his Stratford apartment had no private outdoor space.

'Now I've got Mum's huge walled garden, I'm thinking of getting a cat or two. Lovely to have company on the sofa of an evening.' He bent down to stroke Rosa. Emboldened by the wine, I posed the question that had been on my mind for some time.

'Do you think Greg will move in with you now you're in a bigger place?'

Billy spluttered and straightened up to his full height. 'I beg your pardon! Why would he want to do that?'

My face flushed, and I wanted to change the subject, but he took hold of my arm.

'Don't tell me you thought I was … gay.' His eyes were wide, and his mouth hung open.

'Er, well … honestly? I thought it might be possible.' If only a sinkhole would open beneath me. 'But it's never mattered to me one way or the other, and it wouldn't change anything.'

'Whatever made you think that about me?' He let go of my arm and stood with his hands on his hips. This tempted me to mention his camp stance, but it wasn't the moment for weak humour.

'Billy, I didn't mean to offend you,' I said, my hands on my cheeks to hide my blushes. 'But I've never known you to have a girlfriend … and you often go away with Greg. I jumped to the wrong conclusion and I'm truly sorry.' I didn't mention his flamboyant taste in clothes, which had also made me wonder.

His serious expression disappeared as he burst into explosive laughter.

'Come here.' He wrapped me into one of his comforting bear-like hugs. 'Silly sausage. Greg's a contented, married old pal from uni. His wife won't fly anywhere and, like me, he enjoys travelling. We're just two chums who like seeing the world and manage not to get on each other's nerves when we travel together.'

I lifted my head from his chest and smiled up at him.

'I am sorry, Billy, but it wouldn't have mattered to me if you *were* gay.'

'And there *have* been a few girlfriends.' he said, smiling. 'But nothing serious enough to talk about. I'm a contented bachelor, but if the right woman were available …'

That told me.

CHAPTER THIRTY-THREE

The last time I slept in a single bed, I was thirteen years old. A restless sleeper then, I had a disturbing habit of rolling off the mattress onto the floor. Tired of the thump that often woke them as I hit the floor in the adjoining bedroom, my parents bought me a double bed.

Twice during the first night of Billy's stay, I dreamt that I was falling. And I was. I climbed back onto the lumpy mattress and tried to catch more sleep, but after the second tumble my brain had other ideas.

I felt restless and uneasy, tossing and turning. *All will be well now Billy's here.* He was like a surrogate big brother, always ready with a hug and some sage advice.

At six o'clock, I padded barefooted to the bathroom, to avoid waking him. But, as I discovered after showering and dressing, he was already up. When I went to put the kettle on to boil, I found him at the pine table, a pen and several sheets of paper from the printer stack in front of him.

'Morning, sugar plum,' he said. 'Kettle's just boiled,

so I'll make you a cuppa.' He'd found his way around and settled in.

'You're up early.' I stifled a yawn.

'Years of crack-of-dawn starts. Besides, I was keen to start work on this project of yours.'

As he made the hot drinks, I put out the breakfast offerings on the table. These days I had plain yogurt with a generous helping of chopped seasonal fruit, nuts, and seeds. To my surprise, Billy told me he had the same at home.

We chatted as we munched our way through the first meal of the day, and after clearing away the dishes, I tended to the cats while he checked his iPad for emails.

By the time I'd finished outdoors, he was scribbling notes. He looked up as I came in to wash my hands.

'You must think I'm awful,' he said. 'I forgot to ask about Andy. Will he be back from Japan soon?'

I sighed. 'Ah yes, Andy. Can we talk about it over coffee later?'

I was itching to start on Project Cat Café. With less than three weeks before I had to vacate Otto's property, time was pressing.

WEARY FROM RECENT events and stress, I was relieved to let Billy apply himself to the project. He was doing so with even more enthusiasm than I expected, and our brainstorming session continued all morning.

The next day, he was borrowing the Renault to drive into Palma. He'd emailed his distant cousin to arrange a catch-up.

'Jaume's a well-connected lawyer there, so fingers crossed,' he said. 'I'll pick up a couple of local papers too, for the classified ads. We're more likely to find cheaper properties in those.'

At lunchtime, we took a short break. After checking the contents of the fridge, Billy suggested the traditional local salad known as *trampó*. We stood side by side in the kitchen, chopping green peppers, plump tomatoes, and white onions, which he mixed in a bowl and dressed with a Mallorcan extra virgin olive oil, cava vinegar, and seasoning. It was funny to think of him – a man who'd always lived in England – showing me how to make a traditional island dish.

We sat at the far end of the table, away from the scattering of notes and coffee-time brownie crumbs. The day had become humid, so we ate indoors for comfort. Thank goodness for the electric fan which was at least keeping the air moving.

The delicious salad helped to cool us too. Although simple to make, its freshness was divine, and I intended to add it to my summer recipes back in Stratford. Or wherever I ended up living. Billy and I hadn't yet talked about my work plans.

'I forgot to tell you about Andy.' I dabbed my mouth with a piece of kitchen roll. In the absence of any serviettes, Billy had taken squares of the absorbent paper and folded them like linen napkins in a posh restaurant. Little wonder I'd thought he might be gay.

'Is he okay?' he asked, after swallowing his last mouthful of salad. 'Seems to have been away for aeons.'

I swallowed hard before I spoke. The shock of Andy's announcement had worn off, and I knew my moving to another city to live and work would be easier as a singleton. But because of the stress I was under, tears threatened at random moments. I couldn't cry in

Billy's presence in case I distracted him from his promising start to the project.

Adopting my professional reporter mode, I told him in a matter-of-fact way about Andy's visit to Mallorca and his plans for life in Japan.

'Oh, and he brought his new Japanese girlfriend to meet me too,' I added, with a slight wobble in my voice.

'Laura! That must have been horrendous for you.' He leaned across the table to lay his hand on my arm and paused before continuing. 'Don't take this the wrong way, but it may be for the best. These past six months, you and I have been out together more times than you did with Andy. Perhaps it's your turn to find someone new?'

I grunted, picked up the empty lunch plates from the table, and took them to the sink.

'Too much happening for that kind of thing,' I said. 'My priorities are sorting things here, then returning home to get myself a new job.'

I ran water into the plastic washing-up bowl and squeezed a green jet of Fairy liquid over the plates. Billy stood up, tidied the papers on the table, and peered at his iPad screen before snapping the device shut.

'Result!' he said. 'Reply from Jaume. I'm meeting him for coffee tomorrow.'

I looked at him and forced myself to smile, trying hard to shake off the grumpy mood that had engulfed me.

'That's brilliant, Billy, thank you. I think we've done well today, don't you?'

'Yes, I do.' He glanced around for the tea towel. 'Shall I dry up?'

I told him I was leaving the dishes to drain. I didn't often snooze during the day but, after a poor night's sleep, all I wanted was to lie down and lose myself in a pleasant dream.

As though he sensed I needed time alone, he said he too was 'a tad sleepy'. He came over and gave me a peck on the cheek.

'Let's eat out tonight. My treat.' He rubbed his eyes. 'Let's hope we both have a good nap.'

He really was everything I could wish for in a friend.

I FELL into a deep sleep within minutes of settling onto the bed, even though the small bedroom felt hot and stuffy in the middle of the afternoon. The tiny window had no shutter but let in little light anyway. The gloom in the room matched my mood.

When I awoke, it was six o'clock. After a cool shower, I changed into something smarter for the evening, then crept to the kitchen table and opened my laptop.

I tapped out an email to Dan, telling him Billy was staying for a couple of weeks to help me with my predicament. In it I mentioned my radio interview and how the station manager had offered me a job which, of course, I'd declined.

By the time I'd finished my update, my guest had emerged in a fresh cloud of Penhaligon's, wearing a floral linen shirt, tailored navy shorts, and smart navy deck shoes. I pressed send on my email and closed my laptop.

'This do for you?' He gave me a twirl, showing me his camp side again.

'You look very dapper, Billy. And I'm delighted to see you're not wearing socks.'

He laughed, looking down at his feet. 'That's my Spanish genes.'

After he'd complimented me on my dress, we went out to the enclosures to feed the cats, being careful to avoid spillages on our going-out clothes. Rosa, the fluffy black and white cat, sauntered across, tail up in the air, and rubbed her face against Billy's calf. I could hear her purring from where I stood.

'I may have to take this young lady back to Oxford with me,' he said, bending down to stroke her. 'I could do with a girlfriend around the place.' He seemed smitten. One less to rehome, perhaps?

~

'THANKS AGAIN FOR DINNER LAST NIGHT,' I said to Billy over breakfast the next morning. For our first night out, he'd driven us up the motorway to the town of Inca which, I knew from my guidebook, was famous for leather goods. His choice of restaurant impressed me. It had a cool urban-chic ambience and was in a renovated former shoe factory. We ate delicious cuisine and Billy told me the chef had won a cookery competition on Spanish TV.

'How did you know about that place?' I poured coffee and freshly squeezed orange juice for us both. He laughed. 'I have to confess I didn't. I messaged Jaume for a recommendation. Impressive one, I thought.'

Billy was off to see his distant cousin that morning and had dressed in smarter attire for his meeting in Jaume's office in Palma's old town. I marvelled at how many clothes he'd squeezed into his cabin luggage and that nothing looked creased. *He'd make a perfect butler.*

'Jaume knows his restaurants, for sure. It'll be

fantastic if he's as helpful in the search for a finca to rent.'

'It's a long shot, Laura. He specialises in family law.' Billy blew on the surface of his hot coffee. 'I'm not expecting him to be a lot of help, but he has good contacts, and you never know.'

He stood up and cleared our breakfast dishes to the sink. He was quite the domestic god and, as far as I knew, did all his own household chores at home.

'Mind if I leave the washing-up to you this morning? Before I meet Jaume, I'd like a scoot around some estate agencies – just in case.'

'Of course not,' I said. 'I hope you have better luck than I did in Santa Maria.' My recent experiences of the property sector were still fresh in my mind.

Within fifteen minutes, Billy was on his way, leaving me with my Marigold-clad hands in hot soapy water. After feeding Calvin, who'd taken a liking to our house guest, I attended to my outdoor duties.

A note on the wall calendar reminded me I had to give my charges their tick-and-flea treatment that day. Marylou had shown me how to administer the drops on the backs of their necks, so I followed her advice by doing it while the cats had their heads down, eating breakfast. Only two jerked around to glare at me for my audacity. Bernie, who was grey and had beautiful Wedgwood-blue eyes, lashed out with a paw and scratched my hand, drawing instant beads of bright blood.

Back in the house, I washed and disinfected the slight wound. The place was silent again without Billy. I enjoyed his company and realised how lonely I'd been feeling. Thank God for Silvia and Tomeu, I thought. I'd never had such a limited social life.

El Capitán came to mind and, for the zillionth time,

I wondered how he'd have reacted to the news that I was his daughter. The connection to Zeller might have delighted him. Or not. What Carlos would have felt about having a half-sister – one he'd slept with – didn't bear consideration.

I found myself wondering how Dad's tomatoes were doing and whether Mum's regular Pilates class was becoming any easier for her. I was feeling a little home-sick, and my weekly email to them was due, so I made a coffee and sat at the laptop.

Mum and Dad were oblivious to my problems in Mallorca. I wrote, rather than phoned, because I could paint a rosy picture of day-to-day life in a cat refuge, without facing questions. I told them Billy had arrived for a holiday but didn't mention the news about Andy.

When I read the email through for grammar and typos – the hazard of being a former English teacher's daughter – my life sounded idyllic. They would have been so worried if they'd known the truth.

CHAPTER THIRTY-FOUR

During Billy's absence, I packed Marylou's books into cardboard boxes I'd picked up in the foyer of the supermarket in Santa Maria. It was a slow job as I kept stopping to browse through those with interesting covers or titles.

Finally, the bookshelves were empty. I scrawled 'Books' on the side of the boxes, then went to read in the garden for a while. I was making slow progress rereading Zeller's book, and wanted to finish my notes before I left the refuge and spent a few last days in Deià.

Sitting under the fig tree, I smiled as I thought about the beautiful La Residencia hotel. It seemed a lifetime ago I was there. I glanced down at my old shorts, T-shirt, and flip-flops, and imagined the faces of the staff there if I arrived in such scruffy attire. I'd worn these and the other similar garments so often, I planned to dispose of them all before leaving Mallorca. It wasn't only their scruffiness and age, but the knowledge that these clothes would always remind me of this fraught period in my life.

I was wondering how Billy was getting on in Palma, when my phone rang. His name was on the screen.

'Hi Billy. Had a good morning?'

It was afternoon, and I guessed that Billy and Jaume had gone for lunch in town. My stomach growled, reminding me I'd eaten nothing since breakfast.

'Not bad, Laura. Tell you all about it when I'm back. Just thought I'd let you know I'm leaving Palma now.'

I wished him a safe journey then went to make a sandwich before he arrived.

~

BILLY DROPPED the bundle of newspapers he was carrying on the table and looked at me.

'Come here, young lady.'

'Thank you. I think I needed that,' I said as he released me from one of his comforting hugs. 'Been packing Marylou's books today, and it made me sad for her; she's facing such a big change when she returns.'

'It's not your fault. You've done your best to keep her informed, and if you ask me, you're going above and beyond to sort out the situation.'

'If only I hadn't volunteered to look after this place.' Tears welled and I blinked them away. 'I'd be at home, sorting out my own life.'

I sat on the sofa, and Billy dropped down beside me, placing his arm around my shoulders.

'You know what they say: no good deed goes unpunished.'

If I heard that phrase again, I was likely to do someone a terrible deed. Billy broke the few minutes' silence.

'What *are* you doing about a new job?'

'Not a lot yet. It's difficult, not knowing how long I'll be here in Mallorca.'

I told him about the potential job in Bristol and my hope to move there when the station launched.

'Don't answer this if it's too personal, but will you be okay financially?'

Coming from Billy, the direct question didn't offend me.

'I should be. Zeller left me some money and her home. If I get desperate, I could sell either the house or my place, but it shouldn't be necessary in the short term.'

'You know there's a room you could have in Oxford,' he said, gently rubbing my back. 'When the studio's ready, we could both use it for voiceover work.'

What was Billy really offering? I wondered. He had always been a caring person, but he seemed different – more intense – since finding out about Andy. Or was I imagining it?

I slipped out from under his arm and stood up. 'I'm getting a cold drink. Fancy something?'

'Any beer? Then I'll tell you about my morning.'

I poured us both a chilled San Miguel and we went to sit in the shade outside.

Billy told me he'd wandered around the city centre, looking in the window of every estate agency office he came across.

'I had no idea Palma had so many … or was such an expensive place for property. Huge foreign demand has pushed prices sky high, for both renting and buying.'

His meeting with Jaume had been an overdue reunion. Like me, Billy's relative was unable to attend Carme's funeral, as he was handling a protracted divorce case. It sounded as though the two men had enjoyed their catching-up time.

'It was a pity he didn't know any suitable properties, but he promised to get in touch if he hears of anything. I'm sorry, Laura, but I tried.'

By nature, Billy was cheerful, but both his smile and the twinkle in his blue eyes had disappeared.

'Hey, it was a long shot, and thank you for your efforts. Maybe we'll have better luck with the newspaper ads. Now, tell me about your lunch.'

My dear friend was a gourmet; talking about the creative cuisine they'd eaten made him smile and twinkle again. The restaurant had a Michelin star and the food sounded delicious. Because Billy was driving and the lawyer had an important client meeting later, they had an alcohol-free meal.

'Then it must be wine time by now,' I said when we'd finished the beer. We opened the bottle of local Premsal Blanc wine, which was chilling in the fridge, and set to ploughing through the newspapers. Even if we found nothing in the classifieds, at least I'd have plenty of paper to wrap Marylou's china and glassware before packing it into boxes.

THE NEXT MORNING, I drove to Santa Maria for some food shopping. Billy stayed at the house to do some work on his voiceover website so it would be ready when the studio was operational. His ability to build a website was another surprise to me, and from what I'd seen so far, the site would be impressive.

Sardines or tuna steaks? I stared at the glistening seafood on the supermarket fish counter. Which would Billy prefer to BBQ that night? I rummaged around in my shoulder bag so I could call him and ask. *Where the hell's my phone?* Then I remembered I hadn't picked it up from the kitchen table. This called for an executive decision.

'Two tuna steaks, please.' I used the Spanish phrase I'd found on a translation website. Incorrect Spanish, it seemed, as the white-plastic-aproned assistant frowned and shrugged her shoulders in response. I gave her an apologetic smile, pointed at the fish on the counter and said, '*Dos,*' holding up two fingers to clarify my request.

Afterwards I was drawn, like felines to catnip, to the garden café at the interiors shop; I was sure Billy would appreciate the extra time to concentrate on his website. Before I'd even sat at my favourite shaded table, the friendly waiter came to ask if I wanted my usual Americano. Being recognised and having my drink preference remembered made me tingle with pleasure and feel more like a local than a temporary resident.

Enjoying the buzz from the delicious coffee and having indulged in my fantasy-garden daydream, I drove back to the refuge singing along to the radio. As I belted out Joe Cocker's 'With a Little Help from My Friends', I had no idea how helpful my dear friend Billy was about to become.

CHAPTER THIRTY-FIVE

'Time to get changed, sugar plum,' Billy said, striding towards me as I came through the door. He took the heavy basket from me and heaved it onto the table.

'Really? Why's that?' I flexed the fingers of the hand that had carried the shopping; buying the watermelon had seemed a good idea at the time, but the extra weight had been a challenge for me and for Marylou's basket. I'd need to replace the old straw shopper with a new one before her return.

'We're off to Palma. To see a woman about a finca.'

My mouth fell open.

'What? How? Now?'

'So many questions, Laura. Come on. I said we'd go as soon as you returned, and you've been gone for ages.'

Not a good time to mention my coffee stop. From the look of the table, Billy had worked without a break since I left, although I did notice he'd changed into smarter clothes.

'Ah, there's my phone.' I picked it up from the table

and dropped it into my bag. 'Ten minutes and I'll be ready.'

BILLY VOLUNTEERED to drive us into Palma. I was a competent driver back at home, but he'd deduced – correctly – that I was less confident when a temperamental vehicle and driving on the other side of the road were involved. I welcomed the opportunity to be chauffeured for a change.

'Has Jaume come up with something?' I didn't think it was likely within a day.

'No, he hasn't,' he said. 'This is all down to that radio interview you did before I came over. But if it looks workable, I shall ask Jaume to make sure it's all legal.'

'How do you know about this?'

'I have to apologise. The phone rang on the table while you were out, and I answered it without realising it wasn't my phone. The caller was an Antonio Duran, ringing on behalf of his neighbour, Isabel Rosselló.'

I cocked my head and frowned. *Never heard of him. Or her.*

Billy told me Señora Rosselló, who had married into a wealthy family, lived in a mansion in Palma's old town. She'd recently inherited her parents' finca in the countryside outside the Via Cintura, the city's outer ring road.

'It's called Finca Es Refugi,' Billy said, beaming. 'It means "The Refuge". Could be a good omen, don't you think?'

The woman had grown up on the property in question, where her hardworking father farmed agricultural produce. Besides the fertile land, there was a one-storey, two-bedroom house and, on the roadside, a small, abandoned building. This had once been a simple restaurant, where her parents offered traditional Mallorcan lunch fare. The place closed after Señora Rosselló's mother died, and when her father later died, she inherited the property.

'And this woman listens to the local English-language radio station?'

Billy laughed. 'She's too posh for that and doesn't speak any English. But the man who phoned is her next-door neighbour. He's a professor at the local university and listens to any English broadcasts he can. When he and Isabel got together for one of their occasional games of chess, she mentioned the property she didn't need or want; he remembered hearing your interview and told her about the refuge's plight.'

Isabel asked Antonio to arrange a meeting with her to discuss an idea. He phoned Britannia FM, where Mike gave him my mobile phone number.

'What amazing news,' I said. 'I wonder where the place is.'

'Don't get your hopes up yet, Laura. We don't know whether she wants to sell or rent the property, and either may be unaffordable. But at least it's a potential lead and the only one we have so far.'

We were meeting at her home and Billy would interpret. As thrilled as I was about the prospect of a possible solution to the refuge relocation problem, I was also itching to see inside one of Palma's many grand properties known as *palacios*.

BILLY PUSHED the doorbell button next to the gleaming brass plate bearing the name Ca'n Sabater. I looked up at the impressive building, wondering if it all belonged to the woman we were to meet. A few minutes passed before the door opened, revealing an attractive young woman wearing a grey dress, starched white apron, and sturdy white shoes.

She beckoned us into the house. Billy and I shot a glance at each other, and I mouthed 'Maid?' at him. We followed her along a wide and gloomy passage, lined with old oil paintings, into a glorious light-filled room with high ceilings, wooden beams and panelled walls, antique furniture, and two glittering chandeliers. I suppressed a gasp at the sight of such grandeur.

Three sets of French windows opened onto a beautiful courtyard where large terracotta pots overflowed with vibrant nasturtium flowers. In the centre of the space, an elaborate stone fountain played. The sound of the water made me feel cooler after our brisk walk from the car park.

The young woman motioned for us to follow her outside, where an elderly couple sat under the shade of a palm tree in the corner.

The man was in a wheelchair; Isabel – we presumed — was elegant and could have been in her seventies. She stood and came towards us and we all shook hands; this was not one of the usual hug-and-cheek-kiss situations. After a few minutes' conversation between her and Billy, she gave me a benevolent smile and invited us to join her and her husband at the table. She had such a regal bearing I had to stop myself from curtsying.

Billy excused himself and turned to me. 'We're going to speak in Catalan; Señora Rosselló is thrilled I can speak it.' He gave me a wink which the good señora would not have seen.

It seemed an auspicious start to the meeting. I understood not a word between them, but their body language suggested the conversation was flowing well. From time to time, Billy would stop to explain a point she'd made or ask me a question on her behalf.

The young woman in the uniform returned with a silver tray bearing glasses and a crystal jug of home-made lemonade, then poured the four drinks.

'Señora Rosselló says the lemons are from over there.' Billy indicated the sagging branches of the heavily laden citrus tree. My mouth watered at the thought of the zingy lemon tart I could make with some of that fruit.

'This lemonade is delicious.' I beamed at the señora, hoping my smile and my slow enunciation of each English word would convey the right message. A thumbs-up sign seemed a bit crude in this woman's presence.

Isabel's husband, Arturo, spent the entire time with a faraway expression on his face. Now and then, she would pat his knee and speak softly to him. The poor man appeared to have been the victim of a stroke, and I imagined Isabel's professor neighbour was a valued source of stimulating conversation for her as well as an occasional opponent over a chessboard.

Almost an hour later, Billy turned to me.

'Señora Rosselló has made an excellent proposal.' He smiled back at the elegant woman who, even in the privacy of her own home, was dressed for a ladies' lunch. She wore a double string of pearls around her neck and her manicured nails were glossy with pink varnish. I doubted those hands ever plunged into a washing-up bowl.

'I'll explain it all to you when we've left and, if you're happy with the arrangement, we'll let Señora Rosselló know later. Then we can set up a time to meet with our respective lawyers tomorrow.'

I had no idea of the outcome of their discussions, but the mention of lawyers sounded positive. The timing was encouraging too, and I couldn't help but smile at the imperious-looking woman.

'*Gracias,* Señora Rosselló.' I gave a small bow of my head and hoped she would forgive my appalling accent.

She smiled and raised an elegant hand to her chest. My eyes widened at the quail's-egg size of the diamond in her engagement ring.

'*Por favor, llamame* Isabel.'

'*Gracias,* Isabel.' I guessed the meaning of her words. '*Muchas gracias.*'

As soon as the heavy oak door closed behind us and we were back in the shaded narrow lane, I grabbed hold of Billy's arm.

'Well, what was all that about?' My heart was pounding and I couldn't wait to hear the outcome of the discussion.

He laughed. 'Come on, Miss Impatient. Let's have a bite of lunch and I'll tell you everything. And I think a celebration may just be in order.'

We walked arm in arm through the city's streets, Billy humming an unfamiliar but cheerful tune.

CHAPTER THIRTY-SIX

'Is this where Jaume brought you?' I asked, looking around the smart, contemporary Marc Fosh restaurant.

'Yes,' Billy said. 'It has a Michelin star, but the lunch menu is a steal, frankly, for the price. And Marc, the chef-patron, is English too. Only British chef in Spain with a starred restaurant.'

Impressive. We ordered, and the sommelier arrived with the wine list. We chose wine by the glass because one of us would have to drive home, but first, she brought two glasses of cava.

'With our compliments,' she said in accented English. 'You were here yesterday, sir, weren't you?'

'I was! And I'd eat here every week if I didn't live in England.' He laughed, and the pretty sommelier giggled and turned a little pink in the cheeks. I'd noticed in the past how he could charm women without trying – or apparently realising. His warm and generous nature and impeccable manners ought to make him quite a catch for someone.

Once we were alone, Billy outlined the details of his long conversation with Señora Rosselló, Isabel.

She was the only child of a smallholding farmer and a cook, and her parents expected her to take over from her mother in the restaurant kitchen one day. But young Isabel was bright and did well at school. Instead of going into the family business, she went to college and became a teacher.

She met and married Arturo, who was a decade older than her and owned a successful shoe-manufac-turing company on the island. As was clear in their grand home, they were wealthy way beyond the point of needing a smallholding on the outskirts of Palma. And had no children to inherit it.

'Isabel would have gifted her parents' place to the refuge but was concerned about the tax implications. Instead, she's offering to let it, initially for five years, for what we'd call a peppercorn rent.'

'Did she give a figure?'

'Put your drink down, sugar plum.' He waited for me to set my glass on the table, then leaned towards me, lowering his voice. 'One hundred euros a month.'

'WHAT?' I slapped my hand over my mouth and my face flushed. I didn't dare look around me to see other diners' reactions to my outburst. 'I'm so sorry, but that was quite a shock.'

Billy squeezed my arm as if to reassure me I hadn't been too embarrassing.

'There are conditions, though. Isabel said the house and the old restaurant premises have been neglected for a few years. They'll need thorough cleaning and deco-rating throughout, the work and cost of which will be down to the refuge.'

I thought for a few moments. Five years was a decent

tenancy length, and Marylou could negotiate an extension later if she wanted. And Rupert's five thousand euros should more than cover the expenditure for decoration and any minor repairs, as well as several months' rent.

'Billy, that's unbelievable. I can't thank you enough for handling the discussion with Isabel – I couldn't have done it, for sure.'

He smiled. 'I did it for you, Laura. Anyway, it was your interview that led to this. The power of local radio, eh?'

Just then, our starters arrived on enormous plates carried aloft by a handsome young waiter with a dazzling smile. The sommelier followed him and poured us each a glass of her recommended Sauvignon Blanc.

'Look at this beautiful food,' I said, in genuine admiration. 'It's a piece of art on a plate.' I pulled out my phone and took a photo to send Mum.

'I had this dish yesterday with Jaume,' Billy said. 'It's divine.'

We raised our glasses to each other.

'To Isabel,' I said.

'To local radio.'

I raised my glass higher. 'And to you, for being the most amazing friend any girl could have.'

AFTER OUR SUPERB LUNCH – Billy's treat, again – we went for a stroll around the city centre, arm in arm as we often did (like a long-married couple). We'd been unable to resist the temptation of a glass of local red wine with our braised beef cheeks main course and needed to put some time between lunch and driving home. I was bubbling with excitement and it never occurred to me we could have bumped into Carlos or El Capitán in town. It was fortunate we didn't.

Later we returned to the car park in companionable silence and Billy drove us back to Refugio Marylou, at a more sedate pace than the journey that morning. As soon as we arrived, he phoned Isabel to tell her I wished to accept her generous offer. Within an hour, a meeting with her and our respective lawyers was confirmed for noon the next day at Ca'n Sabater.

We'd signed the papers, and the bunch of keys for Finca Es Refugi was in my handbag. For the first time in weeks, I felt as though I were breathing correctly again – such was the monumental relief of finding a new home for Marylou and the refuge.

The lawyers were efficient and helpful. Jaume had even volunteered to research the licensing requirements for a cat café. With no existing business of that type in Mallorca, though, he warned us it could take some time.

Until the situation was clear, Marylou could run the former restaurant as an ordinary café, even with cat-themed décor, if she wanted. That would be her decision, and I was grateful it wouldn't need my input.

Back in the Renault, Billy started the engine. Before engaging first gear, he turned to me.

'Straight back? Or shall we visit the finca first?'

I grinned at him. 'What do you think?'

CHAPTER THIRTY-SEVEN

As Billy drove, I worried I might have been too hasty in signing the rental contract. After all, I hadn't even seen the place yet. But I had a good feeling about Isabel, and after we'd negotiated our way through the property's gates and pulled onto the drive, I could see it had potential.

At the house, I fumbled with the key in the lock, my hand shaking.

'Here, let me.' Billy unlocked and pushed open the door; it creaked like something from a haunted-house movie. A musty aroma rushed to greet us.

We wandered around the compact property, making observations as we did so. Both bedrooms were quite small; the largest had a view of the distant Tramuntana mountains. The old-fashioned bathroom had ghastly orange wall tiles and ugly taps, but I thought I could get them replaced at a reasonable cost.

Like Marylou's current home, there was an open-plan living room with a kitchen-dining area at one end.

The windows faced what would be the optimum place to erect the cat enclosures.

'It's not bad, is it?' I said to Billy, amazed at our good fortune.

He pulled out his phone and swiped to the note-taking app.

'Shall we make a list of jobs to do?'

'Brilliant idea. Oiling the front door hinges would be a useful start.'

He removed a stylus from his shirt breast pocket and tapped at the screen with surprising speed. Other than perhaps replacing the bathroom tiles and taps, the house needed little more than a thorough cleaning and painting throughout. I imagined myself up a ladder, brush in hand, paint in my hair. Maybe even some on the walls.

After we'd finished indoors, we wandered around outside. Although overgrown with weeds, the land was flat and had plenty of space for the cats' enclosures. There was even a suitable plot if Marylou wanted to grow her own produce, although, having seen the state of the herbs in her flowerpots, I thought that was unlikely.

A small stone building with a filthy window and a wooden door stood behind the house. Billy searched through the bulky bunch of keys and tried the smallest one in the padlock securing the entrance.

'Think the lock's rusted up.' He frowned as he wriggled the key. 'Got a hacksaw in your handbag, by any chance?' Suddenly the lock clicked. 'Bingo!'

He pulled open the door, revealing the contents.

'Ooh, look,' I said, wide-eyed. You'd have thought we'd discovered the Holy Grail. 'Gardening tools and a ladder. And what could be the world's oldest lawnmower.' We laughed. I doubted the mower would work, but the grass was so sparse, a pair of scissors would do the job.

'I'm sure we can find a use for some of this stuff though.'

'Shall we check out the future cat café?' Billy said, turning towards the former restaurant. His optimism was such a tonic. If Marylou hated the idea of running a café, she didn't have to use the building at all. At least she'd have a new home for herself and the cats.

The customers' car park could be cleared of weeds and new gravel laid with moderate effort. But as soon as we went inside the old eatery, I could see – and smell – the challenge we faced. It would take more than a pair of Marigolds and a bottle of bleach to get that place ready for decorating, let alone fit for serving food and drink.

'You could fry an egg in the grease on this worktop.' Billy grimaced as he studied his fingertip, which he'd wiped over the kitchen surface. I shuddered.

Inside the oven, I found a roasting tin containing a Curie-style culture: UFF! Unidentified Former Foodstuff. I wrinkled my nose at the horrible aroma and slammed the door. 'I think I'll prioritise the house and land.'

'Sensible idea. Gives us time to buy a hazmat suit.' My scribe added some notes to the list on his phone, then slipped it into his pocket. 'Seen enough yet?'

'More than, thanks,' I said. 'Let's go. I'm thinking bubbles, and there's a bottle in the fridge back at the refuge.'

～

BILLY AND I shared the evening cat-feeding duties and once we'd locked the felines' enclosures for the night, we assembled a light supper of *pa amb oli* with smoked salmon. We ate and drank under the fig tree, enjoying the buzzing of the cicadas and the scent of the wild Mediterranean vegetation in the warmth of the evening.

It was a memorable time. Perfect, in every way. We laughed at silly things and became more animated as the level of the cava in the bottle fell. A peacock shrieked somewhere nearby and Billy replied by imitating its call. Bird and human had a hysterical, shrieky conversation for a few minutes, until it set off a dog barking somewhere nearby. It sounded like Otto's Bruno. We laughed until we were bent double on our chairs, tears rolling down our faces.

This is what fun feels like, I reminded myself. For the first time since the eviction notice arrived, I knew I'd be able to sleep without worry. The relocation of Refugio Marylou was in progress, all thanks to Billy's help. I felt a surge of affection for my old friend.

'Oops!' I hiccupped and held the now-empty cava bottle upside down. 'All gone. Shall we open a wine?' I stood and planted a kiss on Billy's cheek before going to fetch more laughing juice.

Well, we *were* celebrating.

WHEN I WOKE up early the next morning, the sun still hadn't risen. The room wasn't fully dark, though; I could make out the light fitting hanging from the ceiling … which appeared to be moving. *Ugh! Way too much to drink last night.*

As I rubbed my temples in the hope of erasing my throbbing headache, two thoughts came to me. One was that we'd polished off an entire bottle of red wine after the cava. The second? There was no ceiling light fitting in Marylou's spare room.

CHAPTER THIRTY-EIGHT

I sat bolt upright. I was in my room; well, Marylou's. But that was where Billy was staying. His head was on the pillow next to mine. Holding my breath, I watched for a few moments as his chest rose and fell rhythmically, relieved to see he was sound asleep. The hint of a smile on his face gave me some concern, though.

Oh my God. What had we done? I didn't remember even coming to bed, let alone anything else that might have happened afterwards. I slowly lifted the sheet and rose from the mattress. It was a relief to find I at least still had my underwear on.

Careful not to make a sound, I crept across to the open door, then went into the spare room. I collapsed onto the single bed and stuck my head under the pillow. *How will I face Billy this morning?*

I MUST HAVE FALLEN into another deep sleep because I awoke sometime later to sounds coming from the kitchen. I picked up my phone to check the time: ten o'clock. *The cats' breakfasts!*

After untangling myself from the bedding, I got up, wondering why I was still wearing my bra and pants. And then I remembered. I pulled a T-shirt dress over my head, brushed my hair, and went to face the man whose bed I'd shared for the night.

'Morning, flower,' Billy said when I emerged from my temporary bedroom. 'Cuppa?' He stood at the kitchen worktop, stirring a mug of tea.

'Paracetamol. I need Paracetamol,' I groaned. 'But tea is also essential, thank you. Must feed the cats first, though; they'll be starving.'

'Don't worry. I've fed them already. And cleaned the enclosures. Thought you needed to sleep in.'

We faced each other. He showed no signs of a hangover and looked bright-eyed and happy. Far too bright-eyed and happy for someone who'd been cleaning so many stinky litter trays that morning.

'Tell me: did we—?'

'No, we didn't.' He stepped forward and hugged me, speaking into my hair. 'Dear girl, we'd both had far too much to drink for anything like that. You were very tipsy and emotional – not surprising after the few months you've had. We only cuddled up together and fell asleep. It was rather lovely, I must admit.'

Phew. 'Thank you. I'm sure you're right, Billy, but I don't remember a thing about it.'

'You have my word, sugar plum. You know I'm not the type to take advantage of a woman who's tipsy.' He rubbed my back. 'Especially not a woman as important to me as you are.'

A wave of heat and nausea came over me. I needed to steer the conversation in another direction. Outside forces intervened: Billy's phone rang. He picked it off the table and answered it. I fished the tea bag out of my mug and took a tentative sip of the steaming liquid before going in search of Paracetamol in my handbag.

When I returned for water to take with the pill, a few minutes later, Billy had finished his call and was sitting at his open laptop.

'That was the company supplying my studio gear,' he said. 'They're ready to deliver and install and want to do it on Tuesday, but that means I'd have to fly home on Monday.'

'Oh!' His frown surprised me; he should have been excited about being able to start his voiceover work sooner than expected. 'That's good news, though, isn't it?'

'But there's such a lot to do here.' Billy glanced at the master list of jobs we'd drawn up, then reached for his phone. 'I think I'll ring back and ask them to stick to the original date.'

I stepped towards him and placed my hand over his to stop him making the call. 'I don't think you should, Billy. You've done so much to help me already, and it's time you focused on your own project.'

BILLY'S last evening with me was on Sunday, and although we'd talked about having a final dinner at Luigi's, we were both tired and decided to spend the time in the garden, enjoying the balmy temperature and sounds of the cicadas and stone curlews. We concocted and ate a delicious al fresco supper together.

After we'd cleared the dishes, we went outside again to review the list of jobs and brainstorm ideas for achieving them. This time, we sustained ourselves with soft drinks rather than alcohol. I'd decided I'd never drink it again. Well, at least not for a few days.

ON MONDAY MORNING, I drove Billy to the airport for his journey home. He closed his eyes in the car, on the pretext of needing a pre-flight snooze. I glanced over at him occasionally and smiled. My fondness for my old friend had grown even more during his stay, and I was going to miss having him around.

In Palma's bustling terminal, I accompanied him as far as the security gate.

'This is it, then.' Billy stopped, gesturing towards the notice warning that only passengers could go any further. 'Bye for now, sugar plum, and thank you for having me.'

'Thank *you* for everything. You've been brilliant.' I opened my arms to him. 'I'm going to miss you so much, but I'll be in touch soon. I'd love to come and see your new studio and home.'

Passengers passed either side of us as we stood and hugged.

'You must,' he said, squeezing me tight. 'Meanwhile, take care of yourself and call me anytime if you need to talk.'

'Oh, I shall. Not sure how I'll manage without you now,' I said in a light-hearted tone, lifting my face from his chest and the familiar Penhaligon's fragrance. 'Thank you, Billy, so much. Again. You're my hero.'

He kissed my forehead and released me from his arms.

'Better go, or I'll miss my flight.'

I watched through watery eyes as he trundled his cabin bag towards security. He turned to look back, and I blew him a kiss.

'Bye, Billy. See you soon,' I said to myself in a quiet voice. 'At least, I hope so.' Then the tears that had been bubbling up inside me all day broke loose. My friend was going home. And I had two weeks before Eviction Day.

I MUDDLED around Marylou's house for a few hours, hating the silence without Billy. Then I pulled myself together and started one of the many tasks, to keep myself busy.

China and glass. One by one, I wrapped the items in newspaper and packed them into a box, which I marked 'Fragile'. I left a couple of plates and mugs in the cupboard, to use until moving-out day. Wrapping and packing took ages but gave me time for some focused thinking.

Should I look for a new job and a place to live in Oxford, so Billy and I were close together again? We had a special bond, and I could imagine living in the university city … but not sharing his home. I wanted to preserve the status quo of our friendship and had a feeling that would be difficult living in the same house.

The irony of the situation was inescapable. Billy was a good, kind man and seemed to have genuine, deep feelings for me, although I could only hazard a guess at their nature. He would make a wonderful life partner, or even husband – but not for me. I could never imagine us having a sexual relationship; he was almost twenty years older than me. I loved him, yes, but as the big brother I'd never had.

Then there was Carlos: gorgeous, sexy, fun, and possibly as smitten with me as I was with him. Making love with him had been like discovering a missing part of myself. He'd turned out to be my half-brother, but my thoughts about him were far from those of a sibling.

By that time, tears were sliding down my cheeks. I stopped my packing to wipe my face with a newsprint-stained hand and felt a nudge at my left calf. I looked down and saw Calvin rubbing up against my leg. He had become friendlier during Billy's visit and once or twice had vacated his smelly old armchair to sit next to me on the sofa.

Now, his low rumbling purr was like a balm for my soul. He bashed the side of his head against my calf as if to say, 'I'm here for you. Make a fuss of me.'

'Hello, Calvin.' I bent to stroke the smooth fur on the top of his head. 'Are you missing your mummy?' To my surprise, he let me pick him up without trying to wriggle out of my grasp. I held him close, kissed the top of his head, and buried my tear-stained face into his warmth. A faint whiff of Billy's cologne reminded me my friend had also become fond of Marylou's feisty feline.

With Calvin still in my arms, I went over to the sofa, sat down, and released my hold on him. I expected him to jump down to the floor and stroll back to his armchair, but he curled up on my lap and closed his eyes. I could feel the vibration of his purring under my hand. It was so soothing …

CHAPTER THIRTY-NINE

My phone's ringtone woke both of us. I leapt up and ran to the table to answer the call. I couldn't believe I'd been asleep for more than an hour, but the wall clock confirmed it. The ringing stopped before I reached the phone, but I saw who the missed call was from and rang straight back.

'*Hola* Silvia. Sorry I didn't get to the phone in time. How was the conference?'

'Informative, but dull,' she said. 'But I returned home to find something surprising that'll interest you.'

'Oh?' I hoped it wasn't another pair of abandoned kittens for the refuge.

'It's a message from Marylou on the answering machine. Do come over and listen when you have time.'

'Would now be okay, please?' I was eager to hear what the American had said.

Silvia invited me straight over. Without stopping even to comb my snooze-dishevelled hair, I grabbed my bag and keys and set off in the Renault for Santa Dolores.

'Hi, Silvia. It's Marylou here.' The recorded message echoed in the small room the vet used as her office. 'I don't have Laura's phone number and wanted to let her know I'm coming home. My flight from Madrid gets into Palma four o'clock on Friday, July twenty-sixth. Could you please ask her to pick me up at the airport?'

We stood together, listening to the message for a second time, then exchanged quizzical looks.

'It doesn't sound as though she's received your emails.'

'No, it doesn't. Or seen the missed phone calls,' I said. 'Could you check the number she called from?'

The vet pressed a few buttons and scribbled on a notepad on her desk. I compared it to the one Silvia had given me a while back.

'It's different. Maybe her mother's?'

I opened the calendar facility on my own phone and added the date and time I needed to be at the airport.

'She's going to have a terrible shock when she gets home.' I felt nauseous at the prospect of telling her everything that had happened.

Silvia nodded. 'Maybe you should call and tell her before she leaves?' She glanced at her wristwatch. 'It's morning over there; you could try now. Use this phone if you like.'

'Thank you so much, I'll do that. But first, may I bring you up to date with a few exciting developments over the past few days?'

'Of course. Let's talk outside.' She gestured towards the door. 'Go through, and I'll fetch us a cold drink.'

'Wow, you have had a successful time with your friend,' Silvia said when I finished telling her about Billy's visit and the refuge's new home. 'At least you have some good news to counter the bad when you talk to Marylou.'

I hesitated, thinking about my own situation. Losing Zeller had been upsetting enough, but to have the news about my job and then Zeller's actual role in my life so soon afterwards almost overwhelmed me. And I was in the fortunate position of having some support. Who knew whether Marylou had someone she could lean on – other than Silvia?

'Thinking about it, I'm not sure it's a good idea to tell her before she returns. She's just lost her mother, so she'll be dealing with all sorts of emotions on the long journey back. I think it'd be better to give her the news in person.' I made a mental note to take a box of tissues to the airport.

We discussed this for a few minutes, and Silvia agreed.

'Okay, so here's what we could do,' she said. 'I'll call and tell her I've passed her message on to you. I'll put the phone on loudspeaker mode so you can listen in.'

We went indoors to her office again, and she dialled the number she'd noted. After what seemed ages, I heard Marylou's voice.

'Silvia, hi, how are you? You got my message then?'

'Yes, I did. I've already spoken to Laura, and she'll be at the airport to pick you up.' She hesitated. 'I am so sorry about your mother, Marylou.'

'Aw, thank you. Mom and I had some real quality time together, despite her being woozy with painkillers. The end was … sudden, but peaceful.' In the quiet of the small room, I heard the catch in her voice. 'I'm so grateful to Laura for making it possible for me to come here – even though I had an awful start to my visit.'

Oh, if only she knew, I thought, with a sense of dread. But her last words gave me pause, and I leaned forward in the chair so as not to miss a word.

CHAPTER FORTY

What a story it was. Marylou had landed at Miami after an uneventful journey from Palma, via Madrid. She left the terminal and was walking to the rank to get a taxi to her mother's home in the suburb of Coral Gables, when it happened.

Just a few steps away from the building, an opportunistic thief snatched and sprinted off with her cabin bag, which she'd propped on top of the wheeled suitcase she was pulling. The theft happened with such speed she saw only the man's back as he disappeared with his haul.

'Not one person chased after him,' Marylou said. 'The bag itself wasn't worth much, but my phone and iPad were in it.' She said the police were unhelpful because she couldn't describe the thief in enough detail.

'Thank God he didn't swipe my purse, or I'd have lost my passport, bank cards, and cash.' I remembered 'purse' was what Americans call a handbag. She'd been lucky there.

'I didn't want to waste my precious time there shopping for new devices,' she said. 'I had Mom's landline to make calls, but she didn't own a computer, so if I had any emails – which would be rare anyway – I haven't yet seen them.'

'What a terrible thing to happen.' Silvia looked at me with her eyebrows raised.

I nodded in response, biting my lower lip as I listened. *How much bad luck can one person have?*

'Sure was, but, hey, they were only possessions … and nothing compared to losing Mom. I'll buy a new phone and iPad in Miami Duty-Free on the way home. D'you think Tomeu would set them up for me when I'm back?'

How fortunate that the American was, as she'd described herself to me, 'a techno klutz'. She was unlikely to check her emails before she was back in Mallorca.

'He'll do it with pleasure,' Silvia said. The two women said goodbye and the vet replaced the phone handset on its cradle.

'Well. We know now why she didn't respond to your messages.' She let out a deep sigh. 'What a rough time she's had.'

Yes. And it's going to get even rougher soon.

I thanked my vet friend, and we exchanged the cheek kisses that had become as habitual for me as they were for the locals.

'I'll be in touch,' I told her. 'Some major planning to do before Marylou returns.'

THE NEXT DAY, I created and worked on a file I named 'The Battle Plan' on my laptop. My concentration was such that I didn't notice Billy's message arrive until it was too late at night to call him back. His text message thanked me for his stay in Mallorca and said he missed the sunshine. I'd speak to him the next day, sure he'd be interested to hear about Marylou.

My priorities were to clean and decorate the American's future home, ready to house her things. I also needed to find someone to dismantle the cats' enclosures and re-erect them and their contents in their new location, having first tidied the land there.

Time permitting, I intended to get the little restaurant spruced up so Marylou could see its potential as a future cat café – if Jaume could arrange the relevant licence. I'd had a taste of Marylou's lifestyle and believed generating some income for the refuge would be helpful.

It would be ludicrous to attempt all the work myself before she returned; I needed some helpers. Sleep would be impossible if I didn't first make some progress, so I stayed up until almost two in the morning, scribbling down names of people who might help me.

One name I underlined three times.

Despite my head hitting the pillow a lot later than usual, I was up early to feed the cats and do the cleaning. Once I'd done those chores, I was back at the kitchen table surveying my list.

How lucky was I to find a couple of British men whose business on the island was doing odd jobs and maintenance? With the prospect of no language problems, I rang the number on their advertisement in the local English newspaper. A man called Reg answered and, after I'd explained what I needed, he promised to come the next day to look at the enclosures and give me a price for the job.

I put a tick on my list, writing 'Pending' next to it. *First thing achieved.*

Then I dialled the next number I'd written down. After a couple of rings, I heard a familiar voice.

'Britannia FM, how may I help you?' Barry had never answered Bard FM's phone, apparently believing it was beneath his status. Mike was a different type of manager, in every way.

'Mike, hello. It's Laura Lundon … with another favour to ask, if I may.'

'Hello there! This is a very pleasant surprise.' I could hear the sincerity in his voice. 'Ask away, Laura.'

I told him how my previous interview had just resulted in me securing a new home for the cat refuge, but I now needed some volunteers to help clean and decorate the place. Over the coming weekend.

'Superb news about the premises. Well done,' Mike said. 'Pleased to help, too. Could you come in tomorrow morning, and we'll do an appeal together on the breakfast show?'

Result! I knew Mike would be astute enough to recognise the public relations value to the radio station of a successful public appeal.

We agreed the interview would be live, after the eight o'clock news bulletin during the next day's breakfast programme. The only negatives were the extra-early start and the prospect of driving in Palma's rush-hour traffic. The potential positives far outweighed those challenges.

'Thank you so much, Mike. See you tomorrow morning.'

Silvia rang just before two o'clock. It had been a busy morning and I was buzzing from having made progress.

'Had any lunch yet?' she said. 'Only I've made enough pasta salad for two and wondered if you'd like to join me? I was sure you'd be too busy to make yourself a proper lunch.'

Lunch was sacrosanct for Silvia. Like most locals, everything stopped for this important meal. Only the occasional veterinary emergency caused her to reopen the practice doors before four o'clock.

I grabbed my bag and keys and set off for her place, knowing I would soon have to say goodbye to Silvia and go back to England. Her friendship and kindness would forever be among my fondest memories of my time in Mallorca.

'I need as many volunteers as possible for a working party this weekend.' We were eating lunch in Silvia's courtyard; between mouthfuls of her appetising pasta salad, I'd told her about my morning's achievements. 'After the radio tomorrow, I'm going to that big DIY store in Palma to buy what I think we'll need.'

What I didn't spend on the relocation project would be in the refuge account for Marylou's use after I'd left. It was even possible she'd be able to pay for future veterinary treatments, saving Silvia some money.

I knew incentives were useful when looking for volunteers, and I told Silvia I'd also booked a street food truck, run by a friendly young Spanish couple who spoke fluent English.

'They follow my Moggies in Mallorca Instagram page and commented a few times. I rang them and explained what I wanted to do, and they offered me a low price for their services. They'll be around for four hours both days at the weekend. So, the volunteers will have free food and soft drinks.'

'I'm sure Tomeu would love to help,' Silvia said. 'Many of his friends live in the Palma area and he can be very persuasive. And free refreshments will be a great incentive for hungry teenagers.'

We laughed.

'To be serious,' she added, 'I could help on Saturday and could spare Sunday morning too. I enjoy decorating, and I'll bring Tomeu with me.' It was her regular one weekend off in the month, when a locum vet covered for her.

Silvia to the rescue once again.

I ARRIVED at the radio station in Palma a quarter of an hour early. From my own experience, I knew it was always a relief to see a guest had arrived on the premises before their interview was scheduled to begin.

Within a couple of minutes of my arrival, an American girl who introduced herself as Nancy came to escort me upstairs.

'Mike's doing a phone interview with the tourism spokesperson right now.' She sighed and shook her head. 'Another drunk English tourist jumped off a Magaluf hotel balcony last night.'

Nancy invited me into the glass-walled booth, next to the broadcast studio. This was where she operated the phones and acted as show producer.

As the interview finished, Mike glanced over to the booth, smiled, and waved me into the studio. He greeted me like an old friend, and I was sure he'd put any nervous guest at ease.

'I've allocated a half-hour segment to this,' he said. 'We'll do the interview in three parts, with songs between. Sound okay?'

'Sounds fantastic. Thank you so much, Mike. I can't tell you how much I appreciate this.'

He opened the microphone fader and the red on-air light came on; it was my cue to remain silent.

'If you're a cat lover, stay with us for details of a special project in Mallorca that needs some volunteers to help this weekend. Britannia FM has all the details for you, after this.'

I smiled when I recognised the introduction to Al Stewart's 'Year of the Cat'.

Off-air, we agreed the structure of the interview, and as Al's song was ending, Mike said, 'Let's do this!'

Our conversation couldn't have gone better. We had good on-air chemistry, and he seemed as keen as I was to attract as many volunteers to the site as possible. The fact Rupert was a friend of his might have had something to do with it.

The previous evening, I'd prepared a one-page document including a map to the new refuge site and my phone number for further details. Fingers crossed I would have a busy day answering calls. I'd emailed the document to Mike, and Nancy was going to send it to anyone who contacted the station to volunteer.

At the end of the interview, during a commercial break, we both stood, hugged, and kissed cheeks. I felt high from the buzz of doing live radio again.

'Thanks again, Laura, you were great,' Mike said.

'Still planning to go back to the UK? Or could I persuade you to come and work here?'

'Sorry, Mike,' I said, chuckling. 'Home beckons once Marylou's back. But if I ever return for a holiday, I promise to come and say hello.'

We paused for Mike to do a time check after the break and announce another song, and then a beaming Nancy came into the studio.

'That was amazing!' she said. 'The phones are ringing like crazy.'

It was encouraging news, but I knew from the past that callers to radio stations don't always deliver on their promises.

CHAPTER FORTY-ONE

'Hello … it's Laura, isn't it?' I was unloading industrial-sized pots of white emulsion from the DIY superstore's enormous trolley into the back of Marylou's Renault, and turned so suddenly I cricked my neck.

Until the girl in front of me raised her sunglasses so I could see her eyes, I didn't recognise her. She looked taller than I remembered.

'Oh! Hello, Claire, fancy seeing you here.' I put down the pot of paint I was holding and shook my aching arm. 'How's Jet?'

'Gorgeous,' she said, beaming. 'He's got me wrapped around his little paw. He's such an affectionate cat, and we love him to bits.'

I saw her glance at my carrier bags full of brushes, rollers, cloths, and rubber gloves.

'Did I hear you on the radio this morning? I caught only the last part of the interview, but it looks like you're gearing up to decorate the Marivent Palace!'

'Yes, that was me.' I laughed at the idea of painting

the Spanish royal family's Mallorcan summer residence and nodded towards the load on the trolley. 'I'm just taking this lot to the new refuge premises. Don't suppose you have any spare time this weekend and fancy wielding a paintbrush for a bit?'

Claire laughed. 'I'm useless at painting, but I *lurve* cleaning ... so therapeutic. I'd be happy to come early Saturday and start on that.'

Who'd have thought it? With her well-manicured hands and immaculate make-up, she didn't look the type to don a pair of Marigolds and get down and dirty with a scrubbing brush.

'If you're free, that'd be fantastic. I'll email you a map to the place later. Thanks so much.'

We said our goodbyes, and I watched her totter towards the DIY store entrance in platform sandals that must have added three inches to her height. *Maybe wear something a bit more practical on Saturday?*

A GREY VAN arrived at Refugio Marylou just ten minutes after I'd returned; I went out to meet the driver.

'Reg, I presume?'

'Nah. My father-in-law's out on a job. I'm Rob.'

We shook hands and he followed me round to the enclosures, a biro behind his right ear, and notebook and retractable metal tape measure tucked under one tattooed arm. I told him I intended to move the wood-and-wire-netting enclosures to a new location near Palma, and he grunted.

Oblivious to the suspicious gaze of the cats that were awake, he prodded at the wooden frames with the business end of his biro and tutted.

'Not gonna happen.' He shook his head. 'The wood's rotten. Take 'em down and they'll fall apart.'

I had a sudden urge to burst into tears. Everything had been going so well. Too well, perhaps. I should have expected a stumbling block somewhere.

Rob, his builder's bum poking out of his denim cut-offs, didn't look like a man who'd know how to cope with a crying woman, so I swallowed hard and focused on my problem.

'Would you be able to build new ones in situ? Just outside Palma? Within a few days?' I was asking a lot, I knew.

At last, a smile. Well, more of a greedy grin; I could almost see euro signs flashing in his eyes.

'I'll talk to Reg. We're not too busy at this time of year – getting too hot to do much, if I'm honest.'

Relatable. I dragged the back of my hand across my damp forehead. When I asked for an estimate of the cost, he scribbled in his notebook. I spluttered when he told me the figure.

'That's a lot of money,' I said, although I had no idea whether it was a reasonable sum for the materials and work involved. It was just as well I'd made only a minor dent so far in Rupert's donation; I didn't have time to shop around for something cheaper.

Rob must have realised I had no choice.

'I could measure up and get Reg to send a written quote.'

He handed me his notebook and pen and instructed me to write the measurements he called out as he set to with his tape measure. Could I claim a discount for doing part of his job? I wondered. He didn't look as though he had a sense of humour. Neither did he look like the discounting type.

Silvia phoned a short while after Rob did his Lewis Hamilton impression on the drive, spraying earth and gravel as he went.

'Your interview was *muy bueno*.' She had been dropping the occasional Spanish words into her conversations with me, perhaps hoping to inspire me to learn the language. As I'd soon be returning home, this was unlikely.

'Two friends who work in the big vet hospital in Palma are coming to help on Saturday,' she said. 'I'm going to pick them up and bring them, so they can't change their minds.'

'Great! Thank you so much. And I met the woman who adopted Jet today, and she's coming too. We won't be alone, it seems.'

Then, with a wobble in my voice, I told her the bad news about the enclosures being too fragile to move.

'I'm waiting for a quote from a builder for new ones, but they may not be ready in time.'

'Have faith,' she said. 'It'll all work out, don't worry. And if they're not, we'll find a solution somehow.'

I didn't have faith and felt sick with worry. But I knew she'd do everything possible to help if the worst happened.

'You're right.' I did my best to sound convinced. In the distance, I heard the doorbell ring over the practice entrance.

'I must go.' Silvia spoke in a quiet voice. 'I have a constipated Cockerpoo to see.'

'HELLO, dear girl, I've been wondering how things were going,' Billy said when I phoned him later.

'Been busy since you left.' I outlined the progress I'd made in recent days.

'You're a wonder woman, sugar plum, you really are.'

'Got to get it sorted; Marylou's coming back next week. And I found out why she didn't respond to any of my calls or messages.'

I told him what had happened to the American just after she'd arrived in Miami.

'Lordy, how dreadful,' Billy said. 'On top of her mother being terminally ill, too.'

'Isn't it? And now her mum's gone, and you and I both know what that feels like.' I paused. 'I decided not to tell her about the eviction until she gets back.'

Billy exhaled at the other end of the line. I didn't want to debate the wisdom of my decision, so changed the subject.

'How are you? And how's the new studio?'

I could hear the excitement in his voice as he talked me through the installation process, which had gone without a hitch. He'd recorded and already sent his showreel to some major production companies. His first commission – voicing a double-glazing commercial for a national radio station – had arrived only that morning.

'When you're back, come down to Oxford to see the studio and we'll make you a proper showreel to send out with job applications,' he said. 'Any idea when you'll be coming home?'

'Best guess would be another couple of weeks.' I thanked him for his offer. A professionally produced showreel would help in the radio industry's shrinking jobs market. 'I'm going to help Marylou get settled into the new place and introduce her to Jaume, so she knows who's looking into the cat café licence. Then I may take a few days to chill out in Deià before I come back. Heaven knows I could do with a bit of luxury and relaxation.'

'You certainly deserve it.'

'Yes, this weekend'll be full on for me, but I can't wait to see how it looks afterwards. I just hope some volunteers turn up.'

Billy laughed. 'Don't be too despondent if there aren't as many as you're hoping for. People can be fickle when it comes to volunteering.'

Then he told me some news that warmed my heart. On his return flight he'd been sitting next to a Mallorcan woman who had visited her elderly mother on the island. By coincidence, she also lived in Oxford, where she taught Spanish at Oxford Brookes University. Billy and Araceli – who was in her early-fifties – had since been out for dinner together in Oxford a couple of times.

'We have such a lot in common,' Billy said. 'And I must admit I'm quite taken with her.'

'That's wonderful news, Billy. You deserve every happiness. I hope I'll get the chance to meet her when I'm back.' We chatted for a few minutes longer, until I heard a doorbell in the distance.

'Got to go, Laura, sorry. That'll be the man to fix the immersion heater. The trials of an old house, eh? Speak soon, sugar plum.'

We said our goodbyes. It was time to feed the cats and lock up the enclosures for the night. Then I was going to check my emails and pour myself a large gin and tonic to have in the garden, before an early night.

CHAPTER FORTY-TWO

The cats had a crack-of-dawn breakfast on Saturday morning because I needed to be at the new refuge site by eight o'clock. A message from Claire had confirmed her early arrival for the marathon cleaning session, and I wanted to open the house to get some fresh air through it first.

I had only one other email, from Reg the builder. My heart was racing as I opened the message.

Hello Ms Lundon,

Rob told me your existing enclosures are in a poor state and you need new ones to replace them.

I heard your radio interview, and as it's a quieter time of the year in our trade, we could make these for you and install them this coming week.

We'd prepare them to the same measurements and material specifications of the old enclosures.

As the work is for an animal refuge, we'd like to offer a heavily discounted price of five hundred euros, inclusive, and hope this will be acceptable.

Please confirm ASAP if you want us to proceed on this basis.

We could buy the materials tomorrow and make a start, so we can have the job finished for you on Wednesday.

Regards,

Reg

Without delay, I wrote back to accept the kind offer. The figure was half what Rob had suggested and, thanks to Rupert, was affordable.

I WAS UNLOCKING the gates at the future refuge when I heard a car horn behind me and turned around. Claire waved from the driver's seat of her VW Golf; another woman sat next to her. Many hands make light work, I remembered Mum used to say when I was a teenager, whenever she was getting me to help with household or garden chores.

I returned the wave and smiled, then climbed back into the Renault to drive into the finca, followed by Claire. We parked in the former restaurant's parking area, which I hoped would fill with volunteers' cars during the day.

Claire introduced me to her neighbour, a smiling Mallorcan woman called Catalina, who spoke no English. She was a cleaner at a hospital in Palma and was, I learnt, happiest when she was scrubbing something to within an inch of its existence. Apparently, whatever Catalina was scrubbing, she imagined it was her cheating ex-husband's face. The Mallorcan grinned at me, ready for action; not a woman to upset, I thought.

'*Bienvenida*,' I said, hoping it was the right word to welcome her to what could be an exhausting day.

I had a list of jobs I hoped we'd do that weekend and consulted my clipboard.

'If we start by cleaning the two bedrooms in the house, I'll get those painted first. That way, the smell may have gone before anyone sleeps in them.' I looked up at Claire, who turned to speak to her Mallorcan friend in Spanish. If I'd told Catalina that the island's tennis supremo, Rafa Nadal, would join her to help, she couldn't have looked more excited.

'Suits us,' Claire said. 'Lead on and we'll get started.'

I smiled to see she was wearing old clothes. And trainers on her feet rather than the vertiginous platform sandals she'd worn to go shopping at the DIY superstore. After unlocking the front door, I led the two women in.

'This'll be lovely when it's all done.' Claire translated her words for Catalina's benefit; the Mallorcan woman agreed, with vigorous nodding.

They tackled one bedroom each, and before long I could hear Catalina singing, happy in her work. I went around the house throwing open windows and shutters, and soon a blend of hot outdoor air and floral-scented cleaning products replaced the musty ambience of earlier.

One window refused to budge and seemed to be swollen and stuck in its wooden frame. I grunted from the exertion of trying for a final time to push it open.

'Here, let me have a go.'

I turned around and grinned. 'Mike, this is a pleasant surprise.'

'Well, I could hardly not turn up, could I?' he said, laughing, as he came to apply some muscle to the stubborn window.

One push and it creaked open.

'What next, boss?' He winked at me.

'Thank you.' I picked my clipboard off the floor and looked at the list.

'Since you're a whizz with windows, how about giving them all a clean?'

Mike gave me the thumbs-up sign.

'I'm on it – glass and frames, inside and out, yes? What shall I use?'

I led him over to the corner where all the cleaning and decorating materials were gathered. He picked up what he needed and went outside. At least the house was only a single storey, and he was tall enough to reach all the windows.

It wasn't yet nine o'clock, and we were already making progress. I looked in on Claire and Catalina, who were working hard. The Mallorcan was scrubbing a stubborn mark on the ceramic floor tiles when I poked my head around the bedroom door. She glanced up, a look of concentration on her face.

'*Todo bien*,' she said and returned to her endeavours. All good. The room was already looking much better, even before decoration. Which of the two would Marylou choose for her bedroom? I wondered.

'*Hola!*' I heard a young voice call from the open front door. I went to see who it was and found three teenagers standing there.

'Laura?' The boy pronounced my name the Spanish way. The way El Capitán had said the name of his late wife and Carlos's mother.

'That's me. Friends of Tomeu's?'

They nodded, then introduced themselves and said they would do anything. The one named Alberto suggested they weed the gravelled parking area; I'd forgotten to put that job on my list, so I was pleased they'd spotted it needed doing.

～

By late morning, more than a dozen volunteers had thrown themselves into the working party. True to her word, Silvia had brought Tomeu, who joined his friends in weeding duties outside.

I tuned Marylou's portable radio to Britannia FM, and the music seemed perfect for keeping us all moving. From time to time, the presenter reminded listeners of the need for volunteers to turn up and help prepare a new cat refuge that weekend. I owed Mike a big drink.

I was busy with sandpaper, rubbing down a door frame and swinging my hips to Hot Chocolate's 'You Sexy Thing', when he appeared at my side.

'Food truck's arrived, Laura — want it anywhere in particular?' I grinned, passing him the sheet of sandpaper so he could take over. Then I wiped my dusty hands on the back of my denim shorts. 'Thanks, Mike, I'll go out and sort it.'

'By the way,' he said before I went, 'I hope you don't mind, but I contacted the editor of the local paper. He's a good friend, and I thought this would be a great story for him.'

'No problem at all.' The exposure could be useful for Marylou's refuge and the volunteers might appreciate it too.

'I've given him the bones of the story, but he may get in touch later for a few quotes.'

'You're a gem, Mike.' I stretched up to give him a kiss on the cheek; he hadn't looked like the type to blush.

I went out to meet Xavier and Lola, who were standing next to their brightly painted street food truck. It was the same type of vehicle as the ice-cream vans that used to stop near our house when I was a child, but this one was adapted to serve hot food.

We made our introductions, and I suggested a parking place.

'Thank you so much for offering such a great deal for this weekend,' I said. 'The free-food incentive has attracted plenty of volunteers.'

Xavier laughed and replied in perfect English. 'We were lucky. We spoke to our meat supplier about it and they donated the burgers and sausages, and a drinks company gave four dozen cans of Coke. Made it easy to give you a good discount.'

'I appreciate it, and the team will too later.'

I left them to set up in their tiny kitchen space and was walking towards the house when I heard a large van arrive. I stopped and pointed to a place where the driver could park – noting the absence of knee-high weeds now – and went to meet him. He introduced himself as Reg.

'Just a quick visit,' he said. 'Thought I'd have a look at the site and see where the enclosures should go.'

I took him to the side of the house and he stood, arms folded, surveying the land.

'That looks flattest.' He pointed to the area I'd identified as ideal. 'We'll need to clear all those weeds, though. Are you here tomorrow?'

I told him we'd be working throughout the weekend, and he promised to return the next morning with his brush cutter to tidy the entire garden space.

'I can't put a concrete floor down for the enclosures,' he said. 'Not enough time for it set properly. So, if it's okay with you, we'll lay paving slabs.'

'Sounds perfect, thank you. They'll be easy to keep clean, too.'

As Reg drove off in his exhaust-fume-spewing van, Xavier called to me from the food truck window.

'Give us half an hour, Laura, and we'll be ready to serve.'

'Thanks. I'll make sure the hungry hordes come out a few at a time. You don't want a mad rush!'

BY MID-AFTERNOON, work on the house was progressing well. The whole place was thoroughly clean, and one bedroom already painted. A few volunteers were at work painting the second. It seemed achievable that the house and land would be ready by the end of Sunday.

An injection of energy, enthusiasm, and confidence that Finca Es Refugi would be a suitable new home for Marylou and the cats had replaced the stress of the past few weeks. Even the finca's name seemed fitting, being Mallorcan for 'refuge'. I just hoped the American wouldn't mind being so far from Otto …

'Someone from the newspaper outside.'

I was crouching, stirring a fresh pot of varnish before I tackled one of the wooden doors, and looked up to see Johnny, one of the volunteers, his face freckled with paint.

'Thanks, Johnny.' I stood up straight and stretched my arms to ease the stiffness. Even looking after the cats over the weeks hadn't prepared me for the physical work of that day.

Mike had said the editor would call me for some quotes, but perhaps he'd come in person. I dragged my fingers through my unruly hair, then went outside into the bright sunshine.

I had such a shock. If I'd been a panna cotta, I'd have had the perfect amount of wobble. But that's not a good look on a human being.

CHAPTER FORTY-THREE

'You're the Laura I'm here to see? What are you doing here?'

'Hello, Carlos,' I said, my voice as shaky as my legs. I spotted the aluminium case slung on a strap over his left shoulder. 'You here from the *Bulletin*?'

'Well, yes, it looks like it,' he snapped, tapping the metal with his hand. 'I thought you'd returned to the UK.' He slid his camera case off his shoulder to the ground and stood looking at me, his face devoid of a readable expression.

'I'm so sorry. You deserve an explanation, I know.' I glanced back at the house. 'But it's a long story, and I guess neither of us has time for it this afternoon.' He didn't reply. 'You'll be wanting a photo of all these brilliant volunteers. Come through.'

Carlos picked up his case and walked a few steps behind me.

'Laura, stop!'

I turned to look at him.

'I need to know what happened. Why did you just

disappear like that? I was sure we'd found something …
with potential.'

His shoulders slumped and there was no trace of the
gorgeous smile that had made me shiver with pleasure
before. I still had an urge to hug him, there and then.

'Believe me, I thought that too. Every moment we
spent together was special, and you've been on my mind
so often all these past weeks.'

'What went wrong? I don't understand.'

'It's difficult to explain. I hadn't told you the entire
story about why I came to Mallorca. I should have had
the guts to reveal what I found out, but I didn't.' I
paused, realising I ought to tell him everything. 'Please,
Carlos, could we talk about this another time?'

He put his hand on my arm and his voice softened.

'When do you finish here today? I could come back
later.'

'Would you? I'll wait here until you arrive. I should
warn you not to have any thoughts about us becoming a
couple. As much as I'd like that.'

His frown turned to a smile. *Ooh, there's the shiver!*

'We'll talk later, then. Now, I've got a job down in
Andratx after this, so let's go and get that photo done for
the paper.'

SILVIA AND MIKE were the last to leave that Saturday.
Tomeu left a little earlier, collected by a friend who'd
passed her driving test and borrowed her mum's car.

During the day, I learnt Mike was a widower, with no
children. His wife had died a few years ago from cancer,
and he hadn't been in a relationship since. He threw
himself into his work at the radio station, which he'd

turned from a once-ailing business into a local success story.

I hoped he would ask Silvia out on a date. They were both warm-hearted and generous-spirited people, with the potential to become a wonderful couple. They spent the afternoon painting the bathroom together, and I heard peals of laughter as they worked in the limited space.

'Thank you both so much.' We stood outside the front door of the house at the end of the afternoon, enjoying the peace after everyone else had left. 'I can't believe all the progress we've made today. If we have a similar response tomorrow, I think we'll have finished by lunchtime.'

'I'd say so too,' Mike said. He had a splodge of white emulsion on his face, and I watched in fascination as Silvia removed a clean tissue from her pocket, dampened it with water from the aluminium drinking bottle in her straw basket, and rubbed gently at his cheek to remove the mark.

'I think in English one would say "you're good to go".' Silvia balled the damp paper and dropped it into her basket. Mike laughed and put his hand on her shoulder.

'*Gracias*, Silvia. I don't know about you, but today's work has given me quite an appetite. Would you like to have some tapas in town with me before you go home?'

Silvia blushed and smiled, then glanced at her watch (although I already knew she had no plans for the evening).

'Thank you, Mike, sounds a great idea.' She looked at me. 'Laura, would you like to come too?' I glanced at Mike, whose face revealed he was planning on tapas for two, rather than three; he was in luck.

'Thanks for asking, but a friend's coming over for a chat soon. Need to spruce myself up a bit first.' I felt wretched after a long, hot day of physical work.

We hugged and kissed cheeks and they left – Silvia in her car, following Mike in his. My love life was going nowhere, but I had a warm feeling there could be a potential relationship budding for these two people I'd become fond of for their kindness and generosity.

Would Carlos return? It wouldn't have surprised me if he'd changed his mind. Before I went to freshen up, I reviewed the day's progress. Clipboard in hand, I ticked off jobs completed and made a few handwritten notes.

Tomeu and his friends had done a superb job of weeding the gravelled part of the property; Reg would come the next morning with his brush cutter to get rid of the unwanted growth in the garden area, and return on Wednesday to erect the new cat enclosures. I hoped.

The house looked much better; every room was sparkling clean and the painting of the bathroom and two bedrooms was finished. We must have set a record for the number of people trying to paint one room, and despite almost tripping over each other at times, it had been a fun afternoon.

The next morning, we'd paint the main living-cum-dining area, which also included the kitchen corner. I hoped enough volunteers would turn up to finish decorating the large space in one day.

I took my handbag into the bathroom to attend to my appearance. The room looked so different: the sanitary ware and taps gleamed as though new, and the white paint made everything seem lighter. Even the orange tiles were acceptable after a serious clean and renewed grouting.

The cool water refreshed me as I washed my face. I

had to pat my skin dry on one of the rough paper towels from the industrial-sized pack bought with everything else at the DIY megastore. Not a beauty tip to adopt at home.

As I brushed my hair, looking in the now-spotless mirror above the bathroom sink, I remembered how much effort I made to look good during my holiday, before I saw Carlos. This time, he'd seen me grubby, dishevelled, and sweaty from hard work, with my hair in desperate need of a hairdresser's attention and wearing the scruffy clothes I used during my cat-care duties. I looked at my hands; the immaculate manicure he'd admired one evening was a distant memory. Instead, I had nails of differing lengths and a cat scratch or three on the back of my hands.

If Carlos didn't return, I wouldn't blame him. Not just because he'd seen me looking such a mess; I'd already warned him we couldn't continue the relationship we'd started.

Scrabbling around in the bottom of my bag, I found a lipstick and the small spray of Chanel Cristalle perfume. A liberal spritz of the fragrance and a slick of colour across my lips left me feeling a smidgen more presentable.

The air outside was still hot but the house felt cool indoors, thanks to its thick stone walls. Carlos and I would have to sit on the floor or stand up, but I doubted he'd stay long once he heard what I had to say.

His car horn alerted me to his arrival and I went out to meet him, my heart thumping. Bringing the Toyota to a halt, he climbed out, and I felt a surge of longing when I saw him. He must have been home after his Andratx assignment; he was wearing different clothes.

'Hi, Laura. All done for the day?' He sounded cheerful.

'Yes, thanks. And we've made significant progress. We may even finish by tomorrow lunchtime.'

Carlos walked around to the back of his car and opened the boot. He removed two folding chairs and a large straw basket.

'I noticed earlier there was nothing to sit on, so I brought these. Indoors or out?'

I suggested we went into the house. He set up the chairs in the middle of the room and we sat down. Then he bent down and delved into the straw basket.

'Thought you'd be hungry after a day's work.' He pulled out two foil-wrapped packages. 'Smoked salmon and avocado baguettes.' He passed me one and then retrieved a half-bottle of cava and two glasses from the basket. 'And maybe a little thirsty too?'

I watched in silence as he popped open the bottle and poured. This was not intended to be a celebration.

'Well?' Carlos said, passing me a glass of fizz.

I thanked him for the drink and food and enjoyed a fortifying sip of the delicious, chilled cava.

'It's quite a long story, I'm afraid.'

'No worries. I'm free all evening.'

Thankful I'd thought all this through earlier, I began.

'When I told you that Zeller Floyd, the writer, was an old friend of mine, it wasn't the whole truth. Having only just met you, I didn't want to bore you with recent events in my life. You and I were having fun, and the full story would have put a damper on that.' I had another sip of my drink, then placed it on the floor by my chair.

'Zeller was my aunt. In April this year, she had a

massive stroke and died without regaining consciousness. We were very close, and it devastated me.'

Carlos gasped. 'I'm so sorry, Laura.'

'Then, not long after the funeral, my parents told me Zeller was, in fact, my birth mother. She'd returned from Mallorca pregnant and, on learning her sister and brother-in-law were unable to conceive, allowed them to raise me as their own. Zeller was single and a successful travel writer who enjoyed her independence. On reflection, she wouldn't have enjoyed motherhood, but she was a terrific aunt. However, learning the truth was a terrible shock.'

Carlos leaned across and rested his hand on my arm.

'You sure you're okay talking about all this?'

I coughed away a lump in my throat.

'Yes, I have to be. And it is relevant, as you'll hear.' I picked up my glass and took another sip. My stomach was rumbling, but this wasn't a story to be continued between bites of baguette.

'At about the same time, my boss at the radio station told me he was moving me to the breakfast show – which, for various reasons, I didn't want to do. I resigned, which gave me an opportunity to come to Mallorca. I wanted to get to know Deià, where Zeller wrote her book.' I paused for a little more cava. 'But I was also curious about my biological father. Zeller never told anyone who he was. I had an overwhelming need to find out his identity, but not to reveal myself as his daughter.'

'And did you also tell El Capitán that Zeller was a friend?'

'Yes, but I didn't expect him to know her, to be honest. It turned out that he did. Very well, in fact.'

I paused, unsure what to say next. Carlos gave me the perfect excuse to take a break.

'Hey, I missed lunch today, so do you mind if I start this?' He peeled back the aluminium foil, removed the baguette, and took a bite, chewing methodically and gazing into the distance.

I opened my own parcel and nibbled the end of the filled roll. It was delicious and made me realise how hungry I was. When we'd both swallowed, and Carlos had topped up our cava, I launched back into my story.

'There is no simple way to tell you this, Carlos – otherwise I'd have done it earlier. When I should have.' I paused. 'But everything your father told me suggested he's also *my* father.' I stopped to let that nugget of news sink in.

'*What?* My dad is *your* father too?' His eyes were wide, and his face had drained of colour. Who knew a lifelong Mediterranean tan could disappear like that? 'Which would make us—'

'Half-siblings, yes. I just couldn't face you with that discovery. Not after … what we'd done. It was easiest to disappear from your life, with no explanation.'

'But why do you believe we have the same father?'

'You had to be there to hear everything El Capitán told me.' I blew out my cheeks and sighed. 'To be honest, I've tried to block all his answers from my mind, because of what it meant for us.'

'Now I think I understand why you left the island in a hurry.'

'Only I didn't,' I said. 'I'd actually booked a two-week holiday, with the second week in Deià. I left Palma and went to the mountains a few days earlier than planned. I thought I'd be able to forget everything that happened here once I was back at home and looking for a new radio job.'

Carlos was silent and leaned forward on his chair, his elbows on his knees, and head in his hands. Had I offended him with my last words?

'I really liked El Capitán,' I said. 'If it hadn't been for the fact that you're his son, I'd have been delighted he was my biological father.'

'But where does the cat refuge come into this story?'

Starting with the storm, when I first met Marylou, I explained the subsequent timeline of events. I was almost hoarse by the time I finished.

We sat in silence for a few moments and then Carlos stood up, took the rest of the foil-wrapped baguette from my hand, and put it back in the basket. He pulled me out of the chair by my hands and looked at me with watery eyes, before wrapping me close to his chest and hugging me tight. I could hear his heart thumping fast, no doubt because of the shocking news I'd given him.

'I don't know what to say, Laura, except I'm sorry you've had such a tough time.'

What I wanted more than anything at that moment was a long and loving kiss from this gorgeous man. But that was impossible because of what we both knew. From now on, I had to learn to love him as a half-brother.

CHAPTER FORTY-FOUR

Carlos released me from his arms and looked me in the eyes.

'I think you should tell Dad the full story.' He took both my hands in his and squeezed gently. 'It may thrill him to know he has a daughter. He used to wish I had a brother or sister.'

'Did he?' It appeared Carlos had already accepted my new role in his life, which gave me mixed feelings.

'Yeah, often. Look, why don't I arrange for us both to see him tomorrow evening? I'll be with you for moral support when you tell him.'

I knew I'd feel better once the truth was out, although I had doubts El Capitán would be filled with paternal joy to discover, after such a long time, he had a daughter.

'Okay, if you think it's a good idea, I'll do it. I hope he has a healthy heart – could be a bit of a shock.'

'He's as strong as an ox. No worries there.' He smiled at me and my insides did a cartwheel that wasn't an appropriate response to a half-brother.

'Now, changing the subject, satisfy my curiosity, Laura,' he said. 'That little building at the front, was it once a roadside eatery? I'm sure I came here as a child but can't recall its name.'

'It was. And it could become Mallorca's first cat café, if Marylou likes the idea. It'd be a way to cover the running costs of the refuge.'

I offered to show him inside and jangled the bunch of keys, and we crunched across the gravel together. I hadn't been back into the building since Billy and I first saw it, and it looked just as filthy as I remembered. Grime covered everything from the windows to the worktop in the kitchen.

'They must have done a lot of frying in here,' Carlos said, wrinkling his nose. The smell was an ancient mix of stale oil, nicotine, and damp. I couldn't imagine sitting in this space, drinking a coffee or tea, and enjoying a brownie or slice of carrot cake.

'Hmm. I'd forgotten how bad it was in here. Even an army of volunteers would fail to get this in a decent state before Marylou's back. And who'd volunteer for a job as horrible as this?'

Carlos did as Billy had done and ran a finger across the bar counter. He shook his head and grimaced as he showed me his filthy fingertip.

'What about using a specialist cleaning company? You said you'd had a donation, and after a professional clean it'd be only a matter of painting.'

So far, I'd spent less than half of Rupert's money. If Marylou decided to open the place again for business, the local equivalent of an environmental health inspector would come calling. Carlos's suggestion was what my dad would call 'a no-brainer'.

'That's a brilliant idea.' My enthusiasm for the cat

café project went up a few notches. 'D'you know any companies I could contact?'

'Leave it with me. I'll sort something out. And once it's cleaned, I'm sure I could give you a hand with the painting. We could even rope my dad in to help.'

I stopped myself from correcting this to 'our dad'. Perhaps Carlos hadn't accepted the situation after all.

SUNDAY MORNING WAS cloudy and cooler, which was a relief. Mike was already waiting in his car outside the locked gates when I arrived, so I wouldn't be the only one wielding a paintbrush that day.

'We may have a storm later.' He looked up as I unlocked the front door of the house.

As likely as his forecast might be, the weather hadn't found a place on my list of the day's worries. All I could think about was Carlos taking me that evening to his – our – father's apartment. I'd be needing a stiff drink in advance of that encounter.

'Thank you for coming again today, Mike. I'm so grateful to you.'

'It's a pleasure. Silvia told me she'd be back this morning, so we'll be three at least.' Mike picked up one of the dust sheets and asked where I wanted to start the painting in the living room. We decided on the kitchen corner, where he draped the cloth across the worktops and the cooker.

'Silvia's lovely, isn't she?' I tried to sound casual. 'She's been so much help to me. I feel like she's become a good friend.'

'She likes you too,' Mike said. 'Thinks you've been a

real trooper. And, yes, she is rather special.' I noticed his face had turned pink. *Aw, sweet.*

Over the next half hour, a trickle of volunteers arrived. They included Silvia and three who'd also helped the previous day. Carlos came too, wearing a hideous Hawaiian-style shirt and surfer shorts.

'Pass my sunglasses!' I held up a hand, grinning and pretending to shield my eyes from the lurid shirt. He'd worn nothing like that in the past, and I hoped this wasn't normal attire for him.

'Good morning to you too, Laura.' Carlos beamed. 'Whaddya think?' He twirled on the spot and we all laughed. Somehow I'd make sure the revolting shirt received a few 'accidental' splashes of white paint so it was never seen in public again.

'Bought it for a fancy-dress party last summer, and it's been in my wardrobe ever since. Ideal for a day of painting, I thought.' He'd made up for his garish shirt by bringing his camera case.

'Thought I'd take some shots of the work in progress. Marylou may like to have them.'

His thoughtfulness stoked a warm glow in my heart, and I gave him a sisterly embrace.

'By the way,' he said, 'I spoke to someone last night who owns a cleaning company in Inca. He'll call by sometime this morning to look at the job and give you a price.'

I'd had so much support for this project, and if all went to plan, Marylou's new refuge would be ready for her return. I hoped it would compensate for the loss of her original premises.

≈

By two o'clock that Sunday, fresh white paint covered every wall in the house. As a team, we'd created a place I'd have been happy to move into myself. It would be a much more comfortable home for Marylou than Otto's old place.

As promised, Reg arrived with his brush cutter and tackled the once-lawned area. He told me he and Rob were making excellent progress with the new cat enclosures and they were on target to install on Wednesday, as promised.

The man from the cleaning company arrived at around lunchtime. As Carlos and I took him over to the former restaurant, I hoped he'd already eaten; if not, what he was about to see would kill off his appetite for sure.

'I'm afraid it's filthy,' I said as the man cast his eye around the eating area and wrote a few notes on a small pad he'd brought with him. 'Kitchen's through here, and I warn you, it's even worse.'

The man shrugged.

'I've seen worse than this in functioning restaurant kitchens,' he said. 'They usually call us in when they've been done for hygiene offences.'

My jaw dropped. If I were living on the island, I'd have been pressing him for those places' names so I could avoid them.

'Can I WhatsApp you a price by tomorrow morning? If it's acceptable, my team will be here Wednesday and get the job done in a day.'

Wednesday promised to be a busy day.

～

SUNDAY WAS ANOTHER SUCCESSFUL DAY. After everyone had left, I walked around the house, inspecting the results of the volunteers' huge efforts. It was amazing what could be achieved in two days.

Satisfied that the work to the house was now complete, I moved the remaining pots of paint and decorating materials to the shed outside. I locked up the property and went back to what had been my temporary home for what felt like months.

I had a few hours before I was meeting Carlos again, in a bar near his – our – father's apartment in Palma. Would I ever get used to El Capitán being my biological father? And would I still call him Capitán? Or Dad Number Two?

After feeding the cats, I lingered in the old enclosures for a while, making a fuss of the ones who enjoyed receiving head strokes and tummy rubs. I'd become fond of most of them and knew I'd miss my cat duties. Apart from cleaning the litter trays, I thought, as I started the least enjoyable of the daily tasks.

Work finished, I showered and washed my hair, then selected my clothes for the evening. I didn't need to leave for Palma for another hour, so I set an alarm on my phone and fell onto the bed in my underwear for a much-needed snooze. It had been an exhausting weekend, but the toughest part was yet to come.

CHAPTER FORTY-FIVE

'You look lovely,' Carlos said when I arrived at the bar where we'd arranged to meet on Palma's Paseo Marítimo. He was sitting at a table on the pavement terrace, watching me as I approached. The expression on his face wasn't appropriate for a man to give his half-sister. Perhaps he still had to get used to the fact we were related?

I wore the dress I'd worn for that fateful evening with Andy, being short of other smart options with me in Mallorca. It felt a little looser, and although Marylou had no bathroom scales (she didn't need to), I could tell I'd lost several pounds in weight. Swapping my old sedentary radio lifestyle for a more active one looking after the cats had brought some benefits.

I ordered a gin and tonic from the waitress, who appeared seconds after my arrival. Dutch courage. *Would we have time for two?*

On the first occasion we'd travelled up to El Capitán's apartment, Carlos and I kissed. And what a kiss, I remembered, blushing. This time he only gave my hand a reassuring squeeze as the lift shuddered to a halt.

'It'll be fine, you'll see,' he said as we walked along the corridor to the apartment. He pulled a bunch of keys from his pocket and found the correct one.

As the door swung open, he called out to announce our arrival.

'Through here, on the terrace,' I heard his father's booming, Scottish-accented voice reply.

'Well, hello again, Laura,' he said, standing up and stepping forward to kiss me on each cheek. 'I didn't expect to see you again, so this is a genuine pleasure.'

You may change your mind when you hear what I have to say. He gestured to the two other chairs and Carlos and I sat down.

'Drink? I've a rather fine bottle of Mallorcan Sauvignon Blanc that should be chilled to perfection by now.' Three clean glasses were already on the table.

He didn't wait for an answer but disappeared inside. Carlos and I sat in silence, appreciating the golden glow of the evening sunshine. The expected storm hadn't happened; after five o'clock the sun came out and chased away most of the clouds. It was beautiful weather for what I was sure would be an evening none of us would ever forget.

'Here ye go.' El Capitán came back onto the terrace, holding a corkscrew and ice bucket containing the wine bottle. He opened the bottle with consummate ease, poured the wine, and we all clinked glasses together.

'To your good health,' he said, making eye contact with me. We sipped and expressed our appreciation of the delicious wine. Looking at the label, I wondered if I could find it for sale in England. A few bottles would doubtless fit into my case for the journey home.

'You're so much like her, you know.' El Capitán spoke in a low voice, and I barely heard what he said. He was smiling. 'I must admit I didn't notice the similarity when you were here before. And you did say you were a friend of Zeller's, so ...'

He stood up and went through the French doors into the apartment.

I glanced at Carlos, who shrugged his shoulders and whispered, 'Promise, I said nothing to him.'

The sound of a drawer opening and closing came from indoors and then El Capitán returned, carrying a fat brown envelope. He sat down and extracted a pile of black and white photographs.

'I was sorting out photos last week and came across these.'

He flicked through and pulled a few out, which he placed on the table between us.

'That's Zeller, on the beach at Cala Deià.' He pointed to the middle photo.

'Oh!' I leaned forward for a closer look.

'You *can* pick it up, Laura,' he said, smiling.

I did just that. Zeller was wearing a white sundress, wide-brimmed straw hat, and a radiant smile. Her eyes were sparkling, and she appeared carefree.

Looking at her as a young woman, I could see the strong resemblance between us. People told me I looked a lot like Mum – but that also meant I looked like her sister; I knew they'd often been mistaken for twins when they were younger.

'She looks so happy.' I placed the picture back on the table.

'Ay, it was a special day. Zeller had finished the first

draft of her book and we celebrated with a picnic lunch by the sea.'

He smiled again, appearing to reflect on the day. He must have loved her very much. From her smile, it was obvious she adored him ... but not enough to make a life with him.

'You're Zeller's daughter, aren't you?'

'Yes, I am.' I bowed my head in embarrassment. 'And I'm sorry I couldn't bring myself to tell you the truth.' I took a deep breath, met his gaze, and the words flowed.

'Back then, Mum had found out she could never conceive, and she and Dad were desperate for a family. When Zeller came home from Mallorca pregnant, they made an agreement: Zeller would give her baby – me – to Mum and Dad to raise as their own. They registered the birth, and my birth certificate has their names on it as my parents. There were conditions, of course. Zeller bought the house behind ours, so she played a big part in my life. She was the best aunt I could have wished for.'

I paused for another sip of wine, and not just because I was enjoying the taste.

'Not long after her funeral, Mum and Dad told me the entire story. It was an enormous shock, and I was furious they'd kept such a huge secret for so long. It took me a while to accept it was Zeller's wish to keep the truth from me until either she or Mum died.'

I finished the last mouthful of wine, and without a word, El Capitán topped up my glass.

'Coming to Mallorca was a big step for me – I've never been keen on foreign travel. But my parents gave me a letter Zeller had written on her sixtieth birthday for me to read after her death. She wanted me to come to

Mallorca and get to know Deià. Work circumstances made it possible.'

'That's quite a story.' He reached for his glass of wine. 'And did anyone tell you about your biological father?'

'No. Mum and Dad know nothing about him, and in Zeller's letter ...' I hesitated. She had written that my biological father wasn't 'the one', and I couldn't upset this kind man by telling him that. 'All she said was my father was someone in Deià.'

'Did you intend to find him here?' He asked in a soft voice.

'Well. Yes – and no. I only wanted to know who he was. I didn't plan to contact him in case he wasn't even aware she was pregnant. That would have been a massive shock.'

El Capitán leaned across the small table as though about to share a secret.

'I can assure you he knew. It wouldn't have been a shock if you'd been able to tell him.'

He'd led me to the perfect moment.

'Thank you, that's reassuring,' I said. 'I liked you that first time we met, and although I had mixed feelings – because it complicated things with Carlos – I wasn't disappointed to find out you're my biological father.'

For a moment, the man looked stunned, then he slapped his thighs with his meaty hands and rocked with laughter in his chair. That wasn't the reaction I expected. I turned to Carlos, who shrugged his shoulders in response to my quizzical look.

'My dear lass,' El Capitán said when he'd recovered enough to speak. He wiped tears from his cheeks with the back of his hands. 'I'm not your father. Zeller and I were never … as intimate as that, I'm sad to say. Only ever a chaste kiss and the occasional hug for us.'

My hands trembled in my lap. Could this be true?

'Whatever made you think it was me?'

I thought back to my last visit to the apartment and our conversation about Zeller.

'You were so upset about her death,' I said, remembering things I'd been trying to block from my memory. 'And you mentioned you'd asked her to marry you when she told you she was pregnant.'

'Och. The old two-and-two-makes-five. I think I also said I loved Zeller but never told her. Maybe I can see why you might have come to that conclusion.'

Was I floating up out of the chair? I looked across at Carlos, who grinned at me and grabbed my hand before joining the conversation for the first time.

'Dad, any chilled cava in the fridge?'

'Does the Clyde run through Glasgow? And bring the decent crystal glasses.'

Carlos laughed and hurried off to the kitchen. I turned to his father and asked the obvious question.

'Well, if you're not my biological father, do you know who is? And is he still in Deià?

'Ferdie Collins,' he said. Then he told me all about the man who had captured Zeller's heart … at least for a while.

CHAPTER FORTY-SIX

W hen I opened my eyes at six o'clock the next morning, I couldn't think where I was. The ceiling above me was white and without beams. As I shifted in the bed, I felt a hand reach across and stroke my arm. Ah yes, I'd spent the night with Carlos in his apartment in Palma. We'd been celebrating – in the most enjoyable way possible – the fact we weren't half-siblings after all.

'Morning, Laura,' he said in a muffled voice.

'Good morning, Carlos.' I rolled over and kissed the tip of his nose.

'You're not getting away with that poor excuse for a kiss.' He laughed, then gave me the kiss of my life.

I ARRIVED BACK at Marylou's in time to look after my refuge duties. *How many litter trays have I cleaned since I've been here?* Some were tatty and needed replacing. I was going to replace all of them with new ones and buy a bulk supply of cat food from Silvia's practice.

After finishing feeding, cleaning, and fussing the cats, I went indoors for my own breakfast. I was ravenous after my night with Carlos and boiled two eggs instead of having my usual yogurt and muesli combo.

While they cooked in the bubbling water, I switched on my laptop. I was expecting an estimate for the restaurant cleaning.

Dan's message was the first email I read; the words 'BIG NEWS' in the subject line caught my eye. Had he found a new job? No, but Barry had – or maybe not. Whatever, he was no longer station manager at Bard FM. Dan explained there had been some irregularity regarding advertising revenue; he would give me the 'gory details' when I returned to Stratford. Meanwhile, a woman called Sarah Owen had succeeded him and, to quote Dan, was 'a fantastic manager'.

'Good riddance, Barry,' I said aloud, punching the air with delight for all my friends at the station. Nobody at Bard FM would miss the toxic man-at-the-top, except, possibly, Odette. I tapped out a quick reply, thanking Dan for the brilliant news. I couldn't wait to catch up with him and find out more.

As I ATE my eggs with some toast, I reflected on the best weekend I'd had since arriving in Mallorca. But in a few days' time, I'd have to explain to Marylou what had happened in her absence. Although I was thrilled about the new refuge, my stomach churned and made me queasy every time I thought about facing her.

My phone's upbeat ringtone broke into my worries just as I swallowed my last mouthful of toast.

'*Hola*, Silvia.' I saw her name on the screen. 'Thank you – and Tomeu – so much for all your help at the weekend.'

'A pleasure,' she said. 'I had fun, and it was a pleasant change from sticking thermometers up dogs' bottoms.'

Hmm, you sound very jolly this morning.

'Anyway,' she continued, 'I was ringing to suggest I come with you to the airport on Friday. Moral support.'

Was this woman a veritable saint?

'Silvia, if you have time, I'd love that. I was just sitting here dreading the prospect of telling her she's lost her home—'

'And gained a new – and much better – one,' she reminded me. But would Marylou see it that way? If she were as close to Otto as he'd suggested, how would she feel about the increased distance between them?

'I'll keep the afternoon free of appointments and leave an alternative number for urgent cases,' Silvia said.

She also offered to arrive early to check the cats ahead of their move. The refuge owed her so much thanks and I hoped Marylou would still use her practice in the future.

I had more packing to do. Eviction Day was Monday, which meant Marylou would have the weekend to pack her clothes and other personal items from her room. It wouldn't take long; she had few possessions and lived a simple life. Apart from the kitchen clock and branded kitchen calendar – a gift from a local greengrocer's – the walls were bare. The pristine white walls of her future home could use some pictures. I added a note on the pad that was my constant companion.

While I waited for the kettle to boil for my coffee break, I checked my emails again. The quote for cleaning the former restaurant had arrived. I gulped at the figure on the bottom line but reminded myself what a vile job it would be. Definitely one for the professionals, so I emailed straight back to accept the quote.

It was courtesy of Rupert that I could do that, and it prompted me to add another reminder to my notepad: introduce Marylou to Rupert. I hoped she'd invite him over to see what his generosity had made possible. Should she have an official opening party and invite the generous benefactor to cut a ribbon?

'No, Laura,' I said aloud to myself and to Calvin who, as usual, was dozing on his ratty old armchair. 'That'll be up to Marylou.' I had to distance myself from the project and start thinking about my own future.

I woke at five thirty on Wednesday morning, unable to get back to sleep thanks to my constant mental reviewing of the day's agenda.

My time caring for the cats would soon be over. By the following week, Carlos and I would be staying for a few days in Deià, getting to know each better at La Resi. I envisaged cocktails on the terrace at sunset, romantic candlelit dinners overlooking the village, and walks up to the Mirador (I'd be fitter this time). Bliss was within my grasp.

We'd already planned to have lunch down at Cala Deià. And he was going to show me the house where Ferdie Collins lived until recently. El Capitán had drawn us a map also showing the precise location of the small cottage Zeller rented during her stay, so we'd check that out too.

Being on Mallorca had been an enlightening experience for me. Who'd have believed what I could achieve? Certainly not me. Overall, my time on the island had been far more enjoyable than I'd expected. Of course, the most surprising thing to happen was finding Carlos. I'd have to tell Mum and Dad about Andy when I was back, but when they heard about my new boyfriend – and my feelings for him – I was sure they'd be happy for me.

It was feasible that Carlos and I could have a future together, even though almost a thousand miles separated our homes. One volunteer who'd helped decorate Marylou's new home on Sunday told me she lived in Palma with her children, and her husband commuted to London for work every Monday morning, returning to Mallorca on Friday evenings.

I imagined us taking turns to fly to visit the other for regular weekends together. Working in Bristol would be ideal, with its vibrant city life and a convenient international airport.

A few evenings back, I'd sat down to review my financial situation. Although I had no salary coming in, I had a small amount of savings and the money Zeller left me. If I was careful, I could afford my mortgage payments and other bills for a few months, if necessary.

After giving a lot of thought to Zeller's house, I'd concluded I wasn't going to live there. It was too large for my taste, and besides, I didn't think it would be healthy to live so close to my parents. I was going to put the house on the market, but wasn't looking forward to breaking that news to them.

My experiences in Mallorca had shown me I was

more resourceful than I'd thought. It was time I stopped relying on Dad to solve every domestic problem or car-maintenance issue and became more independent.

With so much rolling around in my head, sleep wouldn't return. I threw off the sheet, got up, and pulled on my shorts and T-shirt. Cats first, then I'd prepare myself for another action-packed session at Finca Es Refugi.

After my sojourn in Mallorca was over, I'd miss tending to the cats; they were the focus of my daily life on the island. Most of them would allow me to pick them up for a cuddle, and I understood why Marylou felt contented here in the refuge. As I placed adorable Harry down on the ground after our morning smooch, I remembered I had to ask Silvia about the practicalities of taking him to the UK with me. Andy's cat allergy was no longer a barrier to my adoption plans.

By the end of that day, the refuge was fit for Marylou and the cats to move into.

The cleaning company had performed a miracle in the former restaurant; every surface, horizontal and vertical, gleamed as though never used before. If Marylou pursued the cat café idea, there was still enough of Rupert's donation to invest in some basic tables and chairs, and modules for the cats to climb and sleep on, like the ones I'd seen in Valencia. I'd send my photos of the place to her for inspiration.

The new enclosures seemed sturdy and practical. Reg and Rob had taken care to ensure they were visible from the window at the kitchen end of the house.

After everyone had completed their jobs and left, I

padlocked the gates and made the short journey to a vast store selling everything a pampered pet would demand if it could talk. Intending to buy only twenty replacement litter trays, I also added a selection of cat toys and half-a-dozen scratching posts to my shopping trolley.

I drove back to the new refuge to put all my purchases in the corner of the kitchen, ready for Mary-lou's arrival. She'd have the pleasure of adding the new items to the enclosures before she introduced the cats to their new home.

One final solo tour of the house reminded me of the massive transformation since Billy and I first visited. Certain he'd be keen to see them, I took some photos with my phone. I owed him an email and would send the most impressive images with it.

My phone rang just as I'd locked the finca gates for the final time. My heart did a somersault of elation when I saw Carlos's name on the screen.

'Hi Laura, how's it all gone?'

'Very well. You wouldn't recognise the restaurant after those guys blitzed it,' I said. 'Everything's finished now and I'm locking up to go back and feed the hungry horde their dinners.'

He laughed. 'Speaking of dinner, would you like to come out tonight? I thought we'd go the windmill restaurant I wanted to take you to before.'

I'd planned to attend to the cats, have a salad supper, and a long, cool shower before an early night. But the opportunity to spend more time with Carlos was too tempting.

'Thank you, I'd love to.'

'Great! The restaurant's not far from Santa Maria. Send me a location pin when you're back, and I'll pick you up. When'd be good for you?'

We agreed a time and he said he'd book a table. And that he was looking forward to seeing me again. I sang along to the music on Britannia FM for the entire journey back to Marylou's.

'IN MY HUMBLE OPINION, Marylou will love her new home after living here,' Carlos said, after he'd had the brief tour of the old house. 'This is pretty grim, Laura.'

'An estate agent would say it has "rustic charm and character".' I laughed. 'It's been okay for a few weeks, but I wouldn't want to live here permanently. Imagine what it's like in winter.'

When we went outside and into the enclosures, I discovered Carlos was a cat lover. Could this man be any better?

'We had a ginger one called Rufus when I was a boy, but when he died of old age, we didn't get another.' He had a note of sadness in his voice. 'I should think about adopting one.'

He bent down to stroke Harry and my heart quickened to see he'd chosen my favourite. 'This one's cute.' He looked around. 'Some great-looking cats here. How about I take some photos? Marylou could use them to decorate the walls in the new place.'

I'd been wondering what we could do to improve the ambience, and framed photos of cats would be perfect. Carlos said he'd come over the next day with his camera.

'But I'll need your help to get some decent shots.'

No problem for me. Everything was ready at the new refuge, and I had only a few minor jobs to do at the old place before Marylou came home.

He looked at his wristwatch.

'Hey, we'd better leave now to get there for our table.'

I secured the cats' enclosures and ran indoors to collect my handbag and keys, then we set off in Carlos's car. How exciting to be eating in a windmill, I thought. But much more exciting was the prospect of another evening with Carlos.

CHAPTER FORTY-SEVEN

Everything about our dinner was superb: romantic setting, attentive but discreet service, and impeccable food. The company? Sublime. We chatted non-stop throughout each course, sharing stories from our past and hopes for our future.

'I'm going to miss you when you go back.' Carlos put down his coffee cup.

'I'll miss you too,' I said. 'But we could see each other some weekends. The flight's only a couple of hours and fares can be quite cheap if you book ahead.'

'You checked already?'

My face flushed. 'Er, yes. Just out of curiosity, you understand.'

He leaned across the table and squeezed my hand.

'Did anyone ever tell you I flew over to look for you in Stratford?'

'My former producer rang me. You spoke to him.' *Is it me or is it hot in here?* 'I'm sorry you went to the expense and trouble, when I was still here on the island.'

'It's okay. At least I can now say I've been to

England. And doing that trip made me realise something important.' He removed his napkin from his lap and put it on the table. 'You once told me you didn't like foreign travel, but if you've checked flights, something must have changed your mind.' He winked at me.

'The lovely people here have won me over.' One wink returned. 'I admit I didn't expect to like Mallorca as much as I do. Almost everyone I've met has been kind and hospitable, and the scenery is beautiful and so diverse. I can understand why Zeller stayed here longer than she intended to.'

Carlos raised his hand and mimed signing the bill to the maître d'.

'Sorry, but I have an early shoot tomorrow in Port Adriano – stonking superyacht for sale – so I hope it's okay if we head off. Perhaps I could come over late afternoon to take some photos of the cats?'

'That'd be great. I'll be there all day.'

He paid the bill and we strolled out, hand in hand, to the car park. Before he started the engine, he turned to face me.

'I wish you weren't going back to the UK.' He took my hand in his. 'I've had plenty of girlfriends but never said I loved any of them … but that's about to change.' He leaned over and kissed me. The thrilling kiss took my breath away and made my heart pound.

Who needed words after a kiss like that? He said them anyway. Once I was able to breathe again, I replied.

'That's a coincidence because I love you too.' But England was calling me. 'I have a potential new job in Bristol and need to find a home there. And I'm putting Zeller's house on the market too, so I have things I need to do back at home.' I was looking forward to my new job but not to all the upheaval involved. And having heard Carlos say the Three Little Words, my desire to return home was waning.

'Maybe I could delay my departure by another week, once we've left La Resi,' I said, 'if it'd be okay to stay at yours?'

He leaned across and pulled me into a big hug, and despite the handbrake sticking into my thigh, I smiled as I snuggled against his warm chest. How lucky was I?

'Of course. And that'll give me a week to persuade you to move to Mallorca for good.'

'And me a chance to see if you leave the lid off the toothpaste or the loo seat up.'

We both laughed, although I knew he was being serious. Was I open to changing my mind about going home? Possibly … probably … but I wasn't going to commit myself yet; I was looking forward to him flexing his powers of persuasion.

CARLOS STOPPED the car outside the door of Marylou's house but didn't come in.

'I really do have to get up at a crazy hour tomorrow.' He gave me a sweet goodnight kiss before I got out of the car. I stood waving, until the dark night swallowed the rear lights of his vehicle and only the sound of the cicadas broke the silence of the rural night.

When I opened the door, Calvin jumped off his armchair and came to greet me. He and I were now friends, and I bent down to stroke him. He purred like a generator then swaggered over to his empty food bowl.

'More dinner? So, this is cupboard love, literally,' I said, smiling. I was looking forward to having more conversations with humans once Marylou was back to take over.

The evening had been perfect, I reflected as I made myself a cup of chamomile tea before bed. Out of habit, I switched on my laptop to check my emails. Mum had sent news of a neighbour who'd won the lottery and spent all the money on crazy-paving her entire front garden. A short email from Billy told me he had a contract to voice a series of building society commercials; things were also going well with Araceli. The third new email piqued my curiosity. What I read had the potential to change any plans I was considering.

Anyone who walked into Marylou's house would be able to tell she was moving out. I'd packed everything in the living room and kitchen that wasn't likely to be used before Monday. Labelled cardboard boxes lined one wall.

Calvin was skittish, and his instincts must have told him something was afoot. When I sat on the sofa to drink a cup of tea, he jumped onto my lap and dropped into a furry comma-shaped curl.

'Your mum's back tomorrow.' I stroked him. Would he settle into his new home? Yes, he'd be at home wherever his armchair lived.

That Thursday, I couldn't face food, knowing Marylou would arrive at Palma airport the next day, thrilled to be back on the island. What I had to tell her would ruin her happy homecoming. But how should I broach the news?

'Guess what happened while you were away'? *No, not helpful, Laura.* I'd have to tell her everything in detail, for her to understand. If she'd been in some sort of relationship with Otto, she was likely to break it off when I told her about his behaviour. I didn't know Marylou well, but was certain he wasn't good enough for her. I shuddered, remembering the incident that had prompted all this upheaval.

And then there was that email, adding to my confused state.

CHAPTER FORTY-EIGHT

Instead of having breakfast that morning, I read the email again. It was from Sarah Owen, the new station manager at Bard FM. The friendly tone of her message warmed me to her … and not only because she'd offered me my old job back, with a substantial pay rise.

I read that Odette had handed in her notice and would soon be playing a nurse in a popular TV series. Sarah said it was fortuitous timing, as too many listeners had complained about her afternoon show and my disappearance from the airwaves. I couldn't help but smile to read that.

Going back to Bard FM would solve my work dilemma and seemed sensible as the Bristol job was still not confirmed. If I stayed in Stratford, I wouldn't have to search for a new home either. Working with Dan again would be preferable to getting used to someone different, and I'd be within reasonable driving distance for evenings out with Billy in Oxford.

Sarah told me management had undervalued me in

the past, and the generous pay rise would enable me to come to Mallorca on a regular basis, cheap flights permitting, to see Carlos. And Birmingham Airport was close enough.

I looked at the clock and decided it wasn't too early to phone Dan.

'Morning, Laura,' he said, as though he'd been expecting my call. 'Get the email from Sarah, did you?'

'You know, then?' It sounded as though Sarah was a communicator, which would be a welcome change. 'She sounds lovely, and made a convincing case for me to come back.'

'She told me you'd get a pay rise. I've had one, so I'm very happy. Sarah's doing a lot to make herself popular. We even have top-notch new headphones in the studios.'

'What's she like to work with?'

'So far, awesome. I see no reason to think she'll change. She's passionate about radio and its role in the community.' Dan paused. 'If I were you, I'd give serious consideration to her offer, rather than taking a chance on a new station that may not work out.'

His suggestion made sense. My head was swimming with possibilities. Once Marylou was back and installed at the new refuge, I would decide my future direction.

CARLOS and I had fun later that afternoon, taking photos of the cats and kittens who stayed still long enough to be captured on camera. We discovered why people say 'never work with children or animals', but he succeeded in shooting ten promising images. And sustained only a few scratches.

He was busy because he was taking a few days off for

our Deià trip, but promised he'd get some framed prints to Marylou as soon as work permitted.

'You need to eat something more substantial,' Carlos said when I offered to make us each a sandwich. Having eaten nothing all day, I was light-headed. But I wasn't the only hungry one; his stomach gave a loud rumble, which made us both laugh. We went to Luigi's in Santa Maria for an early one-course supper.

As we munched our way through a cartwheel-sized pizza, we reviewed everything still outstanding. Carlos had arranged for a friend with a van to do Marylou's removal job at a much-reduced price. He'd also arranged for another friend to come with his minibus to transport the cats. They'd be travelling in individual carrying cases on loan from Silvia and a few of her vet friends, which we'd secure with the vehicle's seatbelts. I'd ticked off pretty much everything on my to-do list, and only the prospect of facing Marylou now gave me a sense of dread.

'I could come with you tomorrow afternoon, if it helps,' Carlos said as we shared a tiramisu, despite our earlier one-course-only intention.

'Thank you, but you've already given a lot of your time to this project. Silvia's coming with me and she knows Marylou well, so that may make it easier.'

'I'm pleased you'll have some support,' he said. 'I'm off to Ibiza on Saturday morning to do a shoot for a new restaurant's website, then I'm staying the rest of the weekend with an old schoolfriend who owns a windsurf school. I'll be back Monday night, though.'

As PROMISED, Silvia arrived well before we had to leave for the airport. She'd brought her vet's bag and set about checking each cat and kitten to ensure they were healthy enough to endure what would be a few stressful hours.

'You've done an excellent job looking after them, Laura,' she said. 'Look at how confident Bambi is now. He used to be such a nervous little cat.' The silver tabby was perched on his back legs like a meerkat, batting with a front paw at the tail dangling from the cat on a ledge above him.

'We were always a dog family, so I didn't have any experience of cats … but I'm a big fan now. They're so independent, and each has its own character. I'm really going to miss them.'

Silvia smiled. 'You should find a sanctuary when you go home and adopt a cat of your own. You'd make a good cat mum.' I still had my heart set on adopting Harry but had to finalise my life plans first. The journey back to England would be traumatic enough for him, without a further move to Bristol if I decided to go there.

When the veterinary examinations were finished, we went indoors for a cold drink before we departed. Silvia volunteered to drive us, perhaps sensing my focus would be somewhere other than on the road ahead.

PALMA'S AIRPORT was as busy as you'd expect for the peak holiday season. Streams of people emerged from the baggage reclaim area every time the automatic doors opened, and Silvia and I craned our necks, searching for Marylou. We commented – trying not to laugh – on the unusual outfits some younger holidaymakers wore. It looked like being a busy weekend for the hen-and-stag-party business.

After what seemed an age, Silvia raised her arm and waved frantically, jumping up and down to catch Marylou's attention.

'There she is!'

The American saw us and waved back, quickening her pace until she arrived, dragging two cases behind her. She stood the cases upright and hugged first Silvia, then me.

'You cannot imagine how great it is to be back,' she drawled. Silvia and I exchanged a fleeting glance. Marylou glanced at her wristwatch. 'Oh, no wonder I'm so hungry. My body clock is right out of kilter.'

'We could have something to eat before we go back,' Silvia said, and I sighed with relief when Marylou accepted the suggestion. I'd be able to explain the entire situation over something to eat, and we could visit the new refuge before we took her home. I'd brought the keys with me, just in case. My prayer – yes, I'd been on my knees that morning – was that presenting both problem and solution would reduce the initial shock.

Silvia knew a decent seafront café only ten minutes' drive from the airport, and during the short journey there, Marylou told us a little about her time in Florida with her mum, before changing the subject.

'And how are the cats, Laura?'

CHAPTER FORTY-NINE

'They're very well,' I said, smiling. 'And I'm sure Calvin's sixth sense told him you were coming home soon.'

Silvia chipped in: 'Wait until you see Bambi – he's become such a confident little cat. And definitely the clown of them all.'

'I'm longing to be in my own place again,' Marylou said. *Oh, no.*

The café served healthy food, and we all ordered salads and freshly squeezed juices. While we waited for the made-to-order dishes to arrive, I told her I had some news.

'I emailed you about it a few times and tried to phone, but, of course, because of the theft, you didn't get the information.'

Marylou frowned but said nothing.

'I hate telling you this, because I know you had some sort of relationship with Otto—'

'Say what?' Marylou leaned forward in her chair.

'Er, well, he told me you and he … Anyway, he came

round one day with a bowl of tomatoes from his garden, which would have been kind if he hadn't also assaulted me. He wanted me to have sex with him, implying I must be gagging for it because I was a single woman. He was aggressive when I refused and stormed out. I'd noticed alcohol on his breath and thought he'd forget what happened. But a few days later, he delivered an eviction order prepared by a lawyer.'

Marylou's face drained of colour. Mine probably matched it. *Please don't faint!* Silvia reached across the table and squeezed her hand.

'It sounds awful, I know, but Laura has sorted everything out.' Her gentle tone of voice was that of a vet talking to the owner of a terminally ill pet.

'Yes, it's quite a saga, and I'll give you all the details later,' I said, anxious about the frozen expression on the American's face. 'What you need to know is you have affordable new refuge premises and a home ready to move into. And I'm sorry I had to tell you your boyfriend is such a shit.'

Marylou's head dropped towards her chest, and her shoulders shook. I delved into my bag to find a clean tissue for the inevitable tears and almost fell off my chair when she suddenly threw back her head and roared with laughter.

'Where the hell did you get the idea that Otto was my boyfriend?'

I told her what her German landlord had said.

'Okay. Here's the thing.' Marylou raised her hands, palms towards us, in defensive mode. 'Yeah, I'm a single woman and every once in a while I like a little action between the sheets, if you get my drift. Otto was kinda convenient, being in the neighbouring property. We slept together maybe three times, more than a year ago, and that was enough for me.'

Three times? Euuggh.

'Then, just before New Year's, he invited me over for a drink and we ended up going upstairs together.' She looked around the café before leaning towards us and lowering her voice.

'We went into his bedroom. And it was there on the bed …'

She paused again and both Silvia and I leaned forward, waiting for more.

'… and there was still some earth from his garden on one end.'

This sounded weird.

'Whatever was it, Marylou?' I couldn't stand the suspense.

'Why, honey, a bamboo cane. He dropped his shorts right in front of me, bent over, and asked me to beat his ass with it.'

'Nooo!' I could only think what a lucky escape I'd had.

'Well, I'm not into all that *Fifty Shades* stuff, so I left PDQ. He's barely spoken to me since.'

I glanced at Silvia, whose wide-eyed expression conveyed more than words.

'Bit of a weirdo,' I said.

'For sure. I don't think he forgave me for that, so the eviction might have been more to do with me than you.'

She seemed to have taken the news much better than I'd expected.

'But I'm devastated you're losing the home you love,' I said.

'That old place? Honey, home ain't about walls and a roof; it's where the heart is and, in my case, also where the cats are.' She placed a hand on my arm. 'I'm just incredibly grateful you gave me the chance to be with Mom at the end. I can never thank you enough.'

'Here's our food,' Silvia said, sounding relieved. Our server arrived, carrying the salads on an enormous tray.

I realised my appetite was back. We toasted each other with freshly squeezed juice, and tucked in.

Silvia stopped the car in front of the property, and I jumped out to unlock and open the gates. As I'd hoped, Marylou wanted to see the new refuge before leaving the Palma area.

'This is a superb location,' she said, looking at the fields beyond the finca and towards the mountains. 'Quiet and rural, but also handy for the city.'

'Come and see the house.' The bunch of keys jangled as I led the way.

'Oh, wow!' Marylou looked around the living space. 'I adore it. And you say the rent is only one hundred euros a month? Are you sure? I've been paying five hundred to Otto.'

'Yes, it's a bargain, isn't it? I'll tell you the full story this evening over a bottle of wine.'

I showed her the bathroom and the two bedrooms, and she immediately went to the window in the larger room.

'Are those new enclosures I see?'

'Yes, they are. I'm afraid the original ones weren't strong enough to move.'

'Honey, how have you afforded all this? I must owe you a whole heap of money.'

'Not at all,' I said. 'Thanks to a generous benefactor,

everything's paid for and you still have some funds in the kitty – pardon the pun. I'll tell you all about it later. Now, there's something else I'd like to show you.'

Marylou, Silvia, and I trooped out to the former restaurant building.

'This used to be a small family eatery,' I said. 'It still has a licence to serve food and drink. If you wanted, you could create Mallorca's first cat café here. It would generate some money towards the upkeep of the refuge and raise awareness of the plight of homeless cats. And I'm sure you'd find some cat-loving volunteers to help run it.'

Marylou said nothing for a few minutes. Did she hate the idea?

'Oh my.' She looked around the space, wide-eyed. 'Just after Mum died, I needed a cat cuddle so bad, I visited a cat café in South Beach. I'd never seen one before and thought it was real neat.'

I told her about Ichika's suggestion and my trip to Valencia to see one in operation.

'In case you're interested, a lawyer is looking into the possibility of a permit for this new concept in Mallorca.'

'Wow.' Marylou appeared dazed.

'There's money still in the new refuge bank account to cover the cost of theming this space.'

She burst into tears. Silvia put her arm around her old friend's shoulders, and I took the American's hands in my own.

'I'm sorry it's so much to take in,' I said, 'but—'

'No, it's not that.' She removed one hand from mine to retrieve a tissue from her jeans pocket. 'It's everything you've done for me and the cats. And you've had to do it all alone.'

'Not at all. I've had loads of help. Silvia's been

fantastic right from the start. A few old and new friends pitched in too. I couldn't have achieved all this without the support of a *lot* of people.'

After locking up the finca, we set off for Refugio Marylou. That had all gone remarkably well.

MARYLOU and I sat under the fig tree, sharing a bottle of wine. Occasionally she stifled a yawn, and her pale complexion and shadows under her eyes revealed her exhaustion. Despite this, she wanted to know every detail, from the eviction notice to getting the new place ready to move into.

By the time we finished talking, she was struggling to keep her eyes open. In contrast, the retelling of the whole saga had left me alert and thoughtful. Not to mention amazed at what I'd been able to make happen.

When we went off to our respective rooms for the night, I lay in the single bed thinking about Sarah's offer of my job back, with a tempting pay rise too. Dan's advice seemed sound. And I knew there were plenty of flights between England and Palma for my future visits to Carlos.

Despite my brain spinning thoughts like a washing machine tossing laundry, I eventually dozed off and had my first unbroken night's sleep for weeks.

CHAPTER FIFTY

Marylou and I spent Saturday morning sorting out the remaining cupboards and packing the last few items into boxes. After a sandwich lunch, she retreated to her room for several hours to pack clothes and other personal belongings and, I imagined, reminisce about her years at the finca.

We were all but finished by late afternoon, leaving unpacked only the basics we'd need before we left.

'I'm so grateful for all your help today,' Marylou said as we sipped the cups of tea I'd made. 'How about supper at Luigi's tonight? My tab. I'll ring and invite Silvia as well.'

'That'd be lovely, thank you.' It would give me a chance to say goodbye to the Italian restaurateur, too.

A few minutes later, she'd spoken to the vet and made a table reservation for supper.

~

'I'M GONNA MISS YOU, LAURA,' Luigi said when I told him I was going back to England.

'I'll miss you too, Luigi. And your terrific tiramisu.'

He treated us to one of his explosive laughs.

'And I'm moving to a finca nearer to Palma on Monday,' Marylou said, 'but I'll still be eating here from time to time.'

Luigi took Marylou's hand and bowed to kiss the back of it. 'My favourite American lady is welcome anytime.'

He made even more of a fuss than usual, giving us a complimentary bottle of Tuscan Brunello di Montalcino and extra-large portions of tiramisu. As we said our goodbyes, he had real tears in his eyes. He wasn't the only one.

WHEN WE DROPPED Silvia back at her home, she invited us to a paella lunch the next day at their little country *casita*. Mid-morning on the Sunday, Marylou drove us to Silvia's, where Tomeu soon had the American's new technology purchases set up and working, and she was finally able to read the emails I'd sent her. She shed a few more tears and thanked and hugged me yet again.

Afterwards, we all piled into Silvia's car and went to the *casita*. This time, Tomeu had done none of the preparation.

'I'll get the fire going,' he said, glancing at his mother.

'Laura, you can't leave Mallorca without learning to make a proper paella,' Silvia said, handing me an apron. 'Tomeu's offered to give you a lesson, so I'm afraid you'll be working for your lunch today.'

Within minutes, I was preparing and chopping ingredients at the table, under the guidance of my teenage tutor.

'It's important to have everything ready before you begin to cook,' he said, a serious tone to his voice.

It wasn't long before the delicious aroma of olive oil heating over the wood fire was drifting across the garden.

MY FIRST ATTEMPT at making the iconic Spanish dish was a surprising success. It was much easier to make than I expected, and I knew I'd be buying myself a paella pan from John Lewis on my return home so I could add it to my repertoire of dishes for entertaining.

'Almost as good as mine.' Tomeu winked at me as he wiped his mouth with a serviette. He leapt off his seat and bounded indoors; I hoped it wasn't for indigestion tablets. Minutes later he returned, carrying a large object wrapped in brown paper.

'For you.' He handed the parcel to Marylou.

'*Me?*' She glanced at me, as though expecting me to know what was within.

I shrugged my shoulders and raised my hands – a Mallorcan gesture I seemed to have adopted for those haven't-got-a-clue moments.

Marylou tore off the paper with all the enthusiasm of a child at Christmastime.

'Oh my! It's just beautiful,' she said, holding the object at arm's length to inspect it. '*You* did this, Tomeu?'

I craned my neck and saw he'd painted a new sign for the sanctuary. It showed two cartoon-like cats wrapped around each other in an embrace, sitting on a lawn. I felt a lump in my throat to see how the gift had touched Marylou.

'You could put it on a pole, or on the gate at the new place,' the artistic teenager said.

'Thank you so much, Tomeu, it's just darling. That old sign needed replacing and I couldn't ask for a better one.' She placed the sign on the table, stood up, and hugged the young artist. If he'd been a British teenager, I imagined he'd have wriggled out of the embrace of an older woman who wasn't family, but Tomeu returned her hug with affection and kindness.

As this was happening, Silvia went indoors and returned carrying a shiny new paella pan with a red-ribbon bow tied around each handle.

'And this is for you, Laura,' she said. 'The next time I come to England, I hope you'll invite me for a paella.'

I gulped away a lump in my throat as I accepted the gleaming gift and hugged both Silvia and Tomeu. How I was going to miss these people.

SILVIA and I went to our rooms early that night, knowing the next day would be a long one. Even after a day of little activity I was bone-tired, but my mind kept returning to Sarah's offer for me to return to Bard FM.

If I went to work in Bristol, I'd be presenting the mid-morning show, finishing at noon. On a Friday after-noon, I could go straight to the airport and catch a plane to Mallorca. By early evening, Carlos and I would be on his terrace, planning our weekend.

Hosting the afternoon show again in Stratford would mean driving to Birmingham Airport in the Friday evening rush-hour. I'd arrive in Palma just in time to go to bed. Not a bad thing, I thought, remembering the last time we'd made love. At least I could fly back early on Monday morning, rather than on Sunday evening as I'd have to do if I went to Bristol.

My head was spinning with options. Both jobs would give the possibility of spending two nights in Mallorca with Carlos. His trips to England to see me would be more flexible because he could arrange his workload to accommodate them. Where would he prefer to be when he visited? Bristol or Stratford? Both had plenty to offer.

I sat up in bed and exhaled. Thinking about Carlos made me long to hear his voice. I picked up my mobile phone from the bedside table. Eleven o'clock was early by Spanish standards, so I was sure he'd be awake.

It took only a few rings before someone answered the phone. But it wasn't Carlos.

CHAPTER FIFTY-ONE

'H*ola?*' The woman who answered Carlos's phone had one of those deep velvety voices used on TV commercials for chocolate bars. I could almost imagine her reclining in a bubble bath, her scarlet-lipped mouth open to receive a piece of luxurious dark chocolate. Not from Carlos, I hoped. Had I dialled the wrong number?

'I was expecting to speak to Carlos,' I said, my stomach aflutter.

'He's in the shower.' She sounded English, rather than Spanish. 'This is Fran. Shall I get him for you?'

An unpalatable image flashed through my mind.

'Er, no, please don't disturb him. I'll catch him another time, thank you.' I pressed the red button to end the call, my heart thumping with fear.

When he'd said he was going to stay with an old schoolfriend, he didn't tell me Fran was a woman. There was I, assuming Fran was short for Francis or Francisco.

He's in the shower. Shall I fetch him for you? Those words kept ringing in my head, and none of the various scenarios that flashed through my mind improved my mood.

I threw off the sheet and padded into the bathroom, where I vomited. Had I been naive to think a good-looking man like Carlos would be satisfied with a girl-friend who didn't look like a fashion model or sound like Miss-Smooth-as-Silk-Chocolate Woman? I filled my cupped hand with cold water from the basin tap and drank it down to wash away the unpleasant taste … and the unpleasant truth.

Then I returned to the small bedroom, flipped open my laptop, and replied to Sarah, telling her I'd meet her at Bard FM on Friday afternoon.

'Have the van and minibus arrived?' Carlos called the following morning. He sounded cheerful, and I tried not to think about the reason for that. I was supervising the removal of boxes from the house and hadn't seen who was calling before I answered my phone.

'Oh, hello. Yes, they're both here, thank you.' I cleared my throat. 'Good weekend?'

'Yeah, great fun. And you?' He didn't wait for a response. 'Fran said there'd been a call while I was in the shower but forgot to tell me until this morning. I just checked and saw it was you. Sorry not to get back to you.'

'Right.' I turned my head and called out to the removals man lifting a box marked 'Delicate'. 'No, not that one yet, please!'

'Pardon? Everything okay, Laura? Or is it not a good time?'

'Well, we are in the middle of trying to move out of

the house,' I said with a snap in my voice. 'But as you're on the phone, there is something.' I paused. 'It was a surprise to hear a woman answer your phone. And that she offered to fetch you out of the shower, where you were presumably naked.' I knew I sounded like a jealous bitch, but felt I deserved an explanation. 'You didn't tell me your old friend Fran was female.'

Carlos laughed, which I thought was inappropriate in the circumstances.

'Didn't I? I'm sorry, it never occurred to me. If you're worried about that, there's no need; Francesca's gay and married to an Ibizan girl called Natalia. They run the windsurf school together.'

That silenced me. He must have thought me suspicious.

'Hey, you didn't think …? Laura Lundon, have you been making assumptions again?'

My face suddenly felt hot and I didn't know how to respond. It didn't seem right to discuss the matter over the phone. Too embarrassing.

'Listen, I have to help Marylou get the cats into the carrying cases. See you tomorrow morning?'

'Sure. I'll be there around ten. Good luck with everything today.' He ended the call without saying goodbye, which made my stomach churn again. Had my apparent jealousy changed things?

He was due to pick me up from the new refuge on Tuesday morning and drive us to Deià for our stay at La Residencia. Assuming he still turned up, I'd make up for my misunderstanding when we were there. The Fran situation was a relief – if embarrassing in the circumstances – but I wasn't looking forward to telling him I was flying home on Friday morning, back to my old radio job, rather than staying a couple of weeks more with him at his place.

GETTING ALL the cats into the travelling cases took two pairs of hands and some coaxing with treats. At last, they were all secured in the minibus, which Marylou had sprayed liberally with a pheromone product designed to calm cats. Judging by the insistent yowling, the calming effect was yet to kick in.

The removals man took out the old free-standing cat sleeping pods and climbing frame to load into the van, leaving the enclosures standing forlorn and empty. Otto would have the job of taking them down.

'Well, this is it, I guess.' Marylou's eyes glistened as she took a final look around the house. Her voice echoed now the rug and soft furnishings were no longer there. Only one thing remained on the kitchen table: the Tupperware bowl in which Otto had brought me the tomatoes. I hadn't returned it to him, not wishing to see him again.

'I'll take it back with the keys,' Marylou said. I offered to go with her for moral support, but she declined.

After locking the house, she took a final walk down the drive and I sat waiting in her Renault outside the house. She was a small woman and I was concerned about her being on her own when she faced her landlord for the final time.

I needn't have worried. Ten minutes later, when she strode back up from the gates, she was smiling.

'All okay?' I asked when she climbed into the driving seat.

'All good,' she said. 'I told him exactly what I thought of him. Y'know what he did?'

I shook my head.

'Only asked if I wanted to go to bed with him one last time.'

My mouth dropped open in shock. 'Unbelievable!'

'Yeah. Unbelievable. Let's go.' She grinned at me and started the car. The removal van and minibus followed us on that last drive away from the old Refugio Marylou.

∼

I COULD SEE the joy in Marylou's face as she instructed the removal men where she wanted her furniture placed at Finca Es Refugi. Later, she would unpack boxes and find new locations for their contents. It was clear she'd be happy in her new home, and Calvin had already settled in. His armchair looked even scruffier in its pristine new surroundings; would Marylou dare replace it one day?

My final night before leaving for Deià would be spent in the smaller of the two bedrooms. The house still had a faint whiff of new paint, but that was preferable to the mustiness before the property's transformation. Now my departure was imminent, it seemed as though I'd been in Mallorca for only a short time. But so much had happened, and my life had changed in so many ways.

While Marylou bustled around, finding the right places for her possessions, I turned on my laptop and set up an email introduction for her and Jaume; the lawyer replied almost immediately, promising to contact her as soon as he had news about the permit but adding it could be 'a while yet'.

Then I wrote to Isabel Rosselló to inform her

Marylou was back and would set up a bank transfer for the rent. I emailed Rupert to thank him again for his generous donation. As promised, I detailed what I'd already spent and introduced him electronically to Marylou.

My work here is done, I thought with a sigh of relief as I closed my laptop. I wasn't going to look at it again until I was back home in Stratford-upon-Avon. As much as I was looking forward to staying again at La Resi – I hoped still with Carlos – I craved seeing my home, parents, and friends again.

MARYLOU and I spent a quiet Monday evening together chatting. She'd found the perfect shady spot for her outdoor table and chairs, where we shared a bottle of cava to celebrate the start of a new chapter in her life.

'I'll never be able to thank you enough for everything you've done for me and the cats,' she said. 'It's such a pity you're going back to England and we may never meet again.'

'Actually, we probably shall, Marylou.' I smiled. 'I've met someone special here on the island and I'm planning to visit Mallorca some weekends and for holidays with him. And I'd love to see how you're getting on here and find out whether you launch the cat café.'

I went to bed contented that night, although I still had a lot on my mind. Uppermost in my thoughts was the concern that Carlos, deterred by my apparent jealousy, might not turn up the next day.

CHAPTER FIFTY-TWO

Why had I worried? When Carlos arrived on Tuesday morning, I went out to meet him and tried to apologise for my reaction the previous day. He placed his finger on my lips to silence me, then we kissed.

'Thank you, Carlos,' I said, when I could speak again. 'Come and meet Marylou.' I pulled him by the hand into the house and the three of us spent almost an hour drinking coffee and chatting, before Carlos and I left for Deià.

ON FRIDAY MORNING, we checked out of La Residencia after a leisurely breakfast on the terrace by one of the swimming pools. We'd had three wonderful nights' stay in a luxurious hilltop suite with a terrace and view of the Mediterranean. We enjoyed sumptuous breakfasts, lazy laps of one pool or another, strolls up to the Poets' Walk and Mirador, late-night drinks on the terrace under the stars, and candlelit dinners with views of the sea on the terrace of the hotel's posh El Olivo restaurant. As we'd promised ourselves, we also walked down to the cove Zeller loved, to have lunch at the waterside restaurant Ca's Patró March. As we feasted on plump Sóller prawns and perfectly grilled sea bass, I told Carlos I'd seen that restaurant featured in the TV series *The Night Manager*, never imagining I'd be eating there one day. Our time in Deià couldn't have been any more romantic if it had been a honeymoon.

Exploring the village, we strolled along the steep, narrow lanes and admired the glorious views. Using El Capitán's sketch map, Carlos took me to see the house where Ferdie Collins had lived until a while ago, and we went to look at his new home. After a long walk down a steep lane, which turned into a dirt track – *inappropriate shoes, Laura* – we arrived at a tiny stone cottage which appeared to have been abandoned.

'According to Dad's map, this is the place Zeller rented when she was here.'

'Really? It's so cute.' I had my nose pressed to the glass of the grimy window next to the old wooden door, trying to see inside.

Carlos laughed. 'Could do with a bit of TLC, don't you think?'

'I'm surprised it's like this,' I said. 'I thought Deià was a highly sought-after location for property.'

He grinned at me and used his finger to rub the dirt off the tip of my nose.

'It is, these days, but the steep access and its location right at the bottom of the village probably don't work in its favour. And it *is* very small.'

I couldn't stop thinking about the place all the way back to the hotel and wondered how I could find out more about it. Javier's grandmother came to mind.

'I WISH you weren't going back,' Carlos said, hugging me tight to his chest at the entrance to the airport security gates. 'It feels like I only just found you again, and I'll miss you so much.'

I blinked away the tears threatening to fall, wishing I hadn't acted in such a hasty manner after that fateful phone conversation with Fran in Ibiza.

'You'll be fine.' I wished I could say the same for myself. 'I'll be back soon, I promise.'

We had a long and passionate public kiss, prompting one of a passing group of lads wearing Liverpool football shirts to shout, 'Get a room!' Then we prised ourselves apart and I walked towards the security gates, dragging my wheeled cabin bag behind me.

As in all memorable airport farewell scenes in movies, music played; when I turned my head for a final look back at Carlos, he was grinning and playing the ukulele. *So that was what he'd had in his backpack.* I laughed and ran back to give him one more kiss.

Before I loaded my case and handbag onto the scanner conveyor belt, I turned to wave. Carlos still stood there, but his ukulele was now out of sight. We exchanged waves and blew kisses to each other, then I walked on.

'Goodbye, Carlos … goodbye, Mallorca,' I whispered, tears streaming down my cheeks.

CHAPTER FIFTY-THREE

'They're here!' A big beam lit up Anna's face. With headphones clamped on my head and my focus on the script notes in front of me, I hadn't noticed the station's new receptionist push open the heavy studio door.

'Oh! Early.' I glanced at the clock on the wall. 'Can you tell them I'll be about a quarter of an hour?'

'Sure.'

I took a couple of deep breaths to slow my quickening heartbeat, then opened the microphone on the broadcasting desk. 'That's it from me today,' I said, smiling. 'I hope you'll join me on Monday, when my guest will be local author Maggie Crane, who's just published her first cosy crime novel. Have a good weekend and stay tuned for Ben Bradshaw, after the news.'

As the first bars of the final song began, I pulled off the headphones and stood up to gather my papers into one pile for a speedy exit. After watching the minutes and seconds tick by, I pressed the red button to give broadcast control to the news booth.

I<small>N THE OFFICE</small>, I slid my papers into my designated filing-cabinet drawer and pulled out the red folder marked 'Monday'. I flicked through the contents and, satisfied that everything was ready for my next show, slipped it back into place and pushed the drawer shut.

Two months had passed since I said a tearful goodbye to Carlos at Palma's Son Sant Joan airport and flew back to England. I'd now been at Britannia FM for four weeks and, so far, had no regrets about having told Sarah that I'd decided not to return to my old job at Bard FM because I was moving abroad.

When Dan and Billy came to my place for supper, they were surprised to learn my decision. But not as surprised as I was to be taking a first step into a new – and yes, foreign – future. On the plane back to Birmingham after my stay with Carlos at La Residencia, I'd realised that, as it had for my birth mother, Mallorca had worked its magic on me.

But it wasn't just the island; like Zeller, I'd also fallen in love. Unlike Zeller with Ferdie, I wanted what I had with Carlos to last. The early signs were encouraging. Since I'd moved into his apartment, he hadn't once left the cap off the toothpaste or the toilet seat up.

I grabbed my jacket from the coat rack and bounded down the stairs to reception, where Anna was chatting to my guests. She loved any chance to speak English.

'Mum!' I ran into her outstretched arms. 'It's so good to see you here.' Extracting myself, I turned to embrace and kiss Dad, breathing in the familiar scent of Old Spice.

'Wow, love the shirt,' I said as I stepped back to look

at my beloved father. I couldn't remember ever seeing him wear one that wasn't plain and pastel coloured.

'Your mum bought it for me,' he replied, raising an eyebrow. 'Not my usual style, granted, but it's only for the holiday.'

I chuckled. I'd describe my dad's wardrobe as conservative. Oh, to have been a fly on the wall when he peered into the carrier bag Mum handed him and saw the jazzy number inside.

'Well, it's perfect for Mallorca' – I glanced through the window at the gathering grey clouds – 'although the forecast is for rain later today.'

'We're not here for the weather, sweetheart,' Mum assured me, placing her hand on my arm. I noticed she'd had a manicure, which was a rare event for her. 'We've come to see you and this island you've fallen in love with.'

'Let's get on with it, then. Checked in yet?'

'All done.' Dad said. 'And our room has a lovely view of the bay, which we didn't expect, so thank you for that.'

Anna came out from behind the reception desk, kissed my parents on both cheeks, and complimented Dad on his shirt. He blushed, not being accustomed to such friendly greetings from strangers.

'*Buen finde*, Anna.' I wished her a good weekend in her own language, then opened the door onto the street and ushered my parents through.

'YOUR SPANISH IS COMING ON WELL.' I heard the note of pride in Dad's voice. We were in Firenze, the cosy Italian restaurant a few doors along from the radio station.

'Could be a lot better, but I'm making progress. And I've even picked up a bit of Italian, eating in this place.'

Paolo, the restaurant's rotund owner, brought the bottle of Barolo I'd ordered as soon as we sat down at the booth table I'd booked. He poured us each a glass of the red wine with all the panache of a sommelier presenting a decanter of Vega Sicilia in a Michelin-starred restaurant, then brought the menus.

Once we'd placed our orders, I picked up my glass and held it towards them.

'Cheers!' We clinked glasses, I took a quick slurp, and then I sat back and looked at my parents.

'I have something to tell you … but I don't want to upset either of you.'

They glanced at each other, then at me.

'Well, let's hear it, then.' A small frown creased Dad's brow.

'I found my biological father.' You could have heard a dropped strand of raw spaghetti land on the floor. 'In Deià.'

'Oh my God!' Mum clapped a hand over her mouth. 'Whatever did he say when you met him? What's he like?'

'I didn't meet him. I never intended to connect or speak with him. For my sanity, I wanted to know who he was and what sort of person Zeller had fallen in love with.' I let this sink in and then raised my glass again. 'Anyway, that's what I had to tell you. Happy holidays!' My shoulders dropped. I smiled and sipped my wine.

'Is that it?' Dad said. 'Aren't you going to give us any more details?'

I glanced around the almost empty trattoria and saw only one other table occupied. The locals ate lunch later than tourists and this was now early for me too.

'Do you remember a pop song called "Laura"?' My parents were classical music buffs and looked at me with blank expressions. 'Mid-seventies. Anyway, the singer-songwriter was a man by the name of Ferdie Collins. "Laura" did well in the UK charts, but Ferdie was a one-hit wonder. He moved to Mallorca and bought a little house in Deià with his music royalties and a generous inheritance. He planned to build a career here performing for holidaymakers.'

'Your biological father was a famous pop star?' Wide eyed, Mum sat up straight in her chair, the manicured fingertips of both hands gripping the table edge.

'Well, famous only for a few weeks, I gather. But it explains why Zeller insisted you call me Laura. She didn't love him enough to spend her life with him, but she cared enough to name me after his only hit song.'

Mum sighed and shook her head. 'My sister can still surprise me, even though she's no longer with us.' She looked at Dad and spoke for them both: 'We always imagined he'd be a journalist or a teacher – something more cerebral – didn't we, darling?'

'Nothing like that,' I replied, smiling and leaning back in my chair as a server arrived with a tray bearing three bowls of steaming minestrone.

'Zeller with a pop singer. Who'd have thought it?' Dad shook his head. As the server left, Paolo stepped forward holding a sizeable chunk of Parmesan cheese. He grated a generous portion into each bowl of the aromatic soup.

'*Buon appetito!*' He gave a small bow before he went to wield his grater at another table.

'It could have been worse, I suppose.' Dad watched Paolo waddle across the trattoria. 'At least this Ferdie character wasn't a waiter.' We all laughed, easing the slight air of tension that had hovered over us. It was time to focus on the food.

'THAT WAS QUITE A LUNCH.' Mum balled her napkin and placed it on the table. 'No wonder the Spanish have a siesta if they eat like that in the middle of the day. I could do with a nap myself.'

'Why not?' I was surprised to see it was nearly four o'clock. 'Sorry, but I need to leave for my weekly Spanish class. Look, it's due to rain soon so it may be an idea to go back to the hotel, settle in, and enjoy the facilities. You could start your holiday with a relaxing evening together, then we'll make an early start tomorrow.'

I signalled to Paolo for the bill and smiled at my parents. 'I'm so pleased you came to visit. We'll have a great week.'

CHAPTER FIFTY-FOUR

The next day, I drove the three of us to Deià in the RAV4. Carlos had a publicity shoot that morning for a Spanish newspaper; it was only five minutes' walk from the apartment, so he didn't need his wheels.

'This boyfriend of yours must be keen if he's letting you drive his car,' Dad said.

The news about Andy had been a shock for them when I returned to England. I knew they were curious to meet the new man in my life and was sure they'd like him when they did.

'He is. And I wouldn't have moved in with Carlos if we weren't serious.'

My dad fell silent for a few minutes. I glanced in the rear-view mirror at Mum, who was gazing with a dreamy smile on her face at the cerulean blue of the Mediterranean way down below the road.

Dad, who sat next to me in the front, pointed to his right. 'Are those olive trees?' Stately manor houses, ramshackle stone huts, grazing sheep, and countless olive and holm oak trees studded the mountainous landscape.

'They are. Some have been there for hundreds, even thousands of years.' Fierce coastal winds had twisted their trunks into what Carlos called 'nature's sculptures'. He loved photographing the ancient, gnarled trees, and framed black and white photos he'd taken early one misty morning decorated the walls of our bedroom.

My talented boyfriend now had a new focus for his personal photography. After I returned to England, he delivered the promised cat photos to Marylou … and adopted Harry while he was there. Our adorable ginger cat was the subject of several cute poses Carlos had captured on camera.

'There, that's Deià!' We swept around a bend and the picture-postcard village came into view. 'That's where Zeller lived.' And that's where she conceived me, I reminded myself yet again. *I'm a daughter of Deià.*

'Will we be able to visit Robert Graves's house?' Dad had read about the writer's home-turned-museum in the guidebook he bought at the airport.

'Yes, of course. You don't think I'd dare bring a retired English teacher to Deià and not let him see that?' We all laughed. 'We'll park in the village centre and walk up to the church and cemetery to see his gravestone first. Then we'll go to La Casa de Robert Graves and afterwards have lunch.'

I gave them no hint of what would follow after we'd done all that.

DAD LOOKED DOWN at the headstone marking Robert Graves's grave. The simplicity of it made him shake his head.

'I'd expected a quote from *I, Claudius* or another of his works.'

We stood in the peaceful cemetery, listening to birds in the trees and looking out at the spectacular views.

'Not an unpleasant spot for a final resting place,' Dad said, taking a photograph of the headstone with his phone camera.

'There's something else I want to show you. This way.' I guided him by the elbow to a different part of the cemetery. Mum followed, reading the old headstones along the way.

We stopped in front of a newer stone and I studied Dad's face as he read the words inscribed on it: 'Ferdie Collins, 24th June 1948–19th April 2019'. He tutted, put his arm around my shoulder, and gave it an affectionate squeeze.

'Oh, I'm so sorry, my love. You didn't get a chance to see him.'

'It's all right, Dad, it doesn't matter. I told you, I didn't want to meet him; I only needed to know who he was and what he was like.'

'Look!' Mum's hand shook as she pointed at the stone. 'He died the same day as Zeller.'

I hadn't registered that fact when Carlos brought me to see the stone previously. I clapped a hand over my open mouth and fought back tears. What a tragic coincidence. I wondered whether Ferdie ever got over losing Zeller; El Capitán told me the singer never married and described him as 'a restless soul'. It made me shiver to think that both my biological parents died on the same day.

As we stood in silence, I closed my eyes for a few moments and said a small prayer that they'd find each other again in the afterlife, with a happier outcome this time.

We left the cemetery and picked our way down the stone steps to return to the village centre. After the sober reflection among the graves, I'd planned the rest of the day to be fun – and one they wouldn't forget.

'Next stop, Robert Graves's house,' I said, holding up my hand and pointing ahead, like one of those tour guides taking cruise-ship passengers on whistle-stop excursions. It was a longer walk than I'd realised and thank goodness we weren't doing it in the heat of summer. To their credit, neither of my parents complained, although Mum was wearing court shoes more suited to a lunch out than a hike to a museum on the outskirts of the village.

After exploring Ca n'Alluny and seeing where Graves used to write and live, we set off back towards the village. The prospect of lunch and a much-needed cold drink hastened our steps towards our destination.

'This is it,' I said as we approached the cluster of honey-hued stone buildings. 'We're having lunch here at La Residencia.'

'It looks beautiful,' Mum replied. 'It's such a lovely day. Can we eat outside?'

'I've booked a table on the terrace. You'll love it, Mum.'

'Do you think anyone will mind if I take off my shoes during lunch?'

'Not at all. It's much more relaxed here than you'd expect.'

We walked through the gates and along the path, stopping by a low stone wall to admire the lush lawns of the garden below. The previous evening's rain had given everything a wash, as though in preparation for our arrival.

'It looks so luxurious.' Mum tugged at Dad's sleeve. 'Look at that gorgeous lawn, darling.'

'Richard Branson bought the place and made it luxurious,' I said.

'*The* Richard Branson? Is he here now?'

Mum's eyes widened at the prospect of bumping into the bearded entrepreneur. I laughed.

'No, he sold the place some time ago. But he put his stamp on it, and I'm told he still stays from time to time.'

We continued along the path, passing the gnarled trunks of ancient olive trees. Mum paused to read the names on the wooden plaques placed on some olive trees. I told her the people named were sponsors of that particular tree; it was a scheme designed to help fund the maintenance of the estate's numerous ancient olive trees.

'Apart from the sponsored trees and the sunshine, it has the feel of an English country house hotel,' she said.

We walked past the drinks terrace and around the corner to the Café Miró terrace. I told the waiter my name, and he led us to the table I'd chosen and booked for the occasion. He pulled out the chair for Mum, who fluttered her eyelashes at the handsome young Spaniard. Dad raised one eyebrow at me and grinned as the waiter shook open the folded starched linen napkin and draped it across Mum's lap.

'I think your Mum approves of the five-star service,' he said once the waiter had left to fetch the menus.

'Well, not that five star' – Mum canted her head

towards the additional place settings – 'otherwise he'd have cleared those away. We're only three.'

'We're going to be five,' I said, when I spotted the rest of our party heading towards us. Mum followed my gaze to see who was joining us. I stood to greet them, and my parents did too.

'Mum, Dad, I'd like you to meet El Capitán and his son, Carlos – my boyfriend. Capitán lived in Deià at the same time as Zeller and, believe it or not, she often used to babysit little Carlos.'

After introductions and the obligatory hugs, I suggested we should sit down. The morning's exercise had honed our appetites for food.

'Capitán, please sit next to me.' Mum patted the seat of the empty chair next to her. 'I'm sure we have a lot to talk about.'

'Oh yes, Geraldine, I think we do. Zeller was a very dear friend of mine.' He gave Mum's arm a gentle squeeze as he sat down next to her, and I could tell they were going to get on well.

I sat next to Dad, and Carlos was at the head of the table. His knee rubbed against mine, giving me a warm feeling, and I smiled at him.

The waiter returned and El Capitán said he'd like to order a bottle of Bollinger.

'My treat. Such a pleasure to talk about Zeller with her sister.'

We spent a few minutes sipping the chilled bubbly and studying the menu, then placed our orders. I couldn't help grinning. Things were going very well indeed.

Almost two hours later, we had all done justice to a delicious lunch. After some discussion about the bill, which I had planned to pay, Dad and El Capitán settled on splitting it between them.

'I THINK that was the best lunch I've ever eaten,' Mum said as she and I went into the hotel building to use the ladies' room before we left. 'And not just because the food and wine were so delicious.'

Zeller's old friend had shared some interesting – and amusing – stories about my birth mother, and waves of laughter swept across the terrace from our table. What shone through in his various anecdotes was his genuine love for my birth mother. I felt a tug at my heart when he told Mum her sister left Mallorca without saying goodbye to him.

'Zeller's friend is charming,' Mum said, drying her hands with a small towel from a pile by the washbasin. 'Carlos is very pleasant too, but he could have been a bit more talkative, I thought.'

He had little opportunity. I suppressed a smile. El Capitán and Mum had dominated the conversation over lunch.

When we joined the men, waiting for us on the terrace, I smiled at Carlos, who winked at me.

'Perhaps a little stroll around the village, after that delicious lunch?' I suggested, hoping Mum's feet felt better after their lunchtime liberation from shoes. I needn't have worried; Mum beamed at El Capitán and slipped her arm through his. Dad raised his eyebrows at me and shook his head from side to side, a what's-she-like? grin on his face.

Holding hands, Carlos and I led the way out of the

hotel gates and along the main road a short distance, before turning into a narrow lane. We'd done this walk a few times. We spoke in low voices, expressing our relief that the lunch had gone so well. Mum, El Capitán, and Dad were behind us, out of earshot and chatting like old friends.

'I wonder what they'll say when they find out,' I said. Even El Capitán was in for a surprise.

THE END

'Where are you taking us?' Mum called out from behind. 'Only these aren't the best shoes for this type of surface.'

Carlos and I stopped and gave the others time to catch up.

'We're here now,' I said, pointing to the cottage that had been Zeller's home.

I saw Mum and Dad exchange quizzical glances.

'This is where Zeller was staying,' El Capitán said, stroking his beard with one hand. 'Looks as though nobody's done much to the place since.'

I opened my handbag. 'We can go in if you like. I borrowed the key.' I inserted it in the lock and turned it, but Carlos had to put his weight against the door to push it open.

Rustic would be the most appropriate adjective to describe the property's interior. Cobwebs draped across the corners, and the furniture that remained wore a blanket of dust. I blushed when I spotted the heart and our initials Carlos had drawn in the dust on the drop-

leaf dining table during our last visit. It was an appropriate name for that piece of furniture: one leaf had
dropped off onto the floor since our previous visit.

The ground floor was an open space with a tiny
kitchen area in one corner. A narrow staircase went up to
one bedroom and a bathroom which had been new in
Zeller's time but, decades later, was now dated.

'I remember Zeller mentioned this in her book,'
Mum said. 'There wasn't a bathroom in the place when
she arrived – just a loo in a shed outside. She charmed
the landlord into installing a bathroom in what was once
the second bedroom.'

'Zeller always was very persuasive,' I said to Carlos,
the only one of us who'd never met her.

'Thank you for arranging for us to see the place,'
Mum said, peering through the dusty bedroom window
down at the tiny courtyard. 'I can imagine her down
there under that fig tree, thumping away on that noisy
old typewriter of hers.'

Mum came over and took my hands in hers.

'Thank you, darling. I can almost feel Zeller's presence here, and I'll never forget visiting this little house.'
She tipped her head towards the window. 'If she were
still renting it, she'd be asking the landlord for a courtyard makeover.'

We all laughed. I looked at Carlos and he gave a
barely perceptible nod.

'There's another reason we're here.' I took a deep
breath. 'I'm thinking of buying this place.' Three mouths
dropped open.

'Zeller's old landlord died a long time ago, leaving
this to his two daughters. But they're both well off and
live in Madrid with their families and have no interest in
the place at all. They had an elderly tenant here for

almost twenty years, and since he died, the place has been left empty and neglected. I found a local who looks after the keys, who put me in touch with the owners. We're in the process of negotiating a price.'

Dad's eyebrows shot up. 'Can you afford to get all the work done this place appears to need?'

'I'm hoping what I get for Ophelia Drive will be more than enough to cover the purchase and the renovations. And Carlos and I are going to do as much of the work as possible, as a project. It won't be luxurious, because we want it to be rustic and as authentic as possible, but it will have twenty-first-century necessities and comforts.'

El Capitán beamed at us. 'I'll be happy to pitch in with the work if you'll let me. It'd bring back some marvellous memories of evenings Zeller and I shared in that courtyard, with a bottle of wine and young Carlos playing on a rug on the ground.'

Mum was the only one of the three who hadn't responded to the news. She walked over to the window again and looked out.

'I think you're a little bit mad to be doing this, but how wonderful you're taking on something from Zeller's past.' She came over, put her arms around me and kissed my forehead. 'She would be so proud of the way you've coped with all the recent events in your life. And that you're doing this.'

'If all goes to plan, we'll have a little place here in the mountains to use for occasional weekends, and you'll be able to come and stay in it whenever you like – you too, Capitán. Just not all at once, of course!'

I told them that we planned to rent out the tiny house as a cosy holiday let during the height of summer, to offset some of the renovation costs.

'We plan to make it a blissful hideaway for a couple,' I said. 'It'd also be perfect for a writer like Zeller to come and create their own literary masterpiece.'

'And it'll the perfect romantic place for a honey-moon,' Carlos added, taking my hand. 'Maybe even ours?'

El Capitán and my parents weren't the only ones surprised by that suggestion.

A SMALL REQUEST

I very much appreciate that you took a chance on this debut novelist by choosing to read *Daughter of Deià*. Sincerely, I hope you enjoyed it.

If you did, I'd be most grateful if you could take the time to write a short review on Amazon. Even just a few sentences can help a novel from a new author gain some visibility on the bulging bookshelves of Amazon.

A big thank-you from me.

ABOUT THE AUTHOR

Cambridge-born Jan Edwards left her career as a BBC local radio presenter in Oxfordshire in 2004 to move to rural Mallorca with Richard and their two rescue cats.

The move gave Jan more time to pursue her lifelong passion for writing. She authors two blogs - *Living in Rural Mallorca* & *Eat Drink Sleep Mallorca* - and produces and presents the podcasts *Living in Rural Mallorca* & *Authors in Mallorca*.

Jan's currently working on a memoir about their early experiences of life at their rural finca.

When not writing something - a rare event - Jan may be cuddling one of the various cats that have adopted the finca as their home and restaurant.

ACKNOWLEDGEMENTS

My thanks to Nicky Taylor Editorial for her work on this novel. How fortunate was I to meet such a brilliant editor right here in Mallorca?

My husband, Richard offered support throughout the long process of getting this novel from inside my head to the book you're now holding.

And Pip, our youngest cat, helpfully refrained from sitting on the keyboard as I typed.

Printed in Great Britain
by Amazon

76545006R00220